STAR FORGED

BOOK 5 OF THE GIFTING

Star Forged

A blurb is typically a 1-2 line endorsement provided by a celebrity or well-known authority. You can also use this specially formatted page to share an editorial review.

When publishing th *The Gifting Series #5*

Macy is feeling a little left out, as usual. Who would have thought moving from one planet to another wouldn't change that loneliness? She is never alone these days since Etterians guard human women with an urgency she understands. But the lack of companionship is like a dark aching abyss inside her chest. On some days, it threatens to implode, and Macy Mitchell would cease to exist. Looming is her impending meeting with King Xeus of Etteria. How is she supposed to keep her shit together when presented to royalty? Not after she ran from the last king she met.

For Xeus, the void expands daily. Duty, honor, concern for his dying people, and endless loneliness fill his life. Having decided to search for pairings among other worlds, he is pleased his son found his soulmate among human women. It doesn't mean that Xeus's loneliness and longing haven't ended until he stumbles upon a crying female. Meaning only to soothe, he is spellbound when her presence brings him peace. Unable to resist, he forms an attachment to a female he can never have.rough KDP, the first few pages of your book can be seen using the "Look Inside" feature on Amazon, and blurbs are a great way to capture interest and show social proof for your book.

Also by Sevannah Storm

The Blood of Legends Series

The Huntress

The Healer

The Gifting Series

Soul Forged

Fate Forged

Sun Forged

War Forged

Star Forged

Shadow Forged

Earth Forged

Lust Forged

Standalones

Xiaxan Fox

Ire of Silver

The Shikari

Sol Survivor

Contents

1. Chapter One — 1

2. Chapter Two — 10

3. Chapter Three — 16

4. Chapter Four — 27

5. Chapter Five — 37

6. Chapter Six — 42

7. Chapter Seven — 49

8. Chapter Eight — 54

9. Chapter Nine — 63

10. Chapter Ten — 72

11. Chapter Eleven — 84

12. Chapter Twelve — 93

13. Chapter Thirteen — 97

14. Chapter Fourteen — 112

15. Chapter Fifteen — 124

16. Chapter Sixteen   131

17. Chapter Seventeen   135

18. Chapter Eighteen   149

19. Chapter Nineteen   158

20. Chapter Twenty   164

21. Chapter Twenty-One   178

22. Chapter Twenty-Two   197

23. Chapter Twenty-Three   207

24. Chapter Twenty-Four   216

25. Chapter Twenty-Five   223

26. Chapter Twenty-Six   237

27. Chapter Twenty-Seven   252

28. Chapter Twenty-Eight   264

29. Chapter Twenty-Nine   273

30. Chapter Thirty   284

31. Chapter Thirty-One   295

32. Chapter Thirty-Two   308

33. Chapter Thirty-Three   327

34. Chapter Thirty-Four   334

35. Chapter Thirty-Five   344

36. Chapter Thirty-Six   353

37. Chapter Thirty-Seven   360

38. Chapter Thirty-Eight   367

39. Chapter Thirty-Nine   378

Glossary   384

About the Author   391

SOUL FORGED   393

FATE FORGED   395

SUN FORGED   396

WAR FORGED   398

SHADOW FORGED   400

EARTH FORGED   402

LUST FORGED   404

CHAPTER ONE

XEUS SWUNG HIS GREATSWORD, colliding with his opponent's, setting off a shower of sparks as Maloidian steel met. With their blades locked, he lunged forward, grunting as he drew on his strength, his muscles shaking. Sweat beaded on his lip, but he clenched his jaw and narrowed his eyes. The magnus sun burned his bare shoulders, his braid stirred up dust, and his heels dug into the gray sand. Exhaustion pounded his thoughts and determination. This male was his sixth challenger, and as king, Xeus had to be the best.

So tired. Quit. Let him win.

He dared not cast a glance at the great teacher, or lima kuu, on sparring master duty today. The temptation to beg for relief was great, more so of his stupidity in accepting another challenge from a male so young.

The only one to save Xeus was himself.

He ducked and spun to the right of the male, who stumbled. Xeus brought an elbow back to strike across the male's exposed back, splaying him into the sand.

"And match," Lima Brac called, ending the challenge.

Thundering broke across the crowd as his males stomped their appreciation, their heavy boots raising dust clouds.

Xeus raised his chin and gazed at the expansive skies of Etteria as he drew in gulps of air. His limbs twinged and trembled. He clasped the forearm of his opponent—a young warrior fresh from his four-year service on Gikaet. Xeus curled his lip and scanned the proving grounds. Did his males fear him? Fewer and fewer were willing to spar with him, leaving the inexperienced and still emotional youngins to chance it.

He squared his shoulders, tucked his greatsword under his arm, and cut a wide berth through the males gathered. All pressed their fists over their hearts in a sign of respect. He strode to where Cales, his closest battle-bond, waited. With shaking knees, Xeus climbed the hill, refusing to show an ounce of weakness. He couldn't as king.

"Impressive." Cales grinned and held out his palm, asking for the sword.

Xeus moaned. "Is it just me, or are we training them better?" He handed over his sword and accepted the towel, dabbing his flushed cheeks.

"Six battles, Xeus, would tire anyone."

Xeus snorted. "I doubt Remi knows the meaning of exhausted." Six, ten, fifteen battles wouldn't be an acceptable excuse to Base Commander Remi—the respected male who trained the youngins on Gikaet. Gesturing to the proving grounds, he arched a brow at Cales.

"Not today. I shall test my mettle tomorrow, perhaps even best the Great King Xeus."

At Cales's wide smile, Xeus chuckled. "You have yet to, so perhaps tomorrow the Maker will bless your strength, footwork, or senses."

Cales fell into step beside him as he headed for his office. "And may the Maker bless your ability to keep your friends."

Xeus weaved along the intricate paths of his beloved gardens, pausing to gather a hahyt blossom into his palm for a deep inhale. The sweet scent triggered memories of his damu days when the weight of Etteria didn't rest on his shoulders. "My friends would accept my challenge to spar." He snuck a glance. "Intimidated? Is it my impressive physique? The length of my honor? The—"

"Size of your ego?" Cales grinned.

"Tell me, Cales, why are fewer willing to challenge me?"

Cales stilled. "Truth?"

"Truth?" Xeus faced him. "When have you not told the truth? And besides, we are Etterian. We do not deceive."

"Very well. Your strikes have been almost lethal."

Xeus frowned. "So?"

"So, they do not wish to perish on proving ground soil. There is no honor in that."

Xeus flicked a dismissive hand. "I would not kill my males while sparring."

"They do not know this, my battle-bond, and your visage is terrifying to behold."

Xeus scowled. "They cannot fear me, Cales. What weak warriors is Remi training if they are frightened to face me?"

Cale smiled. "Prudent ones?"

"Then you shall sacrifice your time and energy as my permanent opponent." Xeus strode off, done with this conversation.

"I—" The clang of the sword striking the gray gravel on the path preceded Cales tackling Xeus from behind, taking him to the ground.

He locked his elbows, not willing to smash his face across the coarse stones. Cales looped his arm under Xeus's and cupped the back of his neck. With the weight of the male pinning Xeus, he struggled to rise. Instead, he pushed off and flipped them, landing on top of Cales. His battle-bond grunted, but wrapped his legs around Xeus's waist, closed his arm across Xeus's throat, and squeezed.

Xeus grinned and brought his elbow back into Cales's stomach. Despite the grunt, Cales's grip across Xeus's throat didn't loosen. With each strike or fumble for freedom, Cales held on until spots circled Xeus's vision. When he tapped Cales's forearm asking for release, air flooded his lungs while his friend rolled away.

He lay there, panting, his lungs burning. "Strike when your opponent is distracted," he huffed.

"That I do not spar with you does not mean I neglect my training, Xeus." Cales rose and offered Xeus his hand.

Accepting it, he allowed his friend to hoist him to his feet. "I know this, but I do not like that my males fear me or grant me the win. This does not improve my skills."

"Agreed." Cales closed the distance between them and rested his palm on Xeus's chest. "Then from tomorrow, we shall show these youngins how to battle like honed warriors."

Xeus pressed his palm on Cales's chest, just below his collarbone. Gray dust coated his white tunic and his braid. "I shall hold you to that, my battle-bond." He chuckled, scooped up his sword, and gestured to the throne room. "Come, let us begin this day. There is much to be done before my announcement."

He stomped to his office, reminded of what awaited him. Under the water's spray in the cleansing room, he corralled his thoughts to now, this moment, not wanting to dread the upcoming gathering. The decision was made, yet, despite the peace in his soul regarding it, he anticipated much disapproval and arguing from his ambassadors.

Raising his palms above his head, he splayed them on the white wall, dipping his head under the spray. In this, he would tolerate none of their opinions.

He stood under the air-dryer, his hair whipping around him, revealing his agitation. Grabbing the clip, he whispered, "Malia pa," and waited for his hair to braid itself before he caught the end and snapped the clip in place.

After tugging on his armor, he hovered his hand above his dark-blue-and-gold cloak—the colors of his bloodline. Gritting his teeth, he flicked it on and allowed the magnetic clasp to connect at the base of his throat. He could dress like the ambassadors in loose pants and tunics in their colors, but he was a warrior at heart, and donning the armor reminded all that Etteria was a battle-ready nation. Cales wore both, depending on his tasks for the day. Xeus did not have that luxury. He had to be consistent, always displaying what his people expected.

As he strode from the cleansing room, Cales held out a glass of giyua juice—the sharp scent making Xeus's mouth salivate. He downed the refreshing liquid then squared his shoulders and marched into his throne room.

Standing center of the dais, he delivered his announcement. Etteria was dying. Couldn't they see that? Why did everything have to be a discussion? He gritted his teeth, narrowing his gaze on the 'trouble-makers.' Finding a compatible species for his males was paramount. They needed mates. Etteria needed females birthing females. Even as he dismissed the naysayers, his gaze strayed to his son, Enyl, standing to the side. His matching eye color of dark blue had made this decision easier for Xeus, for his son's future. No matter what happened, he would hold to that.

XEUS ADMIRED ARAZYL, A former lover and the mother to Enyl. Still supple in form, her cheeks glowed with happiness, her dark blue eyes sparkling. The thick braid down her back announced her honor, something he had experienced first-hand. Despite her suitability and the genuine bond between her and Xeus, he had to let her go. When they'd parted, he'd wished her happiness, and she had done well for herself. A glance at her lover, Droal, had Xeus nodding. Yes, she had chosen well. His thick braid brushed his heels, and as far back as Xeus could recall, Cales had never cut it in punishment.

Droal was an honorable male, blessing Arazyl with many sons and one daughter. That was such a gift from the Maker. But Etteria needed more females to save them. His thoughts lingered on the announcement he'd made earlier, to search the known worlds for candidates, no matter the species. If they drew forth the Ethera, their ancient mating bond, then that too would be a blessing. But he'd value any females who birthed more females to bolster their diminishing numbers. He sipped his giyua juice, sparing his half-eaten kreso a dismissive glance.

Food had lost its appeal, along with the day-to-day life as king of Etteria. He longed for peace or a battle worthy of his skill, yet debates, trade agreements, and the impending war with Yithia consumed his time. He yearned for the joy of a youngin when the void didn't press so hard on his control, when his life loomed with possibilities. Now he couldn't spare the time to travel to Gikaet for a battle rush, and any emotion he experienced brought the darkness closer. It blurred the edges of his soul, bleeding the light from within.

He'd bid Enyl farewell, sharing his son's need to find peace in exertion, in conquering a known enemy. But as king, Xeus's life remained here, enduring endless politics, having every decision judged. He would remain firm on this one, though, needing to find suitable candidates for Enyl, Cales, and his males.

"You are quiet," Arazyl said with a sweet smile.

Xeus grunted, acknowledging that she'd always had the ability to sense his moods. "It has been a trying day."

He wasn't willing to discuss the state of his soul with her. She need not concern herself when her future belonged with Droal, as was right. She did look beautiful in her silver and green ceremonial gown. Her thick black braid rested over one breast, and her dark blue eyes glowed with contentment. Had she found her Eth in Droal, having experienced the Ethera, her eyes would've been the lovely pale blue as at her birth. Droal's too.

Yes, Xeus had made the right decision. Doing so would save their females from a life of chasing daughters. To move from male to male, despite her feelings, until birthing a daughter didn't encourage a healthy society. Many males matured without their mothers influencing them. No matter how much honoring females and those weaker was drilled in during a male's service on Gikaet, the way females now behaved had the males believing females chose to spread their thighs for tokens, treasures, or pleasure. That some females did so, found solace in things as their souls faded, lay heavy on Xeus's shoulders. But some, like Arazyl, remembered why they chased birthing daughters.

Xeus frowned, wondering what they taught females from age four. Males received extensive training in all aspects of Etterian life, from weapon mastery to security, to data analysis, even to farming kreso. His stomach gurgled as he glanced at his plate. It was hard to imagine such hardy beasts remained a staple of Etterian diets.

"Greetings Lady Arazyl, Lord Droal," Advisor Cales said, entering Xeus's chambers unannounced.

"Cales, what a lovely surprise." Arazyl offered a small smile, careful not to seem too pleased to see him. She rose to her feet and held out her hand to Droal. "It is time we took leave. I do believe Cales has many things requiring your attention, my king."

"Thank you for the meal, King Xeus." Droal clasped Arazyl's hand before escorting her from Xeus's chambers.

"My thanks," Xeus said to Cales, downing his juice before slamming his cup onto the table. "Did you have something specific I need to attend to?"

"Yes," Cales said, approaching the display vid on the side wall. He moved the magnetic-based chairs to the side before pulling two Maloidian swords off the adjacent wall. "I suspect your skills are somewhat lacking," he teased, tossing a sword at Xeus.

He chuckled, and despite his twinging muscles, snatched the sword out of the air before swinging it with practiced ease. The familiar weight tightened his grip, and the rush of a challenge fired along his veins. For a fleeting moment, joy sparked to life in his chest. Then with a battle roar as old as time, he leaped in the air, bringing the blade down.

Chapter Two

MACERA GAPED AT HER ex-boss like a fish out of water, her disbelief a parody of a horror vid in the mirror behind his bald head. The idiot squirmed in his seat as if she gave a damn he was uncomfortable performing this task.

"What do you mean you're letting me go?" She worked, past tense, at the curio shop in the casino's lobby. It wasn't much of a job, but at least it kept her fed and a roof over her head. "What am I supposed to do now?" She slammed her palms on his desk.

He jumped, his face paling, but she kept his gaze, flipping her mass of brown curls out of her eyes to do so.

"We will rehire you back once the revamp is complete...I think."

Her eyes widened. "You think? No work for, what, six months? Maybe even a year?" She yanked her access card off her pocket, tearing the fabric, before slapping the card down on his desk, startling the little twerp again. She snatched the severance pay out of his hands then glared at him, resting her hands on her wide hips. "This had better be decent or so help me." She stormed out of his office, ignoring the curious and nervous glances thrown at her. The jungle sounds peppered with lion roars fired her blood en route to the parking lot. *The bastard.*

She slid into the car she'd inherited from her grandmother. It was so old, the rust held the car together, nor was a S.A.D.I, Standard Automated Driving Intelligence, compatible with the car's antiquated software. Despite it being solar powered, it ran on prayer and violent cursing. She banged the door a few times until it stayed shut, only to sit there stunned with her hands gripping and releasing the bus-sized steering wheel.

What am I going to do?

The salary had barely covered her expenses. Her savings were non-existent. She owed the funeral parlor for Gran's burial, and there were outstanding bills for the house, such as it was. Old, dilapidated, a double story in a shady neighborhood, selling it would get her nothing. Not that she wanted to either. She had to live somewhere, and the house was cheaper than renting another place.

Biting her lip, she relished the sting, praying it held back the tears. The moment she let them loose, she'd cry for days, like she had after Gran's death. The car started at the second attempt, and she drove to a brown nondescript building in the same shady neighborhood, not too far from her home.

She needed music and an alcoholic beverage that promised to make her forget her woes for the evening. Not that she could afford to waste her tokens on booze. She parked her car in front of the building's entrance, not concerned with the possibility of an opportunistic yet blind individual stealing it. No one would touch it.

She slammed the door and leaned on it. At least the previous paints on her car were harmonic, which shone blue, green, and the final coat of white through the rust. She locked the door. The car had no S.A.D.I, no alarm system, no special anti-theft mechanism inserted through the steering wheel, nothing to deter would-be thieves. They simply weren't interested in it. Their loss, she chuckled, bouncing on her heels, excited about drowning her sorrows in illegal music and whatever drinks were the cheapest.

The weathered steel door had once been painted red. Now it showed as much character as her car. With a glance from side-to-side, she yanked the door open and skipped down the steps into the bowels of the building. The deeper she ventured, the more the bass of the music vibrated up her soles. The stench of smoke, sex, and stale perfume carried a welcoming sweetness. She burst into the room and smiled. They were playing the classics, the ones she loved. There was talk of the powers-that-be eradicating the ban on vids, music, and online games. She hoped they decided soon. It had been centuries since the vid that had triggered epilepsy in over a hundred-thousand teenage girls, killing them. Something about girls of a certain age being more susceptible to seizures. Gran had tried to explain, but it had gone over Macy's head. Now all restaurants, casinos, and radios played were ambiances, hence the lions at the casino. Studies had shown that the rumble and cries of predators triggered a flight or fight response so people gambled more recklessly.

People, of course, had taken the industries underground, and often, a newish song would make the popularity rounds. Until the Media

Police shut them down and sent them to Mars' penal colony. She shuddered at the idea of never dancing or singing again. Music fired her soul, empowered her to lose a few moments in joyful dance, where the state of her life and bank account didn't matter.

She chose a table, not in the back and not too close to the bar. It tended to get disruptive near the bar, and the booths enshrouded in darkness promised an unpleasant experience if she sat there. She was in no mood to deal with the undesirables who would accost her. A plain girl like her needed all the loving she could get or some such nonsense.

No, she did not.

"I'm surprised to see you at this time of the day," one of the regular waiters said.

She ordered her usual house white wine and added a shot of tequila—a special request just for today.

"Bad day, huh?" the waiter asked, and it wasn't due to an interest in her. The place was quiet with business having yet to pick up. So the poor dear was fending off boredom by forcing unpalatable conversation onto a depressed woman.

"You could say that," she said, taking pity on the guy. She swiped her wrist across the paypoint embedded in the table. "As soon as that's up, chase me home," she said before downing the tequila, sans lemon and salt. Since she was a regular, she could trust him. Not that she had ever asked his name. Nor had he offered it, for that matter. "And keep it coming, please." She gulped her wine, letting it join the fire in her belly—from anger and blessed tequila.

By the third glass of wine, she was nearing intoxication—the kind where she didn't care anymore. The kind she needed. She belted out choruses of songs she recognized, putting far more energy into the singing than she had in her previous job.

Yup, that was about the crux of it. She'd probably been let go since she hadn't proven herself and was redundant. Some guy tried to charm her, but she glared him into silence. She didn't have the energy to deal with a desperate man and his issues. She belted out another chorus and chuckled, now sipping the wine in front of her to have something to do.

"I like the way you sing," a man said, his voice not oily or insincere.

His honesty broke through her walls. She raised a wide-eyed gaze to meet his. He stood, taller than she'd expected, in some sort of expensive suit—charcoal gray if she wasn't mistaken. Not that she was a connoisseur of fine suits, just of broad shoulders.

"Thank you, I think." She flashed him a wobbly smile since her lips had entered Numbville.

He glanced at the wine in front of her and the empty tequila glass her waiter had yet to remove. "Bad day?"

"Yup, lost my job." She shrugged as if her imminent starvation wasn't important. Not that she would reveal that. She widened her smile, trusting her numb lips to convey some sort of friendliness. But when the song playing neared its chorus, she held up a finger, asking him to wait, then belted out the lyrics as if her last moments on this forsaken planet counted on her level of enthusiasm. "That felt good." She smirked, lifted the glass to her lips, and frowned at it taking a few tries.

"Why don't you sing for us?" He gestured to the stage.

Her eyebrows arched, and she laughed. "Sure, I will. You have a band playing all the time. Why the hell didn't I think of that?" She rolled her eyes then gripped the table as his face tilted. Best not to do that again. "Listen, dude, your stage is never used."

"You can sing to the music playing on the speakers." He dropped into a chair, uninvited. "I'll pay you for every night you perform."

"Are you serious?" She blinked at his blurred image, trying to assess his sincerity when she couldn't see his eye color.

"You can start tonight, as a trial, since you're here."

"But I'm...drunk." She hiccupped for added emphasis.

"You have just over an hour to sober. That's when the crowds start to arrive." He jumped up and held out his hand. She accepted it for a firm shake. "Ask the barkeeper for the mic. I look forward to hearing you perform,...?"

It took a while before she realized he waited for her to supply her name. "Macera Mitchell." She flashed him what she hoped was a bright smile.

"Dave, the barkeeper, may also have discarded dresses in the back if you want to shine tonight." He glanced down at her black trousers and boring, button-up white blouse with the torn pocket.

"Thank you, again." She watched him walk away, unable to contain her hope, her breathing erratic, her heart pounding. She gestured to the waiter and ordered coffee, hoping it would sober her as well as calm her nerves when she'd never sung in front of a crowd.

But she couldn't back down now. Music and singing were illegal, therein lay the attraction. That the Media Police might raid the club added a zing to her blood, bolstering her voice. She couldn't abandon the thrill for fear of capture.

Besides, she needed to eat.

Chapter Three

Planet Etteria
The Royal City of Issneen
The Royal Court
Months later

XEUS MOVED AROUND HIS office like a caged *sogair*—prowling, intense, ruthless. That he hadn't seen a *sogair* in years, with its dark red coat, sharp fangs, excellent vision, and hearing, didn't, in any way, affect his ability to prowl like one. He couldn't spare a smile if a life depended on it. Something troubled him, and he wasn't dealing well with it. Enyl escorted the first compatible female from another species. This was the *only* species so far to trigger the Ethera and as such was Etteria's salvation. This could be disastrous or life changing.

He had sensed Cales hovering behind him during the interaction. He had done so all day, soothing ruffled feathers as well as steering Xeus clear of oversensitive ambassadors. Xeus grunted, recognizing that Cales interceded more and more of late. He drew in a deep breath and glanced through his transparent walls to the vacant court.

The beauty of it was lost on him. The high vaulted ceilings were painted with poignant images. The dark blue and gold tapestries contrasted boldly against a white polished stone floor. His thoughts remained on what he knew of Earth and its inhabitants. More importantly, what he'd seen of this alien female.

She'd shown incredible skill, utilizing a fighting style they themselves employed. They called it Hatimaye, and he had believed it was unknown to all but Etteria. Was her species a warrior race to such an extent that the females also trained? What kind of males would endanger such treasures?

Regardless of how impressed he'd been, not only by her actions but her unusual coloring, he had to remain calm, strong, and confident. None of which he was managing. He glanced around his office and lingered on his white Fuyra desk. What it stood for, the generations of kings before him, the expectations of his ancestors, his people, and Etteria's future pressed on his shoulders until the thought of taking a step sucked the life from him.

He had just met his new daughter, Oriana, and he wondered, not for the last time, what she saw when she looked upon the Etterian species. They all had bronzed skin and long black hair that was fish-tail braided to their bootheels, honor willing. To lose honor was to lose a foot of their hair—a visual representation of one's failure. Their features were bold, dominant, their eyes dark blue unless the Ethera occurred between pairings. But those were rare. He couldn't recall the last pairing or gazing into adult ice blue eyes until today.

Centuries before, a civil war had broken out among them, and many lives were lost. Their king, Pius, Xeus's ancestor, approached the wise Durn for guidance. The Great Durn had devised Etteria's current approach—the extensive training, the development of a passionate people into a warrior race now feared and respected. The Durns modified Etterian genetics, and thus, the Ethera was born. He suspected that the Durn, revered for their higher intelligence and their statistical focus, hadn't anticipated the decline of the Etterian female birth rate. Now their males faced the void, unable to find contentment in meaningless liaisons, to end their lives in battle just to avoid the darkness consuming their souls.

Xeus was such a male.

When the herald had announced the entrance of Enyl and his princess, Oriana, this had stunned Xeus. *Princess?* He'd thought Enyl had selected a female to claim without the Ethera blessing the pairing. Such was an irresponsible, dangerous risk, and his son must've done so for a reason, one Xeus had soon learned had nothing to do with choice and more to do with the Maker's blessing.

His son had a Dar Eth.

And now Xeus had a daughter. A beautiful creature with ocean-red hair and bright green eyes, the same vivid green of their Ferusi gems. She was tiny in comparison to Etterian females, but she scented like delicious fruit. And there lay the crux of the matter.

He'd found his daughter appealing.

Her scent, softness, incredible beauty, *and* her inner strength made her a great find.

Maker.

He scowled, the rage building deep within him as his arousal throbbed. This was unacceptable and dishonorable. And he wasn't the only male who suffered so. He needed to bring these human females to Etteria. But how? Any decision he took could affect the survivability of Earth, long-term, as in hundreds of years into the future. He understood what his ancestors must've gone through before the decision to modify their race. He didn't want to harm Earth, but he *needed* to save Etteria.

"Alodon's balls, Xeus. She is exquisite." Cales marched into Xeus's office. "I've never...*felt* like this."

"Yes, therein lies the dilemma. We need to find human females with extreme urgency. I cannot have our males testing the strength of the Ethera between Enyl and Oriana."

"Yes... The urge is there." Cales sank into a comfy chair, resting his elbows on his bent knees. "Even her voice made me *feel*. I wonder what our ancestors would say if they saw how we react to such a creature."

Xeus grunted. Cales had the right of it. He did *feel* and the darkness in his soul pulsed with hungry eagerness. "Our males might fight the temptation to kidnap a female for themselves. We are not savages nor slavers."

"Agreed, the temptation is great." Cales frowned. "Also, it could be a female and not a species thing. Perhaps the Ethera has chosen this specific female. We would need to discover whether other human females spark the Ethera in our males."

"Yes, but how, Cales? That is what I am struggling with." Xeus paced, the white walls of his office pressing in. "If we approach mid-grade Earth in an ambassadorial role, we violate the Global Council. We cannot stoop to kidnapping either."

"And yet Yithia has no such qualms," Cales grumbled. "Perhaps we could *allow* a few Yithian slave ships to kidnap females then rescue them?"

"That seems like the only option at this point." Xeus clenched and unfurled his fingers. "Though, to endanger females does not sit well with me, Cales."

"Neither with me. We can only do what we can, Xeus. Protect the planet and rescue kidnapped females."

"True. To stand by and do nothing to prevent their harm is as dishonorable." And he would throw the full might of Etteria in this task. Guard earth with a battalion of battleships and have Malo's operatives infiltrate and monitor human bases between Etteria and Earth.

"Perhaps we need to approach this as if it were a battle? A multi-faceted strategy?" Cales said, now deep in thought.

"Continue." Xeus gestured that he was listening despite pacing the stifling confines of his office.

"Have you heard the buzz about sex-cybs?" Cales's words were so off-topic that Xeus shook his head. "They are cyborgs developed to bring pleasure."

Xeus jerked to a halt. "Cyborgs? As in mechanical creatures?"

"Yes. As you know, we relieve the tension once a day and view it as a chore. It is safe to do so since our hands do not summon the void. Would the cyborg not perform the same function?"

"Release into an inanimate object?" Xeus shuddered at the thought of it.

"An object that is the shape of a human female, or so I am told."

Xeus blinked at Cales. "Truth?"

"They have a sex center in the backwaters of space for...weary travelers." Cales punched into his O.D.I. and projected the location onto the extended display vid.

Xeus strode toward it, mesmerized.

"It is in Earth's system. Trust these humans to invent such an object," Xeus said, even though his heartbeat pounded in his ears.

An image of a sex-cyb appeared. They groaned. Her appearance was that of a human female with flowing hair the color of sunlight and pale green-brown eyes. Her body was perfect with large breasts that looked incredibly soft, a cinched-in waist, wide flaring hips, and long legs easily discernible in the small garment she wore.

"Do you think they could spark the Ethera?" Xeus asked, his voice a little too hoarse as he adjusted his armored pants around his arousal.

"I suspect only biological females are able to." Cales shrugged. "Hence why we should send a delegate."

"Do so. Choose a few volunteers sensing the void and have them test out whether releasing into...*that* brings the void closer."

"Done." Cales punched into his O.D.I.

"It is a pity we couldn't have them here." Xeus ran a lone finger down the display vid, tracing the curve of the sex cyb's cheek.

"Yes, that is a pity."

"Test first, then we shall decide." Xeus rubbed his hands together. "For this, I will insist the Global Council allow trade negotiations with Earth."

Planet Etteria

King Xeus's office

A week later

"WELL, THAT WAS QUICK," Xeus rasped, though grateful for the confirmation.

He'd just ended a communication with Supreme Commander Ulriq. The male's ice blue eyes were the defining factor. He'd also stated that one in his unit, Kanzo, son of Lenzo if Xeus recalled correctly, had also discovered his Dar Eth.

"Three Eths," Cales boomed, his excitement palpable.

Xeus grunted in response, wishing he could rouse as much enthusiasm, especially for something he'd instigated, prayed, and longed for.

"And all human females." Smiling, Cales sat in the comfy, his hand raised in mid-O.D.I typing.

Xeus could seek the void, now that his males would, at last, find contentment. It seemed their salvation was at hand. And once he received the results of the genetic compatibility tests done on Oriana, then he might even experience peace. An elusive concept for him. Though, whether humans were breeding compatible remained unknown. Perhaps the tests might confirm this? He doubted that the Ethera would choose a species unable to bear Etterian offspring. That seemed implausible.

To discover the Yithians had abducted both Dar Eths from Etterian custody made his vision haze in red. At least anger he could still experience without consequences. Teric's betrayal stung. Honor above all, but to stoop to this? "Have you tasked Operations Commander Malo with Teric's investigation?"

"Done, Xeus. I've informed Xan of the impending rescue attempts."

Xeus pinched his lips as he fisted his hands, relishing the tightening of his muscles. No species would stand in the way of Etteria's salvation. That Ulriq had to violate Global Council laws didn't bother Xeus. The council members were a bunch of sanctimonious males with no self-control. They had a marked lack of honor, integrity, respect for themselves, for the species they represented, and for other species in general. He was grateful Ulriq had informed him of this, lest the council blindside Xeus at the next assembly.

He slumped, the weight of his age, wisdom, and experience dragging on his shoulders. "I do not recall having as much enjoyment when we were their age, Cales."

"You say that as if we are ancient, Xeus. You and I are in prime condition, though that cannot be said for all our males." Cales didn't glance up from his O.D.I. "I do approve of the new law you implemented, even though the males in your court are displeased. A distressed ambassador is a joyful advisor." He grinned at Xeus, implying he was the joyful one. "Wait until they discover this does not mean on Gikaet. We have mines, farms, dockyards, and town disputes requiring their assistance." Cales shifted in the comfy. "Discussions I cannot wait to have with each complainant."

Xeus drew in a slow breath, not willing to break his bond's high spirits by informing him that the law excluded the two of them. There would be no trips to Gikaet. He let Cales have this moment. Soon, he'd come to realize they had no one to replace them during the month's warrior service he had implemented into law.

Planet Etteria
Xeus's Office
After an Evening Meal

Xeus paced his office under Oriana's vigilance. He struggled to contain his reactions with strange emotions pelting his control. "How do you plan on approaching Earth, my daughter?" He glanced at her for a moment before he resumed pacing.

"I will set up an appointment with the ESA's director. That's Earth Space Agency. They control Earth's interstellar travel. Malo will masquerade as the Etterian ambassador to lay down our terms. The negotiations will commence from there."

"It is simple but effective. I have yet to conceptualize how human females will be introduced to our males, though." Xeus gripped the back of the comfy, channeling his restless energy into stiffening and releasing his muscles, starting with his legs to his shoulders and down again.

"Battleships of females delivered to Etteria would be preferable." Cales chuckled from his position against the wall.

"Yes, I agree, but we will need protocols in place. How will we recruit females? Where to house them once they reach Etteria?" Xeus said.

"If they do not have an Eth, they will not leave Earth." Oriana laced her fingers through Enyl's. He flashed her a sensual smile and caressed her hand with his thumb. Their bond grew stronger each day, proving the Ethera had chosen well. "Etteria cannot cater for women indefinitely. My proposal is this... A dating website."

"A what?" Xeus frowned after his O.D.I. had updated him. *Dating? Date? What did a fruit have to do with a Dar Eth?*

"A dating website is where humans go to find love. If we create such a central point, we can invite your males to browse the females eager for a match. We just need to make sure full-length images of the women are available. That is what triggers the Ethera."

"Yes, that could work. A directory of sorts," Enyl said.

"They can apply if they agree to off-world life and alien matings. Perhaps we can offer incentives like what Coldar did with me." She laughed—a delightful tinkle that reverberated off Xeus's white walls. "An education, Ferusi gems, or tokens."

Xeus paced again. For Etteria, the combined cost of the incentives would be negligible.

Still smiling, she said, "Malo will have to play the charmer, smiling for the audiences, showing off his Etterian physique, convincing the director that he is an engineer-cum-ambassador."

Enyl grinned, no doubt imagining Malo being amenable. "I'm sure he will rise to the challenge."

"He is not going to like this plan." Cales smirked.

"It is for Etteria. He does not have an opinion," Xeus said, anger hardening his voice. His unusual mood had Enyl studying him, concern darkening his features. Xeus scowled.

"Perhaps you should do the negotiations, Father... If they anger you, and they will, you can detonate a building." Oriana teased Xeus, and for a moment, his lips twitched.

But his presence on Earth would be ill-advised. If he couldn't manage self-control with his daughter's scent, how would he cope surrounded by unclaimed human females? It was for this reason he'd tasked her and Enyl. It would remove the temptation of Oriana from his males and him.

Volunteer males were en route to the sex center on the moon Calisto. It would be a two-week journey at full fusion pulse. Two weeks? He wasn't certain how he'd survive this evening, never mind fourteen days.

"When do you intend to depart?" Xeus asked.

"The closest battleship is the *Chikara*. It arrives tomorrow. We should be on our way by the setting of the magnus sun tomorrow evening," Enyl said.

"Excellent. Keep me informed. All of Etteria is with you." The urge to flee his office drove Xeus. He made to do so, only to halt when Enyl called his name. His son bounded after him, a frown marring his temple. Xeus drew in a deep calming breath and waited. "What is it?"

"You do not seem yourself." Enyl squeezed Xeus's shoulder.

"It has been a trying day. I need to swing my greatsword. If you have Gika hidden in your chambers, please do inform me." Xeus's attempt at humor brought Enyl's brief smile. He clasped his son's forearm. "Return safely." He marched off with an unexpected heaviness in his chest he couldn't name.

Chapter Four

MACY STILLED AND LOWERED the towel, despite her wet tresses curling and cooling her neck. The scratching repeated, skittering shivers down her spine. She unknotted the towel covering her damp body and yanked on a nightshirt and gown. Bolting across her bedroom, she paused to slip on slippers then padded to the back door.

Through the window, she studied the unkempt backyard, peering into the bushes and to the wilds beyond. She'd played there as a child, spending summers careening down the embankment and into the stream below.

At the whine, she slumped, releasing a long breath. "Arnie?" Swinging the door open to the old mix-breed, she tried not to meet his soulful gaze. All she had was noodles with no tokens to purchase anything remotely good for a dog.

"Are you hungry, my boy?" She opened the door wide and scurried to the antiquated kitchen to make her last packet of Ramen.

While the water boiled, she crooned to the mutt. She carried the bowl to the back door where he sat on the threadbare mat. He whined as she huffed at the steam—the aroma of roast chicken was so far from what she could remember eating, but beggars couldn't be choosy.

She placed the bowl before him and sat on the step, ruffling his coat. He slurped the noodles the way she did after a day without food. When the bowl shone squeaky clean in the fading moonlight, he rested on his haunches and whined again.

"That's all I have." She curled in her shoulders, unable to help this desperate soul. "You might as well find someone else, Arnie. I have no job, no tokens—" She sniffed.

He rested his paw on her leg and dipped his head, settling the full weight of his bottomless gaze on her.

"I'm serious, my boy."

His head whipped up, and with a heartbreaking whimper, he fled, disappearing into the bushes.

She scrambled to her feet and followed. "Arnie. Please." Ducking to peek under a bush, she called to him. A rustle to her left had her facing it, hopeful she'd find him. "Come, you can sleep by me tonight."

A light flickered on in the house next door.

She winced. "Sorry, Ms. Carstens."

The light went off.

"I tell you, Arnie. I can't feed you anymore. I don't even have enough for me." The vise grip on her heart tightened at the thought of abandoning him. A sob tore from her. She smothered it with a deep breath. "But at least you can be warm." She raised her gaze to the thick velvet navy sky and shivered, pulling the nightgown closed. "Or if you know someone with food...?"

Her singing gig didn't pay as well as she'd hoped, and it wasn't as if jobs for shop assistants grew on trees. She snorted. The real issue was her lack of support of any kind. She had no family, not since her gran had died. Her mom, Calida, had died when Macy had just turned thirteen. Her aunt Caldera, as well. They had gone out to celebrate their birthday, being twins it had made sense at the time. Macy couldn't fault them for that, even though she'd railed at the universe for months after their funeral.

That their accidental run-in with an automated tanker had been just that, accidental, yet it was the start of her cursed karma. Her father? Some *dumbass*—her mother's words—had knocked her mother up and run for the hills. So no help from that quarter. If it hadn't been for her gran, Macy would have fallen to the foster system to raise. Gran would've followed her daughters if she hadn't had to care for her granddaughter. Looking back, Macy understood what a devastation that must have been, to lose her children at the same time.

She could remember lying awake at night listening to Gran's crying. And every year, on the anniversary of their deaths, they would traipse to the cemetery to place flowers on the gravestone the twin sisters shared. Followed by the appearance of a bottle and Gran's ragged sobbing into the early hours of the morning.

Once, Macy had tried to console her. That hadn't ended well. It had left a gaping wound in their relationship with no words spoken for days. She knew then to never mention her mother, her aunt, or their deaths.

"No work, no food." She crept farther into the backyard.

She glanced over her shoulder at her gran's old dilapidated home. Her shoulders slumped as she fought the sorrow of her situation, of losing the last link to her family. But she had no choice. She'd put it on the market tomorrow.

"Arnie, come now. It's cold."

Something moved in the shadows, too big to be a dog. She gulped, trailing her gaze from its booted feet to black eyes. A squeak escaped her. She shook her head, trying to clear her vision. But when she focused on the shadow splitting into three, she stumbled back. Pressing a hand to her chest, the pounding of her heart beating a staccato rhythm, she cried out.

With the damp grass penetrating her bedroom slippers, she spun on her heels. Bright light flashed, highlighting the house, its cracked windows, and worn, stained walls.

Fire exploded across her shoulders. She fell forward, splaying onto the ground. A scream lodged in her throat, words came out garbled, and her body stiffened as her limbs tingled and numbed. *Crawl, dammit.* But she couldn't command herself to move.

Dark shapes loomed over her, cutting off her vision of the night sky and Ms. Carstens' bedroom light. "Help me," formed in her mind, but her lips remained shut.

Another flash of light preceded a fiery tingle across her skin.

She convulsed, and blessed darkness claimed her.

"It's okay," a woman said.

Macy struggled into a sitting position, groaning as the throbbing in her head doubled and blurred her vision with shards of pain piercing her skull.

"What happened?" She kept her eyes closed while rubbing her temples. Nausea hit her, churning her stomach. She moaned, swallowing in desperation.

"Here, eat this. It's a protein bar and tastes like shit, but it might help the nausea." Something sticky was pressed into her palm.

She opened her eyes and frowned at the unfamiliar surroundings. A sickly yellow light along the bulkhead worsened her nausea. A bubble of bile formed in her throat. She shoved the tasteless food into her mouth, gagging at the strange texture and bitter flavor.

"Are we in a cell?" She darted her gaze from side-to-side, fighting the numbing fear gripping her. The walls were a dark gray, like metal sheets with precise gaps between the panels. "On a submarine?" The door to the room was like something out of *The Hunt for the Red October*, a classic vid her Gran had had an illegal copy of. The contraband was her treasure due to the *yummy* man in it, her Gran's words. He did have a nice voice, though.

"We've been kidnapped," the stranger said.

"What?" The trembling of Macy's hands worsened. "Why? I've no tokens, no family. I'm not even attractive." She grimaced at the woman with her pale blond hair falling around her face in a halo of curls. She had pretty eyes as well. Macy harrumphed.

"I'm Cyndi Stanford. I'm sorry you got taken too."

Apologies made no difference, but it felt good to hear it. On the other hand, why did Cyndi feel the need to apologize? She was in the same predicament.

"Macera Mitchell, but you can call me Macy." She rose to her feet, stretching the kinks out of her back and stamping her left foot which had fallen asleep. "How long have you been in here?"

"Maybe two or three days." Cyndi shrugged, well tried to, but her slumped shoulders made it difficult.

"You've been here all alone?" Macy squeaked, horrified at the thought of seeing these walls without someone to speak to.

When all Cyndi could do was sniff, Macy hugged her. This opened the floodgates. Cyndi cried heart-wrenching sobs.

Macy patted the girl's back, though what comfort she could offer was minuscule. "We'll get out of this. There has to be a way."

Cyndi shook her head. "It's worse than you can imagine." She sniffed. "They put a device in my ear so I can understand them. This is their first visit to Earth, and they plan on many more."

"So, we're guinea pigs?" Macy asked.

Cyndi nodded before taking a deep breath and dashing her tears away with shaking fingers.

"For what?" Macy leaned back to meet Cyndi's gaze.

"I think it's to do with an arena. They mention bets and winning big."

"What? Arena? Like from the Greek and Roman days?" Macy frowned.

"Yeah, their champion escaped, and they're searching for a replacement."

"I'm so not following here. You said Earth like they're aliens or something?" At Cyndi's silence, Macy scowled. "I know aliens have made contact somewhere in our known galaxy, but I didn't think it was to enslave us." She tried to summon the image she could remember of the alien—green, loads of tentacles? They hadn't seemed threatening or welcoming.

Or the recent contact with a warrior species known as Etterians. Her heart fluttered, and she held her palm to her chest as if it might soothe her. With the way her life had spiraled out of control, running into one of those was never going to happen. She sighed, dreaming of a tall, broad-shouldered man in military garb storming into the cell and sweeping her off her feet. With those muscles, he'd be able to carry her. She glanced at her dimpled knees and winced.

"Well, the Yithians are desperate. Their Earthian champion was a female, and she brought them great wealth."

Yithians? Macy mouthed. Nope, not a word she'd heard before. "Earthian?"

"Their word, not mine." Cyndi tugged on her wrinkled pencil skirt. "I don't know how many women they've taken. There are cells through that door so there might be more of us."

"I don't mind traveling the stars. It's not as if Earth's special to me," Macy said, hoping to change the subject or highlight a hidden silver lining. She was desperate to believe there was hope, and that perhaps, she was having a nightmare. Aliens kidnapping humans had been the subject of many novels and vids. *That shit couldn't be real, right?*

"Me too. What do you do for a living?" Cyndi scooted back to rest against the inclined metal wall.

"I lost my job as a shop assistant. I've tried to make ends meet by singing at an underground jazz club." Macy pulled up her legs to tuck them under her nightshirt. The cell was cold, and the warmth of the thin fabric sent goosebumps across her skin. "You?"

"Personal secretary to a lazy, arrogant CEO's son." She shifted closer to Macy bringing her body heat with her. Macy shivered, wishing the damn aliens had warned her so she could've dressed warmer.

"Can you sing something for me?"

No, she wasn't in the mood, but Cyndi's tremulous smile made Macy succumb. "Sure, what would you like? Happy? Sad?"

Cyndi folded her arms across her chest and curled her shoulders inward. "Anything. I've just been so lonely in here."

A sad song might not be such a good idea, with the fresh tears pooling in Cyndi's eyes. So Macy belted out something about happiness and sunshine.

By the end of the second rendition, Cyndi swung her bare foot to the rhythm. "Good choice."

Macy patted Cyndi on the hand then rocked on her backside until she rested against the wall. When she sang, the weight of their situation had lifted for a few minutes.

"You have a gorgeous voice. I bet you had your male audience panting." Cyndi pulled on her skirt again, trying to get it to cover her knees.

Macy snorted. "Yeah, something magical and biologically impossible happened. Wouldn't surprise me if those old farts came in their pants."

"Ew." Cyndi giggled.

"Sing with me, Cyndi."

Cyndi held up her hands as if in self-defense. "I suck."

Macy gestured to their 'crowded' cell. "Does it matter? Who will hear you?"

Even when Macy switched songs, Cyndi sang along, breaking into laughter between verses. The noise they were making didn't seem to penetrate the cell walls. The door remained shut. Peering into the cell's dark corners, she searched for security cameras while doubting she'd be able to recognize alien tech.

They sang a few more times before falling into silence.

"Thanks, Macy. That was fun. Let's make it our theme song."

"Interesting choice. It's all about hot sex, you know that, right?" Macy wiggled her eyebrows. At least Cyndi wore a grin. That was progress. "What the hell." Macy curled onto her side on the cold metal floor and rested her head on her bent arm. "Any chance of a rescue?"

"No," Cyndi said after a few minutes had passed.

"We're humans. I bet you these aliens have never dealt with us before."

"You're right. We're stubborn, opinionated, willful." Cyndi raised her face which the yellow light painted in a jaundiced glow.

"If they knew us well, they wouldn't let us anywhere near their planets," Macy mumbled as sleep called to her. Trapped on a spaceship, she couldn't worry about her gran's house, unpaid bills, or finding work. None of that mattered anymore.

"Yeah. We haven't been kind to ours."

"Or to each other." Macy smothered a yawn. "Night, Cyndi."

"Night, Macy. Thanks for keeping me company."

Macy sighed. "I won't say it's a pleasure."

"I won't expect you to."

CHAPTER FIVE

"WHAT IN ALODON'S HELL is going on, Cales?" Xeus ended the comm with Supreme Commander Ulriq and a Yithian Commander Pyo. Said Yithian was seeking an alliance for a rebellion against their king, Urio. "We are finding our Dar Eths, have formed an alliance with the Gika, and are assisting in a rebellion against Yithia." His body trembled. Each limb tugged downward as if weighted. His inability to find joy or energy thrust a fiery burn of anger along his veins. His impatience and intolerance grew with each passing day. As it was, he spent hours swinging his greatsword, hoping to stave off these volatile emotions. "I now have two daughters, and Maker willing, a new addition to our bonds will soon be announced."

"Adopting Erox was honorable, but had I been the king, I would have killed her father, Xeus." Cales stilled mid-typing on his O.D.I. "Such a male does not deserve life."

"And what if Lady Erox held a little affection for her father?" Xeus shook his head. "I could not in good conscience bring further pain onto her."

"Hence why you rule and I do not. Lady Ava has done wonders in reviving Lady Erox's damaged spirit." Cales flicked through the holographics hovering an inch above his arm.

"She has. I do hope what offspring Oriana births will carry the warmth and fortitude of the humans."

"You want more offspring?" Cales raised his gaze.

"For Enyl, yes. Oriana's test results were conclusive. Her human genetics are compatible with ours. It *is* possible for her to conceive, though the results couldn't explain their unusual glow." What had worn him down regarding the longevity of the Etterians had faded upon receiving the confirmation the Ethera would be successful. And yet, there was no relief for him, no ability to breathe easier, to wake up rested.

"Compatibility would mean any Eth with a human Dar Eth may sire offspring. Would you have another if you could?"

Xeus's breath caught. A crushing pain held his chest captive. *To have more offspring? I would, without a doubt, but with the void closing in, the* Maker *would never grant me such a blessing.* "You know my time has gone, Cales." He cleared his throat.

"What talk is this? You can still bear offspring." Cales leaped out of the comfy to place his hand on Xeus's shoulder and held him still, forcing him to meet his matching dark blue gaze. "Remember, I am as young as you. When you succumb to the void, so will I, my battle-bond."

"That is unjust, Cales," Xeus said, his voice rising. "You cannot place that responsibility on my shoulders. Remove it." He threw all his authority behind the words, but it made no impact.

"Why? So, you can cease to fight the void without consequences? I will not." Cales tightened his grip. "Previous kings did not experience this much change happening at once. None of your ancestors had to endure this, conquer so many obstacles as you, Xeus. Etteria *needs* you."

Xeus grumbled his discontent, but he forced himself to admit Cales was correct. He couldn't allow the void to consume him, not until Etteria was secure on all fronts. Perhaps, Maker willing, he could die on the battlefield in the war with Yithia. He squared his shoulders, refusing to succumb to the dark void threatening to overpower him. *To feel is to fail*, that was their Etterian creed, and it applied to negative emotions, as well.

"Thank you, Cales." With a nod, he acknowledged the loyalty his battle-bond displayed. He stepped back, drew in a deep breath, and sank into the comfy behind his desk. "I am pleased that Ladies Jacqueline and Ava are secure. The repercussions of these Yithian incursions we have yet to realize."

"These females have endured much, my king." Cales released a long breath. "Lady Jacqueline had to battle a *sogair*, and Lady Ava was a gift for King Urio and bartered for like a crate of omeika."

"Truth?" Xeus stilled. "Have you seen this?"

"No, Sub-Commander Nerx mentioned this in a report. He is serving on the Battleship *Kushin*."

"Nerx? Tarx's son?" Xeus asked to which Cales nodded. "His father was an unpleasant male."

"Nerx commed a sec vid prior to Lady Ava's teleporting. Interested?" Cales flashed Xeus a cheeky smile.

Xeus grunted and bounded up, striding to the extended display vid. He preferred this larger vid to the smaller one on his desk.

The vid played. A tall, sunlight-haired human female jumped into the shuttle with a blaster held in her hands. Her stance was military and vigilant. Cales paused the vid just as she peered into the camera. Xeus analyzed the features of Ulriq's Dar Eth. After a few moments of silence, Cales activated the vid and continued until it fell upon a black-haired female who was Kanzo's Dar Eth. Xeus's sucked in a breath at the pain on her features, how she held herself tense, keeping her emotions to herself. No one in the shuttle had noticed her stillness. And when she screamed Kanzo's name, her fear was palpable with her wide and exquisite green eyes.

The human male who had instigated this adventure was as pale-haired as his sister. And in the vid, there were two other females. One was tiny with white-blue hair. She clung to the human male. The other female shivering with fear had red-gold hair and brown eyes.

Protective instincts reared to the fore. A scared female shouldn't sit well with a warrior, no matter her ethnicity. This shuttle had held two frightened females, and worst of all, none of his males had attended to them.

Xeus activated his O.D.I. and messaged Remi. Xeus needed him to reinforce their creed and the importance of tending to *any* female. Once done, he returned his gaze to the display vid and the tiny red-haired female.

Victoria, Xeus recalled, was Teric's Dar Eth. That male now had two females under his protection. He was also the first Etterian intent on living on Earth, with his daughter and Victoria. Xeus had no intention of requesting permission from Earth's authorities. Let Earth attempt to deny an Etterian male residence, and there would be hell to pay.

Chapter Six

THE SWISH OF THE door opening woke Macy. She sat up and rubbed the sleep out of her eyes when a *thing* walked into the cell. Images flashed in her mind of shadows with black eyes and thick boots. It looked like a man with a shark head—a great white shark, not a hammerhead. The light reflecting off its skin made her shudder. It shimmered like a wet slimy fish. The sharkman stared at her, its black eyes showing no warmth or emotion as it held something out to Cyndi, speaking to her in strange hisses and clicks. Cyndi responded adding an almost melodic quality to the sounds. Macy's eyes widened as she clambered to her feet, pulling her pajama gown closed around her sleep shirt. At least it reached her knees, but the knowledge of her nudity underneath didn't help her feel any better.

"Ew," she said as soon as the door closed behind it. The lighting flickered from white to yellow again. "And you can talk to it?"

"Yup, thing in the ear, remember?" Cyndi offered a smile. "Here, one protein bar for you and water packets. Finally." She handed a bar and packet to Macy before sitting. "They don't often bring water."

Macy consumed the meager fare. When Cyndi tossed the packets onto the floor, Macy did the same but squealed when the wrappers disintegrated into thin air. She leaped to her feet and darted to the farthest corner. Cyndi laughed.

"Not funny," Macy mumbled.

Cyndi's laughter dwindled into giggles and ended with hiccups.

They sat in silence for what felt like two hours before Cyndi asked her to sing something. Macy sang a modernish love song, as in released the last few years before the media ban.

"Are these the usual ones you sing?" Cyndi snuggled against the wall.

Macy slipped off her nightgown, settled beside Cyndi, and draped the nightgown across their laps. "Nope, I sing some of the greats from Frank Sinatra or Nina Simone."

"I would've loved to have seen you perform." Cyndi's expression turned wistful.

Macy arched a brow then dipped her chin to her chest. She'd never had friends who supported her. It would've been wonderful to know Cyndi was in the crowd, cheering for her.

"Why is that surprising?"

Macy raised her gaze and attempted a shrug. "I see you more as a pop fan if music wasn't illegal."

"I am, of course, but the greats are...classic." She flashed Macy another smile.

Tossing her nightgown onto Cyndi's lap, Macy jumped up, grabbed the imaginary microphone, and belted out a classic from Nina Simone.

Cyndi clapped, singing along with far more enthusiasm than skill. At a scraping, like metal along stone, she tackled Macy to the floor, yelling at her to keep her eyes shut. Thick, sticky foam rained on them, saturating them, and bringing on the shivers.

Time slowed as they lay sprawled in the icky substance and waited, their breathing ragged. When all was clear, Cyndi pushed off Macy.

"What the hell?" Macy sat up, wiping the stuff off her face, not willing to open her eyes until she was sure it was safe to do so. That took a few swipes before she was confident enough to try a peek. Cyndi held out the nightgown. Macy accepted it and buried her face in it. Having been trapped between Cyndi and Macy, it was dry.

"Some sort of detergent. It burns the eyes," Cyndi wrung out her hair that hung limply over a shoulder.

With trembling fingers, Macy gathered the dank mess of her hair. Tears burned at the backs of her eyes. She let them flow while she twisted the remnants of foam from her hair.

"Just give the foam a few minutes. It evaporates."

Macy shivered at the thick, soapy feel of the foam coating her skin. *Oh, what I'd do for a shower. And a coffee.* Ramen noodles would be wonderful about now. She sucked in a sharp breath. With Cyndi's gaze on her, Macy couldn't lose her shit. Her new friend needed her to be strong.

Forcing a chuckle, she said, "Dammit, Cyndi, I lost my mic."

"My folks are on an arctic cruise. Mom saved up forever for it." Cyndi sucked on the protein bar as if it tasted like a grilled cheese sandwich.

Macy shuddered, staring at hers, untouched and resting on her lap. A sharkman must have delivered it while she slept. "But I thought ship cruises had fallen away."

"Nope, just fewer, I guess. When the polar ice caps melted, there wasn't much to see. Now that they're frozen again and losing large chunks of ice, the cruises are available." Cyndi licked her thumb and grimaced. "My younger brother Allen is a pilot for ESA."

"Earth Space Agency?" Macy clasped her hands to her chest. "Does he fly into outer space?"

"Sometimes, though mostly between Earth and Lunar Base." Cyndi dipped her head and sniffed. "He always wanted to explore space, and here I am beating him to it." When she raised her chin, tears had pooled on her eyelashes. "What about you, Macy? Who are you leaving behind?"

Darkness crushed Macy's chest, and she struggled to breathe. She blinked the haze aside and focused on Cyndi. "I...have no one. My gran just died, but I lost my mom and aunt years ago."

"I'm so sorry." Cyndi squeezed Macy's hand.

Macy usually shrugged off sympathy, but this time, she covered Cyndi's hand. "So, I can venture into space as free as a bird."

Cyndi grinned. "I like the sound of that."

"Will you be missed?" Macy draped her nightgown across their laps. As thin as it was, it provided some relief from the cold.

"Only from work. Allen doesn't check in on me unless Mom asks him to. We don't have a close relationship. He's quite a bit younger than me."

"I wonder how they scout us out?" Macy frowned. "I mean, you and I were miles apart and alone. They can't have thousands of aliens lurking in the shadows ready to nab an unsuspecting woman."

"They scan the city, searching for unguarded female lifeforms."

Well, that explains it. "So owning a sex-cyb wouldn't have saved me." She grinned. "Good to know."

"Ew, Macy." Cyndi giggled. "Would you do a cyborg?"

"Hell, yes, when the alternative is—" she flashed her palms, "fresh air."

"They do come without emotional baggage."

Macy laughed. "Yes, yes, they do."

That day of girlish chit-chat went far to bolster Macy. By the time she found herself confronting an alien, she knew almost everything about Cyndi, from her favorite color to the worst childhood memory. Macy had shared as much.

When the sharkman had stepped into the cell, as her alien first contact, color her unimpressed. Part of her had hoped Cyndi had misheard Yithians for Etterians. But alas, what stepped through that door was in no way bronze-skinned and gorgeous.

It had entered again—Scarface, Cyndi called it. Macy watched the arrogant son of a bitch—without a doubt. And the way he spoke down to Cyndi, his words clipped, his gaze unwavering as if he addressed a lesser species, shot fire through Macy until her heartbeat deafened her and a wave of heat flushed her body from her toes to her ears.

What gave them the right to steal women? Yes, yes, the fittest survive, she got that. One would think aliens were superior with better things to do than kidnap defenseless people and cart them off to who knew where. What if she'd had a child? What if she had a sick parent? And the least they could have done was provide a freakin' blanket. Last night, she'd slept like shit. Freezing cold, shivering on a rigid surface with damp clothing due to their idea of sanitation, all thanks to these idiots. She'd be lucky if she didn't get pneumonia.

She'd had enough. From whence she got the courage or stupidity, she would never know. While *Scarface* hissed at Cyndi, Macy stormed up to it and poked it in the chest. The thick armor bruised her fingertip, but the pain didn't stop her. She only wished it had or if her conscience—in her gran's voice—had been vocal. It hadn't. It had, in fact, been unusually quiet. Probably scared shitless, which she realized in hindsight may have been the better approach.

Cyndi's eyes were wide when Macy shoved past her. "Macy, no," she whispered, dragging her fingers along Macy's arm as if to yank her back.

Macy shook her off and faced it, poking him again with another finger. "Listen here, fish breath. I demand you free us. Who the hell gave you the right to take us?" Macy huffed, gripping her hips.

He placed his three-fingered hand in the middle of her chest and shoved, sending her flying. She stumbled but caught her balance.

"Don't touch me," she yelled, her fist raised.

He hefted his black gun with the yellow blinking light and, without hesitation, fired at her.

She hadn't seen that one coming. Why hadn't she noticed the damn thing in his hands? *Idiot.* Her gran's voice echoed in Macy's head as she writhed on the floor, the fiery tingles that had preceded her kidnapping once more traversing her body, numbing her limbs, and smothering her ability to speak.

On a whimper, she froze, now immobile. Scarface stomped across, hissed something at a jabbering Cyndi then fired at Macy again.

Chapter Seven

Planet Etteria
The Royal City of Issneen
Later than preferred.

CITUS PORTED ONTO THE docking bay, sighing at the first sight of his home. Weeks had passed since he'd left the Kushin, en route to Etteria. So much had required his attention, from one ambassador to the conflict at the Fuyra mines. Now he was home. The sky was perfect today. The scent of the ocean carried on a delightful breeze.

He strode toward the hover, eager to see his brother. Eager to impart all he'd experienced and the cost to Etteria. The expense was a necessity, the negotiations a success. But Citus longed for the GC to hold the Yithians accountable for kidnapping, slavery, and violations of their global laws. Something he would reiterate when he saw Xeus.

"Drop me off at the garden entrance, Pilot," he said.

"Yes, my prince," the pilot said, and the craft rose in a swift yet graceful elevation.

Within minutes, Citus found himself disembarking. He leaped down to the soft ground covered in blue grass. Drawing a deep breath, he strolled along various paths, stopping to pick a white hahyt blossom before bringing it to his nose to inhale.

Maker. How I've missed Etteria.

Like the expansive sky with dark clouds roiling in the distance and the magnus and minus suns painting green across the red sea. Maloid's dark gray skies, with constant electrical storms, were mesmerizing to behold, but the wide-open expanses of Etteria's pink sky was far more beautiful to him. There was a sense of freedom to it.

He meandered his way to the court and upon discovering it vacant, strode to Xeus's office, bursting in without requesting access. Xeus sat at his desk, Cales on a nearby comfy. It seemed as if time made no impact on their lives. His brother's head shot up at the intrusion, his eyes widened, and he bounded up to grasp Citus on his forearm. The small smile that played across his lips was all he expressed.

Citus frowned and sliced a glance at Cales, who nodded. *Alodon's hell.* The void couldn't and wouldn't claim his blood-bond. But when it came time, there was nothing Citus could say or do that would stop it.

"Citus, at last." Xeus gestured to a comfy.

"How is Lady Ava?" Citus sat close to Cales, the male he needed to speak to the most.

"She is well, as are all the Dar Eths under our protection." Xeus slumped into a comfy, as well.

The excitement that had added a bounce to his step and allowed him to wake rejuvenated faded. Citus gritted his teeth. If Xeus wanted to discuss the Dar Eths, then he would...for now. "How many?"

"Four so far. We have placed a perimeter of battleships around Earth to thwart Yithia. I have tasked Malo to act as ambassador."

"Malo? Do you not trust these humans?" Citus hadn't noticed any dishonorable traits when he'd spoken to the females.

"It is at my daughter's suggestion." Xeus rubbed his chin. "She advised Etteria not to trust them."

"Daughter? Yes, Ulriq mentioned Enyl has a Dar Eth."

"Have you met a human woman, my prince?" Cales asked him, drawing Citus's gaze from Xeus's face, the dark circles under his eyes alarming.

"Yes, I met Ladies Ava, Jack, and Tory during the rescue. It is the reason for my delay. I attended to what we owed Ambassador Barro, and even though I added our navigation charts to the Scimitar as agreed, I had the forethought to remove Earth's location."

"Wise indeed. Our attempts to prevent Yithians from stealing our females would be further compounded by Maloid's involvement." Xeus leaned forward, resting his elbows on his knees. "And your thoughts on the human women you met?"

Ah, so this interests my brother? "Their scents are intoxicating, fertile, and their variety of features are incredible, so appealing. Not once had I considered the possibility of choice. To prefer yellow hair to red or brown?" Citus grinned. "And they're not weak, able to endure much without breaking. Ava enthralled Barro, and had he not been so greedy, he might have kept her."

"As was King Urio impressed," Xeus said. "He stated in a written missive that she was a delight, beautiful, and it was understandable why we kept our females hidden."

"He still believes she is Etterian?" Citus chuckled.

"Yes, he sold her since she was too honest for his court. He was not apologetic that his males had kidnapped her nor that they had violated

GC laws. I have long suspected that many GC ministers are bribed to remain silent in the face of these injustices." Anger blazed in his dark blue eyes, and for a moment, they paled, alarming Citus who shot another glance at Cales.

"We need a non-Etterian to infiltrate the council," Cales said.

"Yes, one acceptable to the members with our interests at heart." Xeus rubbed a hand over his face. "Remain for a while, brother. I might need you to assist in the negotiations with Earth. Malo is not as patient as you."

"He should be more so as our head assassin," Citus said, even though the idea of staying on Etteria for a while did appeal to him.

"Ulriq is en route to Earth to deliver Lady Tory and Medic Teric then will return to Etteria with the two Dar Eths."

"I am excited to see how Kanzo is treating Lady Ava,' Citus said, unable to curtail an eager smile.

"As if an Eth would mistreat his Dar Eth?" Cales chuckled.

Citus agreed. The concept of such occurring was absurd. "As my first human female, she made an impression on me."

"Without a doubt. Oriana is as memorable." Xeus scowled.

Citus stiffened. *Why does Xeus's expression not match his words?* "Where are Enyl and his princess?"

"En route to Earth, which was a wise decision considering her knowledge of her home world." Cales sipped his giyua juice before placing the cup on the table. "Not to mention she scented so good, it was a true test of our self-control."

"Truth?" Arching his eyebrow, Citus glanced from Cales to Xeus, who bounded up and headed for the door.

"I will see you at the evening meal." He left his office post-haste.

Citus stared out the transparent walls watching Xeus stride across his court. "How close is it?"

"It is not, but he believes it is."

"Alodon's balls." Citus jumped up to pace. "Perhaps a trip to Gikaet? I am here. I could attend to any issues that arise."

Cales's smile broke forth, proving the offer a propitious one. "Yes, such a venture would be of value."

Citus ran a hand over his face. Thank the Maker he'd returned when he had. He punched into his O.D.I. informing Remi of his concerns. If anyone could assist Xeus, it would be the Base Commander.

"I will arrange our immediate departure." Cales was out the door, taking the same path Xeus had.

Citus frowned, praying to the Maker that a killing spree on Gikaet would aid both males. For if Xeus succumbed to the void, his closest battle-bond Cales would follow him.

Chapter Eight

Macy grumbled at the phantom hand stroking her hair like her mother used to do. Visions of her birthdays, presents and cake waiting for her. Aunt Caldera dancing around the table with her cocktail raised above her head. Mom teasing her and shooing her away from the fireplace. Gran sitting at the table, still wrapping last-minute gifts morphed into her slumped in the chair in front of a dead fireplace, to her sprawled on the bathroom floor in a pool of vomit. Macy stilled. Gran was dead, so was her mom. So who was touching her? A vision of a massive sharkman stroking her while she slept gave her the creeps.

"Macy, sweetheart. How are you feeling?" the strange voice asked.

Macy mumbled a bit more as she forced herself to sit up. A similar headache as the last time, throbbed in her temples. She rubbed there, hoping this time the mini massage would help her feel better. "Like shit. Blasted shark," she said.

"You challenged him," Cyndi said. "He probably thinks you're champion material."

"Oh, shit." Macy slumped and shifted on her ass to sit next to the new woman, leaning her back against the cold metal wall. "I didn't think of that." She blinked to clear the fuzz from her mind.

"Yeah, their escaped champion took down a few Yithians when they kidnapped her," Cyndi was saying to the new prisoner.

"Why didn't you tell me this before?" Macy snapped, hating the familiar burn of anger in her nostrils and the narrowing of her vision. She drew in a shuddering breath. It wasn't fair to take her fear and frustrations out on Cyndi. She was as vulnerable.

"I'm sorry." Cyndi sniffled. "I forgot."

"It's okay, Cyndi. We know now." Macy leaned across the stranger to pat Cyndi's hand. "Hi, I'm Macy." She forced a lip-curl despite having nothing to smile about.

"Quin. Glad you're okay."

Macy's gaze traveled over the towering Greek goddess. Sprawled in leggings and a gym tank, she was the epitome of everything Macy wished she could be. A thick braid of sunshine blonde hair and escaped tendrils haloed a face with an angled jaw, strong yet beautiful. How had the crazy sharks managed to take her? "You're gorgeous," she whispered, hoping those muscles could help them, but doubted it. What this woman might be doomed to was a life as a gladiator. Macy wouldn't wish that on anyone.

"I know, right?" Cyndi giggled. "She looks like an Amazon warrior."

"Do you think they'll believe you're a champion?" Her concern for Quin didn't surprise her. Lumped together under these circumstances would change the normalcy of her life. She sighed, dismissing the strangeness of it all as par for the course.

"Nah, even though Quin towers above me, they're taller." Cyndi clasped her hands. "Let's hope they see us and think puny Earthians."

"Earthians?" Quin pressed four fingers to her lips, hiding a grin. "You can't be serious."

"It's what they call us." At the scraping noise, Cyndi screamed at Quin to close her eyes. Cold, wet foam rained onto them again, smelling like antiseptic and dousing them in seconds.

Macy had reacted, as well, the desperation in Cyndi's voice driving her to obey. She now understood the correlation between scraping and foam party.

"Shit, I hate that stuff," Cyndi muttered, once more drenched like a drowned rat.

"It's supposed to keep us clean, I think." Macy wiped her face with her sleeves before standing up to stamp her slippered feet. Argh. She wanted a long bath with no bubbles.

"They do it every second day." Cyndi twisted the foam out of her shirt. "I made the mistake of glancing up the first time it happened. Damn shit burns." The remnants of the foam on the floor and the cell walls evaporated after a few minutes, but not from their clothes or bodies. Macy plucked at her drenched nightgown and scowled. The cold saturating the wet fabric had her shivering in. Rubbing her hands along her arms brought some warmth back.

"How were you taken, Mace?" Quin asked her while she squeezed her braid.

Macy gaped at Quin, so tall that Macy's temple reached her shoulder. Towers over her, Cyndi had said. Damn right, the woman was a giant.

"About midnight, I went into the backyard to help a stray dog," she said, recalling the hopelessness that had paralyzed her. Some people prepared for any attack, but Macy had never believed it could happen to her. What idiot prepared for alien abductions? Well, not her. "Didn't see this coming. Damn dog is probably sleeping on my bed now."

"If we get free, would you want to return to Earth or travel the stars?" Quin asked.

Not return home? Macy smiled. What an intriguing question. As she thought about it, she tilted her head and studied Quin. In normal life, she'd never have thought Quin or Cyndi could be her friends, but circumstances changed everything. And if it meant they were friends for the rest of their short, tormented lives as shark-slaves, then she'd be grateful for it.

"I always wanted to see the stars but never as a prisoner." Cyndi's voice was wistful.

"I wouldn't mind if I had one of those sexy aliens," Macy said, relishing a wave of heat as hope swept through her. Images flashed in her mind's eye, and she rubbed her palms together.

"Macy, no." Cyndi giggled, having picked up on Quin's nickname. Not that Macy minded, she liked the sense of familiarity as if they weren't on an alien ship heading toward a doomed and painful end.

"Hell, yes, I am. They're damn hot." Macy's smile deepened, building a tightness on her foam-stiffened cheeks. *Oh, to have one of those Etterians claim me.* She shivered but this time, not from the cold.

"What sexy aliens?" Quin frowned.

"Quin, where have you been?" Macy laughed, relishing the joy bubbling inside of her as if she'd snubbed the sharks and her fate.

"Gorgeous aliens have found us women to be just what they need. Four or five women have mated, so far."

"Mated? Like with bears and wolves?" Quin widened her hazel eyes.

Macy did a little dance. "I saw one once, on the homepage of Trash-e. They were paparazzi-style pics, but damn, sign me up for that ride." She ignored the nasty voice that whispered that a gorgeous alien would never choose her, that there would be no more rides for her...of any kind.

"Let me guess, tall, super buff, bronze-skinned, long black hair down to his ankles?" Cyndi ticked off on her fingers. "And sexy as hell." She smirked.

"Yup, sounds about right." Macy chuckled, but she'd lost the joy, the excitement, her inner voice having drained her hope.

"Damn, how come I didn't know?" Quin said.

Macy couldn't answer that. Sure, the news had been about green-tentacled aliens making first contact in the outer reaches of the galaxy, and only recently had images of Etterians reached the masses. She was an average human in an average world living a less-than-average life. What chance did she have? She scanned the cell. None.

After a few minutes of silence, Cyndi nudged her. "Macy, sing for me, please."

"Anything?" Macy's heart wasn't up to singing. The sheer miserable life she had weighed on her, but the expectant and needy expression on Cyndi's dirty face tugged at her resolve. When Cyndi nodded, she chose a song with a catchy tune, hoping the beat would restore some happiness to the cell. Quin joined in the moment she recognized the archaic song. The three of them belted out the lyrics, uncaring of their situation and their tremulous future.

Quin hugged Macy. "You have an amazing voice," she said, her praise warming Macy as nothing else could have. *Okay, so I may not be the prettiest, but I can, at least, do this. It's better than nothing.* Cyndi hummed on, proving her tone-deaf self-assessment. It didn't bother Macy. She was happy her friend could get her mind off their situation, even for a little while. And she had to admit, singing helped her feel better too. It always did, even under such a dire cloud.

Into the silence, Quin said, "Did they mention sexual slavery?"

Macy slumped, her eyes drawing together in a scowl. *Sexual slavery? Shit, why didn't I think of that?* Then she took a deep breath. *They'd go for me last since Cyndi and Quin are far more attractive than I could ever be.* She chastised herself for her unkind thoughts, but a glance at her friends only confirmed their beauty.

"Yithians don't find Earthians attractive. We're arena fodder if they cannot find a champion among us." Cyndi's words had relief shooting through Macy who released a held breath in a rush.

"What do they look like, Cyn?" Quin asked.

Macy shuddered, remembering the hardness of his skin under her finger and the solid-black gaze Scarface had leveled on her. She shot a glance at Cyndi, letting her answer Quin.

"Like sharks, gray, slimy with eyes too wide apart."

"Wearing some sort of body armor," Macy said. The texture was like leather but a synthetic kind, mixed with plastic or something harder, not so supple.

"Any weaknesses?"

"Weaknesses?" Cyndi scowled. "Oh, no, you don't, Quin. They'll shoot you like they did Macy."

"Just tell me." Quin's voice dropped to super-serious.

"Eyes wide to see all of the room." Macy split her fingers and pointed at her face. She lifted her chin to the pale-yellow light as she recalled as much detail as possible.

"Excellent peripherals." Quin pursed her lips. Her level of confidence warmed yet frightened Macy at the same time.

"What about a blind spot, right between the eyes?" Cyndi tapped the bridge of her nose. "You know, like a hammerhead."

Quin shook her head. "It would be too tricky if he did have such a blind spot. A step to the left or right, and he'd see me. Anything on his body that could be targeted?"

"They have balls, well, I assume they do. One of them grabbed there suggestively as our men do." Cyndi raked her fingers through her filthy hair and tried to braid it.

"Good to know. And their necks?" Quin asked.

"Like a shark's, wide to their shoulders, thickly muscled." Cyndi gestured with her hands, touching the crown of her head to the edges of her shoulders.

"So only eyes and balls. That's not much." Quin's shoulders slouched for a moment before straightening as if her posture was under scrutiny.

"Maybe if we distracted Scarface, you can attack from there?" Macy indicated the corner closest to the door.

"That could work. I'd need to get his gun. Once I have that, we can blast our way through them, arming ourselves and some of the prisoners, as well."

A sliver of icy fear slithered down Macy's spine. "Shit, Quin, you don't think small."

When Quin frowned at her, she glanced down, hoping no one thought her a coward.

"If we kill the guard, sweetheart, it's not going to help. We need access to the command room and communications. We need to send out a distress signal or message." She jumped up to pace. "There's bound to be more prisoners than Yithians, right?"

Cyndi shrugged. "So what? You get the gun, we leave, and start shooting the guards?"

Macy blinked at Cyndi as sparkling excitement coursed through her. But mostly there was fear with her gran's voice screaming at her that she was damn insane. If she died while escaping, it was a shit ton better than an arena, or worse, slavery.

"Yeah and let's take the time to get the stunned guards into the empty cells. I don't want them taking us from behind."

When Macy glanced at Cyndi, 'what the fuck?' crossed her mind. Quin pressed her ear to the door and missed the look Macy shot at Cyndi, who had paled. There was a confidence, a stubborn strength that ran through Quin, and it scared Macy. And since neither of them could form the words to argue with Quin, it seemed as if they were about to attempt an escape. Sheer mindless terror gripped her, and she sucked in needed breaths, hoping to calm her trembling limbs.

"Also, we need to check before we open doors. For all we know, there are alien monsters destined for the arena."

Macy almost snorted, as if finding alien monsters was as common as replacing a toilet roll. "Monsters for an arena? Like *Gladiator* the vid?" As an ancient Earth movie with a handsome lead actor, the Roman world had seemed so far from her life. Never had she thought she would one day find herself on her way to such a place. She pinched her arm and winced. No, not a nightmare, which meant escape or die with a blade or claw in her belly.

Quin opened her mouth to answer, but the cell lit up, bathing their wretchedness in bright light.

"Shit. I'm not ready," Cyndi said, panic cementing her face in ashen gray.

"Go to the corner, Mace, and lie down. Cyn, pretend to kick her. Mace, I want you moaning like she's killing you."

"What?" Macy gaped. She shut her mouth with a click and clenched her jaw at the thought of her impending death.

"Just do it."

She threw herself onto the floor, shivering against the cold. Wrapping her arms around her head, she sobbed, groaned, and wailed, putting her heart into her last performance.

"Stupid bitch, why don't you die already?" Cyndi yelled.

A glimpse between Macy's splayed fingers revealed Cyndi's face contorted in anger. She stilled for a moment, impressed then grimaced, releasing a scream as the air moved where Cyndi pretended to connect with her foot. Macy jerked back as if struck, 'crying out' again. She fought the urge to freeze when the door swished open and continued to moan as if her life depended on it.

Because it did.

Chapter Nine

"My king." Remi bowed as Xeus strode down the lowered ramp. The Base Commander glowed with health and peace, as if the encroaching void didn't bother him. Xeus almost snorted. Even the void feared Remi, and the small smile that twitched Xeus's lips proved this visit was just what he needed.

He looked forward to testing his skill on the battlefields. An energy hummed through his veins, despite his chest aching as if he'd lost something or missed someone.

"My king, he says," Xeus teased him. "As if rank means anything on Gikaet."

"It does not, this you know. However, until you have completed the diplomatic portion of your visit, you will continue as my liege."

"Alodon's hell," Xeus grunted as the hum's intensity decreased.

"Lord Tjakik heard of your arrival. He awaits you outside the neutralization zone."

Xeus squared his shoulders and with his long legs, he strode toward the zone, greeting warriors as he passed them in the passages. He didn't suit up, ignoring Remi who held out a suit of armor for him. He had no greatsword on him, just his blaster strapped to his thigh.

"Xeus, I will not have you die on my watch." Anger twisted Remi's features.

Xeus ignored him. "Then *you* suit up." He marched through the zone and out onto the monochromatic sands of Gikaet.

The gray desert planet with its matching skies didn't give him pause, despite the need he had to visit here. What almost faltered his approach was the thousands of Gika warriors in perfect military formation. They spanned out on three sides with Tjakik waiting in the center. This display of military bravado was impressive, but Xeus saw not the purpose of it. *Is this to intimidate me? Is Tjakik nervous to meet with me alone? Does Tjakik not trust me?* Regardless, sensing no fear or intimidation, he strolled toward the Gika Lord with two of his most trusted males behind him, Cales and Remi.

Gika had variegated gray exoskeletons and eight legs, of which two were red oversized mandibles with razor-sharp pincers. At the tip of each leg supporting its great bulk, sharp claws could tear asunder or form a skewering spike. Venom dripped from its mandibles, lethal and acidic. A face of some sort peered at Xeus. Two large eyes sat near the 'forehead,' a long-drawn flat surface fell to a straight-lined mouth with serrated tusks, and on the sides of the 'face' were another set of elongated eyes.

"Lord Tjakik," Xeus clicked in the Gika language still activated on his O.D.I.

"Welcome to Gika, King Xeus," Tjakik chirped. "I wished to meet the king who saved my people."

Xeus almost flinched. Gratitude didn't sit well with him. His decisions were his duty and didn't require a response, good or bad. "I live to serve," he said by rote, wincing at his stoic words. *That is the sum of my life, I serve, unceasingly.*

"My people didn't approve of my decision to return, not trusting the Etterians to keep their vows. Yet I know you are an honorable people. You have proven my belief. I, therefore, wish to align my people to yours in the upcoming war."

Xeus's breath stilled. He wasn't surprised that Tjakik had heard of the impending war. But he was stunned at his offer of alliance. Gika soldiers were fearless and fearsome. To have them fight on Etteria's side could save lives and perhaps end the war before it began.

"Of course, we will not conquer other planets. Gika is our home-world, and it is sufficient for our needs, more so after your assistance."

"Do you require anything further?" Xeus grasped onto this topic, preferring it to professions of gratitude.

"Medical technology would be appreciated. We are losing too many of our *kamiq*, our offspring."

"No, that is unacceptable. Remi, send out our medics." Xeus glanced at Remi before facing Tjakik. "Your *kamiq* are precious as our *damu* are. If our medics cannot assist, we shall search the galaxies."

"Your words and continued assistance prove my belief further, King Xeus."

"Since we are both rulers, Xeus will do." He flashed a smile, one he almost felt.

Tjakik inclined his great head as if to agree. A flicker of iridescent color behind the ruler had Remi tensing. A few Gika females scurried around Tjakik to lower stone boxes at Xeus's feet. He didn't blink. The exoskeleton of the females fascinated him—darkly shimmering from black, gray, purple, and cyan, the play of color bewitching.

"Your females are beautiful, Tjakik. It is honorable that you keep them hidden and protected." Xeus settled his gaze on Tjakik, lest his staring offended.

Tjakik inclined his head again, and with a flick of a pincer, the females returned behind him and faded into the Gika.

"Thank you, Xeus. We discovered these during harvest. We have no use for them. Perhaps they are of value to you?"

Cales crouched in front of a box, flipped a lid, and leaned back on his haunches at the light that burst outward. He scanned it with his O.D.I and shook his head. "Unknown mineral."

Yet the stones glowed brightly, their power source a mystery. Xeus palmed one before placing it back in the box. "I will have our *lima kuu* research these. The sale of these might bring opportunities to better your lives."

"It is a gift, Xeus," Tjakik clicked, bobbing his great head.

"You have given me a gift, Tjakik. These," Xeus gestured to the boxes, "are a joint venture." A dozen Etterian males jogged up to stand at attention behind Remi. They were the medics he'd summoned.

"It was an honor to meet you, Xeus." Tjakik bowed his head and skittered away. The medics followed the departing ruler. Then in perfect military style, the legions disbanded.

"That was...*impressive.*" Remi rumbled his approval.

"Agreed," Xeus said, watching the dust clouds settle.

"And now we have Gika soldiers for the war. I almost pity the Yithians." Cales chuckled as they turned back to the zone, grabbing a box in the process. Remi and Xeus did the same, handing the boxes over as soon as they strode through the neutralization zone.

"Now will you suit up?" Remi asked.

"To appear fully armored is a sign of distrust..." Xeus accepted the suit Remi held out to him. He removed his current standard armor to tug on the Gika-proof suit.

"Or a sign of prudence?" Cales said.

Xeus shot him a glare. "Do you two intend to talk me to death or will you join me?" He unstrapped his blaster from his discarded armor to re-strap it to his thigh. He hid a lip-twitch as Remi and Cales donned their armor with more efficiency. He grabbed a greatsword off the rack to sheath down his back before pulling the helmet on.

With the visor still up, he stepped through the zone and paused to survey the gray sands with more appreciation this time. He drew in a deep breath, nostalgic as he recalled his first Gika kill. Since then, he attempted to duplicate the initial rush of emotion he'd experienced, the sense of achievement. He flipped his visor down and strode north, away from the zone.

The outline of Gika soldiers undulated as they skittered toward him, a solitary Etterian warrior. Two charged at once, the burn of the challenge lanced through him, setting his blood aflame, and filling him with a flood of unbridled energy. Yet, as he sunk his greatsword through the thorax of one soldier, distaste made his mouth bitter. *This was wrong.*

"Stop," he clicked at an approaching soldier.

It drew to a halt, wavering, confused. Etterians weren't known to speak to Gika soldiers on the field.

Xeus stood there stunned for a moment, disbelieving what he was thinking of doing, what he believed to be the right thing to do. "Summon Tjakik," he said to the soldier.

It hesitated before scurrying off. As it did so, it gave a shrill cry, the ululating was like nothing Xeus had heard before. All Gika soldiers withdrew from their individual battles. Astonished by the unexpected withdrawal, his warriors lowered their swords. It was dishonorable to attack a retreating enemy. They gathered at the zone where Remi gaped in silence.

The sight of Xeus striding toward him must have broken through his daze. "What...what have you done?" He barreled past Xeus to assess the empty landscape.

"They are our allies, Remi. How would you address this?" Xeus flipped his visor to glance at his battle-bond. "We need every soldier. We need to train them. For all we know, traveling in a box in space might not be good for them. There are too many unknowns. This I do not need." He drove his bloodied greatsword into the soil. "It was *wrong* killing that soldier."

"To kill an ally is dishonorable. It is betrayal," Cales said, standing beside Xeus as they watched Tjakik scurry toward him—traveling at an incredible speed. It wasn't something Xeus had considered before. They ought to, with eight legs. This could be an advantage.

"Tjakik, thank you for speaking to me." Xeus bowed his head, then, on second thought, ripped off his helmet and tossed it to the floor. "I cannot condone the killing of soldiers. We need them for the war."

"But...," Tjakik clicked, his mandibles opened and closed with no sound.

"I propose we change these pointless killings to something of more use. Your soldiers are fierce, as are mine. If we combine our strengths, address our weaknesses, together we can build a formidable armada."

"In what way will I punish my males?" Tjakik's clicks transformed into the snapping of his jaws—a Gika displaying anger. "This is how it has been done for centuries."

"We are rulers on the cusp of a profound change, we either flow with it or break under it. Set your convicted to build homes, hospitals, or to redeem themselves in our armada. It is better to improve your people than to lose what knowledge they may have."

Tjakik stared at him for a few moments. "Very well, Xeus. How do you wish to proceed?"

"Our males will spar with your soldiers, good or bad, using soft greatswords. They will remain fully armored should your saliva inadvertently touch them. There will be accidents, and hopefully, not to the death. Any injuries will assist in training our medics, yours and mine, to heal on the battlefield for both species." Xeus paced as he warmed to the subject. "We would need to build classrooms to cater for all, Remi. See to it. We must learn everything about each other and Yithians, perhaps even include Maloidians in this. I do not trust them."

"As you command, my king." Remi relaxing his shoulders had peace coursing through Xeus. It meant his battle-bond supported him.

"Inform our males why I have made these decisions. Should they have issues, they must bring them to you or me. I wish to address any negative influence. Disobedience is punishable starting at three feet of honor. Some will view this as heresy. I do not want them *accidentally* killing a Gika due to their short-sightedness."

"You have those too?" Tjakik clicked repetitively, sounding like laughter.

Xeus released a drawn-out sigh. "Tjakik, send up your general. He will work with Remi."

"Mkaok is my general, but be warned, Base Commander, he does not bear your warriors great love."

"We value strength of conviction, Lord Tjakik." Remi bowed with respect.

Tjakik threw back his head and ululated. A tremor rumbled under their boots, and a legion burst through their cavern entrance, not too far in the distance. Within minutes and in a cloud of dust, Gika soldiers drew to a halt behind their ruler.

"This is Mkaok and his legion, Akluke, the finest we have."

"My lord." Mkaok skittered forward and bowed to Tjakik, his front pincers brushing the ground. This Gika general was more battle-hardened than any soldier Xeus had come across. He had a jagged scar running over his eye, making it whiter than usual. He doubted the general could see out of it. One of his legs was missing, and the scratches that crisscrossed his thorax were impressive. He also seemed old, as in ancient. How long was the natural lifespan of a Gika? Xeus was ashamed he didn't know this.

"For now, our facilities do not cater to your height, General Mkaok. Perhaps we could utilize your war room to strategize?" Remi gestured to the cavern.

The general inclined his head, and as Remi turned, he ripped off his helmet and tossed it to Cales before following the ancient Gika general.

Chapter Ten

Still on a Yithian Slave Ship
Same Cell

Beating up someone in real life didn't sound like it did in the old vids. Soft thumps and grunts snuck through Cyndi's yelling, but when she stopped fake-kicking, Macy peeked at Quin. Macy sat up, just missing Cyndi's swinging foot. She was in time to catch Quin's kick to Scarface's head. She twisted the gun from his twitching fingers with an ease that calmed Macy. *This woman knows her stuff.*

Quin spun and shot him in the face, the action warming Macy who clambered to her feet.

"Damn right, fish breath." She bent over the Yithian and poked him in the chest again. "It worked." She straightened to gawk at Quin.

"Great performance, Cyn, Mace." Quin grinned then took a moment to study the gun in her hand. She stepped over the Yithian's body and peeked through the door. When she faced the cell again, her eyes were narrowed in calculation. "Cyn, I'm putting you in charge of prisoner release." She tapped the side of her head, indicating Cyndi's interpreter. "Mace, I'm getting you a gun. I want you to shoot the shit out of these aliens. As many times as you'd like."

"Like paintball?" Macy grinned, rubbing her hands together. *Revenge is sweet, indeed.*

"Give me a moment." Quin lay down on the metal grating of the passage, took careful aim, and fired three short blasts. Macy chewed her lip, straining to hear anything. *Did she get them?* When no alarm sounded, she released a long breath. But when Quin jumped up, Macy stiffened, only to lunge forward when Quin disappeared into the passage. Macy glanced at Cyndi, unable to hide her worry and shock, wondering what she had to do now. She peered into the passage then beamed at Quin who was jogging toward her. The sight of slumped Yithians everywhere made her ecstatic. Excitement gripped her—an uncontrollable flame against the recent rollercoaster ride of fear.

Quin offered them each a weapon. The weight of it was like nothing Macy had held before, but so comforting. She clutched it to her chest with both arms. *This is my future.*

"Hold it with two hands; they're heavy." Quin hefted hers as if it was nothing but a bag of rice. "Now, help me drag the bodies into our cell."

Five minutes later and Macy was sweating, breathless, and wishing she'd done more than sing and stock shelves. *Shit, they were heavy.* In the end, she and Cyndi had dragged them inside, then rolled them like they were tortillas. Quin shot the four of them again in the face and punched a button on the door, closing the cell. "Get to the prisoners."

Cyndi ran down the passage, peering into the cells. She opened one door and spoke in clicks to the prisoners.

"Ask them if anyone knows this ship's design," Quin said.

The plan she'd mentioned, reaching the bridge and sending a distress signal, now seemed possible with the downed Yithians and the weight of the gun in Macy's hands. She grinned and rocked on her heels, nervous energy coursing through her. They'd made it this far. She studied Quin and her chest swelled. What an amazing woman. The Etterians would consider her more than desirable. Macy glanced at her slippered feet and sagged. She lowered the gun and rested an elbow on the butt. She didn't stand a chance next to Quin. She sucked in a sharp breath. But then again, what were the odds of meeting Etterians? If no one responded to their call for aid, she could easily imagine Quin piloting this ship to Earth.

A midnight-blue alien man stepped through the door and strode toward Quin. Hard angles marked his jawline and square chin, with V-shaped lines from forehead to nose, and lateral grooves in his cheekbones. He was humanoid for the most part, with broad shoulders and two arms, and wore a sleeveless tunic and yoga pants in beige. Sandals of some sort adorned his blue feet. Macy watched him with fascination. Unbound white hair cascaded around his face, ice eyebrows twitched above his white eyes. He was her second alien sighting, and he was gorgeous. She sure hoped he was friendly. Although, there was a certain lethal quality about him, something that transcended physicality. She snorted at her nonsense.

"That's Illan; he's a Durn. He says he knows the design," Cyndi called while directing prisoners.

Macy shrugged and stood next to Cyndi as a variety of species crowded the door. Browns, greens, tentacles, and many heads, too much for Macy to process now. Cyndi answered questions in a calm tone, and the hope on their faces was recognizable yet painful to see.

I mean, Macy harumphed, *it's just the three of us women.*

"Cyn, tell him there are two guards outside the door." Before Cyndi spoke, the blue alien pressed two fingers to Quin's forehead. When she staggered, Macy hefted her gun and aimed it at the alien. She bolted, crossing the passage to go to her friend's aid, concern rushing through her.

"What the hell did you do that for?" Quin rubbed her temple, looking none the worse. Anger hardened her features and summoned a harsh glare. Macy expected a dead blue alien.

He mumbled something in a soothing tone, and at Quin's gaping, Macy relaxed, but she shuffled closer. Just in case. Quin exchanged whispers with the blue alien, then she frowned with her eyes widening in awe. Macy scowled and tightened her grip on the gun. *What the hell?*

Whatever it was, Quin recovered from it to open the door, then they were both firing. Macy sighed, glad the blue guy was with them. She'd dreaded having to shoot any prisoners who were in the same boat they were in. *Or ship, in this case.* She smothered a giggle.

Quin glanced back, and so did Macy, at the released prisoners. "Move." What happened next was almost in slow motion. Quin's mouth contorted as she bellowed while sprinting to the back door. She was still running when she fired two more shots as soon as the back door opened. Both Yithians crumpled. Quin dove through the opened door but didn't fire again. *Shit.* Macy gulped. *That was kinda awesome.* She hurried to help drag the bodies into an empty cell. Blasting them afterward made her cackle, despite her sweating and breathlessness. Their captors may have been big and slimy, but they were also damned heavy.

"Cyn, tell them that we have four more slave compartments. We'll help to take out the other guards. You free the prisoners and usher them down to the escape pods."

"I don't know where the pods are," Cyndi said, panic twisting her features. Another blue guy broke from the crowd to touch Cyndi's forehead. Macy didn't worry this time. Uncertain of what to do, she stood around trying to hold up the toy-like gun—constructed with black blocks and a yellow glowing one. She was too scared to touch the other black buttons in case she set off a self-destruct mechanism. *That would suck.*

"What are you thinking, Quin?" Macy asked with a hand on her hip when she noticed Quin's calculating expression.

She gripped the gun barrel in her other hand and used it to lean on, her focus was on her new friend, though. Regardless, it was more comfortable than holding the heavy weapon indefinitely.

"Illan and I will storm the bridge. You and Cyn get everyone to the pods, just in case we fail."

"I'm coming with you." Macy crushed the gun to her chest, grateful for her breasts acting as some sort of shelf. Quin opened her mouth, but Macy leveled a steely-eyed glare on her friend, the one Gran had perfected. That shut Quin up. She was determined to help, and Quin had to learn to let her.

"We'll clear the guards. You focus on the prisoners," Quin said to Cyndi.

After clearing the remaining four compartments and as they headed for the bridge, Macy was useless. She hadn't been able to shoot a single guard. She'd helped drag them into the cells and shoot them again where they lay, but that didn't count. She and Quin waited as the blue guy, Illan, stopped in front of something console-like. He tapped a few holographic buttons, but his frown deepened. He glanced at Quin, and she stared at him, and their heads bobbed. Expressions crossed Quin's face. Macy rubbed her ears, suspecting she'd somehow lost her hearing. Leaning against a bulkhead, she tapped the gun against the metallic panel. Just once, not too loudly, but it was enough to confirm her ears worked well. Quin glowered, tilted her head, and bulged her eyes. Ice drenched Macy from her scalp to her slippered toes. No way. No, she couldn't believe it. She narrowed her gaze and focused. Shit, they were communicating telepathically.

Damn. As awesome as that was, she was even more excluded.

"Mace," Quin's whisper startled her. She jumped a foot and barely managed to swallow a yelp. "We're going to lure them out."

Macy gulped and hefted the gun into her hands, showing she was ready as needed. The door slid open, and Illan shuffled along the passage where the three of them could hug the metal-paneled walls. Macy mimicked Quin's posture, trying to hold up the gun, which seemed to be growing heavier with each passing second. She smashed her back against the wall, copying Quin's attempt to minimize her body.

Sharp pain lanced through Macy's shoulder, and she bit her lip to stifle a cry that tore up her throat. Fire throbbed through her shoulder with warmth saturating her nightgown and pajamas, telling its own story. *Shit.* She gritted her teeth, glancing at Quin, wondering if she should tell her.

But she didn't have any time to dwell on it when a Yithian stepped into the passage. He was a big bastard, bigger than Fish-breath, and a slimy nefarious feeling oozed from him. She raised the heavy gun and fired on him instinctively. She wasn't alone. Three blasts hit him, hopefully in all his vulnerable spots. She grinned, despite being unsure where she'd shot him but glad to have helped.

The ship tilted, and she flung out a hand to steady herself. The gun's nozzle tipped to the floor, her one arm unable to handle the weight on its own. When Quin bolted, Macy gaped. Her friend barrel rolled into the room. The blue guy muttered something that sounded like a curse and followed her. Three blast sounds followed.

Macy entered the room, gun upright again. Quin held hers to a Yithian's forehead. Macy couldn't halt the grin as she imagined a famous actress in that position. The Yithian didn't seem frightened, though. Had she been asked, she couldn't say whether a scared Yithian would cower. No recognizable expression crossed his solid-black eyes, but he didn't glance at her or Illan. Sprawled around Quin were other Yithians.

"Sweet," Macy said, fist-pumping the air.

Quin fired the gun not bothering to watch the alien collapse. "Mace, come stand guard."

Macy rushed to do just that, while Illan helped Quin drag the big bastard from the passage into the bridge.

"Guarding," she sang with forced happiness, ignoring the guilt that whispered she'd killed someone. What they'd put her through, they deserved it. She shot each one again. "Just in case." She chuckled, then stiffened, fresh pain radiating outward from her shoulder. Wouldn't it be ironic to die from this? She almost rolled her eyes. Typical her.

Illan studied the bright lights on a large console and pressed a few.

Macy glanced from the bodies to Quin when she dipped to speak to the colorful buttons. "Mayday, mayday, we're escaped prisoners on a Yithian slave ship, requiring immediate aid."

"Will they understand English, Quin?" Macy asked.

Quin blinked then glared at Illan. He spoke in clicks. Quin's lips twisted into a smirk before she shifted closer to Macy.

"Greetings, Yithian slave ship. This is the Etterian battleship *Phoenix*. Please confirm assistance is still required." A deep voice penetrated the quiet and in English. Macy's mouth fell open as excitement and relief gripped her. Her shoulders relaxed. She whimpered and shifted, trying to find a posture that didn't hurt. *So quick? What are the odds? And the male is Etterian with the sexiest voice I've ever heard.*

"Uh, hello?" At Quin's response, Macy giggled. *Smooth, Quin.* "Yes, we still need help. We don't know how to operate this ship. Hell, I don't even know where we're headed or what the blasted name of it is."

A deep chuckle came through.

Macy liked the sound of that voice. *Like chocolate.* Her stomach growled. Perhaps the Etterians had food that wasn't in paste form.

"We are ten minutes from your navigation point. We will need to breach your vessel. Is this acceptable?"

"Hell, yeah," Macy squealed, jumping up and down. "Breach away." *Yes, please, sexy-Etterian, I'll submit to a breaching.* She giggled, wishing she could share her naughty thoughts with Quin. But Macy paid for that little display of joy. Her vision spun, and she almost threw out a hand to catch the wall, not wanting to faint.

But Quin playfully punched her on the shoulder and wiggled her eyebrows before saying, "We have prisoners at the docking bays ready for evacuation. I can have them launch the pods, though chasing them down might not be fun."

"Gorgeous aliens," she whispered to Quin who chuckled. Macy caught movement to the right of her and fired another yellow blast at the Yithian big-bastard. As soon as Quin faced the console, Macy sagged against the wall, sucking in great gulps of air.

"Was that a blaster?" an Etterian asked through the console.

"Yes, the Yithian commander moved," Quin said in clipped tones, even as she threw a wink at Macy. The answering Etterian's chuckle had hope pooling inside Macy. "Are any of you hurt?" Quin glanced at Illan then at Macy. Illan shook his head. Macy grumbled, looking anywhere but at Quin. She didn't want to admit she'd gotten herself injured when everyone else was perfectly fine. "Where, Mace?"

"A sharp something cut into me." She showed her shoulder. When Quin gasped, Macy realized it must be bad. *Felt like shit.* The pain gripping her wouldn't let her shrug, and she didn't want to, not even to put Quin at ease.

"Why didn't you tell me?" Quin hugged her, a little awkwardly, taking care not to touch her wound.

"If we're successful, help will come. If we weren't, then what injury would matter in the face of death," Macy said.

"That's my brave girl," Quin whispered into her hair. "Etterian? We do have a few injuries."

"We will attend to these, milady."

Milady? What a strange honorific to use, but I didn't care what they called us.

"Who is with you, human female?" another deep voice demanded.

Macy fanned her face. *A nice dark smoky voice, yummy.* She sighed. *Damn, I need to get laid.*

Quin didn't find that voice as awesome since she slammed a hand on the console. "Listen, whoever you are, I'm tired and sore, surrounded by aliens I didn't know existed. I don't know what they are or who they are or how they came to be here. I don't want to waste time detailing who the hell is on this piece of shit. I want off, I want a coffee, and for the love of it, a damn shower."

Holy shit. Macy pushed herself off the wall, worried Quin's anger would drive their rescuers away. She nudged her out of the way to face the console.

"Mace," Quin moaned, but Macy leveled a steely gaze on her, shutting her up again. Her gran's do-you-want-to-die expression sure came in handy.

"Hello? Hi, I'm Macera Mitchell. I'm so happy you guys found us. I was a little worried we might go from the fire into a volcano. Quin's a little stressed right now so please don't take her pissy attitude personally. On the bridge, it's just us and Illan. You're a Durn, right? My other friend Cyndi is at the escape pods with the released prisoners. Is that the answer you were hoping for?"

"How did a Durn get on a Yithian ship?" the voice asked.

"I fail to see…" Quin fell into silence and locked gazes with Illan, confirming Macy's telepathy suspicions.

"The comm is still active, Supreme Commander," the original Etterian said.

"Yes, it is." Macy hurried to assure them the connection hadn't dropped. "They're talking telepathically. I find it quite rude, to be honest."

"Mace," Quin huffed. "Illan says he will be happy to explain it all after we're rescued." The Etterians were silent. "I don't know why you don't bloody well talk to him," Quin said to the Durn.

"We are two minutes away," the original Etterian said. "You should be receiving a visual of our approach, milady."

"And which button would that be?" Quin's tone dripped with enough sarcasm to transcend cultures. Macy sympathized with the dilemma. The damn console had more lights than Lunar Vegas. "I'd prefer my people join the others in the docking bay."

"This is acceptable, milady."

"You and Illan go, I'll wait here," Quin said to Macy and Illan, using her no-nonsense tone.

"Nope, sorry, can't make me," Macy sang back. Two could play this game. She had no intention of abandoning her friend, not until they were finally off this ship.

"Damn it, Mace. Cyn might need you," Quin said.

Unless she used logic. Macy scowled, hating to admit that Cyndi only had one blue guy and loads of prisoners to protect.

"I don't know where the bay is," Macy mumbled.

"Which is why I need Illan to go with you." There was again silence as they argued, Quin's face morphing with a variety of expressions, like an insane person. She grunted in frustration and resignation. "Iddan is on his way." She muttered, "Stubborn Durn."

"Tether extended," the voice said.

The ship lurched, which was strange on what she suspected was a large ship.

"Breach in progress," stated the voice.

She shot each of the Yithians again, just in case.

When Iddan stepped through the door, Macy glanced at Quin, but followed him, still hating going. She stomped behind him, well as best as her slippers would let her. He didn't say anything and was courteous, helping her down the ladder, letting her go first for her modesty.

When they breached a massive warehouse-like room, she hesitated, gaping at the metal-grated ceiling. A solid-looking door occupied one side with the same appearance as the submarine door in their cell. She shivered, praying nothing could pry it open. Being sucked out to space wasn't her idea of fun. The prisoners gathered in groups around the room. Some sat, but most stood, their movements twitchy as if they were anxious or scared. Cyndi weaved through a group, running up to Macy to hug.

The pain from her shoulder made her bite her lip again, but she endured regardless.

Chapter Eleven

As short as Macy was, seeing all the prisoners was a struggle. She had no idea if one would attempt to kill Cyndi, but then again, the way Iddan guarded her, maybe not. Still, it wouldn't hurt to be…higher. The tallest point was crates stacked in the center of the warehouse-like room. She grimaced. Which meant climbing in her slippers, with a gun, and a sore back.

On her tiptoes, she pushed the gun on top of the crate, gripped the edge, then gripped the edge, locking her knuckles in place. A whimper slipped past her clamped lips. No matter how much she willed herself to pull her body weight up, she couldn't. Her limbs refused, made stubborn by the fire bathing her shoulder. Huffing, she scanned the area, searching for tiny crates or a toolbox, anything to give her a little leverage. If the universe didn't hate her, a stepladder would appear out of thin air. She blinked. Nothing, not a shimmer of light or something useful appeared. *Yup, well, universe, the feeling's mutual.*

Crates, barrels, and heavy-looking rolls of thickish material filled her line of sight. In the corner, sheets of metal rested against one wall. She tapped her chin. That could work. If she laid it like a ramp, she could walk to the top of the crate.

She weaved through the crates and the prisoners, climbed over a roll that had the texture of canvas, and squeezed between wall and crate to reach the metal sheets. The edges were curled inward which made gripping it easier, and it was as light as a feather. She put it down, picked it up again just to be sure she wasn't losing her mind, then waddled to the crate.

"Excuse me," she muttered over and over, even though she doubted they understood her. Still, they let her through but lingered to watch her balance the sheet. As light as the sheet was, it was cumbersome, but when in place, she stood back to admire her brilliance.

She made it halfway up before she slid down, landing in a disheveled heap at the bottom. Heat flushed her body, from the wound and sheer embarrassment.

"Now if you had listened to me, we'd be on top already." She glared at her arms. Rocking onto her hands and feet, she clambered to her feet, offered a sweet smile and a curtsey to her avid audience, took several steps back, and bolted, sprinting up the ramp.

She slipped and scrambled but managed to reach the top just as the sheet fell. Brushing the hair from her sweaty face, she hefted the gun with a gasp and clutched it to her chest, fearing and relishing the warm stickiness on her back.

Dizziness assailed her as she stood on guard, trying to be vigilant in a multi-colored sea of species. Her feet throbbed, her vision blurred, but when she lowered the alien gun to lean on it, a fresh wave of agony lanced across her shoulder. Her nightshirt pulled tight, stuck with blood to her skin. Still, it was warm, barely keeping the chill of the warehouse at bay.

Damn, she could sleep for days. A soft bed, a hot shower, and something solid to sink her teeth into like a burger, or an apple... Oh. She gasped. A hot cup of tea would be amazing.

"I am told to speak Earth English?" an older man with yellow skin said. The thick tentacles he had instead of hair undulated in soft sweeping movements regardless. Dark spots traveled from his temple, fading into his tentacles, and his black eyes saw too much.

She smiled. "Yes, thank you."

"I am Pannos, a Maloidian." He smiled and didn't move along, choosing instead to lean heavily on a metal rod.

She studied him, noting the many wrinkles that lined his face, like slow-drying paint. "I'm Macy. A pleasure to meet you, Pannos."

He tapped his rod. "Please, address me as *Lommia*." He gestured to his body. "It is a term of respect for one of my age."

"Of course." She winced. "I meant no offense."

"No, not one as sweet as you." He chuckled. "It is also an endearment." He pointed to her collapsed ramp. "I watched you. It was most entertaining and revealing of your character: stubbornness, ingenuity, determination. Truly remarkable, Macy."

She shrugged, not sure how to respond to his compliments. "I'm short. I tend to find myself in situations requiring resourcefulness."

When the hole appeared in the wall and crates were shoved aside, the tall man who entered the bay through a makeshift hole made Macy gasp. *Shit. They don't make them like that on Earth.* She glanced at the other angelic-looking Etterians, who had marched through the breach to stand on guard, and sighed. *Yup, nothing like that where I'm from. And just as gorgeous as those paparazzi pics. Damn, I sure hope there's one for me.*

Pannos followed her gaze. "Ah, our rescuers. They are a good species and stubborn, just like you."

Casting a glance at him, she chuckled. "I can't claim stubbornness for my kind. I think it's determined by character, no matter the species."

Pannos chortled. "And wise." With a shudder, he tightened his grip on the pole.

She frowned at him. "Are you all right? Do you need a doctor?"

"Doctor?" He shook his head. "In time. For now, I am grateful to be out from under those Yithians. Their intentions were not honorable."

She raised her gaze to admire the Etterians. "We were lucky."

Pannos tapped his metal pole. "Maloidians do not believe in luck, Macy. We spend our lifetime mastering fate." He lifted his stick and pointed at the prisoners. "The Etterians will see to our needs. Come find me when you can." He toddled off.

Smiling, she stared after him.

A few Etterians spoke to Cyndi and Iddan, then gathered the prisoners into lines. In sync, they crossed the makeshift tunnel. Macy peered down it, trying to see inside. Which was silly when she'd find out soon enough. She huffed. Teetering, she hurried to straighten before she toppled off the crate.

"Milady?" An Etterian gripped her hip with his bronze-toned hand. Even in the yellow lighting, his skin shimmered.

She blinked at him.

"You are safe," he said.

"Duh." She grinned.

A smile teased his full lips but didn't fully form. *Wow, so gorgeous.* Up close, he was better than the paparazzi pics. She sighed, then winced when the weight of the too-heavy gun pulled on her arm.

"I scent blood. Are you injured?" His brow furrowed while he ran his deep-blue gaze over her.

She twitched, tempted to throw an arm across her body as if it could hide her overabundance of curves, her ratty clothing, and overall lack of hygiene.

"Yes." She chose honesty, especially when the heavy-metallic scent of her blood lingered in the air.

He held out his palm. "Can you walk?"

Knights in black armor, sexy-as-sin, and built like brick shithouses? When a man like that offered his hand? She took it, no questions asked and with not an ounce of hesitation.

A squeak escaped when he ushered her toward the edge of the crate, then with the gentlest of swings, whipped her to the floor.

"Thanks," she rasped, stepping back and taking her hand from his. Up and up she lifted her gaze until her neck muscles twanged. From the crate, she hadn't grasped how tall these Etterians were. "I'm...Macera or Macy."

"Sub-Commander OyazetBoaz. Please, this way, Maceraormacy."

She giggled. "No, my name is Macera or you can call me Macy."

He nodded. "Thank you for clarifying, milady." With a sweep of his massive hand, he gestured to the hole. "Let me escort you to the medic."

Sub-Commander? She handed him the gun and "strolled" down the tunnel. The aliens veered around her. Each step drained her. Her breathing labored, and her vision spun, forcing her to palm the metallic wall to keep her balance.

Not once did OyazetBoaz rush her. She cast him a smile, even if it was weak. Gran hadn't raised an impolite woman.

By the third stop-for-breath, she couldn't muster a word, glance, or smile. Just kept her head down, eyes squeezed shut, as she willed her trembling limbs to keep her upright.

"May I carry you, milady?"

She gasped and threw up a hand, caught it trembling, and snatched it back. "I...can do it."

He smirked. "Are all Earthian females this stubborn?"

"We don't claim ownership of that trait, but we do have a fair share." The break had helped. She trudged onward, gliding a hand along the wall. "How far is it?"

"Far."

He'd hesitated, which meant a lie. She met his gaze and rested her good shoulder on the wall. "Fine. Carry me...please."

And she was airborne. In the seconds it had taken him to hoist her, he'd made sure not to harm her. Neither did his long strides jar her nestled in his arms. She hadn't been carried since she was a child. The floating sensation was strange.

His men parted without a word as he turned corners, marched along narrow passageways, and into a crowded square room. Against one wall was a counter and metal trestle tables before it. Against another wall were what looked like exercise equipment and weapons mounted to a wall. In the middle, beneath many feet, was a mat sunken into the floor.

OyazetBoaz crossed the room to the corner resembling a trauma ward. Folded beds lined walls not filled with cupboards or counters. In the center sat a bed, bright lights above it.

"Milady is bleeding." He lowered her onto the bed, then paused to tuck a swath of her icky hair behind an ear. "Medic Rior," OyazetBoaz growled.

She yelped, the hairs on the back of her neck rising.

"Sub-Commander." An elderly Etterian appeared from among the prisoners. The slight wrinkles around his eyes and mouth denoted his age. Other than that, he was as buff and tall. He shoved a black box at another Etterian and gestured to a tentacled lime-yellow alien.

"Lady Macy requires attendance."

She gaped at OyazetBoaz. "No, please, see to the others first." She climbed off the bed only to find herself lifted onto it again.

"Females are served first." OyazetBoaz splayed his hands on either side of her thighs, keeping her there.

"What?" she squeaked, then scoffed. "You can't be serious."

He leaned back. "Why is this alarming?"

"The severest injury should be attended to first." She sliced glances between them, frowning when they blinked at her. Why did she have to explain this? "Listen, my life isn't more important than another's." At their continued stares, her face flushed hot as if she had a fever. That churned nausea in her gut, threatening to bring up half-digested paste. She cupped her mouth just in case.

First impressions mattered, and she'd shot hers to hell with her bedraggled state. No need to add vomiting on his biker boots to the list. She giggled. Maybe they'd think it was an Earthian greeting?

"I scent blood." The medic sniffed, then followed his nose to her back. He activated images and lights from his wrist and scanned her.

Twisting to watch him shot agony through her. She cried out, faced forward, and folded. OyazetBoaz caught her before she fell off the bed.

"I will have to remove your garment, milady."

At Medic Rior's words, she whimpered but raised her chin to meet OyazetBoaz's gaze. *What the hell? Might as well add nudity to the situation.*

"Males to me." OyazetBoaz's growl lifted the hairs on her neck again. Would he stop doing that? Every time he made that noise like a wild animal prowled around her, she almost peed herself.

Etterian men emerged out of the crowd, standing to attention with their fists pressed to their hearts.

"Lady Macy requires privacy."

As one, they formed a circle, their backs to her, shoulders touching shoulders. Heat burned her cheeks. Right, like stripping was made easier surrounded by a wall of masculine men? She arched a brow at OyazetBoaz.

"Please, milady, lay on your front. I will peel away only what is necessary to attend to your wound."

For that, she loved Medic Rior. Without further ado, she sprawled, taking the time to cover her ass and tuck her hair under her.

"Sub-Commander Oyaz, please step aside."

Oyaz? She smiled. So much easier than OyazetBoaz. Was etBoaz his last name? She met his gaze, but when he hesitated, she threw out a hand and caught his wrist. "Stay."

His eyes widened, then he settled back on his heels and folded his arms across his chest.

Cool air bathed her shoulder, and the pain faded.

"Describe what you're doing, please," she mumbled. "I'm curious."

"Medic Rior has sprayed your wound with a sanitizer and anesthetic. He is cutting your garment to expose your shoulder."

"I don't feel a thing." She closed her eyes and hummed a haunting song her gran had said was Irish. Macy didn't care about its origins. For once, she was comfortable, not in pain, and...safe. "What will happen to us, Sub-Commander Oyaz?" She met his gaze.

"My supreme commander will comm our king, but I suspect you will be returned to your homeworld if you choose."

She sighed. *Go home? Mm. Starve on Earth or starve in space? Mm.* "And if I stay with you? Is that possible?"

"You are most welcome, Lady Macy. If you choose to, you will be escorted to Issneen, our royal city on Etteria." Oyaz shuffled closer.

She grinned. Decision made. She doubted the Etterians would let her starve.

Chapter Twelve

Planet Gikaet
Northern Base, Aluna
King Xeus's Satellite Office
A day or two after Quin's daring rescue.

FOR THE THOUSANDTH TIME, Xeus replayed the sec vid Supreme Commander Xan had communicated to him. Xan finding his Dar Eth had pleased Xeus, but that initial surge of joy had dwindled to despair. And judging by the skills his female demonstrated, Xan was a blessed male. She had extensive military training, yet despite all her talents, she appeared soft and feminine.

Alodon's balls. Her hair was the color of molten gold. The various colorings of these human women intrigued Xeus, and he had yet to see duplicated physical features. The pairings were happening rapidly, the more his males encountered human women. And when she'd fired the kill shot, ending the life of Prince Yada—the arrogant fool—anger had vibrated through Xeus. It still did.

He knew feeling anything was dangerous now, yet the anger still rose within him, strong, overwhelming. He had no right to feel anything this potent. Lady Quinlan had killed to survive, and her lack of remorse was clear in the words she'd spoken to the Durn. Xeus could recall them with perfect clarity.

"Illan, they would've tossed us into their arena and laughed as we died horrifically, so no, I don't regret killing them."

She was correct. The Yithians would have done so. Xeus scowled in response to his unreasonable anger. Nothing he said or did at the GC had made any difference. The Yithians continued to endanger humans. That Lady Quinlan had been placed in this situation lay on his shoulders. Perhaps he should direct his fury at the Yithians? The temptation was great.

He replayed the sec vid, more as a distraction from his depressing thoughts, opting instead to study the other two women with Xan's Quinlan. They were dirty, their hair hung around them, their faces smeared with grime, yet their bright smiles were glorious. The vid had captured their energy and their ability to remain calm yet cheerful was truly a marvel.

Their shapes were different too and not in an unacceptable manner. One was lithe with light hair, the other was shorter with amazing curves and wild, dark hair. How Quin tasked them revealed aspects of their personalities. The one who ushered the prisoners to safety was adept at organizing, sorting, and commanding. And the woman accompanying Lady Quin was softer, more light-hearted with moments of steely determination.

She had an incredible voice too, husky, alluring, and she often spoke in birdsong. It was strange yet pleasing. Lady Macera Mitchell was her name. Her sense of humor had made Xeus's lips twitch—it was something he appreciated. She'd been delighted when Etterians had rescued them, whispering *'gorgeous aliens'* to Lady Quin, implying she found his males attractive. She'd make a wonderful Dar Eth to one of his warriors.

That the Yithian Prince Yada had died at the hands of a human woman jeopardized the well-being of Earth. Xeus wasn't concerned should Etteria go to war, they'd bred for it. And now with Gika's alliance, were more than prepared for it. His greatest concern was the possible destruction of Earth, more specifically their women. And in his opinion, the cost of war for the prevention of Etteria's extinction was acceptable.

King Urio of Yithia had drawn forth further anger within Xeus when he kidnapped Enyl with the intention to kill. A son for a son. It confirmed that war was inevitable. The anger that had coursed through Xeus at Urio's audacity still hovered under the surface. He had felt out of control, his vision stained with red.

Then there were the Durns.

Their presence pleased Xeus. As an endangered species, any sighting or interaction with them was a rarity. Xan would escort the Durn blood-bonds to Etteria where they would remain, protected. They weren't Etterian prisoners and may have other plans. Xeus would share the Etterian archives on the Durn culture in the hopes that they'd accept his protection.

They were a remarkable race, one that needed cherishing since the annihilation of their planet and culture. None knew how their end had come about, though the buzz suggested the disease may have been at their own hands. It didn't matter. They were welcome to make Etteria their new homeworld.

Cales had already commanded more battleships to protect Earth. Xeus took the opportunity to send communications to his allies on the Global Council including Citus in the requests. He had to notify his fellow councilmen of their salvation, issues, needs, and the possible outcome of Etteria's struggles with Yithia.

Xeus returned to his chambers to request another set of Gika-proof armor, hoping to join the war room discussions with Remi. From there, he would launch the first strike. He prayed to the Maker that his restlessness would still long enough for him to decide wisely.

Chapter Thirteen

Etterian battleship Phoenix
Their shared quarters
A day later.

IT TOOK ALL OF Macy's strength not to roll her eyes. Slumped in a comfy, she shot glances between Illan and Quin staring at each other, their eyebrows wiggling while various expressions crossed their faces. Cyndi had escaped with Iddan, but Macy would've been in the same position had she gone with them.

She slapped her knees. "It's lovely to watch you two chat. Riveting stuff."

When Quin winced, Macy leaped off the comfy but hesitated. Leaving the room would mean what? Strolling the endless corridors? Chatting to herself like a mad woman? A hobby would be helpful, but what? If she knitted Illan a sweater, would he wear it? She clapped a hand over her mouth to smother a giggle, imagining his expression when one sleeve stopped at his elbow and the other dangled off his fingertips.

Maybe start with a scarf?

She glanced at the replicator. Would it know what knitting needles were? Or a ball of wool?

"I'm sorry, Mace." Quin yanked Macy into a hug.

She squealed, crushed within her friend's tight embrace. "I'm fine. Just bored," she mumbled with her temple smashed against a collarbone. She wiggled to free herself and managed to…just. As soon as she could, she lunged away from Quin, lest she wanted another hug. "You two, go, do your thing. I'm going to…" She twitched her fingers as if they were knitting needles.

Quin and Illan ignored her to converse in silence again.

Leaning over the replicator, Macy punched in her requirements and stared at the variety of colors available. Well, at least there was wool. A rainbow-colored ball snagged her attention. Merino would be lovely but then it pilled, with tiny fuzz balls forming on clothing. Cashmere would be super soft but it wasn't strong. What she wanted, and this was her gran speaking, was a blend of Merino and silk. She'd lamented for years about the cost of such wool. Biting her lip, Macy ordered four balls. She released her breath with a whoosh when they appeared on the glass surface. She glanced at the front door, half expecting an irate Etterian to storm in.

Her shoulders slumped when the door remained shut. Now to choose the needles. Something big was preferable. There was no way she was going to knit with tiny needles. The scarf would take her forever.

When she selected size six, the machine beeped. She ordered the needles again. *Beep.*

"Illan?" She faced him. "I think I broke the replicator." She stabbed the glass to show him. *Beep. Beep.* Yup. Trust her to break it.

"Impossible, Macy." He pushed off the comfy and settled beside her. "What are those?" He tapped the order button, but it beeped for him too. She would have lost her shit had it magically granted him the needles. "They look like weapons."

She snorted. "If you want to poke someone's eye out, sure."

Quin crowded her from the other side, then nudged her out of the way. She and Illan crowded the replicator, punching, and beeping. Macy huffed, folded her arms across her chest, and tapped her foot. What? Did they think she was an imbecile? Yeah, she did have idiot moments, but she knew how to work a replicator, for pity's sake.

She squeezed between them and flicked their hands aside to order a beach bag for the wool. Nothing too fancy. Bam, there it appeared. So it was the needles the replicator didn't like?

The door chimed. Oyaz occupied the doorway when Quin granted him entry. His gaze settled on Macy. She stiffened, only now considering that maybe ordering needles might not be a good thing. Glancing down at her plump self, she wondered how they thought she could hurt anyone with a pair of knitting needles.

"My apologies for the intrusion. I have received notification of a replicator violation." Oyaz strode toward her where she leaned against the replicator, as guilty as can be.

Gathering her courage, she gestured to the beach bag. "If ordering knitting needles is a violation."

His eyelids fluttered, and he paused, glancing at the rainbow-colored balls of wool. His mouth fell open. "You...create items with that?"

She frowned. "Why the surprise?"

Oyaz took a moment to respond. "Since the introduction of the replicator and rehydrator, there is not a need to craft things anymore."

She gasped at the room in disbelief. "Not even cooking a roast chicken or an apple pie?"

"Why would they need to with a rehydrator?" Illan shrugged.

"Because it smells incredible." Quin drew in a deep breath, her eyes closing as a dreamy smile formed.

"Damn straight." Macy huffed.

"Very well." Oyaz tapped on the replicator, and the needles appeared on the glass surface.

She snatched them as if they might disintegrate, but when he turned to leave, she grabbed his arm. "Do...?" She glanced at Quin and Illan in yet another silent conversation, their arms gesturing, their faces switching between expressions. "Is there somewhere quiet I can go?" She stuffed the wool and needles into the beach bag and clutched it to her chest. "Where I can be alone?"

Oyaz frowned at Quin and Illan then studied Macy. "This way, milady."

"Just Macy, please, Supreme Commander Oyaz." She trampled after him, out the quarters and along the passage.

"As you wish." He smiled. "Earthians are an informal species."

She shrugged. "For the most part."

"Then I insist you call me Oyaz." He didn't glance at her once while he led her down a long passage.

Etterians passed them, peering at her with open curiosity. It was to be expected, but still, she dipped her gaze, preferring to stare at the back of Oyaz's chunky boots. A door opened, which she stepped through, only raising her chin when Oyaz stopped.

The room was narrow and long with built-in benches lining one wall. Above them were windows to ceiling height, displaying the passing stars. She squealed and stumbled toward them, resting a knee on a bench to splay her fingers across the glass.

"This is the viewing deck. We often forget we travel through cosmic beauty. Here, if you miss your home, you can task the display vids to show scenes close to your heart: an ocean, a meadow, a mountain."

She faced him without removing her hand, relishing the chill of the glass. "These aren't windows?"

"No, those would be a structural weakness."

She peered at the stars. "So you have cameras on the outside of the ship recording what we see now?"

"Yes." He tapped a panel beside the door. "When you are ready to leave, touch this and speak. Pilot Msar will send someone to escort you to your quarters."

She dipped her chin. *Right, the man had a job to do.* "Thank you, Oyaz."

He gave her a curt nod and left, the door sliding shut behind him.

Silence settled on her as she planted herself on a bench, curling into its curved backrest. Hours passed as she reacquainted herself with what her gran had taught her, unraveling the various monstrosities until she had the hang of it.

As she lost her thoughts in the monotonous task, she pondered her choices. Knitting could only entertain her for so long. Sure, there were a ton of other hobbies like pottery or mosaic tiling, but to what purpose? Maybe she could beautify their quarters? She frowned. The replicator couldn't manufacture something large like a rug, nor did she think she could lift the white chairs—they seemed fused to the floor.

Mm, she'd give it more thought. If Etterians didn't make things, then what or how did beds and chairs come into existence? Something she could ask Illan.

When her stomach grumbled, she stashed the palm-length scarf, needles, and wool into the beach bag, slung it over her shoulder, and approached the panel. Pressing her hand to it, she leaned forward until her mouth was an inch from it.

"Pilot...?" *Shit, what was his name?* She couldn't guess when that might insult him.

"Yes, milady?"

Relief slumped her shoulders. "Um, could someone please take me to my...quarters?"

A man opened the door not five minutes later, and without a word, ushered her along their metallic passages that were the same as the last one she went down. How was she supposed to navigate this maze of dullness? There were no markers or signs to say, "this way, milady."

She harumphed. Maybe she should talk to Oyaz about that? What could the poor man do though? Change the design of the battleship? She giggled. Pink walls, please?

Mm, pink sounded delicious, like strawberry icing. She winced as a sharp pang twisted her stomach. A cupcake with rainbow sprinkles and a caramel center would be wonderful. Could the rehydrator make one of those? And did she want to know how it created magic?

She snorted. Already her brain was fuzzing over at the thought of asking.

Her usher abandoned her at the door with a bright, "greetings, milady." With a long sigh, she entered and found the room empty. Dumping her beach bag on the comfy, she approached the rehydrator and ordered an array of cupcakes along with an iced coffee. Alone, no one could judge her for her poor food choices, and to hell with it, she needed pink and lots of it.

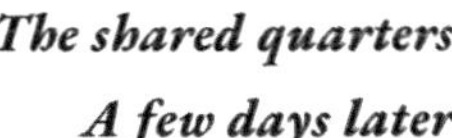

The shared quarters
A few days later

MACY AWOKE TO FIND herself alone again. Her initial excitement had waned, at having escaped from a Yithian slave ship, made two friends, and embarked on a new beginning. Cyndi and Quin preferred to spend their time with Iddan, Xan, or Illan. They hadn't abandoned Macy on purpose, and she supported their relationships, she just wished she had something to keep her mind from circling the drain.

This new beginning promised to be similar to her dull life on Earth. Endless boredom in a pointless existence. She wanted to sob, to wail at the universe, but crying didn't solve anything. Her gran had proved that. With a sigh, she trudged out of bed, not bothering to shower or pin up her hair, and programmed the rehydrator for a coffee. *Who would see me dressed like this anyway?* Her leggings and baggy shirt were comfortable and covered her. She snorted. Even if she walked around naked, it wouldn't matter.

Flopping into a comfy, she activated the display vid and read through the menu items which were what she'd expect to find on a military vessel. The current location of the ship, communication options, cultural studies of alien species... Curious as to what the Etterians had on humans, she selected the Earthian icon. A shiver trailed from her scalp to her ears then down her spine. She giggled, tempted to jump up and dance. Beaming, she selected a section on illegal entertainment. Vids, music, concerts, ancient but also new, as if the Etterians had trawled all online databases—something the Media Police had never managed to do. Focusing on the music, she chose the Four Seasons by Vivaldi. The music swelled and dipped as it swirled through the quarters. She increased the volume until the instrumental notes consumed her and vibrated through her body. The volume was sheer luxury. On a battleship, the chances of the MP finding her were slim to none.

Coffee forgotten, she jumped up, closed her eyes, and twirled with her arms held out wide as if she stood in a green meadow amid rolling hills. Spring flowed into Summer and she swayed, immersed in the notes with shivers racking her body at the beauty of the music. The high quality and volume didn't compare with the sound system at the club. She was in heaven.

Summer flowed into Autumn into Winter, and for the first time in a long time, she was content. As Winter concluded, she drank her cold coffee while she browsed the other options before selecting Beethoven's Moonlight Sonata. She stood there, just holding an empty mug, swaying with her eyes shut. A shadow crossed her eyelids. She turned and squeaked. Oyaz had raised his face to the ceiling, his mouth open and his eyes wide. She lowered the volume with an apology forming on her lips.

"What is that?" he rasped.

"Beethoven. It's classical music. Beautiful, isn't it?" she asked but didn't need a response or his opinion.

"Yes," he said, a little breathless. A smile curled his lips. She loved it when an Etterian showed warmth. "I apologize for the intrusion. Security notified me of a disturbance in your quarters."

"And you rushed over to defend me?" she teased.

"Yes." He gestured to the display vid. "What else can you show me?"

She laughed. "How much time do you have?" She chose Tchaikovsky's Waltz of the Flowers and increased the volume. His face was unusually expressive, revealing his enjoyment.

"Earthians are so passionate." He leaned in to whisper before stepping back with his eyes closed again. His mouth hung open in delight. As it concluded, she changed genres and chose a classic hard rock song about the weather. Louder this time, she watched his face for his reaction. She didn't have to wait long. It stunned him then when the singing started. His eyes went wide, but he tapped his foot, matching the rhythm. She swung her head back and forward, her hair flying with the movement as she let the beat sweep over her.

His chest shuddered with his ragged breathing. "That was amazing. What was it?"

"Hard rock. Not all our music might appeal to you. You'll have to sift through it and find your preferences."

The concept of a treasure hunt must have delighted him because he blessed her with a bright smile, showing his even white teeth. He punched his holographic buttons on his O.D.I., then met her gaze.

"I've notified my males that I am with you for this day. If you do not mind, of course."

She rubbed her palms together, more than up to the task. "Challenge accepted, Oyaz." Chuckling, she flicked through the options. "You will either hate this or love it. There is no in-between. It's called Opera." She selected Nessun Dorma, from the opera Turandot and only because a man performed it.

His eyes stuttered closed, and he raised his hand to rest on his chest. She could have sworn his dark blue eyes paled.

"One more of this genre?"

When he smiled, she chose O Mio Babbino Caro from the opera Gianni Schicchi. His reaction was the same, with a sweet and dreamy smile curling his lips.

"And now pop." She selected one with an addictive beat, and of course, had to dance, since the tune called for it. Her senses tingled, warning her that he watched her, but she didn't care. She adored this oldie and the freedom the music made her feel.

"What are you doing?" he asked into her ear.

She grinned and grabbed his hips, swinging them side-to-side to match the beat.

"Dancing," she said.

He laughed and swayed his hips but his chest and shoulders didn't move. She left him to it since he looked like he was having fun.

"Now something electronic." A remix would be perfect. As the beat and thrum vibrated up her feet, she pulsed and jerked her body as if her life depended on it, the beat allowing her to lose herself in a hypnotic trance.

Once it ended, she flopped into the comfy, panting for air. "Had enough yet?"

"That was incredible, Macy. I liked the..." He tapped his fist into his palm to mimic the rhythm.

"Beat?"

He fell into a comfy next to her, a smile still cracking his cheeks.

"You should choose a genre and set it to random play. There are many artists in each category and some artists cross over." She peeked at him. He'd said the day. Would he...? She straightened. "Wanna watch a vid with me?"

"I have seen your instructional vids on your mating rituals."

Did he mean porn vids? Heat burned her cheeks. She glanced away, not sure how to address that. "Um, no, these are stories in a visual format."

"An entertainment vid?" His eyebrow arched in interest.

Excitement coursed through her, notching a permanent smile onto her face. She hoped he'd spend more time with her. That he'd choose to. "We can watch an action if you would prefer?"

"What kind do *you* like?"

"Romance-Comedy but don't worry about me. We could also watch something sci-fi. You might enjoy that more. Laugh at what we imagined space travel to be like?"

"You choose."

She browsed the available vids, skimming over the porn, and chose a sci-fi vid, a true classic from the year 2016. Before she pressed the start holographic button, she jumped up and requested from the re-hydrator two bowls of buttered popcorn as well as two large sodas. She handed him his then flopped into her comfy, dimmed the lights, and started the vid.

"What is this?" He gestured to the bowl and beverage.

"Standard vid fare. Try it." She flashed him an encouraging smile then faced the screen. "Remember, it's fictional so don't take it too seriously."

He picked up a few kernels to pop into his mouth. He grumbled his appreciation. His wrist buzzed a few times during the vid, but he punched a few holographic buttons and continued to watch the vid until the end.

"So, what did you think?" she asked as she put her empty bowl aside and spun in her comfy to smile at him.

"I loved this." He gestured to the empty containers. "And the vid was good. I believed it would be a waste of time. The space vessels were too pretty and impractical, but some of the technology was believable. I understood why the captain reacted the way he did and agree with his judgments. He was honorable toward the end." Oyaz flashed a brief smile. "There was even music in the vid."

"We call it soundtracks. You should find that under entertainment, as well."

"Thank you, Macy, for this day. It was...enlightening."

"My pleasure." She grinned. "Stand still." He obeyed, and she wrapped her arms around his waist to hug him. She needed one more than he did. "You put your arms around me and squeeze gently."

He did as instructed. "What is this? I have seen you and the females do it often." He rested his chin on the crown of her head.

She sighed at the comforting gesture. For his first time, he was an incredible hugger.

"It's a hug and can be non-sexual like now." She pulled away, asking him to release her. He did so without hesitation. "Thank you for your company, Oyaz. I dreaded spending more time alone." She bit her bottom lip, furious with herself for having told him something of a personal nature.

"If you wish a repeat, you have only to notify me," he said.

At his kindness, she gave him a small smile. Not that she would take him up on his offer unless he was her friend.

"Are we friends, Oyaz?" Her question horrified him. He stiffened then twitched as if preparing to bolt. She turned away, preparing her heart for disappointment. This wonderful man, friends with her?

"Etterians form friends in battle. I do not wish to endanger you, *ensa*."

She shook her head, now understanding his reaction. "Friends on Earth are people who care for one another as a family would and like to spend time together."

He grunted. "My first female friend."

"Thank you, Oyaz. I needed company." She squeezed his hand and stepped back. "I wanted to ask if someone's willing to teach me how to fight?"

"What?" His scowl was ferocious. "You imply we cannot protect you?"

"Of course not." She twisted her hands, heat staining her cheeks at having to explain herself. What if he said no? What if he denied her this? She had to keep busy somehow. "I need to fill my time, or I'll go insane. Even if someone just teaches me to remain hidden, or how to run away, it will be something other than these walls."

He studied her for a minute. She shuffled under his intense scrutiny then clasped her fingers behind her back to hide their trembling.

"It will be so. We will start with fitness." At his choice, she wanted to groan but bit her tongue. He was teaching her, and she was grateful. At least one hour of her day had a purpose. "I will collect you early every morning. I do not wish for other males to bear witness."

"Ashamed of me?" she teased, happy to do so now that she'd gotten what she'd asked for, maybe more than she'd bargained for. Time would tell.

"Never. I do so to protect you, *minus susa*." He frowned then shook his head. Why she didn't know.

"Protect me? Are there bad Etterians who wish to hurt me?" The fear that tore through her snatched her breath and flashed images across her mind. She remembered the Yithian's face who'd abducted her and Fishbreath's reaction when she'd poked him with her finger.

"No one will harm you. My males are curious regarding human females. They will stare at you. I am aware that it makes you uncomfortable."

"Yes, it does," she said with a deep sigh. This was what she looked like and without an immense bank account, this was how she'd remain—alone and unloved. She didn't want these men cataloging her every flaw. But on the other hand, she did want what Quin had—a man who'd love all of her.

"Ask Medic Rior, to implant an O.D.I. It will be easier if we do not awaken the other females."

"Thank you for doing this for me, Oyaz," Macy said, wringing her hands. She liked change, didn't she?

"A pleasure to serve, Lady Macera."

As soon as he'd left, she hurried through a shower to have more time to find the right exercise outfit. In the end, leggings, a baggy T-shirt, and sneakers were easy. It was the blasted sports bra that was the most difficult. By her fourth attempt, she was confident that nothing would escape, jumping up and down to test it. Once satisfied, she dressed in normal jeans, a red blouse, and matching ballet flats before heading to medical.

Chapter Fourteen

Etterian battleship Phoenix
The common

"Milady Macera, how may I assist?" Medic Rior greeted her with a small smile.

Macy liked him. He was helpful, gentle, and kind. He didn't scowl like most of the Etterian males she'd met. Xan wore a pinched expression as if he was horny all the time, but Oyaz was at least approachable. Smiling came easier to him too.

"Rior, please just call me Macy. Oyaz said I needed to get an O.D.I. implant?" She hadn't considered what the insertion would entail. Days in medical? When she'd had the paychip embedded in her wrist, she hadn't been able to use her hand for a week. "Is this possible?"

His smile widened as he gestured to the bed. "Please...Macy. Come sit for me. It is a painless procedure. I slip a device under the skin of your wrist. For the O.D.I. or Optical Data Implant, your internal energy powers it, and it is sensitive to your brain functions. This means that you can send it mental signals, and it will respond."

She gaped. *I've heard of advanced robotics for people with disabilities but not to this extent.* There was talk of security robots and bionic implants for those needing extra strength or a new limb, but she'd never seen either. And the cost of owning a sex cyborg was beyond her. It would take a lifetime to save the tokens.

"What is your handedness?" he asked, and she raised her right hand. He reached for her left, turning it palm upwards. "Would you mind?" Curiosity arched a raven-winged eyebrow.

It was so beautiful against his bronze skin, her finger itched to trace it. She blinked, slow to remember he'd asked her a question. "Mind?"

"Yes, I did not think to ask when I last served you or the miladies."

"You're not asking me now either, Rior," she teased. If he could blush, she suspected he would have. He dipped his chin, but doing so didn't hide his sensual smirk.

"May I feel your skin? Your softness is most appealing."

She offered her exposed wrist to him without hesitation. "If I can feel yours as a comparison."

He nodded before running his fingers from her wrist to her inner elbow and back. "It is so smooth," he whispered then offered her his arm for her to stroke. His was like velvet and firmer as if he worked out. With those bulging muscles, she had no doubt he did just that.

"Even your fingertips are soft." He'd captured her hand to rub her fingers.

An Etterian cleared his throat as he inched closer. "May we?" A few men hovered behind him, their gazes fixed on Rior's hand touching hers.

"If you wish to." She offered them her wrists.

They crowded her, eager to touch, caress, and each male mumbled their appreciation as they stroked her skin. The constant touching stiffened her spine before making her shudder. A scream built inside her, but she forced herself to swallow it and take slow, deep breaths. Sensory overload, she'd hazard a guess. She slumped when they stepped back, dropping their long fingers from her arms.

"Are all human females this soft?" one male asked, the hope in his eyes too painful to behold. *Hope for what? Yes, human females are as squishy as their males.*

"I suppose we are," she said and offered her left hand to Rior for the procedure. Her audience retreated, but Rior pressed her wrist and she twitched, now realizing she was about to let an alien slice her wrist. What if he went too deep? What did they know about humans? "Please, stay, keep me company." She glanced away then back at them to offer a smile. "I'm a little nervous doing this and could use the distraction. If you have questions, I'll try to answer them."

They crowded to the side of her, giving Rior the space he needed. "Your coloring varies. Ours is not so, not even on Lysara and Maloid," another male said. Black military armor adorned his sculpted body, not that the other males wore anything else.

"Lysara? Maloid?" she asked. "Are those places or people?"

"Lysara is the planet, Lysarans the people with similar physiology to us but with the ability to move through their giant trees. Their planet has overgrown forests interspersed with villages," Rior said, swiping his thumb over her wrist to tighten her skin for the procedure.

"Maloid has yellow-skinned people with tentacles for hair. They are a peaceful species," another male said.

She gaped. "Do they have spots that run from their hairline into their tentacles?"

"Yes and solid black eyes." Rior patted her hand then sifted through the metallic tools he'd splayed on a tray.

"And Lysarans? Are they among the prisoners too?"

"I believe so." A male ran his dark blue gaze over her. "Did you truly take over the Yithian ship?"

She gritted her teeth, torn between claiming she helped and revealing the truth. "I didn't do much. I'm not trained like Quin."

"Your honesty is valued," the male said. "Ladies Quin and Cyndi do not share your features. Is that an anomaly?"

Macy chuckled. "On Earth, each human is unique, even our skin tones vary from pale to deep brown. Eyes and hair color too. There are so many combinations, and we change our hair color if we wish to." She babbled on, trying not to acknowledge the tiny sensations on her wrist held firmly in Rior's large hand.

"Human?"

"It's what we call ourselves, humans instead of Earthians, wo*man* for singular, wo*men* for multiple. Not females." She forced a smile, covering her wince as something sharp touched her wrist. It wasn't painful, just alarming, like a pen nib.

"Is this your true hair color?" the same male asked.

"Yes, all me." She ran her right hand through her hair, her best feature in her opinion. "Coloring hair cost tokens. It's best to stay natural."

"Do your...women have occupations?" Rior drew her gaze.

"Yes, we're considered equal to men and, therefore, can do any task we choose to."

"That is illogical. Females are not equal," one of the males said.

She blinked at him. *What did I expect? Theirs is a patriarchal society.* "It's true we don't have your strength, but do you believe my intelligence to be lower than yours?" At her question, he frowned, his gaze thoughtful. "Your viewpoint is one of strength and protection. Ours is of nurturing, care...love. Combined, isn't that a complete union? If women were also of strength and protection, then the joys that make our lives worth living would be lost."

"Beautifully said." Illan slipped between the parting males to stand before her. "I didn't realize you were holding court?" he teased.

"Hey, Illan," she smiled. "These males are as curious about humans as I am about Etterians."

"If you are answering questions, then perhaps you should explain how humans procreate?"

She gasped, ducking her head to hide her burning cheeks.

"I mention it because they do not understand what a true gift a human female is to Etteria."

"Do I have to describe the sexual act?" She prayed she could channel her inner schoolteacher and not catch on fire from mortification.

"Please," a male said.

She studied their faces and saw nothing but interest, no lasciviousness, not that she'd expected any. None of them showed any sign that they saw her as a woman, someone to woo. *Woo?* She snorted before drawing in a deep breath.

"All right." She rushed through the foreplay, touching on names and descriptions with the barest of details. They battered their eyelids often.

She closed her eyes so she could minimize her nervousness as she described the sexual act. When she peeked, more males had joined, and they listened with eagerness. *Holy shit.* She squeezed her eyes shut and took another deep breath. "The same is done to men, licking and sucking, maybe even fondling their..." Flicking a glare at Illan, she wished she could jump off the bed and return to the safety of her quarters. She skimmed over bringing a woman to orgasm, how many ways and how many times. "Same for you?" Her gaze flew open to see their responses.

"No, our females only find fulfillment once per day."

Only once? She opened her mouth to ask for more detail—

"Etterian males are extremely sexual. Would a human woman be able to withstand unions?" The male gestured to Macy. "You appear to be too fragile."

She grinned. Her, fragile? Had they met Quin? "Oh, yes, we are sturdier than we seem."

A male gave her a curt nod. "Your explanation is as per the instructional vids Prince Enyl shared."

Prince Enyl? Wait, what vids? "The what now?" She prayed he meant biological differences and nothing too pornographic.

"What is required of us to mate with a human has formed part of our training," Rior stated as if he hadn't just blown her mind.

"What exactly is in these instructional vids?" She scanned the men.

One man tapped his ear. "The women moan throughout the act. Is this normal?"

"It is most annoying," another man gritted out.

Macy cupped her mouth to muffle a squeal. These men were watching porn as commanded by their prince. "Um, please tell me only you have access to these vids."

"As part of our training, all must learn," the man stated.

"All?" she squeaked. *An entire nation?* Heat exploded across her face, and she squirmed on her ass. *Oh, dear Lord, no.* Who was she to go against a royal decree, but damn, as wonderful as it was that they were eager to please in the bedroom, porn set up unreasonable expectations.

"When you get an opportunity to sleep with a woman, let her guide you. We like different things. One woman might like to be kissed below the ear, another...much lower." She winced. What else could she say? Don't do what the porn actors did? "And wear protection." She sounded like a mom. "Without it, the man's sperm can fertilize her egg. This will attach to the inner lining of her womb, and a baby will be created."

"Protection?" they repeated in unison.

"Yes, to prevent pregnancy." She arched a brow at their confused expressions. "Prevent the creation of children." She pronounced each word as if she spoke to idiots. They weren't, but the horror contorting their faces worried her. *Did I say something wrong?*

"Why would you want to do that? Children are the Maker's gifts," a male roared.

She stiffened then curled into herself, unable to flee, not with her wrist in Rior's hand and the men blocking her exit.

"Tell them how often women are fertile," Illan said.

Now he helped? She glared at him. This was all his fault.

She sucked in a breath, trying to calm her pounding heart. "We are fertile for about a week a month."

The Etterian men rumbled their surprise, their eyes wide as they glanced at each other.

"Now do you see the gift that she is?" Illan asked her audience. "So not only can a human female be a Dar Eth, *but* she can also bare a child every nine months."

Dar Eth? Normally she'd ask, but she wanted done with this conversation. "This is why we use birth control. Our population would overflow the planet's capacity to feed us." They grumbled their understanding. "Having children is a serious matter and should be decided on together."

"It is complete," Rior said and gave her a gentle smile.

She pulled her wrist closer to examine it. The skin didn't have a scar, and she hadn't felt any pain.

"Thank you for your honest responses." An Etterian man bowed his head before moving away.

"My pleasure. Please, if you have any more questions, I'd be happy to answer them." They dispersed with not a smile among them. "That was awkward," she whispered to Illan.

"I apologize for placing you in such an embarrassing situation. They needed to know," he said.

"I'm not embarrassed," she said to which he chuckled, catching her in the lie. "What are you doing here? Are Iddan and Cyndi using your quarters?" she teased.

He winced. "His feelings for her are strong. I cannot deny him this, and since I cannot sever the bond between us, I must endure."

"Now what?" She turned to Rior, his eyebrows rising in surprise. "How do I activate it?"

"I'll show you how to work your O.D.I. then perhaps you reveal why you decided to have one implanted?" Illan said.

"Thank you, Rior." Jumping off the bed, she grabbed his hand for a quick squeeze. She bounded over to Illan to loop her arm around his. "Oyaz said I should get one. He's going to teach me how to defend myself and said the O.D.I. won't disturb Cyndi and Quin in the mornings."

"Why do you need to learn defense?" Illan's eyes widened.

She stared into their white depths. They were striking against the midnight blue of his skin. "I need a distraction. Besides, Oyaz said he'd focus on fitness first." She grimaced, anticipating a little pain in her future. Okay, a lot of pain. She was so unfit that changing her linen had exhausted her. Thankfully, that chore was millions of space-miles away. "I think I'm going to be in pain for a long while to come."

"I assume it is every day?" he asked, to which she bobbed her head, her curls flying around her as she pirouetted. "May I participate?"

"Sure." She shrugged. "I don't think Oyaz would mind."

Illan took a few minutes to explain how the O.D.I. worked. It didn't have access to the entertainment folder, but he explained how to transfer from there to her O.D.I. The space available on that tiny device boggled her mind, and he assured her it could handle quite a few birdsongs.

She tugged on his arm, urging him toward the rehydrator. "Come, I want some ice cream."

"Ice cream?" He repeated her words, but it was clear he had no idea what she was talking about.

She skipped the remaining distance to the rehydrator and punched in her request. A white bowl of decadent death-by-chocolate Belgian ice cream appeared with a dessert spoon. Scooping the bowl off the surface, she punched in a request for an extra spoon.

Handing Illan his spoon, she sat at the table. On the first mouthful, she moaned in delight. She scooped another spoonful into her mouth, not caring if she ate it too fast. It was too good, the kind she couldn't afford. This tasted like real dairy and authentic chocolate, not the artificial stuff that flooded the market.

"It cannot be *that* good," he teased.

"It is," she said and opened her eyes to smile at him. "Try it, and see for yourself."

He scooped an amount into his mouth and stiffened. "It is cold," he mumbled around the protruding spoon then sighed. "And delicious." He went for another scoop. "Even your food is passionate."

"It's not as nice as chocolate, though. Every woman would kill you for a piece." She giggled, imagining women attacking these men not for their good looks but for the chocolate stuffed in their many pockets.

"You have food better than this?" Illan gaped.

"Oh, yes. It depends on what you feel like. Ice-cold beer on a sweltering day. Hot coffee on a chilly day. Chocolate cake when you are feeling naughty, and chocolate on every other day, for whatever reason. Popcorn and soda when watching a vid, and a delicious chicken sandwich when picnicking. Pizza when you're drunk and burgers and fries with friends."

"Truly, milady?" an Etterian male asked from the bench next to her. "And this is?" He gestured to her bowl.

"Chocolate ice cream." She laughed as he scrambled to the rehydrator. Within minutes, each man held a bowl and spoon, including Illan who'd braved the masses to get his own. "Just remember, too much of this can make you..." She glanced at Illan for help. "It's fattening. How do I explain that?"

"It has a large amount of fuel," he announced to the common.

"Yes, and it doesn't have all the nutrients your body needs," she hurried to add.

"I am told you are corrupting my males," Oyaz said to the right of her.

She squealed before breaking into another laugh that reverberated off the walls. Wincing, she tamped it down. Too loud, inconsiderate, unprofessional—yes, she'd been called all those things and more.

"Taste this." Illan shoved his bowl across to Oyaz who did as instructed, taking a small amount as if it was poison. He groaned before scooping a larger amount into his mouth.

"This is almost better than the popcorn and soda," he said, his dark blue eyes crinkling in pleasure. "We watched an entertainment vid this day, Illan. It was most enlightening." He dropped onto the bench next to Illan. "And Macy introduced me to Earth's music."

"Music?" Illan asked with a white arched eyebrow.

Oyaz clamped his spoon between his lips so he could activate his O.D.I. A popular heavy rock song, the same one she'd played for him, filled the common and loud at that. She almost rolled her eyes. *Of course he'd loved that one.* He rocked his head as he scooped in another mouthful of ice cream. She shimmied to the beat as well, her hair cascading around her. Illan listened, not revealing whether he liked it or not. She didn't care, not when she could listen to it on repeat. At the end of the song, the men talked at once.

"Under Earthians, Entertainment, Music," Oyaz said, scraping the last of the ice cream out of the bowl.

She snatched it away from him before he licked it clean. "See, I didn't corrupt them, you did," she said and, with a smile at Illan, dumped his empty bowl into the waste receptacle.

Chapter Fifteen

Etterian battleship Phoenix

Bored, as usual.

MACY WANDERED ALONG THE passages, greeting males who bowed their heads at her. They gave her smiles instead of frowns, all because of yesterday's little sex talk and ice cream. After the music introduction in the common, she'd left Oyaz to explain everything, considering that the whole procreation discussion had drained her. She knew nothing of the Etterian sexual act, and she was certain she'd never get to find out. So, her discussion had been rather one-sided.

Her O.D.I. buzzed, and she glanced at it, still trying to accept having a small comm device implanted inside her body.

The message popped up, and she blinked at it. Oyaz had organized an Earth appreciation evening meal and requested that she select the food. He wished to do it every evening until they reached Etteria, to smooth over relations with his males. Squealing, she did a dance with jazz hands then hurried to type on her holographic buttons.

"Are you up for tonight?" she asked Illan, who strode alongside her.

"What is happening this evening?"

She bounced. "There's to be an *Earthian* meal. Oyaz has asked that I do this every day."

Illan smirked. "After yesterday's ice cream, I'm not surprised." He arched a brow as he squinted at her. "Will there be music?"

"Of course. Though I'm not sure which music goes with pizza and beer." She wiggled her fingers as she mentally sifted through the genres.

Punching on her O.D.I., she called up a hip-hop selection. The sound was good coming from her wrist as if her body was a tuning fork. She adjusted the volume, so it was loud enough for Illan to hear it but giggled at the intense tingles zinging through her. He jerked back and frowned. She chose another hip-hop song and laughed when he shook his head. Next was reggae. He grinned, looking far too handsome for a blue guy.

"I wouldn't have said you were a reggae fan," she teased. "I could see your white hair in dreads."

His eyelids fluttered, but he said no more.

"Tell me, Illan, why did your eyelids flicker?"

"When I do not know a word you use, the O.D.I. flashes descriptions and images." Illan tapped his temple.

Right. Well. She shivered. *Thoughts and photos planted into my brain? Not scary at all.*

They continued to stroll toward the viewing deck, a glow on her wrist brightening when she neared the correct door or passage. O.D.I.s were so helpful.

"What did you show Oyaz? He seemed most pleased with it," Illan asked. "I've browsed your Entertainment, and the quantity is...intimidating."

"We watched a vid from the Science Fiction section. After dinner, you can come over if you like." She looped her right arm around his left one.

"I would appreciate this." He patted her hand resting on his forearm.

"It sucks having no place to call our own," she mumbled.

"Sucks?"

"It's earth terminology for 'it's not nice.' And I can't ask for private quarters when it might hurt Cyndi and Quin's feelings." She paused to admire the passing stars displayed on the large vids paneling the walls.

"Are you well?" he asked as he guided her into a molded bench.

"Of course," she said. "Why do you ask? Am I pale? Covered in a rash?" She laughed at his wide eyes.

"You have seemed sad, Macy," he said.

She frowned at having not realized her mood was visible to others. That they had taken the time *to* notice. She snorted. *They* was just Illan.

"I hate boredom, Illan. It's why I started knitting. Today was better. I like Oyaz's idea for evening meals. It gives me something to do. And if he says I can, I'll do extra sessions to increase my fitness."

"So, you are happier now?"

Was she? Probably not. But at least she didn't have endless alone time to dwell on it.

"Yes." She beamed at him, hoping to convince him and herself. "And you? Are you well?"

"Most of the time." He winced, and she captured his hand for a squeeze. "I am in Quin's mind, and she and Xan are quite...amorous." His cheeks lightened to a pale blue as if he was blushing.

"But aren't you in Iddan's mind too?" Macy remembered the pain lancing across Quin's face when Illan had fused with her. Forming a connection must have hurt. The constant barrage of thoughts, images, and sensations as excruciating. Since Illan didn't writhe in agony, he had to be doing something to shield himself, right? "You've been blocking them all this time? Isn't it exhausting?"

He exhaled a long breath. "Iddan guards the more private moments between him and Cyndi, but I need to teach Quin to do the same."

"Good idea. Why must you do all the work?" Macy gave him an encouraging smile and squeezed his hand before pulling away.

"I hate to ruin this moment, but you do not have long until mealtime."

She blinked, tapped her O.D.I. to check the time then jumped up. "Shit." Clasping her hands across her chest, she jogged to the common with Illan close on her heels. Men crowded all sections of the room. She clung to the doorframe, fighting for breath. When she could speak without rasping, she strode toward the metal tables. The men parted to let her pass. After dressing the tables with red-checkered tablecloths from the replicator, she placed out a variety of extra-large pizzas ordered from the rehydrator.

Following those were jugs and jugs of blonde beer. She set the music at random to play reggae on their intercom system and at a low enough volume to allow for conversation. Illan settled at the back of the eating area to watch her. Now and then, she'd stick her tongue out at him. As the males approached, dropping into their seats, she explained the toppings on the pizzas and the music playing. The beer was an outstanding success. *Typical.*

She served Illan, Oyaz, and Rior with slices of her favorite pizzas. By the end of the meal procession, she'd accepted their compliments and tentative conversations with over a hundred males. She'd taught a few how to shake hands. Their questions ranged from her shoes, height, voice, the music, and her soft skin, of course. She gritted her teeth against the sensation of being pawed, and it was in no way sexual. Their touch had been reverent.

Illan called her, and she hurried over, grateful for the breather. He showed the seat next to him, and as she sank onto it, energy drained from her. Oyaz grinned a greeting before shoving another slice of pizza into his mouth. She shook her head, amazed at his capacity for food. Rior was downing his beer as if it was water.

"It has alcohol in it," she said for about the thousandth time.

"Delicious." He burped, and his face darkened in what she'd learned meant a blush.

She giggled, more at his surprise as if burping was a new experience.

"May we watch the vid tomorrow, Macy? I need to lie down." Illan rubbed his stomach and grimaced. His skin had mottled into monochromatic shades of blue.

"Sure. I'm a little tired myself." A shower then bed. That sounded wonderful.

"Did you at least eat?" Oyaz asked as he pushed a slice over to her. She accepted it and took a small bite, too tired to eat. "What is the next meal?"

Illan scowled at Oyaz. "How can you think of the next feast? I can barely move," he grumbled.

"I am curious." Oyaz shrugged then grinned. "Well?" he asked her again.

"I was thinking of burgers, fries, and milkshakes with rock 'n roll music." The sound of 1960s music blaring had excitement swooping through her. That was the precursor to dance and nightclubs. Oh. She dropped the pizza slice and launched across the table to grab Oyaz's hand, ignoring his fluttering eyelashes. "Can we have a club night?"

"What's that?" Illan straightened then slumped.

She bounced on her seat. "Dancing."

At her response, Oyaz blinked again, and a scowl marred his lips. "You would have to dance in front of all the males."

Males? Not men? Regardless, he didn't like the idea of her doing that, and she wondered why since they would all be dancing. *Why would shaking her backside be an issue?* "I can get Cyndi and Quin to join in, and you know how to dance now."

He grumbled something under his breath.

"Besides, imagine Xan's and Iddan's expressions when they see their women dancing." She giggled. "It will be awesome."

"I do not agree with your *awesome*," Oyaz said before he finished his beer. "Come, let me help you clear up."

Groaning, she pushed herself off the bench. He gathered the platters and jugs to toss into the waste disposal receptacle. She shook off the crumbs from the tablecloths and folded them for tomorrow night's event, storing them on one of the shelves built into the bulkhead.

"Thanks for this." She flashed Oyaz a bright smile. Instead of answering her, he held her arm to access her O.D.I., punching the holographic buttons and setting an alarm.

"I'll see you in the morning. You can meet me here for your session." He turned to Illan. "Set your O.D.I. for 0430."

Illan groaned but did so. She watched Oyaz leave, frozen in place. *Had he said four-thirty in the morning?* "Shit, I'm going to bed," she said to Illan and Rior. "Especially if he wants me here at that time. Goodnight."

"Good evening," Illan said.

With a finger wave, she skipped back to her quarters.

Cyndi greeted her as soon as she walked in. "Hey, sweetheart, where've you been?"

Macy glanced at the display vid and grinned. A classic vid was playing, a rom com for sure. Poor Iddan struggled to stay awake.

"All over." She gestured to Iddan. "Put him out of his misery and watch something else, Cyndi."

"Illan told him about the 'Entertainment' section. So Iddan chose the vid. Said he liked the idea of a sinking ship. It's almost finished anyway." She squeezed Iddan's hand. The Durn winced, his face twisted as if tortured.

"Just going to shower, then I'm hitting my pillow. Oh, and I'm organizing a dance party. You and Quin have got to come."

Cyndi hummed a yes but returned her attention to the display vid.

Macy left her to snuggle with Iddan in peace. Her shower was quick, and she once again dressed in her pajamas. Sprawled in bed staring at the ceiling, she reflected on her busy day. She'd never be able to explain to Oyaz how grateful she was to him. Maybe if she gave him the scarf she was knitting? She beamed and rolled over, tucking her hands under the pillow. Images assailed her of his wide eyes and eager smile. Then she would knit a scarf for Illan. And best of all, sleep claimed her immediately.

Chapter Sixteen

Planet Gikaet
Northern Base, Aluna
King Xeus' Satellite Office

XEUS'S O.D.I. BUZZED UP his arm, not that it had awakened him. He was doing what he did every night, lying on his back and staring at the ceiling. The holographic letters were bright in the lowered lighting. The direct message was from Xan, which included Cales as an afterthought. All correspondence went through Cales and with reason, but Xeus's nephew and supreme commander thought he was above protocol.

With a scowl, Xeus read the message. He froze as he attempted to understand the words. *Earth had underwater ships? Had mastered deep-sea warfare? Could fire missiles with success?* He bounded out of bed before he thought to, striding to the display vid in the central room. He activated it and navigated to their data archives of Earth.

There. *Submarines?*

"Submarine," he said to activate his O.D.I.

A submarine is a watercraft capable of independent operation underwater. These vessels are large and crewed, moving beneath the surface with stealth and speed.

The schematics, images, and archaic vids were extensive with continuous innovation over centuries. Not only were these vessels maneuverable underwater, but they fired a variety of missiles. Etteria couldn't perfect one type, never mind so many others. Alodon's balls. He forgave Xan for his protocol oversight and applauded him for discovering such vessels. This could assist in the war.

His door slid open, and Cales burst in, also in his sleeping pants. He strode to where Xeus browsed through the information.

"Incredible," he said, his smile vibrant and his body vibrating with emotion.

"Yes, it is implausible that such a tiny, blue planet could solve two of our crucial issues." Xeus focused on an image of the inside of a submarine—its narrow and lowered passages and small air-seal doors. "Our males will not fit," he said, disappointment gripping him, tugging his mouth downward.

"Yes, we would need to construct our own. This is a long-term venture; one we may not have time for."

"At least their missiles fire true, perhaps let us focus on this."

"But there are so many. I will bring this to the *lima kuu*. Let them decide on the most viable type to construct and test," Cales left Xeus standing there, still browsing through the many images available.

With a grunt, he entered the cleansing room. He might as well start his day. He dropped his pants and rumbled at his throbbing arousal, realizing he needed to attend to the chore. In his disbelief regarding these underwater vessels, he hadn't felt himself harden. Every day, it was there when he awoke, and he usually dealt with it with prompt efficiency.

Stepping into the cleanser, the water activated, drenching him in seconds. He rested his palms on the white bulkhead, high above his head while ducking his head in and out of the spray. *Will my days ever be more than surviving? Will I be able to look forward to something, an event, seeing a person? Will I experience joy, pleasure, peace?*

With a deep sigh, he lowered his hand to his arousal, wrapping his fingers around the hard girth of it. At his heated touch, images exploded in his mind, startling him. He released his arousal, and the images faded. That had never happened before. He grabbed his arousal again, and the images returned. He focused on them and groaned. They were not of Oriana, thank the Maker, but were of a little human female with masses of brown curls. *Macera.*

He hadn't realized how much he liked her appearance.

As soon as he thought her name, his arousal hardened to its full length. Familiar tingles originated from his balls along his malehood to the head. With two pumps of his hand and a roar, his seed ejected out of him, leaving him shuddering, his nipples having pebbled at the force of his release.

"Alodon's balls," he rasped, his voice hoarse. He wished he understood what had just occurred. Rinsing off his spilled seed, he completed his cleansing lest the images tempted him to repeat the chore. He'd never been this aroused, and even though she wasn't his Dar Eth, her blurred image must have impacted him.

Macera.

He shivered, allowed the wrap to close around his body then strode to the closet. He dressed in his warrior breeches, yanked on his boots, and strapped on his chest armor. He needed to keep his mind active, and he'd do so by checking in with Remi regarding the Gika training before his morning meal. Perhaps these discussions would assist in calming him. Even more preferable if it would eradicate images of Macera from his mind.

Chapter Seventeen

Etterian battleship Phoenix
A day later, when Oyaz's torture began.

MACY AWOKE TO A strange but persistent vibration running up her arm. She wanted to grumble, roll over, and snooze for another three hours when a different buzz rippled up her arm. Moaning, she activated her O.D.I. to find a message from Oyaz.

'Awaken!'

She stifled a snort, swung her legs off the bed, and in a half-asleep state, dressed in her exercise clothes. Tiptoeing from the room, she waved at Quin who stirred but didn't rise. Macy snuck out of the room and grabbed a bottle of water from the rehydrator.

Skip-jogging, she hurried along the now-familiar passages.

She entered the common. "Morning."

Illan and Oyaz were waiting for her. "Good morning," they said in unison.

"What?" she asked the men when they stared at her.

"Your hair." Oyaz scowled.

With a huff, she gathered up her hair. "Sorry, forgot about it." She tied it into a ponytail using the band around her wrist. "Ready."

For the next hour, he made her do exercises her brain couldn't instruct her muscles to do. And judging by her aching body, they were good exercises. By the time he called an end, sweat drenched her clothing, and she fought for every breath. With a whimper, she threw herself onto the sparring mat and lay there, spread-eagled, not caring what she looked like. Illan also struggled. She didn't feel so bad then since he was more muscled than her and should have been in a better condition. He was still standing, at least. *Hoorah for him.*

"I think you killed me," she said between breaths. Groaning, she rolled onto her stomach, hoping to be able to get on all fours, onto her knees, then, Lord willing, to her feet. She squealed when Oyaz picked her up and held her steady until she stood on her own. "Warn a girl next time," she muttered even though she was grateful he'd done that.

"Are you going to complain every day?" A black-winged brow arched, and his lips twitched as if he fought a smile. The bastard hadn't worked up a sweat, looking gorgeous in his warrior pants and a tight vest. She wished she could smack him but couldn't risk moving her arms.

"Yup, get used to it." Unrepentant, she forced a smirk. He shook his head, but this time a small smile claimed his mouth, dimpling one cheek. "I'm going to shower. Come across when you're ready."

Illan tapped his chest with one hand, the other still clutching his side. She assumed the chest-tapping was a yes.

"Watching another vid?" Oyaz asked, interest flittering across his face.

"Yes, I was thinking of playing this ancient vid. It's about a guy that brings music to a town without it."

"Sounds appropriate considering." Oyaz hooked a towel around her neck before patting her shoulder.

With a wince, she tried to stand upright and not tip over. "You're always welcome, Oyaz." She dabbed her temple with the towel. "I'll have the popcorn waiting."

"Popcorn for breakfast?" His wide-eyed expression was priceless.

She couldn't help but laugh. "All right, I'll have something else waiting for you." She watched him leave, her body throbbing in complaint. "Did he hurt us on purpose? Well, he failed. I only half-died."

"Feels like an assassination attempt, though." Illan straightened before he smiled. "Same time tomorrow."

She grumbled. And did so, under her breath, all the way back to her quarters. She took a quick shower, dressed in a long summer dress, then relaxed in a comfy with a coffee. Her body wasn't happy over the treatment Oyaz had put it through.

"Morning, sweetie." Quin grinned, strolling out of their shared bedroom. "How's my favorite singer doing?"

"I'm doing well."

"Cyn and I were thinking of spending the day with you, watching vids, and doing other girly things."

"No thanks, Quin. I have plans for today. But I'm throwing a party one evening soon. I'll need you and Cyndi to show these males how to dance."

"Sure, sounds like fun." The cleansing room door closed and opened again with Quin's head popping out. "What? You have plans?"

"Yup, spending time with Illan and Oyaz."

Quin flashed a wide smile, and the door closed behind her.

Macy grinned and punched in a message to Oyaz and Illan asking them to let her know what time they were coming so she could make sure the food was ready. Both responded that they would be there at 0700. She set her O.D.I. alarm for 0645 and stretched out on the bed, groaning as her aching muscles twitched. Cyndi mumbled something into her pillow but didn't stir otherwise. Macy didn't nap though because Quin returned from the shower, now in her jeans and a T-shirt.

"Heard what you did last night," she said, brushing out her yellow-blonde hair. "It's impressed Xan. Is that why we're having a party?"

"In a way. I kind of like the idea of teaching these guys how to dance, Quin. They're graceful and for them to learn this..."

"Would be awesome," Cyndi grumbled into her pillow. "Morning." She rolled over to peek at them. "What's the time?"

Macy tapped her O.D.I. to check. "0615."

"What the hell? Mace?" Quin leaped to her side to study her wrist. The holographics faded when the O.D.I. deactivated.

Macy shrugged. "Medic Rior implanted it yesterday."

"That's so unfair." Quin pouted.

"Hurts like hell." Macy trembled her lips and sniffed. "I bled all over the place. Rior ran around panicking that he'd nicked my artery. I thought I'd die."

"Someone's bullshitting us." Cyndi chuckled as she sat up, rubbing her eyes with the heel of her palms.

"How come I can never fool you, Cyndi?" Macy thumped the bed with a firm fist, despite grinning. "Oyaz needed to comm me."

"It's a good idea." Cyndi flicked the blanket aside. "We should get one too, Quin. That way we can talk to each other no matter where we are."

"I don't know if it has a limited range. I'll ask Oyaz. Speaking of him, would you guys mind if Illan, Oyaz, and I watch a vid this morning?"

"Vids?" Quin's brow arched.

"Yup." Macy pointed in the direction of the display vid. "I found all of Earth's contraband music and vids on the display vid." *Best find ever.*

"Awesome." Quin clapped, her unbound hair swirling in her excitement.

"We don't mind, Macy. We were a little worried about you," Cyndi said. "I felt so bad leaving you all alone."

"It wasn't you or Quin making me sad, Cyndi." Macy gave her friend a quick hug. "I was super bored. Oyaz and Illan are helping me find things to do."

"What are you going to watch?" Quin asked while braiding her hair.

"Something about bringing music to a dull town." Macy laughed. "It's appropriate."

Quin flicked her braid over a shoulder. "Well, I'll make myself scarce, but let me know if you need any help with the party arrangements."

"You mean besides shaking that ass?" Macy teased.

Quin chuckled and did a quick butt jiggle before leaving the room.

"That's my cue." Cyndi leaped to her feet. "Best hop into the shower and out the door."

"Thanks, Cyndi." As her friend left the room, Macy activated her O.D.I. to check the time and sighed.

She made the bed and had a coffee waiting for Cyndi as she exited the cleansing room. Macy browsed through the music and chose a ballad, mournful, evocative, setting the volume to medium. Cyndi hummed as she sipped her coffee, swaying her hips to the tune. She dropped her empty cup into the waste receptacle and hugged Macy before rushing out.

Macy ordered breakfast and iced coffees, all the while singing along to the song. When it ended, she selected another one from the same artist. The words were about hitting rock bottom then being rescued. She belted out the lyrics, stretching her voice to its fullest range.

"Your birdsong is beautiful," Oyaz said from where he stood in the doorway. A smiling Illan hovered behind him.

"Shit," she gasped. "I didn't realize the door was open. I'm sorry."

"Sorry for?" Illan entered the quarters. "Oyaz was correct. You sing well."

She dipped her chin, straightened, then bounced toward them. "Well, come in, let's get the party started."

"Party?" Oyaz frowned.

"It's just a saying. It means let's start." She gestured to the chairs. "How do we make them face the screen?"

Oyaz tapped on the display vid and navigated to Aesthetics. He pressed a few buttons, and the chairs shifted. She gaped when they moved by 'themselves.' Crowding him, she watched him work the buttons. On the vid was a plan of their quarters. He positioned the chairs, three in a row, right in front of the display vid.

"Magnetic bases," he said.

"Well, that makes life easier." She offered him a sandwich from the platter in her hand.

He took one and bit into it with enthusiasm. His groan of pleasure had Illan reaching for one too.

"These are bacon and cheese grilled sandwiches. My grandmother used to say that bacon should be in heaven." She shared with them before giving each one their iced coffee.

"Your grandmother was right," Illan said, accepting the cold beverage.

Her lips tingled when he watched her wrap them around the straw and suck. He grinned once he'd swallowed a good deal of it.

"What is this?" Oyaz drained the cup.

"It's ice coffee."

"It is wonderful." He focused on her untouched coffee.

She giggled and handed hers over. She started the vid. Illan and Oyaz grumbled at scenes throughout, but by the end of it, their hips twitched to the music.

"I liked it," Oyaz said as soon as the credits rolled.

"Entertaining." Illan reached for the last sandwich, now cold.

"You do not expect me to dance like that, do you?" Oyaz's worried expression had her laughing.

"Of course not. But you are a little stiff when you dance, surprisingly for someone so graceful."

"Stiff? Graceful?" He frowned.

"What is so terrible?" Illan furrowed his brow.

She gestured for them to stand. Using the display vid, she sent the chairs to the walls, giving them a larger space to dance. She chose a classic club anthem, loud enough to vibrate the walls and up through her feet. Shimmying to the center, she closed her eyes and let the music take her. She roved all over the floor, grinding and pulsing her backside, gyrating her shoulders, her arms in the air, reaching for the ceiling. She opened her eyes and dragged a wide-eyed Illan into the middle. He jerked his hips, finding the rhythm.

She gawked. *Damn.*

He gyrated like he'd danced his entire life. Oyaz joined then, encouraged by Illan's skill. At first, he was stiff, but by the end of the song, he swayed and twirled his hips. When he moved a little lower, bending his knees, her pulse screamed 'stripper.'

Their self-confidence solidified as song after song played, migrating them around the floor.

"The last one," she said as the next song started. This one was heavy on the bass. Her chest swelled with warmth and excitement. She loved it. "That was fantastic. I'm so proud of you two." She hugged them before bouncing on her feet. Her thighs burned, and her calves twinged, but she ignored the agony.

"I like the vibrations" Illan hugged her back. "I will practice for this party, Macy."

"Neither of you need to practice. You are both naturals, and see, Oyaz, there's nothing to worry about."

"I am grateful for that," he grinned, pleased with himself. "So, when do you want it to be?"

"After tomorrow's evening meal?" She arched a brow, watching his face for disapproval. Oyaz grunted which she assumed was a yes. "Now, I'll play one or two sexy songs, for Xan and Iddan. So, don't panic. I don't expect you to dance to them."

"Sexy?" Oyaz's eyebrows shot upwards.

Illan frowned. "Is that wise, Macy?" He darted a glance at Oyaz as if to tell him to say no.

She wrung her hands. "If it bothers you, I'll play just one, okay."

"Let me hear it," Oyaz said, his tone commanding.

She sighed and navigated on her O.D.I. to the song she was thinking of.

"Now show me how to dance to this one."

Her eyebrows shot up as her cheeks heated. *A personal 'lap dance?'*

"It's the same, just slow." She squeezed her eyes shut, trying to block out their faces. Swaying her hips in a seductive figure eight, she brushed her sides, past her breasts, over her waist to her hips. She thrust out her backside and swung it side-to-side before she ran her hands back up, flipping her hair out and holding her arms above her head as she swirled her hips. Her mouth fell open ad she spun her head and arched her back.

Oyaz tapped her wrist, pausing the song, halting her in mid-hip-swirl. "Alodon's balls," he gasped and glanced at a stunned Illan.

"No," Illan growled out.

"I agree." Oyaz scowled.

"Why?" She darted her gaze between them. *Was it the song choice? Was it my dancing?* She wasn't *that* bad.

"Are you insane?" Oyaz clenched his hands at his sides.

"You will have every male wanting to mate with you, Macy," Illan said.

"What?" The thought hadn't occurred to her. "Why?"

Oyaz frowned. "To find their Dar Eth."

"Their what now?" Some of the males had mentioned this, but she hadn't asked. Settling her hands on her hips, she met Oyaz's gaze.

"Do you not have the Etterian Language Protocol activated on your O.D.I?" Oyaz reached for her wrist but she whipped it out of reach.

"I don't have time to learn a new language. Just...explain, like I'm a two-year-old."

With a sigh, Oyaz clasped his hands behind his back. "When an Etterian male meets the female meant for him, it triggers the Ethera. The force of this bond will bring a male to his knees. He becomes an Eth, the female a Dar Eth."

"So...if any of your men...males were my Eth, they would kneel?" She pursed her lips as she dredged her memories for any collapsing Etterians. None came to mind, but it could still happen, right? "Is there a time delay?"

"It strikes in an instant." Oyaz shrugged. "Not much is known. A pairing is considered intimate so not well-documented."

She formed an 'oh' with her mouth. Pairing? That had to mean Eth plus Dar Eth like a couple?

"What I do know is that the male must see all of the female in her natural beauty," Illan added.

"You know this for certain?" Oyaz arched a brow.

"She must be naked?" Macy gasped. No wonder no Eth existed for her. There was no way on this metal flying box she would prance around in the nude with her breasts swaying and her flabby ass jiggling.

Illan chuckled, earning a thump on the arm from her. "No, just a full view of her without anything to hide her true beauty...like mud, dust, dirtiness." He rubbed his arm while grinning.

"So I can dance then. No Ethera has happened."

"We can find fulfillment without the Ethera, *ensa*." Oyaz winced, which meant there was more to that.

She gestured to herself. "They would want to mate with me? Don't you mean with Cyndi or Quin?"

He shook his head. "No, with you."

She smothered the laughter bubbling up her throat, but she wasn't going to push the sexy songs if he believed that bit of nonsense. "All right, nothing sexy," she said, hoping this incident wouldn't cost her the club night. She was looking forward to it.

"Good." He sucked in a deep breath.

"What are you going to wear?" she asked, making them jerk back.

"This," they said at the same time, pointing to what they were wearing—Oyaz in his uniform and Illan in his loose slacks and shirt.

She sighed. "Come, put in your sizes." She pointed at the replicator.

Illan strolled over first and helped her size his garments. She chose a pair of dark blue jeans with a white, buttoned-up long-sleeved shirt. It took longer to convince him to try shoes that weren't like his comfortable slippers... and socks.

"Try it on." She gestured to the cleansing room and faced Oyaz. His expression said he wasn't pleased with this new development. "Just try. You might like it."

He grumbled, shifted closer, and let her choose black jeans and a camel-colored V-necked T-shirt. She handed him his clothes and gestured to the bedroom. Tucking her bottom lip over her top lip, she smothered her laugh when he dragged his heels but did as she asked. So like a teenage boy.

Illan came out handsome-as-hell in his jeans and white shirt. As aliens went, he was attractive, made even more so by the pleased smile gracing his lips.

"The shirt is nice, but the pants are a little tight."

"You don't like showing what a nice ass you have?" she teased, delighted with herself when his cheeks faded to a pale blue. "And the shoes?"

"Will take getting used to. Opacity: reflection." He admired himself. "Yes, I see the appeal." He nodded at his backside. "These do suit me." He flashed a smile. "Thank you, Macy. I will wear this to the event. Now, if you will excuse me, there is somewhere I need to be." He left, leaving her a little stunned at his speedy exit, but knowing his circumstances, she understood.

"These are too tight," Oyaz said from the bedroom door, tugging at his crotch in a boyish manner.

Her mouth dried, and she licked her lips. *Shit, he is hot.* The jeans not only hugged his thighs and backside but hung low on his hips, and with his military boots, he gave off a kickass biker vibe. His camel-colored T-shirt hugged his shoulders and biceps, and the V-neck showed off a bit of his caramel chest. The color complimented his bronzed skin and black hair.

"You look amazing," she said.

He grumbled and studied his image in the reflective walls.

"I like the shirt." He grunted, which she was fast learning meant approval or agreement. "But the pants are too tight. How do your males move in this?"

"Do you want a bigger size?" She requested a larger size from the replicator.

He grunted again and strode toward her. She'd forgotten how bulky he was, and with the tight T-shirt and jeans on, he had an intimidating presence.

"Thank you. Now the most important question, what will you wear?"

"I haven't decided yet, maybe a dress?"

He glanced at the summer dress she was wearing with the open shoulders and the floor-length skirt.

"No, not like this."

"Let me see." He faced the replicator, crowding her to see the screen.

She shoved his larger pair of jeans to the side before punching in her requirements. Then chose an outfit she'd never wear—a red elegant dress with a thigh-to-ankle split which made his eyebrows shoot up. She smothered a giggle.

"No."

She rolled her eyes but managed to hide her smile.

"How about pants and a shirt?"

"Can the shirt have an opening down to my belly button?" She didn't bother hiding her grin. Why he needed to make sure she was decently covered amazed her. Like what she wore mattered. "In transparent fabric, so you can see my nipples?" She laughed when his scowl darkened. "I'm kidding, Oyaz." She sucked in breaths as tears slid down her cheeks. "I'm wearing jeans and a shirt. I want to dance not fuck."

He grumbled something and ran his hand over his face as if she tried his patience. Well, she *was* lying to him. Any one of these males would be a killer in bed. They would want the lights off, but she wouldn't mind. She imagined running her fingers down a male's muscled back. *Yummy.*

Oyaz stiffened and stepped away from her. "I will collect you. I want to ensure you wear nothing transparent." He grabbed his jeans and bolted for the door, picking up his discarded uniform along the way.

"Don't trust me?" she teased.

"No." And the door closed behind him.

She un-paused the sexy song he had halted and finished the seductive dance for herself.

Chapter Eighteen

Etterian battleship Phoenix
The common
Late one evening.

MACY SCROLLED TO THE next page, finding the O.D.I. as a reading device unusual. The words were legible against an opaque background, but she couldn't read for longer than an hour before exhaustion fogged her mind. Curled into a corner in the common, the buzz of males coming and going added comfort. She glanced up to smile at no one. Returning her attention to the travails of forlorn lovers, she ignored the pang in her heart whispering that such an all-encompassing love wasn't for her.

"Are you bothering Lady Macera?" a male asked, drawing her attention. Alongside her sat a Lysaran male, one of the prisoners Quin had freed. She hadn't heard him approach, nor felt his gaze upon her.

"Forgive me, milady. I sensed your longing and pain."

"It's all right, Rior." She smiled at the medic, hoping to ease his protective instincts.

Powering off her O.D.I., she faced the Lysaran, wishing she'd taken a moment to prepare herself. "Hello, I'm Macy, are you adjusting well to freedom?" She glanced down, tracing her fingertip along the edge of the table. What could she say? Damn, he was gorgeous with his caramel skin and brown hair. Those amber-gold eyes pierced hers every time she met his gaze. She drew in a calming breath before raising her chin to offer a polite smile.

"I am Myn-ras Bel-nataar. It is a pleasure to meet you, milady." His voice dipped low with his gaze traveling her face. What he searched for or saw, she couldn't say.

"Call me Macy, please." *Is that husky voice mine? Get a grip, woman.*

"I would like to thank you for your bravery."

Discomfort at his admiration lanced through her. She shifted on her backside then straightened her spine. "I did nothing, Myn-ras. Quin's the true heroine."

"I do not believe so." He frowned. "I have saddened you. I am sorry."

She gasped. "I'm not sad." *Or am I? Did I want to be the heroine? The way these men gravitated toward Quin? Yup, hot damn, I'd love to be desirable.*

The man drew in a deep breath and smiled, vampiric fangs dimpling his bottom lip. *Holy shit, now that is sexy.* Awe had her gawking at him. She hadn't believed in vampires, but the man before her had her reconsidering their existence.

His sensual lips split into a wide grin. "Your emotions are passionate and intense. They perfume the air with delicate fragrances." His amber-gold eyes turned molten. Excitement skittered goosebumps down her spine. It felt good to be the focus of such warmth, but alas, she didn't trust it.

"You can smell my thoughts?" She tried to think of nothing—a struggle on its own.

"Emotions, yes. Our people are losing theirs. Without mates, they are withdrawing, and our world is dying."

"Why can't they find their mates? Too few females?" It was a common enough scenario with the Etterians not being able to produce girls.

"No, our females are dying inside and losing the urge to procreate. My kuna is searching for a solution but to no avail."

Dying inside? Of boredom, loneliness? No, I know nothing of that. She smothered a snort. But at least her depression wouldn't kill a nation. "How does that kill your world? Don't you mean species?" Sadness at the thought of a dying people drew a shuddering breath from her. Perhaps they had no idea what the cause was?

"When a male and female mate, the heavens answer their cries of delight and drench our lands with much-needed rain." His eyes became shiny as if he was about to cry. "It has not rained for over a year."

She closed her mouth, aware she gaped like a fish. A planet destroyed for lack of sex? Laughter burst from her, and she clamped her lips shut, heat burning her cheeks. This wasn't a laughing matter.

"I'm sorry. I know it's not funny." But when she glanced at him, he was smiling at her again.

"I am exhilarated in your presence, Macy." He leaned across the table to hold out his hand.

Long fingers gestured to her to accept his request to touch her. She placed hers into his, watching as his caramel hand layered hers. He was hot, like he carried the sun within him. His moan returned her attention to his contorted face, and she chewed on her lip in concern. Deep red blood dribbled from his bottom lip where his fang had pierced it. Was he in pain? Should she find Medic Rior? She glanced around the common searching for him since he wasn't in medical. Where the hell was he? Typical. When she needed him, he was gone.

"I do not want to alarm you, but I find your emotions arousing," Myn-ras rasped.

"What?" she squeaked. Heat burst afresh across her cheeks. She wanted to yank her hand free but didn't dare offend him.

"Are all your females as emotional?" He licked the blood off his lip.

"Yes, so it's not me you're attracted to." There it was. Her usual self-recrimination. Anger burned through her, and she scowled, tugging her hand free. She was miserable too, but it was better to embrace the anger than to cry.

"I meant no insult." Darkness crossed his eyes despite the sexy smile curling the corner of his mouth. "Being near you feels like I am drenched in the warm rays of our yellow sun."

He bounded up and circled the table, looping his arms around her waist to lift her to her feet. At the ease with which he picked her up, she grabbed his biceps, hoping not to hit the floor face-first.

"Come, I need you to meet my friend, Bry-dar. He will not believe me unless he feels for himself."

Dizzy and a little breathless, she chuckled at his eagerness. She should be chasing him away, but he was an alien species, one she couldn't tar with any brush she knew. "Where is your friend?"

"In the common the Etterians allocated to us. He is a late sleeper."

She blinked at the man clasping her to the length of his body. Was he aware of their intimate position? Not that she minded the heat emanating from him. She cherished being held, even as a semi-hostage. His cologne was of an unknown flower with a citrus undertone. Perhaps his world had beautiful flora, and he wished to carry the fragrance with him. A little mesmerized, she sucked it in, wondering if his scent carried pheromones.

"Myn-ras." She darted glances at the Etterian males gathering around them. They were a protective species, a mannerism she found endearing. "Are you aware you're holding me too close?"

A peach-colored blush burst across his face, and he released her, his mouth gaping as he pressed his palms to his cheeks. "I am embarrassed? It is wonderful." He grabbed her hand and pulled her behind him, forging a path through the vigilant bronze warriors.

His strides were long, and she hurried after him, doing double the steps to keep up. Her thighs burned from the abuse, reminding her of what Oyaz had put her through. Myn-ras was too excited, and she didn't have the heart to ask him to slow down. It was understandable that by the time they reached his Common, she was breathless, and a fine sheen of perspiration beaded her forehead. Her knees trembled. She prayed it was muscle-strain and not in reaction to the man still holding her hand.

It was easy to spot his friend among the prisoners. Most of them were Maloidian—a yellow-skinned species with undulating tentacles for hair. She hadn't had an opportunity to chat with many of them yet, well, except for Pannos. The old man had weaseled his way into her heart within a conversation. She missed her gran. Pushing down the constant grief thoughts of her revived, Macy pasted on a smile, watching Pannos amble across the room. In his hand was the metal pole he'd leaned on when they'd first met.

"*Lommia*," she said, accepting his offered hand for a squeeze.

"How fare's my favorite Earthian?" he asked, a bright smile splitting his cheeks.

"I'm well," she said. He arched his unibrow in disbelief. "Struggling to adjust and battling boredom." She shook her head, amazed at how he managed to wheedle the truth out of her. Myn-ras released her hand and gestured to his friend, indicating he'd fetch him. "I'm making changes though, and Rior's implanted an O.D.I."

"Ah, now I see. You love change. A stagnating future saps your energy." Pannos squeezed her hand again before releasing it. "I hope to see my son soon, and if the gods bless me, bring him home. It has been too long." He smiled. "Poor Myn-ras is in a state. What did you do to him?"

"He smells my emotions," she said, disbelieving the words even as she spoke them.

"Visit more often, *mitkaari*. I enjoy interacting with you." Pannos pulled back, allowing Myn-ras to approach her. His friend trailed him with more reticence.

"I promise, *lommia*. I'll visit daily," she said, fighting the urge to beg him to stay with her. Myn-ras was a little too much for her to handle, and two Lysarans might overwhelm her.

"Lady Macera, this is Bry-dar Tol-aryss."

"Please, Myn-ras, call me Macy." She held out her hand for a shake, but Bry-dar clasped it between his large-thumbed hands. His eyes fluttered closed. His fangs pressed down on his bottom lip in the perfect image of ecstasy.

"I did not believe you, my friend," Bry-dar said, opening his eyes with gold swirling in their depths.

Drawn to their beauty, she inched closer to cup his face, marveling at the satin texture of his skin. "You're beautiful." Gasping, she glanced down, praying the heat on her cheeks wasn't recognizable. *Please tell me I didn't say that aloud? Sugar honey iced tea.*

Bry-dar laughed, tightening his hold on her as he drew her closer. "As are you, milady," he said, peering into her eyes.

Me beautiful alongside this Adonis? She snorted, slipping her hand free and removing her grasp on his cheek. *Moving on.*

"We need to inform our kuna of this, Bry-dar," Myn-ras said.

"He will not believe us, as I did, my friend." Bry-dar looped an arm around her and yanked her against his taut body.

She cried out, her hands flying to his biceps. *What was this? Manhandling me as if I'm a sex-cyborg? Hell, no.*

"Will you return to Lysara with us, sweet Macera?" His voice rolled over her senses like molten honey. There was a seductive lure to his words, and she opened her mouth to agree to whatever he asked. She snapped her mouth shut and stepped back, knowing full well that she did so because he let her. Her fingers had touched bulging muscles, confirming his superior strength.

"To visit?" she asked, hoping not to cause an intergalactic incident if she disrespected him, but dammit, they touched her as if they had a right to.

"For as long as you would like."

Myn-ras crowded in as well, engulfing her with their combined colognes. Her heart quivered in her chest, but she wasn't sure if it was from fear or excitement. A purr rumbled through the air, feathering along her skin. She gasped, taking another step back in sheer panic. The urge to stay there warred with her need to run.

"Macy, here you are," Oyaz said.

She spun to face him, her cheeks flushing as if he'd caught her naked. Relief flooded her, and even though she'd like nothing more than to bask in the allure rolling off the Lysarans, Oyaz offered a refuge for her tumultuous senses. She broke away from Bry-dar, not wanting to run but unable to ignore Oyaz.

"Were you searching for me?" she asked, delighted her voice remained steady. Although, her chaotic emotions had to be thrilling to the two Lysarans with the way they grinned at her.

Myn-ras followed and caught her hand, halting her retreat.

Oyaz rattled something off in a lyrical language she assumed was Lysaran. He looked none too pleased. His posture stiffened, and it seemed as if he'd grown taller, more intimidating. Here before her stood a commander and a powerful warrior. She darted glances between them as they conversed, and when Myn-ras released her hand, she slumped, allowing relief to claim her. Oyaz strode toward her to loop an arm around her, securing her to his side.

"We need to discuss tonight's meal," he said, sticking to the ruse.

She flashed an apologetic smile at Bry-dar and Myn-ras and allowed Oyaz to whisk her away. As soon as they were down the passage and alone, he stopped and clasped her shoulders with a gentle touch.

"Are you harmed?" His brow furrowed with what she assumed was concern. Etterians didn't like to *feel* emotions. She had yet to find out why. "You look dazed, and your face has red patches."

She groaned, mortification claiming her fragile ego. "I'm fine, Oyaz, thanks for finding me."

"Take care with the Lysarans, *ensa*. They believe you are their salvation as well."

As well as what? As whom? "So they implied. I'm not, though. Maybe other women but never me." Biting her lip at having revealed some of her inner turmoil, she squeezed Oyaz's forearm and scurried off, wanting nothing more but to find a hole to crawl into.

Chapter Nineteen

Dinner was a success. Each male polished off two deluxe burgers and a few strawberry shakes. Macy couldn't resist the idea that these masculine males drank pink drinks. It appealed to her sense of humor. She mentioned where possible that there'd be a special treat after tomorrow's evening meal. And she did hope they loved it. She was looking forward to it. They were days from reaching Etteria, her new homeworld.

All enjoyed the rock and roll music she'd played. The men...males were more comfortable in her presence, content to talk to her and ask her questions, some of them were bold enough to tease her. They were well-behaved. No one tried to feel her backside or proposition her for late-night activity. And they didn't mention her too-generous curves or her dull coloring. They were the sweetest males she'd ever met.

Regardless of the success of the evening and the barrage of questions thrown at her, she still returned to an empty room.

Quin and Xan had made an appearance but had left shortly after Xan had consumed his second milkshake. The way he gathered her close told her exactly how he felt about her Amazon friend.

Cyndi and Iddan had shown their support, but they hadn't stayed for long. This would mean that poor Illan had nowhere to go. Macy activated her O.D.I. and messaged him to come over if Cyndi and Iddan occupied their shared quarters. In the meantime, she hopped into the cleanser, air-dried, and was in her oversized T-shirt ordering a bottle of water when her door chimed. She commanded it to open. Illan wore his usual soft yoga-type pants, loose tunic, and sandals, ready for bed.

"Welcome, my friend. Want anything from the rehydrator?" she asked him.

"No, thank you, Macy. I fear I've overindulged again with your delicious food." He stepped in then dropped into the closest comfy.

"Some water then to help it digest?" She handed him an ordered bottle before slumping into a seat next to him. Since the comfys were facing the display vid to watch vids, she activated her O.D.I. and selected a docu-vid on elephants. It had him riveted in seconds, and for forty-two minutes, he didn't say a word.

"They are marvelous creatures," he gushed as soon as it ended. "Have you seen one on Earth?"

She shook her head. "They live in secluded parks built in their natural habitat. At one stage, in Earth's history, animals were becoming extinct at an alarming rate and as per music, movies, and games, the government intervened. For the most part, we live normal lives, similar to our grandparents." She shrugged as she ordered another bottle of water. "Little things have changed like we can space travel now and use solar power. All technology has come a long way, I suppose. O.D.I.s aren't common though." She assumed her seat again but twisted to face him. "Our air, water, and soil are still polluted, but we're repairing them and not making it worse. We've always had an abundance of food, yet people used to die from starvation. Our food now has birth control in it. You have to apply to birth a child. Once your application is successful, the government delivers special food to you." She raised a teary gaze to his. "That only applies to law-abiding people. Those dodging the law eat what's available so unwanted babies still happen. It is why we have orphanages. I was such a baby."

"You were an orphan?"

"No, my mother met a man who wasn't...well-behaved. Needless to say, the birth control in the food is for men only. Since their seed contains one hundred million possible babies in one milliliter, it made sense to control their fertility than females who only have a maximum of two eggs a month."

"And since your father..."

"Donor," she said with a dismissive wave.

"And since your donor wasn't consuming government-approved food, he was fertile?"

"Yes, but in all fairness, my mother loved me, even if I was a surprise." Macy flashed him an overly wide smile, attempting to thwart her tears. "My gran too, in her way. It was hard for her to raise me when her two daughters died together."

"She lost both her children?" he asked.

"Yes, my mom was a twin."

His eyelids flickered. "Now I see, two born at once and both died at the same time. There is harmony in that."

"I suppose." She shrugged, trying not to think too much about those first few months. They had been hard to endure, to survive.

"I assume you never knew your donor?"

"No, I don't even know his name." She gestured to his O.D.I. "Message Iddan, tell him to keep Cyndi by him. You can crash with me."

"What? Crash?" Illan frowned.

"Since Cyndi's spending time with Iddan, you can share the bed with me." She grinned when Illan blinked with wide-eyed horror cementing his face. "No, silly, as in sleep only. No hanky-panky."

"Hanky-panky?" His eyes twinkled with humor after their brief flutter.

"Yes, none of that. As friends, we can share a bed, like brother and sister." She requested a blanket from the replicator and tossed it to him.

Despair clogged her throat, but she refused to show it. Even he didn't want to touch her. Her friend. Well, what had she expected? She'd only ever had one lover, and he'd been a one-night stand when she'd been too drunk to care. It had happened shortly after her gran's death. Hell, she couldn't even recognize him if he bit her on the ass. "Now there won't be accidental touching in the middle of the night. That should appease your honor?"

He huffed but trailed her. Within minutes, his private blanket cocooned him. She stared at his back for the longest time, fighting the sorrow burning her eyes with unshed tears. Smothering a sob, she rolled herself inside her blanket, turning her back on hope.

"ALODON'S BALLS, WHAT HAPPENED?" Oyaz watched their human friend charm his males, sharing bright smiles with her hair swirling around her.

"She worked hard today," Illan said, licking ice cream off his spoon.

"She does not look exhausted," Oyaz said, biting into his seventh *hotdog*. Macy had explained that even though it was called a hotdog, it didn't have their dog creature in it, which Illan was grateful for. And that she knew not why it had such a strange name.

"What has you so displeased?" Rior drank his soda, his foot tapping to the music she had chosen.

"I am concerned she will dress in something revealing," Oyaz said, even though she wore blue leggings and a black, buttoned-up shirt, he still didn't trust that she'd remain so.

"She said she would not, and she is a woman of honor." Illan wore the garments she'd ordered for him, as did Oyaz.

"Yes, she *is* honorable." Oyaz relaxed his shoulders. She'd worn what she said she would.

After the males helped tidy up, each receiving a sweet smile of thanks from the adored Macy, she nodded at Kemt. The lighting dimmed.

Bright colors bombarded Oyaz's vision. The music played loud enough to vibrate the bulkheads. Rior gathered his nano-meds to store in his quarters since the vibrations might disturb them. Macy laced her fingers through Oyaz and Illan's and tugged them into the middle of the common. The thumping beat flowed through Oyaz, merging with the beats of his hearts.

He swung his hips, unable to deny the urge to dance. It didn't take long before more males joined them. Ladies Cyndi and Quin wiggled to the music. Xan's lustful gaze was riveted on Quin, revealing that he had other needs on his mind. But under her determined instruction, he too jerked his body. It was yet another success, and hours later, the image of a happy Macy lured Oyaz into an exhausted slumber.

Chapter Twenty

To visit Pannos as promised, Macy stepped into the Lysarans's common, darting her gaze around while hoping to spot them before they pounced on her. Not that she was scared of them, but she worried their sex appeal would seduce her like it did last time. She'd told Illan where she was going and to fetch her in an hour if he didn't hear from her.

"Pannos is not here, sweet Macera." Bry-dar appeared behind her. His voice breathed across her neck, sending shivers down her spine. Stiffening and vowing not to succumb, she faced him with a smile plastered on. She'd forgotten how handsome he was.

"Oh, no. Will you tell him I came by?" she asked, hoping Bry-dar didn't smell anything other than friendliness.

"Macera, sali, please forgive me for frightening you. Your emotional range overloaded my senses." He held up his hand, offering peace. "Come, sit with me. I would enjoy learning about you, if you will share this with me?"

She hesitated, casting a glance at the door. "Where's Myn-ras?"

"He is organizing our departure," he said.

"You're leaving?" She took a seat opposite Bry-dar. The width of the table separated them, but it didn't help. His intense gaze remained fixed on her, spiraling butterflies in her belly.

"The offer stands, Macy. I would love to show you Lysara. It is splendid with its lilac sunsets and pale-yellow skies." His love for his homeworld was evident and for a moment, she wished she could trust his intentions. "Quin is coming with us, just for the shuttle ride."

"She is?" Macy smothered a twinge of jealousy, not that Quin traveled with him but that he knew her friend. She must've been spending time here, as well. A selfish part of Macy wanted to keep Bry-dar's admiration for herself. He made her feel beautiful even though it was a lie. "I will think about it, Bry-dar. I must travel to Etteria in gratitude and support, and visiting with you will delay that."

"Your sense of duty makes you more appealing, Macera. But I fear, once my kuna meets you, I shall have to forfeit any claim to you."

"What?" She blinked at him. *Who spoke like this?* "Claim?"

"Suns above. You do not know how breathtaking you are. This rattles my control, and every day you visit Pannos, I must fight the need to be near you."

"You'll say that to any human woman, Bry-dar," she said with a dismissive flick of her hand. "I'm the only *unclaimed Earthian female* on board."

"True, I might react this way to another of your species."

She winced. His words stung, but she needed to hear them. "I'd like to think of you as a friend, who'd one day claim a woman of your own."

He studied her for a while, his face expressionless yet his eyes swirled. She understood that to mean inner turmoil. "I would cherish your friendship, as would Myn-ras."

"That's a nice thing to say." She flashed a delighted smile.

"I do not say what I do not mean." He frowned. "I sense my words brought you joy, and I am grateful for that."

She chuckled. "That doesn't give you carte blanche to compliment me. My reactions would diminish the more you sweet-talk me."

His lips curled in a heart-fluttering way, and she glanced away, praying Pannos or Illan would arrive to save her from herself.

"I prefer you happy. Your scent is so much sweeter."

"Thanks, I think." She jumped up to order two cappuccinos from the rehydrator then slid one across to him before resuming her seat. Sipping it would serve as a distraction from his gold eyes. He tasted the hot beverage before pushing it aside with a shudder.

"We are fruitarians," he said with a shrug. She giggled. A man who looked like a vampire from the legends survived on fruit? "You find my food choice humorous?" he asked, a grin splitting his cheeks.

"One day I'll explain it to you," she said, cupping her cappuccino.

"Lady Macy," Myn-ras said in greeting, choosing the seat beside her. "Has Bry-dar convinced you to visit our wonderful home?"

"Yes, but not now. I have obligations I need to deal with first." She gave up on convincing Myn-ras to call her by her name. Underneath the table, she stretched out her legs, trying to ease the ache in her muscles. She'd swear Oyaz was trying to kill her.

"You are in pain?" Myn-ras asked, his brow furrowing.

She stiffened, winced, then lowered her feet. "You can't smell muscle pain, can you?"

"Pain has a sour undertone to it," Bry-dar said. "Should I summon Medic Rior?"

"It's not necessary." She sipped from her cup. "Oyaz is teaching me how to defend myself."

"He is?" Myn-ras laughed. "How did you convince an Etterian warrior to allow a female to train?"

"Fitness first, hence the pain." She arched her back, trying to ease the tense muscles, although the action brought some measure of pleasure.

"Why not have Medic Rior add anesthetics to your cleanser?" Bry-dar asked.

"I'm proud, not wanting to ask anyone for help, and I have to endure the pain to believe I'm accomplishing something." She rose to order orange juice from the rehydrator. Bry-dar arched a dubious brow before sniffing then tasting it. When he smacked his lips in delight, she returned to savor her coffee.

"This is better than that." He pointed at her cup.

"When do you leave?" she asked Myn-ras, who sipped his juice.

"Within the hour," he said.

"So soon?" she gasped, shoving her O.D.I. at him. "Punch in your details." She jerked her arm back. "You have an O.D.I.?"

He gathered her hand in his and pressed a kiss to her fingertips. "We do." He released her to activate his implant. He tapped her arm, and a buzz traveled up to tingle in her elbow. Bry-dar did the same. The appearance of Oyaz snagged her attention. Had Illan sent him instead? Was she out of time?

"I'll talk to you daily." She placed her cup in the recycler. When she spun around, both men had risen to their feet. She wrapped her arms around Myn-ras, allowing him to hold her close before pulling away to hug Bry-dar. "I'll see you soon."

"Suns above, sali, I hope so," Bry-dar said.

Hoping they didn't pick up on her sadness, she pinched her lips closed, smiled at them, then dashed over to Oyaz.

"Was this wise?" he asked as soon as they were alone along a passage.

"I promised Pannos I would visit." She raised her chin, prepared to argue about this.

A pulse ticked at the base of his jaw. "I know, *ensa*, however, the Lysarans—"

"Which is why I asked Illan to save me." She huffed. "And besides, it hasn't been an hour, Oyaz." Halting her steps, she faced him. "So why so early?"

"I'd like you to join us in your quarters." He paused. "There has been a...development."

Her spine tingled. She blinked at Oyaz then gestured for him to lead the way. "Of course, my friend."

Trailing him, she pondered what this all meant. And why did he need her to attend? Skipping to keep up with his long strides, she spent the time focusing on her breathing, not wanting to be huffing and puffing after him like a pissed-off rhinoceros.

She let them into her quarters where Iddan and Cyndi waited. "Where's Quin?"

"On her way," Illan crowded Macy from behind, forcing her to step aside.

Oyaz darted around her and leaned against a wall, his posture casual. With the way he'd rushed them to reach here, she didn't believe it. His pulse was going crazy along his clenched jaw.

She chose a comfy and slumped into it, stretching out each leg to twirl her foot. The pain was easing, which was good.

Iddan laughed then sliced a glance at Illan, who wore an expression of amusement. His lips were pursed together, and his white eyes twinkled. She dipped her chin, once again excluded. A peek revealed Cyndi giggling as well.

Yup, just Macy alone against the universe. She picked at her jeans, trailing a finger along a seam. With a deep breath and a slow exhale, she squared her shoulders. It was time to move on, to find a group of people she could call her own.

The door opened, and Iddan smiled as he addressed Xan and Quin stepping into the room. "Idiot? I have often thought him such," he chuckled.

"Only a human would dare to call me that." Illan gestured to Oyaz to reveal this 'development.'

"We are incapacitated, and we suspect the offender is a prisoner, perhaps more than one." Oyaz gazed around the room.

"Sabotage?" Quin frowned.

Macy stilled. It had to be serious. Oyaz wouldn't involve them if they weren't...well, involved.

"I have received strange comms from various sources." Oyaz pushed himself off the wall, stiffened, relaxed, then leaned against the wall again. "Twice in the last few days, the engineers replaced the cylinders for the fusion drives. With no documented defects, they have inexplicably fractured. Pilot Msar deactivated the drives to perform the repairs."

"The sec vids confirm the destruction?" Xan asked.

"No, there is nothing, no suspicious activity, almost as if someone tampered with the data. Kemt is investigating this since only a select few on this ship have the skills and the access to do so." Oyaz scowled and unfolded his arms only to refold them across his chest, his body remaining tense.

"There's more," Xan said.

"Yes, life support malfunctioned, powering up the backup tanks. Doing these repairs has cost us four hours. They tampered with the acceptable oxygen levels, and the emergency failsafe kicked in. As malfunctions go, this was minor but still critical."

Macy took in a deep breath, as if oxygen might be denied to her at any minute.

"So they had to know the ship's design well." Xan watched Oyaz, who stiffened further. "What else?"

"We are transmitting an encrypted signal to an unknown receiver. Kemt has disabled it, but it has compromised our location. The usual comms masked the low-frequency signal. We still do not know what it communicated nor what awaits us en route." He lowered his arms to his side, slumping.

"It is a prisoner. That is the logical conclusion." Xan glanced at Quin then frowned at Cyndi. "Milady, you were with the prisoners the longest. Did anyone act out of the ordinary, any behavior that could raise suspicion?"

She clung to Iddan's hand. "They were happy we rescued them. A few were a little cold toward us, distrustful. I can't say it's unexpected. We're an unknown species."

"Have we documented these prisoners, their origins, the people they contacted?" Quin asked. "I mean, we can't assume they spoke to their families."

"Kemt is investigating this," Oyaz said, "but perhaps he should do a more detailed assessment."

Xan grunted. "See to it, Oyaz. Someone gains by this delay."

"It would mean waiting for something en route to us. That makes the most sense," Quin said. "Here, we can control the battleground. Who knows what they're preparing for our arrival."

"Alter our course, Oyaz. The Yithians would gain the most, and perhaps news has reached them of their prince's death." Xan weighed his options. "Have Kemt delve into any Yithian connections to the prisoners and their blood-bonds."

"Acknowledged, Supreme Commander."

"Are you sure it's them?" Quin gasped. "Did I bring this upon us by killing the prince?"

Macy jerked back. How was this tied to the rescue? If Quin thought herself to blame for this then Macy and Cyndi were just as culpable.

"Your actions were justified, *ensa*." Xan gave her a sideways hug.

Quin flicked a glance at him. "That doesn't mean I made wise choices."

With a punch on his O.D.I., he activated the display vid. Macy leaped off the comfy to crowd Oyaz and Illan, watching the meet-and-greet with the prisoners where she'd met the space vampires.

"No, it cannot be." Oyaz pointed at a familiar Maloidian and scowled. "He seemed so docile, so grateful." There on the vid, Pannos fiddled with a panel while Xan's focus was on Quin.

"That sweet old man?" she squeaked. "He has a son he hasn't seen in a while and hoped he could bring him home."

"Msar, locate Pannos, the Maloidian," Xan snapped into his wrist.

"Last known location was in engine room three." The surprise in Msar's voice came through the device. "That cannot be accurate; it is an access secure area."

"I will investigate." Xan strode to the door, tugging Quin with him. A whispered argument followed.

Macy slumped into the comfy again. What did Quin think she could do? This was a shitstorm of a catastrophe. Macy couldn't believe Pannos had done this. Sure, he hadn't been at the common when she got there. Nor could Bry-dar tell her where he had disappeared to. Still, to sabotage a battleship needed some epic skills, right?

She had to hear it from Pannos's lips. But first, Xan and Oyaz had to catch the old Maloidian in the act.

Etterian Battleship, Phoenix
Sec Center, where Macy shouldn't be.

MACY THUMPED ILLAN ON the arm when he grumbled for the thousandth time.

He yelped and glared at her. "How did you convince me to do this?" He rubbed his arm while slicing glances down the passage.

"What?" she gaped. "I asked you for directions, yet here you are. This isn't on me."

"Oyaz would expect me to dissuade you from this madness, not be complicit in it."

She squeaked and raised her fist.

Illan threw out his hand and leaped away from her. "I am curious." He harumphed.

She schooled her features, folded her arms across her chest, and tapped her foot as if impatient. Damn toes spasmed from this morning's workout, ruining her pissed-off-Gran stance. She twisted and turned to uncramp her toes while trying not to giggle.

Illan blinked at her, watching her do the marionette-dance, his eyes twitching.

"By all means, please do elaborate," she snapped while bouncing on her feet, working free the cramp.

"I cannot fathom why you need to see Pannos."

She tilted her head, implying he was being an idiot. "Oh, well, it's simple. I want to know his motives."

Illan slumped, leaned against the bulkhead, and grinned. "Ah, I see." He straightened. "Then we best have done with this. The security center is down the next passage."

She jerked back and scowled. "So close? I swear, Illan, next time we spar, I'll make sure to knee you where it hurts."

He frowned, not from anger but in puzzlement. She couldn't be sure he wasn't calculating the statistics of her successfully kneeing him in the groin.

"I fail to understand this threat, Macy. Would it not hurt anywhere on my body if you knee me?"

She threw up her hands, grabbed his forearm, and dragged him around the corner. Then stilled. At the end of the passage stood a circular room, glowing bright white. In the center of that was a desk with an Etterian warrior on duty. She shoved Illan against the metallic wall and plastered herself beside him.

"Shit. I hadn't thought about guards," she whispered while Illan peered around her. "Now what?"

"If Quin was here—"

"He'd be on the floor, groaning, stunned, or dead. Yeah, I get I'm not Quin." Macy huffed. She pushed off the bulkhead, straightened her baggy shirt stained from her earlier ice cream binge, and squared her shoulders. "But I'm adorable me, and sweet-talking is my superpower."

"Macy," Illan hissed, but she ignored him and flounced down the passage.

She smiled at the guard and rested her elbows on the counter. "Hi."

"Good day, milady. How can I be of assistance?" The Etterian's gaze traveled her face.

She fluttered her eyelashes in all innocence. "I'd like to visit my friend."

She twirled to study the cells. Seamless metallic panels lined the walls. Dull lighting illuminated the one cell housing Pannos. Why have a jail if honor was everything? Was there such a thing as a dishonorable Etterian? She doubted it but supposed it was possible. There were good and bad people in all cultures.

"I have received no notification of your visit. Is Supreme Commander Xan or Sub-Commander Oyaz aware of your request?"

"Xan's too busy with Quin to care about me. And I'm not talking to Oyaz after he slammed me into the mat this morning and knocked the ever-loving breath out of me." She pressed a hand to her chest. "I thought I was dying."

The Etterian's eyes twitched. She frowned. Was she having this effect on everyone now?

"My apologies, milady. Visits must be authorized."

Shit, were all Etterians this stubborn? She gritted her teeth, about to demand he contact Oyaz.

"An exception can be made, I am certain." Illan strode into the lit circle.

Now he helps? She huffed and damned if the guard didn't salute Illan as if he was effing royalty.

Illan grinned and dipped his head to whisper, "Superpower, huh?"

She shrugged. "Every heroine has off days." She nudged Illan shoulder to shoulder. "Thank you."

With a skip, she crossed to Pannos's cell, wary of the humming. The front was open, though she guessed she needed to avoid the pulsing white line running the length of it. She'd seen enough illegal vids to know to be suspicious of anything unusual. She snorted. Here she was, sneaking into a security center. Nothing odd about that.

"Pannos?"

The old Maloidian male sat on his bed, and at her greeting, his sad gaze rose to meet hers.

"Lady Macy," he said, though his usual enthusiasm was absent as expected under the circumstances.

She sank to the floor to sit Indian style, and in her blue jeans, it was easy. Thankfully, her padded backside softened the hard floor.

"Tell me what's going on, *lommia?* Why couldn't you come to us...to me? You know I would've done everything to help." She studied his downcast head, his slumped shoulders, and sorrow lanced through her. Under the bright lighting, the shadows under his eyes revealed how he'd worried, lost sleep, and allowed this to affect his health. Yet his tentacles swayed like they were caught in a gentle breeze.

"My son..." His voice cracked. "The Yithians have my son, milady. When I commed my blood-bond to let him know I was safe and that you had rescued me from the Yithians, he informed me they'd captured Mannx." His head drooped in despair. "Because of me, they know you took their ship. I did not think beyond my selfish need. For this, I have jeopardized your planet. I cannot ask your forgiveness... I truly cannot."

"I have hope and faith, *lommia,* that everything will work out for the better. And I can't fault you for wanting to save your son. I would've moved heaven and hell to save my child."

"You are not angry with me?" Pannos's solid-black eyes widened.

"Of course not. You were desperate. The Etterians won't understand, though. You did violate their trust." She winced.

"I know. Thank you for speaking to me, Lady Macy." He graced her with a small smile, but it didn't reach his eyes. Not that she could tell in his black murky depths. Expressions were different and yet similar across species.

"Would you mind if I visited again?" She scanned the cell, devoid of anything interesting. As far as she was concerned, if anyone could fix this situation, it would be the Etterians. Did she have an absurd faith in them? Yes, but dammit, who else could sort this out? "Or is this goodbye, Pannos?" Tears stung her eyes, and she blinked them away.

Desperation was all too familiar. It contorted your thoughts and led you down the wrong path.

Pannos sighed. "You are an emotive species, *mitkaari*. I will never regret meeting you." He rose to his feet and shuffled toward the shimmering light. "I would appreciate it if you did visit." He smiled at her, and this time, it crinkled the edges of his eyes like laugh lines. The devil was in the details, her gran used to say.

"Don't give up yet. Xan and Oyaz will do what they can for all parties. They're the good guys, Pannos, and everyone knows good always kicks evil's ass."

"Your faith is that of a child, *mitkaari*, but I thank you for sharing it with me."

She jumped to her feet, threw a beaming smile at the security guard, looped an arm through Illan's, and ushered him the hell out of there. "I could do with apple pie. My treat."

"Do I have a say?" Illan smiled, patting her hand resting on his forearm.

"Nope, and you'll thank me later."

Chapter Twenty-One

Etterian battleship Phoenix
Their shared quarters.

ILLAN SHOOK MACY AWAKE. "Come, ohara, Quin's shuttle was shot down."

"What?" she squeaked, blinking at him.

"I journey now to Lysara, and you are coming with me."

"Why?" she moaned, swinging her legs off the bed she now shared with him.

"I refuse to leave you alone without myself or Oyaz to ensure you stay out of trouble."

She harumphed but pushed herself to her feet. "What time is it?"

"Late." Illan shoved clothes at her—a silent request to hurry up.

Stomping past him, she disappeared into the bathroom, all the while grumbling about having to go anywhere. What about her was untrustworthy? And what could she get up to on a battleship this huge? But she emerged in her jeans, a flowing blouse in brilliant sky-blue, then flopped into the closest comfy to slide on matching slippers.

Along passages they hurtled. She stayed close on his heels, especially when he took routes she'd never been on. They breached a massive warehouse lined with the same dull gray panels. This time, in the center of wall-mounted crates stood a shuttle. Males veered around it, performing their tasks. In the door of the shuttle waited a grim-faced Oyaz.

"Good." He closed the door the moment she passed him.

Illan strapped her to a seat, and while the shuttle vibrated as it powered up, she stared at the display vids showing the pilot aiming for the bay doors opening onto the vast expanse of space. She gaped. Sure, the viewing deck showed the stars and planets, but in her mind, she could dismiss it as a movie or documentary. Faced with traveling through space within the thin metal walls of a box... Tingles chilled her spine, traversing to her toes then returning to her ears with a wealth of heat. Lord above, she wasn't designed to be an astronaut. If the shit hit the fan, she wouldn't know how to survive.

Illan grabbed her hand. Just like that, tension oozed out of her, and she cast him a grateful smile. But with nothing to look at but Oyaz, a few Etterians, Iddan, and Illan, her gaze strayed back to the display vids.

There, zooming toward them was a green planet. Her breath hitched. Bry-dar and Myn-ras had claimed their homeworld was wonderful. She couldn't agree more. Green oceans, purple land, and cream-colored clouds made for a breathtaking planet.

"Initiating quarantine," the pilot called.

She cast a glance at Illan, but he was immobile, his eyes closed while expressions crossed his face. Talking to Quin, no doubt. When she tried to free her hand, he released her. She had nowhere to go since she was strapped to a death box careening this way and that to Lysara.

"Quarantine?" she asked Oyaz.

"Lysara is dying. King Sy-mar is trying to save it by limiting foreign bacteria and diseases."

"Dying?" She studied the world, now realizing the brown spots were dead zones. The great purple trees didn't grow there, and parts of the landscape were desert-like. Myn-ras had said something to that effect, about their women losing hope. Macy understood hopelessness, desperation, and fear.

"When they mate, the euphoria experienced triggers the rain. Fewer fulfillments mean less rain." Illan stated this in a matter-of-fact tone.

Euphoria? Fulfillments? Did they mean orgasms? She cupped her mouth, blinking at him. "Wow. On Earth, it would rain every second of the day."

"Yes, which is why Bry-dar and Myn-ras are so enamored with you, ohara."

"Right. Earthian females can 'save' the universe." She tugged on the strap digging into her hip and rested her head against the wall. This human had yet to save anyone.

When the shuttle touched down, the door opened onto a wide platform. Surrounding it was nothing but clouds. Warmth from the yellow sky kissed her cheeks when she trailed Illan into an elevator. They whooshed down, clouds engulfing the glass structure and closing in on her. She struggled to breathe, sucking in great gulps of air while clinging to Oyaz's arm. Dizziness spun her vision. Nausea churned her gut, threatening to spill her stomach contents.

"Macy, look at me." Oyaz's voice reached through her panic.

She blinked her eyes open, then glanced at the clouds. Her life would end here. She would be trapped in this capsule forever. Heat flooded her face even as she shivered.

"Macy, *ensa*, stare into my eyes."

Oyaz's calmness was an oasis of peace. She dragged her gaze from the clouds.

"Good. Now mimic my breathing." He demonstrated a deep inhale and a slow exhale. She tried to copy him, her dizziness fading the more she breathed. When her gaze strayed, he would speak her name and snag her focus. The grip he had on her shoulders kept her from sliding to the floor.

"Look." Illan pointed.

The glass pod halted on another platform, but this time, a forest spread out. Birds peppered the sky, along with gigantic whale-like creatures in the distance. The air was sweet, crisp, and she drew in gulps of it, quelling her nausea.

"It's spectacular." She squeezed Oyaz's elbows, thanking him while asking for release. He stepped aside, granting her a wider view of Lysara.

Striding toward them were a few Lysarans. One stood out. Gold threads entwined his braids. He was taller than Myn-ras, and regal, his movements graceful. And he had the same swirling amber eyes.

"Greetings from Lysara." He swept his hand to the side in welcome. "Your Supreme Commander is being monitored."

"Thank you, Kuna Sy-mar. I am certain with your assistance, no harm shall befall him and his unit." Oyaz dipped his head.

Illan did the same. "How long will it take to retrieve them, my king?"

"You mistake me. They are monitored. I have not dispatched my males to mount a rescue."

"What?" Macy whispered. Quin was missing, lost somewhere in the wilds of Lysara. And this man...male...king had done nothing? She scowled as she scanned the platform, wondering how she could get off the damn thing and into the forest. With Oyaz and Illan beside her, she could find her friend. It's what Quin would do had their roles been reversed.

"I am bewitched," the king said, capturing Macy's chin in his heated palm.

She gasped, slicing her focus from the platform to his face. The urge to jerk away from him stiffened her muscles, but Illan shook his head.

"What manner of species are you?" The king tilted up her chin. "Beautiful, intriguing, so passionate." He closed his eyes and drew in a deep breath, dipping to sniff her. "Sweet, spicy, exotic, and..." Lowering his hand, he stepped back, his eyes wide. "Arousing. Mm."

"My name is Macy, and I'm human." This was the so-called king Bry-dar thought would claim her? She snorted. *So not going to happen.*

"Hooman?" The king captured a lock from her mussed hair and wrapped it around a finger. "Macee." He smiled and scattered her wits. Fangs dimpled his bottom lip. His eyes warmed to molten, and a breeze carried his sunbaked scent to her, pounding her heart into an unnatural rhythm.

Holy cow, he was gorgeous. She blinked, unable to break their locked gazes, when she wasn't sure she wanted to. Goosebumps spread along her arms, as if he had run his hands over her skin.

"Mm, your scent is delicious. Tell me, Macee, why should I send a unit to rescue this Supreme Commander when he has trespassed?"

What? "A downed shuttle isn't intentional. Regardless, wouldn't rescuing Xan and my human friend Quin be of diplomatic interest?"

"Another hooman?" The king arched a dark-chocolate eyebrow. "I suppose Xeus would expect me to extend all effort." He sighed. "Very well, for you and Etteria, I shall send a unit."

She slumped but beamed at him. "Thank you,...your majesty." She twitched before dropping into a curtsey, not sure how to address royalty.

"Majesty?" His sexy chuckle rasped across her senses. "Come. You shall be my guest."

Casting a wide-eyed glance at Illan then Oyaz, she hurried after the king into yet another glass elevator. As soon as Oyaz stepped inside, she latched onto his arm and squeezed her eyes shut. Fear crawled up her throat like thousands of scratching insects. She held her breath.

"Just trees, *ensa*." He patted her arm.

When she peeled her eyes open, the king stared at her. "So emotive, your hooman."

"I guard her, my king, for her protection and sanity."

"My what now?" She twisted to meet Oyaz's gaze.

"Boredom," Illan said.

"Ah, yes." She peered into the dense forest in the hopes of spotting Quin. Hopefully, the Lysaran team would find them soon. From the elevator, they strolled along a stone bridge toward a stepped pyramid.

When she glanced down to study the markings in the floor, she noticed the king's bare feet. Her gaze traveled up his harem pants to the sash cinching his waist. A tunic hid his torso. She sighed and forced her gaze to the tapestries lining the walls. Sconces flickered with light, and the floor gave off warmth.

Lysarans, male and female, stepped to the side to let them pass. The females wore dresses that wrapped around every curve. The males had similar harem pants and tunics as their king. All had beads, threads, and ribbons in their unbound hair in mocha, gold, and blond with matching amber eyes. Yet their faces varied, like humans did. And of course, their smiles revealed their fangs. She smothered a giggle. Fruitarians, she had no doubt.

"Lady Macy, I am delighted to see you took me up on my offer." Bry-dar nodded at his king before settling beside her. He ignored Oyaz's scowl.

"With my friend missing, Bry-dar, I had no choice but to visit." If only. She didn't glance at Illan, who cleared his throat at her lie.

Bry-dar sniffed her and nodded. "I scent your concern."

"On my planet, sniffing people is considered rude." She huffed.

"It is?" He smirked. "You are on my world now."

His king snapped a few choice words. Bry-dar stiffened, captured her hand for a squeeze, and left the procession. Not that she knew what the king had said.

"Perhaps bringing her with was not wise," Illan hissed.

"We agreed, Illan," Oyaz muttered.

Illan scowled at her. "Try and not be so emotional."

She squeaked then thumped him on the arm. "Try not to be such an ass."

The king chuckled and halted the procession. Striding between them, he snatched her hand, then escorted her into his throne room. She gasped, her gaze snagging on the tapestries, gold décor, the flickering sconces, and the ancient feel of his home—a mixture of Aztec, Egyptian, and old vids.

He settled her on a seat then sank into his cushioned throne beside her. "Tell me, Macee, what of your world? I want to know everything." He captured her hand in his, dragging his thumb across her knuckles, then peered into her eyes, his packed throne room expectant.

She gulped. Every ear tuned in on her as she rattled on about animals and plants, how hoomans had messed up the planet and tried to fix it too late. Not to mention how they'd corrupted the moon and Mars and every damn moon or planet they colonized. But yeah, they had emotions, too volatile, and unpredictable, with periods of darkness as documented in their history.

By the time news of Quin's rescue reached Macy, she was drained, slumping in the chair like a limp tofu noodle. Despite finding the king's interest in her flattering, his 'feeding' on her emotions exhausted her.

Sy-mar straightened in his seat and summoned a Lysaran female. "Tan-rae, escort Macee to the royal terrace."

"As you wish, my kuna."

Gardens? Fresh air? A terrace? It wasn't as if Macy could mount an escape, not when doing so would land her in even more trouble. Alone time would be wonderful. She waved at Illan and Oyaz before trailing the female. When she attempted conversation, interested in a feminine viewpoint, Tan-rae didn't respond. Only when they stepped into the sunlight did she meet Macy's gaze before abandoning her there.

Spinning in a circle, Macy studied the tall arum lilies, the thick bushes in pinks and blues, the orange furry leaves—all creating some sort of maze. She dived in, choosing random paths until only the distant calls of creatures filled the air. Here, in nature, the loneliness didn't bother her. As she raised her face to the warm rays, she basked in the solitude.

Humming a haunting melody, she settled on the purple grass, folded her legs beneath her, and closed her eyes. For once, she didn't cast her thoughts toward inconveniencing Illan or Oyaz when it was time to find her. She was going to take this moment and be selfish, allowing the tranquil surroundings to grace her with peace.

"Your birdsong is beautiful." A deep voice silenced her.

She squealed and scrambled up but couldn't get her feet in place to stand.

"I did not mean to frighten you, milady."

Milady? Etterian? She slumped, letting her backside hit the grass. Had Oyaz sent someone to find her? She scowled.

"Please continue." His chuckle came from behind a thick blue hedge. She tilted from side-to-side, trying to find a gap in the foliage. "I am well-versed in the Lysaran culture, yet did not know of such beauty. It seems Sy-mar has hidden much from me."

"Lysaran?" She smiled. The male didn't know she was human. Anyone Oyaz or Illan sent would know who she was. "I'm not from this planet."

"Ah, yes, Earth English. I should have noted that in your birdsong."

Wait, he'd said Sy-mar as if he knew the Lysaran king personally. She opened her mouth to ask—

"I too am a guest," the male continued.

"I figured that out." She grinned. "You called me milady."

"Yes, I did." Warmth filled his voice as if he smiled. "What would you prefer I call you?"

"Macy or Macera is fine." Silence met her reply. She peered through the bushes, wondering if he'd left.

"*Macera*?" Emotion thickened his voice.

Shit, he'd heard of her, or at least of Quin and what she'd accomplished. Maybe he even knew how worthless Macy had been throughout their great escape.

"Macy?" Illan called from far off.

She groaned, cupping her face as if her hands could hide her. "I've got to go. It was a pleasure meeting you." Finding a low gap in the hedge, she shoved her hand through. The male captured it, his touch hot, sending a zing of tingles to her elbow.

"Wait..." He pressed a kiss to her knuckles and scattered her thoughts.

She blinked, dazzled by the dark head she'd glimpsed. His lips had imprinted on her skin.

"May I comm you?"

The alien equivalent to 'can I call you?' She dipped her chin to hide a grin and stared at her heaving chest. *Right, who would want to comm me?* For some odd reason, she did like the stranger's voice. So pen pal? "As in message? I have an O.D.I. now."

"Yes," he chuckled, the sound resonating and husky.

Yup, love his voice. "Can we keep the anonymity?"

"If you prefer."

Excitement zinged again, playing pinball with her insides. She bounced on her toes while wearing a massive grin. So Lysara wasn't a wasted trip. "What do I call you?"

"Macy, ohara, where are you?" Illan sounded closer.

Why did he have to interrupt her now? She was going to kill him first chance she got.

"Xeu—" The stranger cleared his throat. "Anything you want, *ensa*."

"Zoo it is," she teased, then pulled her hand back.

"Greetings, Macera."

She smothered a squeal as his shadow faded. Just to make sure, she froze her bounce and listened for his breathing.

"Here you are." Illan appearing at her side drew a squeak.

She punched him on the arm. "Quit sneaking up on me like that."

He harrumphed while rubbing his bicep. "You could have answered me."

"I was busy," she huffed. Throwing a pout at him, she asked, "Are we leaving?"

"Not yet," he muttered, wincing then pinching his brow.

Guilt struck, like a bolt of fiery agony, twisting her heart. She could be a pain, of that she was aware. Looping an arm through his, she pressed her temple to his upper arm she'd just bruised. "Sorry, Illan. I can be trying."

He patted her hand as he ushered her out of the maze. "It is not you, ohara. Quin is...in darkness."

Macy bit her lip, tucking herself under his arm to support him when he stumbled. More so when he staggered to the side. When Iddan appeared and slid under Illan's other arm, she said nothing.

Together, they carried Illan to a suite of luxurious rooms she couldn't spare the time to admire. Every muscle throbbed. Her breathing was ragged. Illan was heavier than he looked. Where was Oyaz when she needed him?

Once they had settled Illan onto the bed, she slumped against a stone wall, digging her fingers into the carvings to keep herself upright. "I can stay with him, Iddan..."

"It is not necessary, Macy." He rested his hand on Illan's shoulder, gazing upon his brother's face.

She peeked through the bedroom doorway to the living room and balcony. "I have nowhere else to go."

Iddan offered a tight smile. "Very well." He pushed off and captured her hand to swipe his O.D.I. across hers. Her arm tingled with the new info. "Comm me when he stirs...or worsens."

"Worsens?" she squeaked.

"Nightmares, mutterings, spasms." Iddan strode to the door.

She hurried after him, wringing her hands. "All right." But her response fell on the solid door and deafening silence.

She circled the room, stroking the fabrics, tapestries, fuzzy-skinned fruit in a bowl, and the velvet texture of the gigantic arum lily on the balcony. To linger there was a temptation, but she wasn't sure she could hear Illan, so she migrated back to the bedroom and sprawled on the bed to wait.

ILLAN ROARED, "AWAKEN HER," and was out of bed and the rooms before Macy could wipe the sleep from her eyes.

She staggered after him while punching on her O.D.I., trying to forewarn Iddan, but when she opened the door to follow Illan, Oyaz stopped her...with his chest. She yelped, throwing out her arms. If he hadn't caught her by the elbow, she would have crumpled at his feet.

"Here I am, minding my business," she muttered.

"Come, *ensa*." He gestured to the passage.

She huffed. "Go there, stay here, come with. I was happy in the garden, Oyaz."

"When the kuna summons you, *Macee*, you obey." He chuckled, grabbed her by the shoulders, and forced her to face him. Then with the gentlest touch, he straightened her hair. "I did not tell you to charm the male."

"Charm him?" she squeaked. "I'll have you know—"

"It is your emotions that seduce, *ensa*. It is best to learn control."

She blinked at him then giggled. "You haven't seen volatile. Wait until it's that time of the month."

"What time of the month?" He frowned.

"Y'know, when it's my monthlies." She skipped ahead, not wanting to have to explain in detail, which, she had no doubt, he'd expect.

"You are...*fertile* every month?" Oyaz hadn't moved, frozen to the spot while a wide grin spread 'handsome' all over his face.

"Yeah, and we can give birth once every nine months." She smiled at his delight. "Mind you, falling pregnant isn't a given. It's all about fertility levels. Some say the sexual position plays a part." Capturing his arm, she tugged him, trying to get his feet to move. "The kuna awaits, remember."

When he hurried his steps, she swallowed a sigh, having dodged a full-blown discussion on the birds and bees. Once was enough, thank you very much.

"Macee, please, join me." The king boomed his request, drawing the attention of everyone in the throne room.

Ducking her head, she crossed the room, clinging to Oyaz like a lifeline. If he'd released her, she would have lost her shit. How was this better? How was this keeping her out of trouble? She could've been watching a vid, knitting her scarf, and eating ice cream. But no, she was on another planet, having her insides melted by a gorgeous fruitarian.

Sy-mar captured her hand and drew her away from Oyaz. She cast a pleading glance at her friend, who smiled as if nothing was wrong, like he hadn't thrown her to the vampires.

Once again seated beside the throne, she twisted to face the king, choosing to narrow her peripherals and exclude the avid audience.

"I wish to know whether you would stay...here on Lysara?" Sy-mar peered into her eyes, his swirling amber-gold.

Her breath hitched. Her inner girl squealed a yes, but the tiny percentage that was sane, knotted her stomach something fierce. Staying meant what?

"It is wise to ask."

She gulped at having spoken aloud. A king could command an execution, right? Would dumbass Oyaz rescue her then?

"You would be free to roam the land, learn our culture, share yours, and perhaps mate with one of us." He smiled, but sadness darkened his gaze. "Save my world."

"That's unfair," she whined, cast a glance at the frozen audience, and hurried to add, "my kuna." She captured his hand in hers, arching his brow. "I have obligations. And besides, I'm the only human woman you've met." Maybe if she stayed... No, she wanted an Etterian, had fantasized about them since the first digi-mag she'd seen. She sniffed and raised her gaze to his. "I don't want to be chosen because you have no other options. I want to be loved for me."

"Indeed." He twisted his hand and caught hers, giving it a squeeze. "It *was* unfair of me to place Lysara's survival on your shoulders. And yes, other hoomans would be as welcome."

"More than one would be better," she teased.

"I see why you are so well-guarded, Macee."

She snorted. "They think I'll cause trouble if left on my own." She met Oyaz's gaze, hoping to convey with a look, 'Next time, leave me on the battleship, idiot.'

A male whispered in the king's ear, and when Sy-mar nodded at Oyaz, he strode forward and ushered her to the side. The throne room held their cumulative breath as Quin and Xan walked in. A blue-mottled Illan trailed them.

Peeking around Oyaz, Macy beamed at Quin, looking amazing in one of those Lysaran dresses. Glancing at her own ample bosom, Macy grimaced. She would have resembled an overstuffed sausage.

When Quin bolted toward her, Macy weaved around Oyaz to hug her. "Oh, Quin, I'm so happy you're okay. Illan said you were, but I had to see for myself." She pulled back, checking out the dress that could've been made of silk sashes. "Whoa. Looking hot. What's the occasion?"

"Meeting the kuna." Quin winced.

Macy shivered. Her eyes widened. "He's potent. I had Oyaz, so make sure Xan's at your side. And by potent, I mean your lady bits will explode." She giggled, then lowered her voice even more. "I swear they release pheromones to dazzle us poor damsels."

Quin laughed. "I thought you wanted to snag a sexy alien?" She wiggled her eyebrows.

Macy folded her arms across her chest. "Yeah, without being drugged or coerced, thank you very much."

Illan dragged Quin away, leaving Macy to wander back to Oyaz. Just like that, she was ousted. Not that she could, in a million years, believe Quin would succumb to Sy-mar's sensual wiles with Xan looming. Macy had no one other than overzealous guards. She peeked at Oyaz and smiled. The scarf would be for him, as a thank you.

"Can we go yet?" she whispered.

"We are free to leave once the kuna approves our departure."

She slumped. "So we're trapped?"

Oyaz grinned and settled his dark blue gaze on her. "Lysara is a paradise, Macy. I suspect we'll spend the night and leave first thing in the morning."

"I suppose one night isn't too much to endure."

He patted her hand. "Come, I must speak with Xan. After that, I will escort you to your chambers."

"And food?"

"Whatever you want, *ensa*."

She clung to him as he weaved through the crowd, trying not to lose her mind when the Lysarans touched, stroked, or fondled her hair. Her stomach grumbled at the array of dishes set before Quin and Sy-mar. A few platters held marinated strips of meat. She wanted to ask how this was possible when Bry-dar claimed to be a fruitarian. Then clamped her lips shut. Some folks were vegan, others carnivore. Perhaps it was the same as humans—a diet of fruit being a preference.

The food smelled so good. She drew in a deep inhale, relishing the savory and tart aromas filling her senses. Oyaz gripping her elbow snapped her out of her food-daze. She waved at Quin and skipped after the male, who led her out of the throne room and down various passages before stopping outside a door.

A Lysaran guard let them in. Similar to Illan's suite of rooms, a living room was center stage, a 'kitchen' to the side held a rehydrator and replicator, a bathroom was to the right, and on the left, was a massive bedroom. A balcony spanned the living room, revealing twin suns in a lovely lemony yellow.

"These are your chambers."

She froze. "What?" Alone, again? She marched over to the replicator. "Knitting needles, please."

"They do not have Earthian items, *ensa*."

She whimpered and slumped into the nearest chair. "What can I do to fill my time?"

Oyaz frowned, but when he cast a glance at the door, she pursed her lips. How to keep herself busy shouldn't be his problem.

"Go. I'll think of something."

"They do have a display vid if you wish to learn about other cultures."

She smiled. He was so sweet to her. "I have songs on my O.D.I. How do I transfer?"

He grinned, tapped her arm, then waited for her to navigate to a song. When it played, he flicked it at the vid. The black screen lit up, playing the song seconds behind her O.D.I. "I will see you much later, Macy."

She deactivated her O.D.I and trailed him to the door. When it swished closed, she rested her temple on the strange stone surface. Pushing off, she headed for the bathroom first. There, a massive tub awaited her. She squealed, bouncing up and down while waving her hands in the air. An honest-to-goodness bathtub? She spent ten minutes trying to find the taps. After a thorough stroking of every stone tile, flaps opened, and water gushed out. The temperature was hotter than she liked, but she could eat while it cooled.

The rehydrator was as bizarre. Everything was in a strange cuneiform. At least tiny images kind of hinted at the food, so she chose an assortment of dishes similar to the platters of fruit and meat placed before the kuna. With the feast relocated to the square coffee table, she switched off the water. Before she dived into the dishes, she cast a glance skyward, praying that whatever she ate wouldn't be poisonous or kill her. It would suck to die now after all she'd been through.

She bit into a sliver of meat and moaned. Like roast beef but succulent with a lingering sweetness on her tongue. Emboldened by her first experience, she went through each dish, groaning, sighing, gagging, and spitting. Peppered throughout were her giggles. With her stomach protesting the assault, she licked her fingers while limping to the bath.

She may not look it, but, as she grinned and sank into the bath, she was ready for anything.

Chapter Twenty-Two

Planet Lysara

The Royal Gardens

Xeus watched from the shadows as a Durn escorted Macera from the gardens, granting him a partial glimpse of her wealth of hair, curvaceous backside, and tiny ankles. Excitement swelled within him, rising and falling like the stormy waves of his beloved oceans. He lowered his gaze to his hand where it tingled from her touch. He'd met the female he fantasized about, had touched her, had pressed a kiss to her silky skin.

And her birdsong resonated and replayed in his mind.

Swiveling on a heel, he meandered to his chambers. In Sy-mar's magnificent gardens, Xeus had hoped to have a moment of peace. Instead, his world had shifted.

He would comm Macera later today.

But how to keep his identity from her? She had asked for anonymity, and for the time being, it would be easy to please her. As soon as she reached Issneen, maybe then he could reveal who he was. He winced. Etterians did not deceive. There was no honor in it.

Cales wasn't in his chambers when Xeus strode in. He circled the desk Sy-mar had installed for him and activated the tablet. First on his task list was the sec vids from Xan's adventure. Thankfully, Xeus was planetside to mitigate any diplomatic consequences.

He stared at the tablet, his thoughts drifting to Macera. Raising his gaze, he imagined her seated before him, a wide smile on her dirty face. No... She would look different from the sec vids off the Yithian ship. Her hair had been lighter and glowing with good health. Would her eyes still be dark? Although, he had yet to learn of humans being able to change their eye color.

"What are you doing?" Cales dropped into a stuffed chair beside him to face the large display vid.

The twin suns were setting. How had time slipped away? Xeus's had his finger hooked, about to select Xan's sec vids. Xeus opened his mouth to declare he'd met Macera, but something silenced him. A part of him wanted to savor the memory, not share this with his battle-bond. Another part of him didn't believe Cales would understand. Also, Xeus hadn't mentioned how the image of Macera tormented him. He would've liked to see all of her, to confirm her bright smile to match her sweet voice.

"Just deep in thought." Xeus cleared his throat and ignored his inner voice whispering that omittance was the same as lying.

"Good. Kuna Sy-mar is en route."

Xeus curled his finger and formed a fist. "Where were you?"

"Strolling the grounds. I find the Lysaran air sweeter than ours." Cales studied him. "And you?"

"The Royal Gardens, as usual." ...*meeting Macera.* Xeus smothered a smile. How blessed was he? A few minutes too late, he would have missed her. "Did Sy-mar mention the reason behind the visit?"

Xeus had planned to leave Lysara this evening, their business concluded just that morning. Now he wanted to reach Issneen before Macera did. His scimitar, *Celeeri,* was faster than the battleship *Phoenix.* He'd be home for a day before she arrived.

His finger twitched. Yes, he was eager to comm her and hear her voice. Perhaps she would gift him with another birdsong.

At the knock, Cales hurried to open the door and ushered in a grinning Sy-mar.

Xeus rose to his feet, frowning at the exuberant Lysaran.

"They are breathtaking, these hoomans." He splayed his hand across his chest. "On my soul, Xeus, their emotional range could save my world."

"I am told there are billions on their Earth, my kuna." Cales took up a position at a wall, clasping his twitching hands behind his back.

Sy-mar laughed. "Plenty for Etteria *and* Lysara."

"They are not treasure to be divided between us." Xeus scowled then sighed. "But yes, if they prove to be your salvation, then help me protect them."

Sy-mar sank into a chair and rested his elbows on his knees. "They are in danger?"

"Yithians and possibly Maloidians seek to exploit them." Xeus gritted his teeth, tempted to assassinate all on the Global Council who allowed this to continue.

"What do you need?"

"Support at the GC and soldiers. I have battleships circling their world. These are not fully staffed. I would also suggest you send ambassadors to work alongside mine."

"I will dispatch males immediately." Sy-mar settled back. "Have you watched the sec vids from the jungle?"

"Not yet." Xeus spared him a glance before returning his attention to the display vid, which showed a frozen image of Etterian males and one human woman weaving through the Lysaran jungle. There was no audio, but it didn't matter.

"Stationary research vids recorded their movement through the jungle. They miss large parts of their progress. They did, however, capture Supreme Commander Xan's escape from a gracc." Sy-mar steepled his fingers. "A brilliant strategy I will employ henceforth."

"Truth?" Cales gasped and strode across to watch over Xeus's shoulder.

Graccs were inescapable once their prey fell into their snare. The doomed creature would sink into the soil and the large gaping mouth beneath it. The graccs hid their gigantic bodies below the ground where they would lay in wait. Their mouths were rimmed with razor-sharp teeth, pointing inward to trap the prey. Once it ingests, it will paralyze and dissolve its meal over ten days. With a swipe of a finger, Xeus replayed the scene showing Xan's escape.

"Alodon's balls, that was ingenious," Cales roared.

Xeus kept his gaze on the vid. It was choppy, as if only parts of the recording had been shared. The unit encountered wilanegy. The research vid's angle was toward the watering pool where it caught Lady Quin dragging Warrior Lurz over the side. She rolled down the hill before diving into the pool with what appeared to be an injured arm.

Lurz rescued then dropped her on the opposite embankment. She screamed something at him, which in turn had him reaching for his blaster to fire on the three approaching wilanegy males. Their deaths were quick. The blaster stunned the pool's surface, killing them.

"Xan's report was vague regarding these incidents. He stated that due to Lady Quin's strategic skills they escaped the gracc and wilanegy," Cales said. "But seeing it is so much better."

Xeus hadn't expected a more detailed report after what the male had endured this day. "He also documented that shortly after this, she became distraught over Medic Eira's death. She collapsed over his body, Xan suspects, due to the trauma of the last day."

"Such an emotional species," Cales said. "When he commed me this evening to warn of the Lysaran violations, your presence here caught him by surprise. When I delved deeper, he revealed that Lady Quin's recklessness and his uncontrollable reaction to her had distressed him."

"It is as expected," Xeus said.

Cales glanced at him, having replayed the gracc incident. "We do not handle emotion well, not within us, nor from others."

Xeus grunted in response, trying not to remember what happened at his morning chore. Macera's image appeared every time, despite his efforts otherwise. Refusing to attend to the chore had taught him that avoidance spilled his seed more than once when he succumbed to the need driving him.

"You are most welcome to remain here in Sosu to strategize." Sy-mar rose to his feet.

"My thanks, Sy-mar, but I have duties I need to attend to."

"Macee said the same." Sy-mar paused at the door Cales had opened for him. "Please share the location of her homeworld."

"Consider it done." Xeus's voice was hoarser than intended. Just at the mention of her name, his throat closed. "Also, I will send battleships past Lysara to collect your males." He glanced at Cales. "Schedule this."

"As you command, my king."

Sy-mar grinned. "And I shall visit your Issneen. It has been too long."

"Perhaps a sparring session like we used to?" Xeus smiled. "I have not forsaken my training."

"Neither have I, old friend."

After the door closed on Sy-mar, Cales faced Xeus and growled, "No." Anger hardened his jaw. "Now we must share?"

"As you mentioned, there are billions of humans, Cales."

His battle-bond scowled and slumped in a nearby chair, his expression that of a petulant *damu*.

"Regardless, we may need the Lysarans in the upcoming war. Data Officer Kemt indicated that the Maloidians shot down Xan's *kuta* shuttle. It was in an attempt to gain access to our navigation charts, perhaps to kidnap Lady Quin, likely due to the price Citus paid for Lady Ava." Mentioning Lady Ava had the expected result.

"Lady Ava's skills as a *hairstylist* are what impresses me." Cales chuckled. "I detest being the Enforcer, Xeus, as you are well aware."

"It is a necessary chore and is traditionally performed by the king's advisor." Xeus's lips twitched. "The *Kushin* arrives in Issneen soon bearing the new Dar Eths and the human children we have agreed to harbor. We will need to return to Etteria by then."

"I would suggest we have our *lima kuu* build an appropriate building behind the palace." Cales punched on his O.D.I. "Or we could house them in a vacant barracks, and with Lady Olivia's input, construct their new home?"

"That may be preferable." What did he know about *damu*? The raising of Enyl had been at the hands of the *lima kuu*, of Remi and Malo.

"We know nothing about the needs of human *damu*, and I suspect she would appreciate it if we included her in any decision that impacts *her damu*."

"You have commed her?" Xeus arched a brow.

"Of course, in an attempt to pre-empt their needs." Judging by Cales thunderous expression, he wasn't pleased by the results of the communication.

"How was she?"

"Beautiful, as expected," Cales said. "Stubborn, opinionated, and full of sweet smiles."

"Then what has you so displeased?"

"She is not my Dar Eth." Cales glanced away before meeting Xeus's gaze.

"You are feeling it too?" Xeus rubbed his hand over his face. "When the *Kushin* docks, I need you and Citus to travel to Earth."

"But—?"

"It is a command. Cales, you know how important Earth is to our survival. I send my most trusted males."

"Yes, my king." Cales frowned. "Who will attend to my tasks?"

"Warrior Kanzo. Since his Dar Eth is the new Enforcer, I foresee his role in court becoming more substantial."

Cales relaxed. "He is an excellent choice, solid, reliable except for when the Yithians stole Lady Ava."

"I have seen the vids. He behaved above reproach as I would expect from our warriors. He protected the *damu*. That pleases me."

"I agree."

"I will address this with him at the ceremony," Xeus said.

"Thank you, my king. I shall leave you to organize our return journey." Cales bounded up, now with a little more bounce in his step.

Xeus understood why. He was to visit Earth. Perhaps he would locate his Dar Eth before Xeus succumbed to the void.

As soon as the door closed, Xeus rose to his feet and crossed to the display vid. There he hesitated. Alodon's balls, he didn't know her full name. He couldn't comm her without it. After a hasty scanning of his comms from the day his males first met her, he roared his joy when he found her name. Grinning like a fool, he spent a minute ensuring she would see a blank vid, then enunciated her name.

"Lady Macera?" He peered into empty chambers.

A squeal from afar preceded her face sliding into view. Damp tendrils fell around her, and for the first time, he saw every feature, from her warm brown eyes to the dark brown wings of her eyebrows. Her perky nose cast her pert lips into shadow, and she had the most adorable little chin.

"Beautiful," he whispered, then cursed himself, praying she hadn't heard him.

"Zoo? Is that you?" She leaned closer, her nose almost touching the screen. Spots were sprinkled across her cheeks.

"It is. I apologize for disturbing you."

"Nonsense." She flicked a dismissive hand. "I was off to bed. Ate like a pig, and after a hot bath, I'm beat."

"Beet?" His eyelashes flickered as his O.D.I. hurried to update him—a purple vegetable or exhausted? "I too am *beat*. Just wanted to hear your voice before I bid Lysara farewell."

"You're leaving?" She pouted. "Unfair. We're stuck here for a night."

"You do not like this world?" He considered this a good thing. Perhaps she would find his Etteria preferable?

"I do, but the Lysarans are...overwhelming." She sidled closer and whispered, "Can they suck my emotions out of me?"

He pursed his lips, trying to smother a chuckle. "No." He cleared his throat.

"Feels like they can. I'm so drained after talking to them." She fanned her face with her hand. "And they make my brain fuzzy."

"Fuzzy?" His eyelids fluttered again. "Why?"

"I swear they give off pheromones. I like making decisions without coercion." She raised her hands and unraveled her damp hair.

His breath caught. In that one action, she had gone from adorable to sensual. His malehood twitched, growing harder the longer he gazed upon her.

"Zoo? Are you still there?"

"I am, Macera."

She smiled. "Will you call me again?"

"Yes, *and* we shall meet in Issneen, *ensa*."

"We will?" Her eyes widened with delight. She bounced, swaying her hair. "Best news ever," she sang but garbled the end with a yawn. "Sweet dreams, Zoo, and thanks for the chat."

"Good night, *ensa*." He deactivated the vid and leaned against the wall beside it. Happiness engulfed him in warmth, and for the first time in a while, he didn't care if it brought the void closer.

Chapter Twenty-Three

From Lysara to the Etterian battleship Phoenix
As if the fires of hell were on Macy's ass.

Sy-mar had drawn in a deep breath, gathered Macy's hands in his, and grinned, fluttering her heartbeat. "It has been a pleasure to meet you, Macee. Are you certain I cannot convince you to stay?"

She shook her head. "As I told Bry-dar, it would be rude of me not to travel to Etteria first, after all, they rescued us."

The kuna smiled. "A diplomatic answer, sali. I have scheduled a visit with King Xeus and hope to persuade you then."

She slumped and sidled closer to Oyaz, casting him a pleading glance. Could they please leave now?

Within minutes, she was forgotten as Sy-mar grilled Quin. Soon after, Oyaz escorted Macy to the platform. Aware of what awaited her, she'd darted into the elevator, happy to endure anything if it meant going home.

The moment she stepped into their shared quarters onboard the Phoenix, a sigh of relief tore from her. What followed was a charade.

She dug deep to find her bubbliness when Xan, Quin, Illan, Cyn-di, Iddan, and Oyaz filled their quarters. Macy bounced, danced, sang, and drank champagne, but what she wanted to do was rest her head on her bed and sleep. Exhaustion hounded her, and she couldn't say if it was from the morning's meeting with Kuna Sy-mar or the overall experience.

When Xan stormed out, muttering something about his king, the 'party' fizzled. Slipping into their shared bedroom, Macy grabbed her knitting bag and left without a word. She'd had several hours alone, but the viewing deck called to her. With her ass on the bench and her hands busy on the scarf—now an arm's length—she let her thoughts wander.

Illan found her not an hour later and settled beside her. He didn't speak but dozed, his legs outstretched, his arms folded across his chest.

If she knitted for two to three hours daily, she could finish before they reached Etteria. Oyaz had mentioned it was five days away. With four evenings left, she struggled with what to feed the Etterians. A barbecue came to mind. All that meat might delight them. She could order a variety of craft beers, salads, rolls, ice cream, and pie for dessert? Her stomach grumbled at her neglect. The music would be soft rock. It would be amazing if they could have an actual fire and not just order the food from the rehydrator, but she suspected that would be a hard no.

That was one meal. Maybe an Italian evening could be next with pastas, garlic bread, wine, and something instrumental or folksy playing in the background.

And a picnic? With sparkling wine, roast chicken sandwiches, sausages, tortilla chips, dips, and lemon bars—for their love of *giyua* juice. Music would be jazz as if they were at a concert.

She grinned, liking that idea.

But what for the final dinner... Maybe dishes from cultures like Hungarian goulash, Japanese sushi, Chinese dim sum, Spanish paella, and Indian curry along with their most popular drinks. Desserts could be baklava, Turkish delight, Belgian waffles, and tiramisu.

She activated her O.D.I to capture her thoughts and paused. A message from Zoo waited. Heat flushed her cheeks, and she blinked. Why hadn't the notification tingled up her arm?

Macera, ensa, I awoke with you on my mind. I count the days until we can meet.

Time drags like an eternity. I will comm you this evening, the moment I am free to do so. I long to hear your sweet voice.

X

She stared at the 'x' wondering if that was a kiss. Her insides fluttered, proving she wanted it to be.

"And that smile?" Illan's question drew a squeak from her.

She beamed, unaware she'd been smiling. "I figured out what our next four evening meals will be. You're going to love them." She hesitated, unsure whether she should share how fond she'd grown of Zoo and his frequent comms. As if discussing it gave it more gravitas than she was willing to admit.

But he hadn't fallen to a knee when he met her.

Then again, how could she consider that a meet-cute when neither had seen the other? Mm, with the way her body hummed, she hoped he was the male for her.

Preparations for dinner distracted her, but despite the success of the barbecue, she couldn't eat. She counted each passing second. If Zoo called her mid-meal, she would bolt.

Sitting or standing, she tapped her foot or fidgeted. If anyone spoke to her, she would squeak like a dog's chew toy. As the males finished off their ice cream and rhubarb pie, she shuddered, unable to bear the waiting any longer. What did Zoo even mean to her? He was but a male she'd met in a garden. And yet...when he spoke to her, he sounded eager to learn all about her. Bry-dar's admiration had boggled her thoughts. Zoo's sweetness warmed her without the fogginess. He left her...thrumming—excitement and joy zinging through her veins like a drug high.

Leaning over the table, she caught Illan's gaze. He was on his second bowl of chocolate ice cream. "I'm off to bed. Let yourself in when you're ready."

He paused with his spoon halfway to his mouth. "Ohara?"

"Just tired, Illan." She smiled at Oyaz and Rior. "Night, you two. See you at four, Oyaz." She sprinted along the passages, taking the corners at dangerous speeds to halt outside her quarters, panting for breath.

Showering with the door open was an impossibility. The damn thing opened and closed without her assistance or preference. So she hurried, skipping the air dryer, but as she sat dripping on a comfy, waiting, sipping hot chocolate, then knitting, her eyelids drooped.

When she jerked awake, she had half-slid out of the comfy. Tossing the scarf into the bag, she sniffed and flicked aside her tears. Anger boiled her blood at her silly hope. At having trusted someone to be honorable. She stilled. Zoo was Etterian. Something must have happened to him.

She gasped, touched her O.D.I., and hovered her finger on his last message. Drawing in a deep breath, she hit the reply button.

Zoo? Are you well? You're still alive, right?

She snorted. What could she ask, if he was still breathing?

What if she was intruding? What if he didn't think of her as more than a friend? And besides, she'd known him how long? Why was she overanalyzing this? Squealing, she tried to delete the message, but his response popped up.

Her heartbeat froze then skittered. She opened the message and read...

Ensa, I am well. May I comm you?

She didn't hesitate. Of course.

The display vid on the wall flickered. "Macera?"

"I'm here, Zoo." She gazed into the dark screen.

This anonymity was bullshit and so stupid of her to ask for. It had seemed exciting at the time, like pen pals. But Zoo not seeing her also meant she couldn't see him. She had no idea what he looked like and a part of her ached to know.

"You seem tired, ensa."

Perhaps she was, but he sounded tired. Grateful he couldn't see she'd been crying, she tapped the 'bags' under her swollen eyes. "I'd love nothing more than the beach, sunshine warming me, a cold drink in my hand, and the waves serenading me as they crash onto shore."

"Beautiful." He hummed. "Etteria does have such a place."

"I'll make Oyaz take me there." She clasped her hands behind her back and rocked on her heels.

"Sub-Commander Oyaz et Boaz?" Zoo's voice had thickened.

"Yes, my self-appointed bodyguard. Though what he's protecting me from, who knows." She huffed. "Illan too. You'd swear I was this precious thing." She stroked the screen, imagining she caressed Zoo's unknown face. "Are you well? Is it late by you?"

"It is, but I have tasks...too many if I am truthful."

He was working? The moment he was able, he'd said. And she'd intruded. "I'm sorry to have bothered you."

"This is a welcome reprieve. I could not focus with thoughts of you plaguing me."

She snatched her hand back to fold her arms across her chest. "You say that like it's my fault."

He chuckled, and she loved the way it rumbled over her senses. "Never, ensa."

Rather than address his revelation, she grabbed at something...safe. "You should take a vacation too. It's dangerous for one's health to overdo it."

"If you were not going with Oyaz..."

Did he sound like he was pouting? She peered at the center of the black vid. "Who else can I ask to take me? Besides, he's my friend."

"Ah, friend...now I understand." Zoo cleared his throat. "I would take you to Galaza."

Galaza? It sounded so exotic. "You would?" She bounced then twirled on the spot. "That would be lovely, Zoo."

"Sleep well, ensa. I will comm when I can."

"And I will be patient, I promise. Sweet dreams, Zoo." She smiled, and on impulse, pressed a kiss to the screen. He couldn't see her, so what she did or wore didn't matter. She skipped to bed, slid onto her side, and was asleep seconds later.

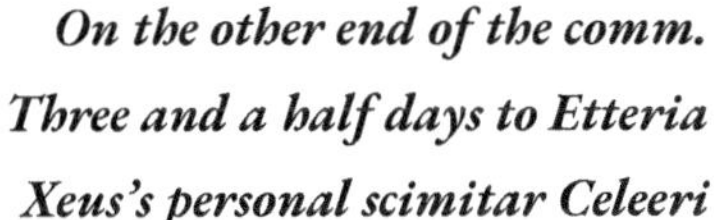

On the other end of the comm.
Three and a half days to Etteria
Xeus's personal scimitar Celeeri

XEUS STARED AT THE display vid, unable to move. Every muscle in his body had hardened. Macera had pressed a kiss to the vid, her lips so close, her silky skin within touching distance but not. When her message had come through, it had taken all his strength not to bolt to the display. Her written words had dripped with concern...and fear that he'd forgotten about her.

For those reasons, he'd ended his comm with Queen Alllero of Maloid and responded to his Macera.

His inner voice warned of becoming too fond of the woman when she would be another male's Dar Eth. But a recklessness took hold of him, and he shook away any warnings. He would take what he wanted, and to hell with the consequences.

Striding to his desk, he circled it and sank into the comfy. He'd had a comm with Xan hours ago where he had advised Xan to take a leap of faith with his Dar Eth. Words Xeus might apply to his own situation if it was warranted.

Sighing, he activated his tablet and blinked at the automated message. If ever a Chokaar was fired, Xeus was notified immediately. With rage burning through him, he forwarded the message to Cales, summoned him, then jumped up to pace.

The moment the door opened to a disheveled Cales, Xeus faced him.

"I cannot fault Xan for this," he boomed, then paced the confines of his quarters, his strides long and forceful. The walls closed in on him. An unknown force crushed his chest. He couldn't breathe. "Alodon's balls. To fire the Chokaar with so little provocation?"

"Xan is an excellent supreme commander. His instincts are seldom inaccurate," Cales said, gripping the back of a comfy. He sat and punched into his O.D.I. "According to Sub-Commander Oyaz's report, Xan destroyed a Yithian vessel. The Yithian commander had attempted to deceive him into believing he was the rebellion representative who'd first contacted Ulriq."

Xeus growled. If Xan's instinct had failed him, he would've ended the rebellion and thus cost Etteria a crucial ally in the upcoming war. "We cannot have our males firing the Chokaar for minor disagreements. There may be repercussions from this. I, we, are left to pick up the pieces." He sucked in breaths, fighting for calm. He couldn't recall when he'd last been this furious. The red haze in his vision and his rapid heartbeats overwhelmed his senses. This level of intensity wasn't a good thing, not now.

"We will deal with it as we usually do," Cales said.

"How can you remain calm?" Xeus glared, his body vibrating with barely restrained energy. "It is unnatural."

"You have enough anger for us both," Cales said to which Xeus grunted.

"Keep an eye on the buzz. I want to know what Yithia thinks of this latest interaction. I want to know even if there is no formal communication on it. I want a comm sent out regarding the casual use of the Chokaar and the caution required." Xeus glanced at Cales to check that he punched into his O.D.I. "I want Xan to undergo a thorough examination to ascertain his mental health." As expected, Cales's head shot up, alarm narrowing his eyes. "I am teasing, Cales. Xan is a good supreme commander." Xeus allowed his lips to twitch, hoping to put Cales at ease. "Perhaps we should include that for all commanders, as a precaution. They do have an extensive arsenal at their disposal."

"A wise decision. I would suggest, as well, that this be done for all males in influential positions?"

"Meaning me?" Xeus arched an eyebrow, wondering if any scans would explain why he couldn't eradicate Macera from his thoughts, dreams, and fantasies. Comming her helped and didn't at the same time. "Schedule it," he said, praying she was a chemical imbalance in his brain and nothing more.

Chapter Twenty-Four

Etterian battleship Phoenix
The shared quarters
Three days to Etteria

Macy shook her hands to ease her stiff fingers. Trying to finish the scarf in the remaining time had her aching. She stuck out her tongue as she looped and slipped the wool over the knitting needles, ad infinitum. The scarf was good enough for her, but super-tall Oyaz would need something a bit longer, like half her damn height extra. Still, it was a thank-you gift she hoped he liked.

This morning, she'd awoken to a message from Zoo—a simple 'good morning, *ensa*.' The leap and dance of her heart and the constant smile said it all, surviving right through Oyaz-torture. She'd been too happy to care that he expected her to stuff her foot into her backside in a butt kick. Not physically possible, but he ignored her grumbling, as per usual.

Romance comedies blared in the background. Favorite scenes were giggled at. Thankfully, Illan had left soon after his porridge-sort of breakfast he called parhp, so no one witnessed her dancing in the comfy, singing along to the soundtracks, or yelling at the actors to kiss already.

Overall, she was content, despite being alone. She hummed as she remeasured the scarf for the hundredth time that morning. Then she sang about sweat dripping down her balls. Most of the lyrics made no sense, but it had a catchy tune.

By the fourth comedy, she was done. As in the scarf could be used as a wraparound dress if she was skinnier. Her stomach ached and twinged at the abuse she'd put it through gorging on candy and soda. Wrapping the scarf six times around her neck, she pushed off the comfy and moaned, bending over to catch her breath. Okay, maybe that last bowl of jelly beans was a bad idea.

She winced as she inched to the door. Strawberry-flavored bile traveled up her throat. She gulped, pressed a cheek to the cold bulkhead for a few minutes, then pushed off it to stagger into the passage.

Males stopped to help her as she inched past them, but she waved them away with a stiff hand and smile. Sweat beaded her temple and upper lip, but she didn't dare try and remove Oyaz's scarf. The quicker she reached Rior, the better.

She didn't make it to the common. Rior barreled toward her, his face scrunched in concern. She had never seen a more beautiful angel. Slumping against the bulkhead, she waited for him to reach her with those glorious long legs of his.

"I'm so glad to see you, Rior." She moaned, clutched her stomach, and doubled over. "I ate too much."

"Many males commed me, Macy. I had to ask Pilot Msar to track your O.D.I." While he berated her, he scanned her with his medical box.

When the cramping eased, she released a deep sigh of relief. "I need one of those boxes, Rior." Or maybe not. That would give her the license to eat like a pig and not suffer the consequences except for an ever-expanding ass. "Have there been many males visiting you after my evening meals?" She would bet her life the poor medic was plagued by all manner of gastric complaints.

"No. Each male has a med-gun and can attend to such minor...ailments." He smiled. "Would you like one, Macy?" He glanced at her leggings. "Though, you will need a pocket."

"And learn how to use it." She shook her head. "I prefer to see you, Rior."

He beamed. "And I you." Stepping back, he punched into his O.D.I. "It is best I update Sub-Commander Oyaz."

She sighed and pushed off the bulkhead, wriggling her backside and stomach to test out her healed abdomen. "By all means, inform my bodyguard that I am well." She huffed. "We don't want him coming down here for nothing."

Rior frowned, hovering his finger an inch above his forearm. "I meant no offense, Macy."

"I know you didn't." She patted his upper arm. "Thanks for the healing, Rior." After a step, she faced him. "Where *is* Oyaz?"

"In his quarters."

"And that would be where?" She pointed down the passage, then in the opposite direction.

Rior frowned then raised his wrist to his lips. "Pilot Msar, guide Lady Macy to Sub-Commander Oyaz's quarters."

"Acknowledged, Medic Rior." Lights flickered from faded to bright, directing her past Rior and the common.

"Thanks, Rior," she called as she jogged to Oyaz's quarters. He was waiting for her when she entered his passage. "Thanks, Msar, a little surprise visit wouldn't have hurt him, y'know."

"My apologies, Lady Macy." And the poor pilot did sound contrite.

Guilt twinged through her, and she hurried to assure the male his guidance had been epic.

"What now?" Oyaz scowled while ushering her into his quarters.

"Well, don't overwhelm me with enthusiasm, Oyaz." She unraveled the scarf and fanned herself with it.

He crossed his arms over his bare chest. Dark-gray yoga pants clung for life to his hips. And the male had an Adonis Belt. She raised her gaze to the ceiling.

"I brought you a gift." She shoved the scarf at him without looking. When silence dragged, she peeked.

"For me?" He hesitated, unfolded his arms, and accepted the bundle. "I...thank you, Macy." He opened the scarf and stretched it out, then jerked to a halt. Groaning, he gathered it into a ball and buried his face into the wool. "So soft. What is it?"

"It's a scarf." She tried to take it from him, but he wouldn't budge. "I made it for you."

"Scarf?" He whipped his head up and met her gaze. "Made with your knitting needles?"

"Yes. Do you like it?"

He smiled so wide, his dimples appeared. "Yes. I shall cherish it always."

"Cherish? You're supposed to wear it."

He frowned then hooked it around his neck, rubbing the ends across his skin.

She rested her hands on her hips and nudged her chin at his bedroom. "Go put on a shirt, then I'll show you how to drape the scarf."

In a flash, he left to do as she commanded. She grinned, dancing on the spot, so happy he liked it.

"Greetings," a familiar voice intruded.

She squeaked and faced the display vid an inch from her shoulder. "Hello," she breathed. *This is Zoo?*

He had a broad forehead and cheeks that narrowed at his strong, square jaw. His nose dominated his face, and his kissable lips were wide, his bottom lip oversized, tempting her to test its softness. He had incredible dark blue almond-shaped eyes under straight eyebrows—black slashes against his bronzed skin.

"Ensa?"

"Well, it's lovely to put a face to the voice." She hurried to clear her throat after that breathless reply.

He chuckled, jarring her heartbeat. *Damn.*

"I have always seen your face, *ensa.*"

She gasped and ran her hands over her unbrushed hair. How many times had she been in a similar state, as if a skunk had dragged her through the bushes backward? "I thought we agreed...on anonymity."

"I could not resist. To look upon your sweet face is heaven-sent."

She blinked, willing the heat traveling up her neck to skip her cheeks. "I..." *Holy cow.* She'd longed to see him, and here he was, an impressive Etterian male. "No fair." She pouted. All those times she could have ogled him? She frowned. How did he know to find her here? "Were you looking for me?" She glanced at Oyaz's bedroom. "Oh, um, Oyaz, you have a caller."

Rocking on her heels, she clasped her hands in front of her and smiled at Zoo. "Oyaz is changing."

Under Zoo's intense eyes, she fidgeted, not knowing what to do or say. If he couldn't see her, she would have stroked his sharp jawline, brushed her thumb across his plump bottom lip, run her fingers over his thick braid, and finished off with a swipe of an eyebrow.

She shivered, her pulse fluttery.

Oyaz stepped through the door and strode toward her, now wearing a shirt-like garment and the scarf. Grabbing the scarf, she flicked the ends, almost strangling poor Oyaz who'd dipped for her to reach. And when she snuck glances at Zoo, it was to find his gaze fixed on her.

Short of hyperventilating, her heart thundering in her ears, she cast a smile at Zoo, waved at Oyaz, and bolted. Outside in the passage, she slumped against the wall and fanned her face. *Holy sweet tamale, Zoo is gorgeous.* His devastating smile enhanced his appeal, and the way he watched her... Whoa. Her body hummed under his attention.

Bursting with energy, she jogged to her quarters, then inside, chose a song about sunshine and walking on it. Hell, yeah, she would dance on a sunbeam, skip, and do the fandango. If she knew how.

"I miss your smile, *ensa*." Zoo's message zinged up her arm.

She giggled, not caring that her face was flushed, that her heart had yet to calm, nor that her insides churned like a good barrel of butter. This excitement, this wild tingle rushing over her senses was what she'd wanted. Even if Zoo turned out to be yet another friend, she would be forever grateful for how he made her feel.

Chapter Twenty-Five

Orbiting Planet Etteria
Etterian Battleship Kushin

BOUNCING AROUND THE COMMON with unharnessed energy, tiny humans giggled, screamed, and, in general, shared their joy.

"They...are exquisite," Xeus whispered to Kanzo, snapping his gaze from female to male damu while excitement and warmth engulfed his chest. Finding Dar Eths among the humans was a gift from the Maker, but these damu and the hope they summoned within him, were the future of Etteria.

"It is hard to believe someone would abandon or abuse them," Kanzo muttered.

"Abuse?" Xeus scowled.

"Yes. Ava mentioned a little of what they have endured. But there is hope, my king. Many of our females have reached out, asking to meet them," Kanzo said, unknowingly validating Xeus's dreams for a human and Etterian world. "And Ambassador Brenin has voiced his concern on the dilution of our race again. Something about the impact this will have on our culture."

Xeus growled, "If we do not embrace change, there will be no Etterian race remaining."

Kanzo chuckled. "As I so delightedly informed him. I must forewarn you, I had an extensive discussion on what Olivia foresees for the...children. When I explained how our damu are trained, to control emotions and learn self-discipline, she stated that both were admirable qualities. She did insist that the girls should receive the same training as boys."

Boys? Xeus's O.D.I. updated him. He grinned. *Boys and girls?* So simple. He laughed, not only at Lady Olivia's audacity but at her strength of opinion. "The...girls as well?"

"Yes, my king. She said they were weaker physically and combat training was wise."

A damu broke away from the group and barreled toward Kanzo, who caught the boy and tossed him into the air amid squeals and pleas for more. A dark-haired woman approached them, her form petite, her smile wide.

"Lady Olivia, allow me to introduce my liege, King Xeus," Kanzo lowered the boy to the floor to usher Olivia closer, her shyness conveyed in a downcast gaze.

"Good day, King Xeus," she said before dipping into a curtsey.

Xeus stared at the woman then offered her his hand. She accepted it but didn't shake it.

Instead, she covered the top of his hand with hers. "Thank you for this sanctuary. I will never forget your kindness."

Her black hair was dark, striking against her pale skin, yet it was her eyes that had him riveted. They were the color of the lilac junix flowers on Lysara. She was a beautiful woman, not that he paid her nose, lips, and angular chin as much attention as her eyes. Maker, he prayed she passed on such a trait to her offspring.

"You and your...children are welcome on Etteria. I do not know if Advisor Cales has mentioned this, but we would prefer to build you a home as per your requirements."

"He has, Your Majesty, and I don't know how to thank you for such an offer. We don't wish to impose or be a nuisance."

"Lady Olivia, your children's well-being matters to us." Using their clasped hands, Xeus drew her closer to whisper, "Etterians struggle to conceive. We will cherish yours. I hope my people will offer to care for a *damu* or two."

Her eyebrows shot up in surprise while her eyes twinkled with delight. "That would be wonderful. They *are* adorable. Would you like to meet them, Your Majesty?"

Xeus agreed, only due to the excitement in her eyes, though he would need to rely on her for guidance.

"Ruby, Saira, gather the children to meet the king," she said.

A tall, dark-red-haired female rushed around the common, gathering the *damu*. They calmed, for the most part, enough to form a line.

"This is Ruby, age seventeen." Lady Olivia introduced the tall, dark-red-haired female with Ferusi-colored eyes, just as vibrant as Oriana's. Her hair was a darker red, like the color of their oceans after the magnus sun had set. It was stunning against her pale, unblemished skin. "This is Saira. She's fifteen." This female had yellow-gold hair and eyes so dark a gray that they glimmered like Maloidian steel. *Beautiful*.

"Then we have Neve, who's twelve." The grumpy expression on the young female's face was one he respected. Once she'd trained alongside Etterian *damu*, her channeled passion would be an asset to Etteria. She was brown-haired and brown-eyed like Macera. He scowled at that thought.

"Neve? It is a good name," he said. The youngin smothered a giggle. He nodded. She had courage and strength, this one.

"This is Mikey. He's eight." The young male had light brown hair and pale blue eyes, almost the shade of an Eth's.

"Still young enough to begin warrior training," Xeus said, and the male responded with a punch to Xeus's thigh. He chuckled and dropped to a knee, offering his palms as punching mitts. The...boy responded, his small fists striking Xeus's palms with accuracy. *An eager warrior.*

"This is Tommy, age seven." The pale-haired male with brown eyes looked at him with caution behind his gaze and posture.

"Another warrior. I will have Kanzo schedule their training." He twisted and offered his hand for a shake. The boy didn't hesitate, sliding his hand into Xeus's before shaking twice. "You have the heart of a warrior, Tommy."

The boy gasped, "I do?"

"I do not lie. It is dishonorable. You and Mikey will make excellent warriors, of this I have no doubt." Xeus rose to his feet and faced the next *damu*, a girl. She was tiny with black riotous curls and bright blue eyes. The scars on her arms and legs caught his breath. He glanced at Kanzo and muttered, "why have her scars not been attended to?"

Lady Olivia spoke before Kanzo could respond. "This is Lily, age six." She brushed the girl's hair off her temple.

"Nerx's Lily?" Xeus studied the small face that had won over his grumpiest warrior.

"I am." The girl thumped her chest.

Xeus couldn't resist lowering to a knee again to shake the little hand she thrust at him. "I am pleased to meet you, Lady Lily." He smiled. *This one has the heart of a warrior, as well.*

"Then we have the twins, Davian and Dagon, age four."

Xeus rose to his feet only to blink at two boys, matching in appearance. "They are identical," he whispered, switching his attention between them.

"Yes." Lady Olivia chuckled. "Born at the same time."

"This happens naturally among humans?" Awe softened Xeus's voice.

"Yes." Lady Olivia clasped her hands in front of her. "These two are in their own world."

They *were* whispering to each other, unaware of their surroundings.

"This is Maddie, she's two." Lady Olivia picked up the girl. "She doesn't speak. We don't know why."

"For medical reasons?" He gestured to a nearby medic to join them.

"She is healthy, my king," Medic Der said. "I have scanned and documented each child and teenager. In Maddie's case, I believe she will speak when she is ready to."

Xeus's eyelids fluttered, the O.D.I. confirming that a single *damu* meant child and youngin meant teenager.

"And baby Jessie is asleep. She's seven months old now." Olivia gestured to Saira who passed to Xeus a sweet-smelling wrapped bundle.

He gaped at the beautiful baby blinking at him, her little mouth pouting. She waved a hand and smiled. His heart swelled, the precious gift she was so fragile in his large hands.

"Nerx." Lily breaking away and scrambling over to the tall male, drew Xeus's attention briefly. Before he gazed upon the baby again, he noted when Nerx caught Lily into his arms and cuddled her.

"She has taken to him." Olivia beamed. "Nerx has requested to adopt Lily."

Xeus froze while stroking aside a whisp of the baby's hair. He scanned through the images and information his O.D.I. shared. "Adopt? As in permanently care?"

"Yes, I'm considering it. He's good with her and adores her. She's blossomed under his care." Lady Olivia made to take the baby from Xeus, but he hesitated before relinquishing the bundle. He clasped his hands behind his back, his fingers twitching.

What she said, sunk in. Torn between disbelief and laughing with sheer joy, Xeus blinked at her. *The irritable son of Tarx?* "My Sub-Commander Nerx?"

What Xeus hoped for, what Kanzo had alluded to with their females, had come to pass. The backs of Xeus's eyes stung with a breath lodging in his throat. For a moment, peace saturated his senses to his toes.

Lady Oliva frowned. "Do you have reasons why I shouldn't approve his request?"

"No," Xeus grinned, "he is a valued male, but I know him to be irritable."

Her laughter tinkled off the walls. "He still is, but I believe they bring out the best in each other."

"I agree." Xeus watched as Lily pressed her cheek to Nerx's. "We have various options regarding temporary housing while your home is under construction, Lady Olivia. Please discuss these with Kanzo. I wish to have you settled and content as soon as possible."

"Thank you again for your assistance, Your Majesty." She dropped into a brief curtsey before hurrying away, taking the gurgling baby Jessie with her.

Had Cales been beside Xeus, he would have admitted to longing for another *damu*. His battle-bond knew him too well.

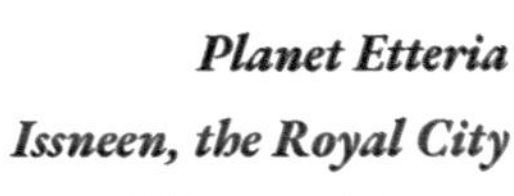

Planet Etteria
Issneen, the Royal City
The Royal Courts

"SHE IS EXQUISITE. HER coloring is almost Etterian," Cales said to Xeus as they watched Lady Ava slide onto Warrior Kanzo's lap. *What a strange thing to do.*

"Except for her softness, her passionate expressions?" Xeus teased, even though no humor creased his eyes or twitched at his lips. He'd just announced that she was the Enforcer of the Foot of Honor since her skillset was one they didn't have on Etteria. Each Etterian attended to their own hair when it was too long and brushed the floor. They would hack at the tips with a sharp blade.

The court had murmured their shock at his announcement, but Xeus didn't care. The fact that he cared less and less every day didn't matter to him either. Lady Ava's new title meant the task no longer fell to Cales. Cales activated his O.D.I. and scowled as he read a message. His body stiffened. His gaze flickered to Xeus, his mouth parted then he pinched his lips into a grim line.

"What is it?" Xeus asked. *Had war begun? Were more humans imprisoned? Had someone died?*

"Warrior Kanzo insists he speak with us in your office, Xeus."

Xeus shot a glance to where Kanzo sat, studying the expressions on the male's face—rage, disbelief, horror. Without a word, Xeus strode to his office, activating his bulkhead to reflect his court without them able to see into the room. Cales held the door open for Lady Ava and Kanzo to enter.

"Thank you for agreeing to see us, my king. My Dar Eth believes there is a mistreated Etterian female, Lady Erox."

"What do you mean you suspect mistreatment?" Xeus faced Lady Ava, glaring at her. She didn't cower under his angry visage, and he admired her for it. His males paled under his stern gaze.

"I've seen the same body language in abused children."

When Xeus thought of each child of Olivia's, a rush of protectiveness swept through him. He hated that he couldn't eradicate their soul-deep scars. If all the culprits could be gathered onto a moon or planet, he'd decimate it. Yet here Lady Ava stood, determined, stubborn, and with absolute conviction that there was such an ill-treated female under his care. She demonstrated this body language—the tilt of a head, furtive glances, jumpiness, and fearful expressions. "I promise you, Your Majesty, she has suffered."

Kanzo gathered Lady Ava's hand in his. "I've seen the same mannerisms in Lily. She speaks the truth, my king."

"Lily?" Xeus gaped, then shut his mouth, realizing he was a king and needed to remain stoic. She hadn't acted as Lady Ava described. Far from it. "How do we ascertain this?" He strode to the bulkhead and scanned the court for the female in question. "She is Ambassador Murox's daughter." *How can I demand Aldur examine Erox? Would not this treatment of her further damage a broken soul?* And as he studied Lady Erox, she mimicked the mannerisms Lady Ava had demonstrated. *It is the truth.* Pure rage raced through his veins, snatching his breath at its intensity. He wanted to rip Murox's head from his shoulders for this violation of their lore and the abuse of a precious female.

"Lily was fearful of my size, of my booming laughter. If any male approached her, she'd cower and search for an escape," Kanzo said to the room.

Xeus gritted his jaw, then whispered to Cales frozen beside him. Cales unfurled his fists and strode from the office. Xeus gestured to Ava and Kanzo to be comfortable while they waited. Medic Aldur burst in, and Xeus explained the situation to the horrified medic, as well as his plan. Minutes later, Cales led Murox and his daughter into the office.

"My king?" the ambassador said, marching into the office as if he owned it. His arrogance irritated him. Xeus clenched his fingers to stop himself from charging this male and killing him. Yet he needed to be certain. *Perhaps it is another blood-bond and not her father?*

"Murox, brought to my attention is an unusual and dishonorable situation with which I require your assistance." Xeus gestured to Kanzo and said, "How should we ascertain whether this male has mishandled his Dar Eth?" Xeus was grateful when Lady Ava performed the mannerisms he required of her. She darted her gaze at Kanzo in fear before glancing at the floor while trying to make her body as small as possible. "What does our law state in such matters?"

"A medic must examine her to verify such claims," Murox said while admiring Ava's curves.

Xeus scowled at the male's lustful expression. *To make matters worse he dares to admire a Dar Eth? And in the company of her Eth?* "And should the male have the right to contest such an examination?" Xeus persevered, to save Lady Erox, not to appease his anger. Though, if justice was served, that would come.

"No, he has no opinion under such suspicions."

At least, the male had stated the truth.

"Thank you, Murox. I request that your daughter escorts Lady Ava for an examination. She might be wary of other males."

"This is acceptable to me, my king. Erox, go with Lady Ava and Medic Aldur."

"As you command, Father," she whispered and followed them into the next room.

As they waited, Xeus paced the confines of his office, trying his best to avoid glancing at a contented ambassador. One look and he might kill him where he sat.

A few minutes later, the solid door burst open with a medic storming into the office. It was as Xeus had feared, now confirmed. His shoulders stiffened. He settled his gaze on his greatsword mounted on the wall. It would take but a leap to reach it.

"It is as we suspected, my king, and confirmed by the female herself. Extensive bruising with evidence of poorly healed broken bones." The rumble that went through the room was alarming, like thunder reverberating in the distance. Kanzo and Cales flanked Xeus, their postures battle-ready, their expressions thunderous.

"Ambassador Murox, what does the law state regarding such abuse?" King Xeus vibrated with barely contained rage. His body was strung tight as if on the verge of pouncing on a prey.

"Etteria should strip him of all he owns, remove his hair, and deny him the right to house a female." Murox smirked at Kanzo.

"Like this?" Cales lunged, and with a flick of his blade, Murox's braid fell to the floor.

The male stared at it aghast.

"*You* have no honor, Murox, for what you have done to *your* daughter," Xeus boomed, then glowered when the ambassador opened his mouth to defend himself. "No words you speak shall ever justify such behavior. I could kill you for this, and believe me, I fight the temptation. Get him out of my sight, Cales."

As soon as the door closed, Xeus faced Ava who had brought Erox into the office. "I must confess, Lady Ava, I know not how to address such a situation. How should we proceed from here?"

Ava glanced at Kanzo.

"Proceed as you would if Lady Erox was your daughter, my king," Kanzo advised, gazing at Ava to ensure he'd answered as she might have.

Wise guidance. Xeus stood in front of Erox. He dropped to a knee and bowed his head. *I'm ashamed I didn't see the signs, that I didn't protect a precious female, that I haven't upheld what is honorable.*

"Please forgive me for not protecting you, Lady Erox. I vow to not fail you again."

She placed her small hand on his shoulder. He stilled. The light weight of it somehow calmed him, as nothing else had for a long while.

"It is not for you to ask forgiveness, my king. You cannot know what my father hid from you." Erox scanned the room while Xeus rose to his feet. "Thank you for freeing me. I am grateful to you all." She glanced at her clasped hands. "What is to become of me now?"

"How old are you?" Cales asked, having returned sans Murox.

"I've seen seventeen years."

"Did you attend the pairing?" Xeus frowned. How many females missed such an event for whatever reason? He would task Cales to investigate their census status.

"No, that would have been a mercy," Lady Erox said. "I am fearful of males, my king, yet an Eth would have been preferable."

"You shall fall under my care." Xeus offered what he hoped was a kind smile, even as it pained him to do so. Only joy shared with Macera lingered in the darkness of his soul.

Ava hugged the girl. "Feel free to comm or visit me. King Xeus has trusted me with a great task, and I may need your help."

"I am pleased to assist, milady."

"It's Ava, just Ava, Lady Erox," Kanzo said, receiving another huge smile from his Dar Eth.

"Lady Ava, Cales, would you please see to Lady Erox's comfort," Xeus said and gestured to Kanzo to remain. As soon as the door closed behind the party which included Aldur, Xeus addressed Kanzo, "Would you recognize such signs in other females?"

"Of course, my king," he said, assuming a relaxed military stance—hands clasped behind his back.

"To even consider that such occurs under our lore, with our honor, it is unthinkable, Kanzo." Xeus sank into his chair behind his white Fuyra desk and rubbed his temple, too exhausted to care that he revealed his inner turmoil. Not even a trip to their northern base Aluna had helped fight this restlessness, only comms with Macera did, but he couldn't spend all his waking hours talking to her. "In the last two years, we have found Dar Eths, are on the verge of war with Yithia, have allied with Gika, and have now adopted offspring from another planet."

"The war with Yithia is a concern, though we have prepared for it, my king."

"True. How fares the children?" Xeus offered a small smile.

"Very well. Some of our males have offered to train the *damu*. I've advised Olivia accordingly. They commence with short sessions tomorrow."

"And Nerx? Has Lady Olivia approved his request?" Xeus held his breath, eager to hear good news.

"She has and believes it is in Lily's best interests. I have notified him."

"Excellent." Xeus slapped his desk. "This bodes well for all Etterians." He rose to circle his desk, approaching Kanzo. "I need you to continue in this role, Kanzo. It cannot fall onto Cales's shoulders as I have tasked him to deal with Earth. We will think of a title for your position at a later stage. I also require that you attend all court proceedings. It is not something Lady Ava should have to endure. You may escort offenders to her for enforcement." He fell silent as it dawned on him. "I now have two daughters." He sighed, wondering how he was able to stand under all of this responsibility. *Endless exhaustion, responsibility, and existence.*

"My king, are you unwell?" Kanzo's concern brought Xeus back to the present.

"Many changes are occurring, Kanzo. Cales will issue a task list for you to attend to in his absence, one in specific is the human missiles and submarines he has assigned to the lima kuu. The construction of Olivia's home is also your responsibility. See to it that the children are content here."

"I am honored to serve Etteria as required." Kanzo stood tall then pressed a fist to his chest in a formal bow.

Chapter Twenty-Six

Planet Etteria

Issneen, the Royal City

THE WAR COUNCIL HAD met, Brenin was tasked to manage the submarines, Enyl and Ori were returning to Earth, and Xeus had just escorted two Durns to the Etterian data archives. As much as this all solidified Etteria's survival in the upcoming war, none of it mattered. With Illan here, that could mean only one thing... Macera was near.

Xeus's breath hitched. He paused mid-stride to press his hand against a stone pillar, trying to ease the dizziness spinning his vision. He shouldn't be this excited. No internal reprimand diverted him from this path. He had to find her. His knees trembled and forced him to lean against the pillar lest he fell. His body's reaction was madness.

"Xeus?" Cales strode toward him.

Xeus barely managed to smother a groan. He cherished his battle-bond, but sometimes a little quiet time would be appreciated. "Have the Ladies Macera and..." What was the other human's name?

"Cyndi. Lady Macera has been allocated chambers. Lady Cyndi is with Iddan."

"With?" Xeus straightened then hopped, testing out his knees.

"Durn version of paired."

"Now that is intriguing." Xeus gazed at the night sky, attempting to not appear too eager. "And Lady Macera?"

"En route to Issneen. Sub-Commander Oyaz has requested two warriors to guard her."

Xeus scowled. He had to slip past more males to reach her? "Why would she need protection in Issneen?"

"From herself, according to Oyaz."

Xeus pinched the bridge of his nose. "In what way is she a danger?"

"I questioned him myself, Xeus. He fears she will become lonely, as she did on the Phoenix."

Xeus rubbed his chest where his heart twinged. His Macera suffered? He grunted. And with his schedule, he couldn't ease that loneliness. Excitement drained from him. She wasn't planetside yet. Nor could he demand regular updates on her location or activities without rousing suspicion. He would find her, though.

"Restrict her access...until she is comfortable in our world." He need only be patient. "In a few days, bring them to court to be formally introduced. The sooner our people meet the human females, the better for all." He almost thumped his chest in victory. She couldn't miss him then.

"Wise, Xeus."

He scowled at Cales, not feeling wise at all. A cool breeze chilled him. He stilled. Feeling? And he was. To feel is to fail, and Macera invoked a riotous explosion of emotions he couldn't begin to sift through. He was playing with his soul, the void... Ice drenched his neck, shooting down his spine. He tested the center of his core, poking the darkness that lived there. The void hadn't grown and wasn't pressing in on him. Alodon's balls, he was losing his mind.

"What are the results from the mental health assessment?" He waited, expecting the worst.

"All good."

Xeus fixed his gaze on Cales, trying to assess if the male lied. Yes, it was dishonorable to do so, but with how his emotions swung from fury to joy, and the void wasn't encroaching, insanity seemed the most plausible. "Truth?"

Cales frowned. "Why would I lie?" He scanned his O.D.I. again. "The results were favorable. You are in peak condition."

He grunted and resumed striding down the passage toward his chambers.

Cales trailed him. "Why would you expect the worst? Are you unwell?"

"I am well, just…" He glanced at the sky again. Beaches, sunshine, with a cold beverage sounded irresistible. Vacation, Macera had called it.

"Tired." Cales gripped Xeus's shoulder. "I shall clear your schedule. Take the time to rest, my battle-bond."

"Thank you, Cales. As always." Xeus stared after him, then headed to the proving grounds. Rest? Not with his thoughts in turmoil and centered around Macera.

Planet Etteria

Issneen, the Royal City

Terra Firma, at last.

MACY GRUMBLED AT MISSING the view of the Royal City as they approached via the shuttle. Oyaz had strapped her in as if she was precious cargo. That he treated her so was sweet and frustrating. She leaned forward to catch glimpses of Etteria on the display vid and sighed at the pink skies and white fluffy clouds. A strong warrior race had a pink planet? She stifled a giggle—a mixture of nerves and excitement.

The shuttle tilted, granting her snatches of red oceans with pale gray beaches. The unusual coloring stunned her. Then bright white buildings appeared on the display vid. They were cube-like with no curves or organic shapes. Made sense in a military culture. Blues, splashes of pinks, greens, and whites of the colorful flora interspersed the buildings. She assumed those were flowers.

As soon as the shuttle touched down, Oyaz unstrapped and pulled her to her feet.

"What's the rush?" she asked.

"My new command is to protect Earth. I leave as soon as I have ensured your safety."

What? He was leaving her? "My safety? Can't Rior do that?"

"Rior cannot, he is a medic and must return to the *Phoenix*," Oyaz said in a matter-of-fact tone.

"You're both abandoning me?" She drew in a shuddering breath. It was no consolation that she could comm them and the Lysarans. She needed someone to speak to face to face, dammit.

"Yes. Two warriors will protect you. I escort you to them now." Oyaz gazed at her upturned face as he led her down the lowered ramp. Protect, escort, but not companionship, not guidance? Besides, she was on a warrior planet, what did she need protection for?

"I'm in danger?" She glanced up then gasped at the full sight of Etteria laid before her. The glimpses had assuaged her curiosity, but the scenery, in its entirety, was breathtaking. Not that Oyaz let her admire the vista. The ingrate.

"You are a human female wanted by Etterian males and Yithians. You need protection. It is not negotiable, Macy," Oyaz said.

While he led her to the waiting hovering craft, many males paused in their tasks to watch her. Spinning on the spot in amazement, she ran her hands over her wide hips, cursing her genetics. Fire burned through her under Oyaz's arched brow, catching her stroking her body. A ferocious scowl settled on his lips. He glared at his males.

"She is not the enemy to observe so," he growled.

She raised her face to the unfamiliar sky and prayed a hole would open, swallowing her.

"My apologies, Macy. They hope for a Dar Eth," Oyaz said, ushering her past them. A few studied her still, while others averted their gazes.

"Me?" Hope flared, bright and blinding. "What must happen for me to be someone's Dar Eth? A blood sample?" She held out her arm as if to say, 'take it, take it now.'

"The annals state a full-body visual," Rior said, leading Cyndi behind them. "From head to toe with nothing to distract."

Macy smothered a groan. This again. How was she supposed to get every damn male to see her? Her gaze caught on Cyndi's ethereal beauty. *Why couldn't I be as gorgeous as her with her pale blonde hair and blue eyes? Not with my cow-shit brown hair, eyes, and skin—dull, dull, dull. Then to top it off, I'm short and overweight. I've tried to compensate by being cheerful and energetic since beauty is skin-deep.* She snorted. *But I have to catch a man's attention first.*

"So, an image of me will do it?" She arched a brow at Rior. "How soon will I know I have an Eth?"

"If you trigger the Ethera, your male will come for you. By Etterian law, you are united," Oyaz said, urging her forward, almost dragging her with him.

She frowned at his eagerness to get rid of her. Still, she dug in her heels. United? She gaped. "Are you saying I could have a husband by dinner time?" She broke into a dance, only to be urged once again toward the hovering craft. *Hi, I'd like to place an order. One Eth to go, please. Sure, I'll take delivery.* The idea of being married by sunset delighted her. To not be alone, to no longer feel disgusted with her company, and to share her boredom with someone? Heaven.

"You want a male?" Oyaz frowned, leaning in to whisper. He darted his gaze around, throwing warning growls at approaching males.

"Oh, yes, very much so." Using the hand he held out to her for leverage, she climbed into the craft. A blast of air, sweeping up from under it, whipped her hair out. "Can we take a picture and send it via everyone's O.D.I.?" She fisted her hair out of her face and pinned it to her chest. Her gaze snagged on her bulging cleavage, heat renewing its barrage on her cheeks even as tears blurred her vision. All their males would study her features and flaws. The number would be way more than the twenty or so who stared at her now or the forty club regulars who had listened to her on stage. At least she wouldn't see them turn away in disgust.

"Such widespread communication is only utilized during war. I can, however, request permission from King Xeus," Oyaz said.

She chewed on her lip, wanting this done. Then she'd know there wasn't happiness for her on this planet. "It would just be for me, right? I don't want Iddan to lose Cyndi."

"No, the Ethera does not work on those who have romantic love in their hearts," Rior said, seating himself beside her with Cyndi opposite him.

"How is that possible?" Macy gasped, amazed at this Ethera's ability to pick up on attraction when the parties involved might not know themselves.

"We do not know. The Durn engineered the Ethera at our request, but we lost that knowledge with the destruction of their planet." Rior's gaze traveled her face, but he said no more. She almost hit him. Talking to him was like pulling water from a stone.

"Why am I not your Dar Eth, Rior?" She pursed her lips, running her gaze over a virile male in the prime of his life. To be his would be wonderful. To be Zoo's would be better.

"I cannot explain this, Macy. I feel warmth and protectiveness toward you, and you *are* beautiful, yet that is all I feel."

She dipped her chin to her chest to hide the heat staining her cheeks. He'd called her beautiful. It was kind of him to say so, even if it wasn't true. "And if I was your Dar Eth?"

"If you called forth the Ethera within me? I would be the most blessed male on Etteria." Rior thumped his chest, whatever that meant.

"You are the sweetest male, Rior. I hope you find your Dar Eth soon."

"And you, your Eth," Rior said, patting her hand.

"If your king says yes? To my image?" She nudged Oyaz, who had, at last, stopped typing on his O.D.I.

"Only the Maker grants a pairing, *ensa*." Oyaz had chosen the seat beside her, within easy reach of her elbow.

The craft followed Xan and Quin's, and even though they arrived at the same landing pad, Macy and Cyndi were led away from the royal court. Quin entered through large doors and disappeared. Rior led Cyndi away while Oyaz kept a firm hand on Macy's elbow. He stopped outside a door two males guarded.

"This is Warrior Azan and Warrior Nuos, I place in your care a treasure infinitely dear," he said, his tone a little too formal for her liking.

She imagined Oyaz handing over a bundled baby saying, 'this is the prophecy child.' Her new guards held their fists to their chests. Ah, as if they were saying 'on their honor?'

Oyaz took the time to grasp their forearms in some sort of warrior-to-warrior greeting before facing her. "I am a message away, my friend. Please, let me know how you are doing and often. And thank you again for my incredible gift."

She bit her lip to hold back the tears then flung her arms around his waist. "Godspeed, Oyaz."

He pressed his chin to the crown of her head and held her for a minute. When he hurried away, he didn't glance back.

She squared her shoulders and caught her new security detail studying her. "You were with Quin on Lysara, Nuos?"

"Yes, milady," he said.

"All right, let's start with that. Macera is fine. Macy's also good. Milady or lady is out. O.U.T." She stared them down.

Azan blinked but said nothing. Nuos showed a glimmer of humor. He would be the first to break in. She couldn't go around with two stiff ironing boards as company.

When they hesitated, she muttered about stubborn males. "What do you call Quin?"

"Milady," Nuos said, a smile spreading across his gorgeous lips. Two dimples appeared, and she sighed at the sight of them.

If she were an artist, she'd carry a sketchbook in which to capture their beauty. Etterian males were gorgeous. She shuddered to think what their females looked like. As it was, Macy felt like a sack of potatoes next to Quin and Cyndi. Next to an Etterian female, she'd feel like a sack of rotten potatoes. She snorted at her unkind thoughts.

Back to the discussion at hand. "And Quin let you?" Macy wondered how that argument had played out.

"There were other issues needing attention," Nuos said.

Right. The shuttle crash and dealing with the Lysarans. "You must tell me about that adventure, Nuos. I spent most of my time on Lysara dodging beautiful males."

"A male cannot be beautiful," Nuos said, his body stiffening.

"A shit lot you know." She gestured to the console. "Is this thing set to me?" Before they could reply, she slammed her palm down, taking her frustration out on the inanimate device. The door slid into the wall. She stilled. Her new prison was like an expensive penthouse apartment—pristine white walls, floors, ceilings, colorful comfys, and huge windows. "Is this mine?" she asked. *Am I to live here all alone? It's empty, cold, and uninviting...like my life.*

"Yes, milady."

She shot Azan a glare for the 'milady' and entered. They waited at the threshold, not stepping through the door to follow her. She frowned, feeling more like a prisoner with them hovering at the door. "Come in. What's the matter with you two?"

"We cannot enter without your permission." Nuos inched through the door, only to assume a guard position next to it.

"Nuos, relax. I'm inside my prison, what could happen here?"

His brow furrowed, the poor dear. "You are not confined, mil—"

"A gilded cage is still a cage." She gazed out the windows.

When she glanced at him again, he'd relaxed his military stance, now a soldier at ease. She familiarized herself with her new home, admiring the light spilling through the windows onto the bright white floor, the massive bed in the enclosed bedroom, and the larger-than-usual replicator with an extended counter surface.

"Nuos, Azan, I'm curious. What if I wanted something too big for this replicator? Like a comfy or a table?"

"We have replicators for those purposes. Inform me of your requirements, and I will see it done."

"So, I can order potted plants, couches, paintings, curtains?" Their eyelids fluttered, and she almost giggled at the look of it. That *had* been mean of her. "And who pays for it?"

"Pays?" Azan mouthed the word. "As in tokens, milady?"

"Yes, cash, gold, whatever currency you use."

"Etteria *pays* for the needs of all Etterians," Nuos said.

"Whoa, don't tell humans that." She held up her hands, palms out. "We go crazy when it's for free. Nothing on Earth is free."

"Truth?" Azan arched a brow.

"Yes, truth." She huffed. As if she had a reason to lie. "And if they say it's free, don't believe it. Do you want anything from the rehydrator?" She may be on another planet, but her gran had raised her. Manners maketh a woman, she'd say.

"Oh, yes, please. Chocolate." Nuos's eagerness was palpable.

"Dark, with nuts, fruit, or plain?"

He blinked at her, so she took pity on him. She ordered plain for him and one for Azan too. Nuos accepted the offered bar while Azan tentatively took it. He watched Nuos rip off the silver wrapper to take a massive bite.

"Addicted, I see," she teased.

Nuos offered a huge grin, then gestured to Azan that they needed to leave.

"Oyaz insisted I collect you at 0430 for your training," Nuos said, calling forth a deep groan from her.

Her shoulders slumped. So thoughtful of him. She'd send Oyaz a snotty message, just so he wouldn't miss out on her complaints. She grumbled about misplaced loyalty, then dismissed her new bodyguards' concern with a wave of her hand. She planned on complaining to Oyaz every morning and super early too, the bastard.

After Azan and Nuos left with instructions to call them should she leave her chambers, she messaged Cyndi. *Cyndi, what happened? Where are you?*

Cyndi commed Macy instead. The display vid mounted to the white wall flickered.

"Hey, Macy. They've issued me quarters...chambers. I'm ordering clothes and hanging them in the closet. What you up to?"

"Nothing much." Macy glanced at her bedroom. Maybe she should do the same? "Any reason you can't order clothes as and when needed?"

Cyndi grinned. "Because we're meeting the king tomorrow."

Macy froze. "What?" she rasped.

"Oh, didn't you know? We're to be introduced to King Xeus and his court. Quin's sort of done it with the war council."

"Tomorrow?" Macy squeaked. No, no, no, she didn't want to. Why would anyone want to meet her? Couldn't they just... She shrugged,...pretend she didn't exist?

"Find something pretty to wear. First impressions count, y'know." Cyndi glanced up as if someone had walked in. Her cheeks flushed a delicate pink. "I've got to go. Let me know if you need help picking out something."

Macy blinked at the black screen. A thousand ants scratched just under her skin. She clamped a hand over her mouth to smother a scream. Meet another king? Sy-mar hadn't been that bad, but this was Etteria's king, the male she had to obey. Pacing ramped her anxiety, and pressing her cheek to the cool window didn't help.

Desperate for something to calm her, she tapped the replicator and ordered knitting needles. She expected a familiar beep. Nothing, just the items she ordered materializing. Huh. Scrolling through the variety of colored wool, she paused and activated the O.D.I.

Zoo? What's your favorite color? She might as well systematically knit a scarf for every male she knew.

His reply was in an instant. *Blue, ensa. And yours?*

I like blue too, or purple, maybe orange. She scanned the colors available. *Dark or light blue?*

The blue of my eyes.

Her breath hitched when she remembered the intensity of his gaze. What could she say? Part of her wanted to gush over his handsome features, another advised caution. *Dark blue it is.*

With needles in hand, balls of Merino-silk wool, and a new beach bag, she sank into a comfy. Click-click, knit one, purl one created an intriguing beat. She swung her foot and sang along. "...leave you all alone? Mhmm. I'm on fire."

Two hours later, she set the scarf-in-progress aside and approached the vid to call Myn-ras.

His familiar face appeared, a bright smile curling his sensual lips. "Greetings, sali. Have you arrived?"

"Yup, Myn-ras, been here half a day, and it hasn't been...good. Oyaz has abandoned me." She smothered a sob as her loneliness crashed down around her. He'd left her on the doorstep as if she were an unwanted pet. The sting behind her eyes didn't match the intense pain crushing her chest. "I'm inside my new home and feel...." She tossed a glance around her sterile apartment. *Trapped.* The walls shrank in on her, the air oppressive, squeezing her lungs until she wanted to run away.

"If I was there, would that help?"

She peered at him. "It's sweet of you to offer, Myn-ras, but you need to find your human." *And not chase after me...*

"I intend to, sali, after King Sy-mar's diplomatic visit to Etteria."

Sy-mar on Etteria? She didn't know how she felt about that. Just as long as he didn't ask her again to make Lysara her home. The way her emotions swung, she might throw caution to the wind and accept.

"You're coming with him?" She'd love to see Myn-ras, but she couldn't monopolize his time. At his nod, she clapped and bounced on her heels. "When?"

"We will arrive at Issneen this day." His gaze darted to the side as if he didn't want anyone to overhear him. "King Sy-mar speaks fondly of you."

"What?" she gasped, stepping back from the vid. "Is he hoping I'll change my mind?" Well, she had said Etteria first...after she met King Xeus.

"But of course." Myn-ras pressed a hand to the screen as if he wanted to touch her. She liked the comforting gesture. "It will be good to be in your company again, sali."

She dismissed his compliment, used to his wiles by now. "I should charge you for each one of my laughs."

"I would pay you whatever you demand."

"Sweet talker," she said, despite the heat staining her cheeks. "Comm me when you arrive. I'll have my guards escort me to you."

With a final smile and wave, she ended the comm. What she should've done was panic and choose an outfit that would flatter her figure as Cyndi had suggested. Instead, she sank into the crimson-colored comfy, wiggled her ass when it adjusted to her shape, then messaged Zoo.

I'm here. In Issneen. She stilled to relish the shiver of excitement coursing through her. Zoo had said they'd meet when she arrived. She glanced at the replicator. Maybe a beautiful outfit would be wise. But she wasn't up to playing dress-up. She winced and typed another message to Zoo. *Already, it hasn't been great. Hope your day is going better than mine.*

She waited a nerve-wracking five minutes, each passing second grating across her senses. But when he didn't respond, it hit her hard. Even Zoo had abandoned her. Dashing aside an escaped tear, she squared her shoulders and sought the comfort of fresh air and two suns shining in a pink sky.

Chapter Twenty-Seven

Planet Etteria
Issneen, the Royal City
Still bored and now abandoned.

As soon as Macy reached the royal gardens, she lifted her face to the warm rays. If she closed her eyes, she could pretend she was on Earth. Not that life there had been all that pleasant. But she couldn't ignore the two suns or the delicate pink of the sky for long. At least here, she wouldn't starve to death.

Etteria.

As stunning as she could've imagined.

The palace of King Xeus loomed, an impressive white building with massive doors and long blue banners flapping in the breeze, their edges glimmering gold in the sunlight. She tried not to think over the last week of pampering onboard the *Phoenix*. Thank God for her gorgeous male friends, despite their lack of interest in her as a woman. Except for the Lysarans. To them, she was a means to an end.

So once again, she was alone. Not even Zoo was there for her, and she couldn't expect him to be. It wasn't fair on him.

Still, it hurt when Cyndi and Quin tried to include her in their changing lives. They were moving on, and Macy wasn't. They had found love, and of course, she hadn't. Plain Macy received no confessions of the heart. The Lysarans offered mind-blowing sex, and despite the temptation of it, it wasn't enough for her. She blamed the romance novels she'd read growing up. Soulmates? Friends to lovers? Alien brides? She snorted, wishing she could write the publishers a few admonishments.

She released a pent-up breath trying to remember when true happiness had last filled her. On the *Phoenix*, with hope for a new life, she'd danced for her imaginary lover. The same damn non-existent love-of-her-life from Earth. The news vids had advertised sex-cyborgs, females only, and even they'd been gorgeous. Now if they'd had males, she would've saved to buy one. They'd guaranteed good sex for the rest of her dull life. But then, she might as well choose Bry-dar or...Sy-mar. No, Myn-ras was the safest. All three were the real thing. They just left her so drained. Surely someone had to know whether they feasted on emotions?

And now she had to meet another king, the ruler of the planet she'd hoped to call home. Meeting King Sy'mar had felt intimate. The Etterian palace was huge which had to mean a massive court, filled to the brim with attendees. All those eyes...watching her. Like they taught royal etiquette at school. Hell, they didn't even cover business etiquette. Just Spanish, which she'd never use now. She snorted. *No Español.*

At the approaching voices behind her, she panicked, remembering too late that she'd promised Nuos she wouldn't leave her prison. She dived through a metal gate and sprinted down a narrow path lined with blue bushes. The sea air thick with salt teased her. She ducked behind a blue bush. When the voices drifted past, she surveyed her surroundings filled with solid pathways. There was a secluded alcove by a white stone fountain with rippling clear water. A blue vine created privacy, shade, and promised to hide her from all the pathways shooting off the alcove. She made a mental note of its location.

She should've been smarter and smuggled food in her pockets. *Tomorrow*, she vowed then scowled. Tomorrow was the king. To avoid having to meet him, she'd need food. She shut off her mental-Gran, who admonished her for her future-rudeness. Macy didn't care. What she needed was true companionship, and as matters stood, Etteria wasn't the solution.

For Nuos and Azan, she was a duty. Neither of them would choose to spend time with her. They wanted to find their Dar Eths and not have to babysit her. Oyaz had taken her image, had spoken to the king, and yet, here she was, without an Eth. A weight settled in her core at how unwanted she was. A loose thread from an epic rescue she had played no part in? How many Etterian males were there, and not one was her soulmate? Rejected by an entire planet... That *hurt*.

She crumpled onto the stone bench and tried to hold back a sob. Crying solved nothing. And once she started, she wouldn't be able to stop. What would they do if she cried in front of them? Their expressions would be priceless. She giggled, on the fringe of hysteria. Well, she didn't have anyone on Earth either, except the stray dog. But meeting Quin and Cyndi had made her feel part of something more and bigger than her worthless existence. Her giggling dwindled into great wracking sobs.

"Why?" she wailed.

"Are you unwell, milady?" someone asked.

She stilled. Had Nuos and Azan found her?

"Why are you sad?" the familiar voice came through the blue vines.

At the thought of Nuos or Azan rounding the vine, she cried out, "Please don't look at me." She suspected her face was mottled like she'd been hanging upside down for at least an hour. Not that her non-crying face would be much of an improvement.

"I will not if you vow to talk to me," the male said.

She tilted her head to listen. Why did he sound familiar? Nuos and Azan would've ignored her request for privacy. "All right, but promise that anything I tell you is between you and the fountain."

"A vow easily made." His sexy voice had her honing in on it again.

It would suck if she spilled the beans and it *was* Azan speaking to her. This stranger's voice was so deep, it made her heart leap into her throat, or were her tears stuck there? She struggled to swallow, to clear her throat. By the way her body reacted, maybe her stranger was Lysaran. Shit, she hoped not.

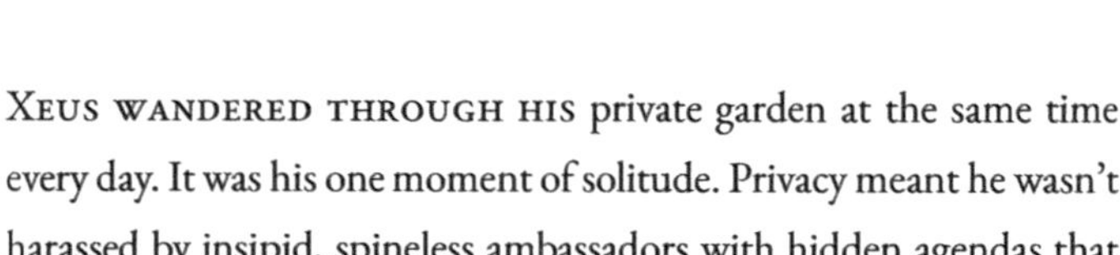

XEUS WANDERED THROUGH HIS private garden at the same time every day. It was his one moment of solitude. Privacy meant he wasn't harassed by insipid, spineless ambassadors with hidden agendas that were in no way for Etteria's good.

Like Ambassador Tamra. Every year, she traveled from Galaza for an in-person meeting he held with each of his ambassadors, especially those in charge of critical aspects of Etterian life—farming kreso or omeika, the Fuyra or Ferusi mines, or the tourist destination of Galaza, the eastern beaches.

And as beautiful and bold as she was, her Etterian appearance tempting, he couldn't bring himself to succumb. Her ceremonial gown had left nothing to the imagination, her scent enticing, yet he didn't dare entertain her offer. He had considered taking a lover, but it was pointless and a burden more than any benefits he received from the union. Not to mention the Etterian female, especially Tamra, would hope he'd form a permanent union with her. Had he been a simple warrior, without status or power, they would never choose him, the male. Regardless, taking a lover without the Ethera would bring the void closer. And in his current state, he couldn't risk it.

He shuddered at the thought of dying to the void. To bring shame to Etteria was unforgivable. He, above all, had to endure.

Nothing he did eased that loneliness except speaking to Macera. He ached to find her, to gaze upon her face, to lose himself in her bottomless eyes. She didn't know who he was, what he meant to Etteria. To her, he was Zoo.

He grinned. And he was free, his schedule cleared. Raising a finger, he activated his O.D.I. to find a message waiting from her.

She was on Issneen...and miserable.

His chest cinched. He punched in a location finder, needing to see her.

Sobbing reached him, penetrating his focus. Crying wasn't a sound he heard often. He paused and listened again. This was of true sorrow. He sat on the bench by the vines just as the female wailed...in Earth English. Anger coursed through him. How could his males leave a human woman so unprotected?

And the emotion, sorrow, was so unexpected, so potent, its sourness coated his tongue as it drenched the air around him. He wanted to comfort the woman, but he didn't wish to startle her. Without thought, he pressed his palm to the blue leaves.

"Why are you crying?" The sobs paused. "Why are you sad?" If it was a tangible thing, like being in pain or missing a bond, this he could assist with.

"Please don't look at me."

The utter terror in her voice froze him. "I will not if you vow to talk to me," he said, wanting to not frighten her. He settled back on the bench and unfolded his clenched fists. Something breathtaking gripped him. Yes, hope, that she'd share her concern, her reason for her unhappiness.

"All right. Promise that anything I tell you is between you and the fountain."

He smiled at how a human woman could negotiate, even when crying. "A vow easily made."

She spoke in a rush. "I just stood by and let Quin rescue us. I was useless, pointless. And now, Quin has Xan and Cyndi likes Iddan, and here I am, as alone as I was on Earth. Kidnapped, on another planet, having crossed galaxies, and yet, nothing's changed." She sobbed again, her breathing ragged. "They try to include me, but I *know*. They don't want me there. Oyaz has gone. Illan is too busy for me. I've only my guards to talk to and that doesn't count when they're forced to be with me." Self-directed anger saturated her voice. "And now I have to meet King Xeus. I'm not comfortable meeting royalty, especially when I don't know what's expected of me. If I could disappear, it would be so much easier... No one would miss me anyway..."

Macera? Pleasure ripped through Xeus, juxtaposed with the anger that had moments ago burned him. The beautiful tiny creature with the amazing voice, who would break into birdsong without warning? The very woman who haunted his nights? He drew in a deep breath, expanding his chest to sniff past her sorrow to the very essence of her. His heart pounded an erratic beat. He sighed at the unexpected warmth spreading there. She was sweet, spicy, earthy like the soil after rain, like the new buds of his hahyt flowers. He inhaled again and trembled. He'd wanted to burst into her chambers to ensure she was well, but to do so would've drawn attention to her. Yet none of that mattered against this longing to see her.

Now that he knew who she was, her sorrow pierced his chest, engulfed his heart, and left him shattered. He was trapped, unable to assuage the need driving him. She'd asked for more anonymity. He curled his fingers into a fist and gritted his teeth. Worse, he'd agreed to it again. Drawing in a slow breath, he shoved his frustration aside and focused on what she needed.

"I have seen the sec vids, *ensa*," he said, his voice too hoarse, but he couldn't soften it. "You *did* help. As an Etterian, I cannot lie to you. As a warrior, I admire courage, determination. You showed all those traits."

"You know who I am?" she gasped. "Zoo?"

"Yes, *ensa*."

As shown by her shadow, she leaped to her feet, took a step toward the edge of the vine then sank onto the bench again, clutching her face.

He gripped the stone, praying its strength would seep into him. "I know who you are, Macera. You are one of three human women who retook a Yithian slave ship." At her groan, he frowned. The sound of it scoured his control, but its implication confused him. "Do you think Ladies Cyndi or Quinlan could have managed the escape without you?"

"Yes," she whimpered.

"It is important to keep your warriors' morale up, no matter the crisis. If you had not done this, there would not have been an attempt made." He wished he could pull her into his arms, that she'd allow him the opportunity to offer her comfort.

"You think so?" Her voice was soft, husky.

He liked hearing it, so close, not distorted by vid audio, and within his reach. The void crushing his chest eased its hold, just as it had done when she'd first seen his face.

"Yes, as a strategist, all three of you doing your part was why it was successful. Now can you answer one of my questions?"

"Sure." Joy saturated her voice.

"Why do you not want to meet the king? Is he a monster?" Her fear of him annoyed him. *What could I have done to cause such emotion?*

"Oh, no, I don't think any Etterian can be a monster. I'm sure he's a male like other males, has needs and wants like the Lysaran king." Her sigh ripped through him, weakening his vow not to see her. "When I sing to a crowd, I lose myself in the music. I don't see the people watching me, I don't have to talk to them. What do I say to a king? To his sycophants? Why would they want to meet me, Macera Mitchell? Dull, unattractive me? And worst of all, I *know*, none of its sincere."

Dull? Unattractive? He scowled. "Maker, you are beautiful," he growled.

"Zoo, you've only seen my face."

"I saw a sec vid of you, as I stated. They are not of superior quality. And yes, I have been blessed to gaze upon your face, *ensa*, and your exquisite eyes," he said, admitting a little of his fascination.

"They're just brown," she said.

That she was dismissive of his words infuriated him. He wanted to grip her shoulders and shake her. "Your voice? Your sense of humor? Your birdsong? Are they brown too?" he demanded. "Lady Macera, an Etterian cannot lie. Doing so is against our code and honor. And if you feel you are being deceived, in court or anywhere else, you bring that matter to me. You comm me immediately."

She chuckled, the joyful sound unexpected and a balm to his ears. Yet another unknown emotion warmed his chest. What was this human doing to him? Or was the void closer than he'd thought? Could he be feeling random emotions before the final plunge? Was he so desperate for salvation that any human woman would do?

"I'll come right to you, my alcove guardian, I promise."

Her teasing spread his smile wide, splitting his cheeks. This was Macera's true character—joyful and playful.

"Why are you in the gardens? Also hiding away?"

Her innocent question struck true, and he jerked back. He drew in a sharp breath. "Yes. I too am lonely. I find the gardens bring me some relief. Flowers do not make demands of me or monitor my every move or second guess each decision I make." His eyebrows shot up at his response and the truth of it. Was that how he felt?

"It sounds like you work too hard," she said. "Maybe work is your purpose? I don't have one, you see. Having a purpose is the reason to climb out of bed in the mornings." Her chuckle was self-deprecating. He didn't like the sound of the false joy that didn't reach her soul. "I haven't had a purpose for a long time." She fell silent for a few minutes. "If you're in such an authoritative position, maybe you're too lenient with those idiots who dare to challenge you. The people who gave you the power trust you to do the right thing, make the big decisions and, above all, uphold your core values."

He shook his head. She was right. They *did* challenge him, and he'd let them get away with it. As an alpha male, he shouldn't have. He needed to be more commanding.

"So, be firm and decisive?" he teased, surprised that he still could and that he felt the need to.

Her answering giggle delighted him. "One or two of those idiots in the palace dungeons or peeling vegetables will teach them manners."

He laughed. It was coarse and unused. His chest warmed. It *felt* good not to guard his emotions, reactions, and the gate sealing the void within him. "If only we had dungeons," he said with a 'deep' sigh.

"Earth has so many. Send them there."

"Alodon's balls, can you imagine how much trouble they would cause?"

Her laughter was full-bodied and rich with emotion. "Then you're on your own on this." Her shadow rose. "Thank you for taking the time to talk to me. I'm feeling much better, Zoo."

"My pleasure, *ensa*. I will take your advice to heart."

"I'm happy if I've been helpful." She turned to go but hesitated, "Will you be here tomorrow?" Her hopeful tone pleased him. Feeling anything joyful, pleased him.

"Yes." And he would be. "I will be here tomorrow even if you do meet the king."

"Shit, forgot about that," she said.

He grinned, he couldn't help himself. It seemed she invoked responses within him that he'd thought had died.

"I better find my guards. I broke my promise. Why do I need protection, Zoo, when nobody knows I exist?"

Her footsteps had faded, but his scowl lingered. Not know she existed? She believed she was worthless. Anger burned. He wished he could force her to see how he saw her.

Cales approaching footsteps drew Xeus from his thoughts. He spared his battle-bond a glance.

"And what, do tell, are you doing?" Cales clasped his hands behind him.

"Regarding what?"

He gestured to the alcove. "Talking to a human woman through the vine?"

"She was crying. I offered comfort." He rose to march down the pathway to his office. Had he told Cales from the start, what would his battle-bond have said?

"Well, it seems like *she* offered *you* comfort. I have not seen you this calm in a while, my king."

Xeus frowned, not at Cales falling in stride beside him, but that his conflict had been so obvious.

"Only to me," Cales answered without Xeus having to ask—their bond was stronger than any blood-bond's. Cales was his usual perceptive self. "What was she like?"

Xeus rubbed his chest where a hot ache had taken up residence. "Like the other human women we have met."

"Yes, but this one brought you peace."

Macera did that and more. "Peace and wisdom, Cales."

"Are you meeting with her tomorrow?"

And he'd comm her later, like he always did. "Cancel the introductions to the court. If meeting me intimidates her, the other human women might be, as well. Perhaps revisit protocol on this."

"If the court questions this?"

"Tell them one single word of discontent and they will find themselves peeling poazo in the palace's kitchens." And to this he strode away, chuckling to himself. *Peeling poazo? A fitting punishment.*

Chapter Twenty-Eight

Planet Etteria

Issneen, the Royal City

An emotional rollercoaster (from Zoo to Myn-ras)

Nuos and Azan found Macy just as she stumbled on a wall running the length of the beach. She'd caught a glimpse of red waves breaking onto pristine gray beaches. Not that they'd let her linger. No, no way, bad prisoner must be returned to her cage.

Nuos had almost bitten her head off for breaking her promise.

She lost her shit.

What followed was a monolog of note. How she was an adult, had been alone for most of her life, wasn't used to being 'guarded,' and that they had to understand, this was all new to her. She'd squeezed out a tear. Best performance of her life.

They'd let her leave her prison but stayed so close to her ass, she couldn't change direction without bumping into one of them. When Myn-ras messaged her, and even though she'd known he would, he caught her with her pants down, so to speak. She was napping on a stone bench like a retiree. Nuos had watched her drool, and, as mortification burst across her cheeks, setting her face ablaze, she suspected, she'd snored too.

"Myn-ras is here," she said, marching past him. Staring at the diverting paths leading from the Royal Gardens, she stilled. "Which way to the Royal Court?" She faced her guards, resting her hands on her hips. She hadn't changed—still in her leggings and a baggy shirt that slipped off one shoulder, baring a bra strap. Having not washed her hair, it fell around her in wild disarray. She didn't care, or so she told herself. Myn-ras liked her for her emotional range. What did it matter what she looked like?

"Myn-ras?" Nuos didn't budge. Both he and Azan fell into threatening stances, their hands hovering by their blasters as if she was in danger.

She stamped her slippered foot. "Listen, he's my friend, and he's here to visit me. I don't know how much time he has, so, if you don't mind, I *need* to find him."

"We have not received information on your friend, Macy," Azan said.

"He's Lysaran, and I met him on the *Phoenix*." She threw her hands into the air when their frowns remained in place. "He's visiting with King Sy-mar."

"This way," Nuos said, striding off to the left, in the opposite direction she had headed.

She hesitated, not trusting him to take her to Myn-ras, but what choice did she have? The arched pathway leading to the imposing doors of the palace came into sight. She broke into a jog, hoping to make up for lost time.

Myn-ras waiting outside the door had her laughing, the joy at seeing his face warmed her chest and pooled in her stomach. She threw herself into his open arms, not minding that he buried his nose in her neck to inhale. She did the same but with less flare.

"You're here," she said, pulling out of his arms when Nuos touched her shoulder. Was open affection forbidden? She proceeded to ignore him.

"Of course. Ah, sali, seeing you pleases me." His easy smiles confirmed his words. "I feel as if the sun hasn't shone its warmth upon me."

She snorted. "I *feel* as if your melodrama is worsening. I'll have the royal medic check your condition."

"Your sass wounds me," he said but ruined it with a chuckle. "Indeed, my friend, it is good to see you."

"It's only been five days, Myn-ras." She wrapped her arm around his as she urged him to stroll with her. The pink blossoms were in full bloom and their fragrances heady. "How long do you have? Time for dinner?"

"Perhaps. King Sy-mar meets with your king now," he said.

Her step faltered. She had to accept that all considered her Etterian, although, she had yet to meet King Xeus. It was inevitable according to Cyndi's comm earlier, but she dreaded meeting any royal for that matter. Myn-ras fell silent as he escorted her along various paths and passages. The silence was comfortable, the heat flowing off his body welcoming and his deep inhalations amusing.

"Okay, quit sniffing me." She gave him a playful punch on his arm.

"You are content here, but a deeper misery has settled on your soul. What ails you, sali?"

She had forgotten how intuitive he was. The vid comms hadn't been along a similar vein since he couldn't smell her emotions across vast distances. "I'm lost," she said. Dropping her gaze to hide her tears was silly since he didn't use his eyes to read her. "I need a purpose, something to fill my time."

"You are finding your way. Have patience, it will come."

His calm response filled her with hope. She grinned at him before resting her temple on his upper arm. Renewed hope was breathtaking, and the way it flowed through her like heated honey opened her eyes to why her emotions swung like a pendulum.

"I have missed you, Myn-ras," she said, coming to a standstill when he paused in front of a door.

"Greetings, sweet Macera," Bry-dar said as the door opened to his devasting smile.

She stilled, her heart rate spiking. She wanted to smack Myn-ras for not warning her, as much as she wanted to bask in Bry-dar's open admiration.

"Macy?" Nuos shifted closer to her, concern furrowing his brow.

"This is Bry-dar, Nuos. He's also a friend, just a more persistent one."

"It is you who soars my soul." Bry-dar stepped back to allow them entry. "Your guards will wait outside."

She shot a glance at a bristling Nuos and sighed. "Then so do I, Bry-dar. They distrust everyone, so let them in and prove them wrong."

With a curt nod, he gave grudging approval. The apartment was a replica of hers with the windows angled to capture the sunlight. Nuos and Azan entered, taking position at the door. She fought an eyeroll but said no more.

"How have you been, sali?" Bry-dar yanked her into his arms, cupping one cheek to peer into her eyes. Gold swirled in the depths of his eyes.

She smiled, despite her best intentions to remain aloof. "I'm fine, Bry-dar, considering it's only been a few days since we last saw each other." She'd spoken more to Myn-ras, his calm a welcome relief from the turmoil of her thoughts. As much as she wanted a male of her own, she needed love and rainbows. Choosing someone because she was lonely didn't make sense despite their impact on her libido.

"Before my king returns, I offer my humble self as your mate."

She arched a brow at 'humble,' but his intense expression said he was serious.

Nuos growled a warning.

She darted her attention between them. "Bry-dar, can't you see you're reacting to my emotions overwhelming you and not to me as a person?" She wrapped her arms around him, giving him a brief hug before stepping back, trying to convey that she wasn't rejecting his friendship. "Like I said before, meet another human woman then we'll discuss my mating you."

"Macy," Nuos said in a warning tone, his posture stiff.

She frowned, facing him. "What? Can't I choose a Lysaran?"

That Etterians might be prejudiced toward other species hadn't occurred to her. Humans had abolished racism to the annals of history when they'd met their first alien species. All colors united under the banner of Earth, and they still celebrated Unification Day centuries later.

When Nuos didn't respond, she stomped her foot, tempted to wag her finger in his face. "You want me to mate an Etterian, don't you? Well, your Ethera decides that, doesn't it?" Anger burned hot and furious, and on its heels were the tears. She blinked them away and drew in a shuddering breath. Oyaz had said it was instant, so either King Xeus had denied his request, or there was no Eth for her. "My offer stands, Bry-dar," she said, marching deeper into the room to claim a comfy.

"Thank you," he said then scowled at Myn-ras, who chose the comfy beside her.

"How long is the journey between Lysara and Etteria?"

"Five days by battleship, shorter with a scimitar," Myn-ras said.

"You must have left soon after we did."

"I did not want to notify you until our arrival was imminent. Many events could occur to alter the plans of a king."

"It's good you warned me. I had so many engagements, I had to reschedule." She fought to keep her gaze down, hoping to hide her teasing from a contrite Myn-ras.

True to form, he reached across to gather her hand in his. "I apologize. I did not mean to inconvenience you."

"I'm kidding, Myn-ras," She threw back her head to laugh. "Oh, your expression was priceless."

A rapid-fire of their lyrical language flew between the two Lysarans with a scowling Nuos growling at them. She didn't know what they were saying, but their gestures were between delight, anger, and irritation.

"What's the matter?" she asked, silencing their tirades.

"I adore the scent of your laughter," Bry-dar said. "Myn-ras will not let me near you. Warrior Nuos is involving himself in our argument when he shouldn't."

His petulance had her laughing for two reasons. Three males arguing over nothing, and here was a male who wanted her but for the wrong reasons. The fates were cruel.

She hopped up and used the vid to push a comfy out. "There, then no one can sit next to me." She settled into her new chair. Bry-dar opened his mouth to speak, but she held up a hand. "Can you smell me from there?"

His expression darkened when Myn-ras nodded.

"What is the meaning of this?" King Sy-mar asked from the doorway.

Myn-ras and Bry-dar jumped to their feet as Nuos and Azan straightened their posture.

In the muted lighting, Sy-mar's skin glowed like soft caramel toffee. A sleeveless vest in ivory revealed ripped muscles and molded edges, all enhancing his broad shoulders. Braided hair, woven with beads and gold threads cascaded past his shoulders in a chocolate and ebony waterfall. Amber eyes rested on her, and she forced herself to swallow past the lump in her throat. His chest expanded as he drew in a massive breath, splitting the opening of his vest to reveal hardened abs. He prowled toward her with intent. The hairs on the nape of her neck rippled, and she closed her mouth, surprised to find herself gawking at him. How Sy-mar did this every time, she couldn't say. She leaped out of the comfy as if to beat a hasty retreat.

"Lady Macee, it is a pleasure to see you," he said, snatching her hand as he shifted closer to sniff her.

Heat from his touch slithered along her body and pooled in her core. A giggle slipped past her defenses, and she stepped back, recognizing the signs of a drug-induced high. This was too surreal for her, as if she were a goddess, gifted with the siren's song. She tugged her hand free, praying she didn't offend him, and took another step back, aiming her backside toward the door.

A scowl crossed the man's face, and she paused, drawing in a deep breath to explain. If she met King Xeus, she didn't want it to be a reprimand for insulting visiting dignitaries. "I see you are well, my kuna," she said, biting her lip when she purred the words. Heat from arousal or shame, or both, burst across her cheeks, and panic thrust another giggle past her lips. "I mean, I'm sorry, but...please excuse me, I'm late for another appointment. Myn-ras, it was lovely to see you." Like the coward she was, she ran, ignoring the Lysaran argument she heard as the door closed behind Azan.

"Sugar honey iced tea." She spat out a string of less polite curse words as she stomped down a random passage. "I've pissed off the Lysarans, haven't I?" She faced a disapproving Nuos, then dismissed him with a flick of her wrist. "Never mind, you'll only chastise me for my stupidity."

A chuckle escaped Azan, then an outright guffaw. "I have not been so entertained in years, milady," he said, fighting for breath. "Nuos should inform Advisor Cales of this incident. He will decide whether King Xeus should know."

"Why?" she gasped, envisioning prostrating herself in front of a larger-than-life Etterian male, begging him for forgiveness. The image left a sour taste in her mouth.

"You just ran from the King of Lysara," Azan said as they watched Nuos leave them, his strides jerky.

Ice chilled her spine, and she shuddered. If she'd accepted King Sy-mar's offer, she would've been in for a rollercoaster ride, one she'd enjoy. It was the lack of control over her senses that she didn't like.

Turns out, across the vast expanse of space, there was nothing scarier than a fruitarian.

She made it to her quarters and slumped against the wall. Azan left her after she promised not to leave her 'chambers.' What she wanted was a stiff drink. She marched to the rehydrator and ordered a brandy. Before she could gulp it down like an uncivilized ingrate, her O.D.I. zinged. She hesitated, expecting to see a summons to the court. Setting the tumbler down, she activated the O.D.I.

Ensa, are you well?

She sighed and tapped a hasty reply. *Zoo, I'm in so much trouble.*

Where are you? I will come to you now.

She paused, glanced at her trembling fingers, at her leggings and shirt, at her mass of hair reflected in the glass surface of the rehydrator, and moaned. *Tomorrow, Zoo. I'm tired, and maybe if I go to bed now, when I wake up, the universe won't hate me so much.*

Macera?

She sniffed then let the tears flow. A lounge singer on a mining colony might be in her future. *Good night, Zoo.*

Chapter Twenty-Nine

"Are you insane?" Macy scowled at Nuos, who made her repeat the exercise. She couldn't wrap her mind or her body around the position he had her do. "I feel like a damned pretzel." She pulled her leg up until her heel touched her hip while lying on her back.

"Oyaz said you would complain all the time."

"I did it to irritate him." She giggled. "Still do." That the big sun had yet to rise both males ignored, because dammit, she was in the royal gardens pulling a body miracle. "Is this payment for not listening to you?"

Heat burned her cheeks that had nothing to do with the pretzel-move. There'd been no repercussions since yesterday. King Xeus hadn't summoned her for decapitation, and Myn-ras had commed her as usual. Despite his sensual appeal, her friend was better from a distance. Safer.

"No," Nuos said, but his brow furrowed as if something bothered him. "Your confidence was lacking. It puzzles me, Macy. What affected your judgment and personality?"

She sucked in a sharp breath, tears stinging her eyes. "Their admiration, as misplaced as it was. I've never experienced that." She changed sides, twisting away from him as she tugged on her ankle. "I'm lonely, Nuos. I have been since my grandmother died."

"So you will mate with the Lysaran if he meets your stipulations?"

"I don't know." She closed her eyes against the temptation of it, to belong to someone. Desperate for a subject change, she glanced at Azan guarding from a distance. "Why doesn't he join us?"

"Someone must be observant. He listens, though." Nuos's grin was cheeky.

She loved it. He wasn't stick-in-the-mud, which meant her plans to corrupt Nuos were well underway. Sadness uncoiled in her chest. She missed Oyaz, and her bed felt empty without Illan beside her.

"Do you know, this morning I couldn't feel my backside. Some exercise Oyaz had me do paralyzed the largest muscles in my body."

"I thought your tongue was the largest muscle," Nuos teased.

"Very funny, smartass."

"Keep complaining, and we will finish with sparring," he managed, his eyes twinkling.

She fell silent, biting her bottom lip to prevent words from escaping. It didn't work. "Damn gorilla," she mumbled.

"We have almost completed this morning's training. Then we can cleanse and have breakfast. A Spanish omelet with a creamy cappuccino?"

"Evil gorilla," she said, but damn him, he did know her favorites. Did Oyaz keep a dossier on her? "I will do ten more of these stupid pretzel-moves if you try my breakfast." Since he adored chocolate, she wanted him to try cheese.

"Deal."

Without further complaint, she did her extra exercises before bouncing on her toes, her usual buoyancy returning. They abandoned her in her chambers to shower and returned fifteen minutes later. Together, like the Three Musketeers, they meandered to the Royal Dining Hall where real food was served. Nothing human yet, but that was only a matter of time if they found more Dar Eths.

She hid her smile and coughed to smother her chuckles when they cleaned their plates. Their appreciation was over-the-top enthusiastic. The idiots, like she couldn't see they'd tried it before. The flavors and textures of the omelet were enjoyable, which the rehydrator somehow did to perfection. She expected the eggs to be rubbery or too mushy, but no, light and fluffy. While sipping her cappuccino and licking the cream off her lips, she pondered how she was going to ditch them to meet with Zoo.

After her tearful performance yesterday, the sweethearts had agreed to give her about fifteen minutes of quiet unchaperoned time. Nuos had been adamant. She wasn't to leave the gardens, mumbling something about risking their hair in doing this for her. Whatever that meant. She flashed them a grateful smile and bolted out of the hall.

So, at the first opportunity, she ditched her guards with their permission and disappeared into the extensive royal gardens. It had a surprising lack of green yet was still breathtaking. Such colors and fragrances, all strange yet comforting. If given half a chance, she'd wander it all day until hunger drove her to 'locate' her guards or their hunger drove them to 'locate' her.

She couldn't complain. Out of all the warriors, she had Nuos and Azan, two of the sweetest guys. They cared, in their way. Although being Etterians, they never showed intense emotion, only anger. But she was working on that. Not for the last time did she wonder what that must be like. To not feel? So, when she managed to make either of them smile or laugh, she considered it a huge accomplishment. Nuos had a naughty streak. She loved that about him. Azan was too reserved. He hadn't laughed since the Lysaran incident.

When they collected her, she directed them to her chambers. Time spent on the scarf was in order. Music in the background and quiet without her guards would be lovely. And she should start a new wardrobe at some point. Living with the same sets of leggings and shirts was becoming boring. Maybe something floral with sandals? Or long skirts brushing the floor? Mm. Splashes of color? She giggled at her plans as she whiled away the time.

After a rehydrator chicken, sweet pepper, and lettuce sandwich for lunch, she waited outside the front door. Bouncing on her toes, she did pirouettes like an amateur while splaying out her arms for balance. Nuos and Azan said nothing while they escorted her to the gardens. When they followed her in, her pulse leaped. How could she chase them away without being rude? A shiver skittered down her spine. Having them eavesdrop put a damper on...well, things. She faced them, but they'd stopped and taken up positions a good distance away.

She waved and meandered over to the alcove, a little earlier than the usual time. Every minute counted. She hoped Zoo came earlier too. A memory of her gran's scowling visage made Macy straighten her spine, as if she was caught slouching. Right, don't get attached. Men...males didn't stick around. Truer now than on Earth. If she grew to love Zoo, what would she do if her Eth or Bry-dar fetched her tomorrow? She was fond of Oyaz and Illan, but neither had 'liked' her, as evident by their willing abandonment. She was being unfair, considering Oyaz was a soldier and his superiors had commanded he leave. And Illan was elbows-deep in a treasure trove of Durn knowledge he'd believed they'd lost for all time.

Zoo made her feel safe, important, like she mattered. He was Et-terian, his choice of endearment wasn't like Myn-ras's 'sali.' But with the Ethera in play, it meant Zoo could never be more than a friend. Still, she hoped he stayed around. That he'd such a sexy voice didn't, in any way, sway her affections toward him. His baritone was deep, sometimes hoarse, but gentle. She'd liked it the moment he'd first spoken to her in Sosu. She harumphed then stumbled as she lost her balance. Bry-dar and King Sy-mar had dazzled her senses, but with Zoo, heat coursed along her nerve endings, flooding her with energy that tingled, but she was still herself. That was good, wasn't it?

When she peeked at Nuos and Azan, they hadn't moved closer. She didn't have the words to explain who Zoo was and blushed just thinking about it. Well, they'd find out soon enough.

The exotic chirps of birds, the suns' warmth on her face, and a cool breeze lifting her hair off her shoulders called forth a smile. She burst into song, her choice melancholic and about seeking love. She hadn't belted out a song in a while, not since the *Phoenix*. Perhaps that was why the loneliness was winning. She skipped through the gate to the fountain and grinned at a carafe and glass waiting on the bench. *How sweet.* Zoo's rather large shadow darkening the vines was missing, so she seated herself on her side, poured a glass of blue liquid, and carried on singing.

If he couldn't make it today, she'd be fine with that. He had thought of her, and that was all that mattered.

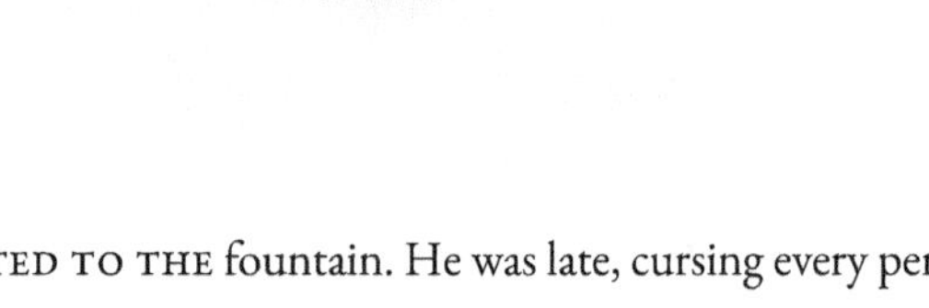

XEUS SPRINTED TO THE fountain. He was late, cursing every person and task that had led to his delay. He couldn't understand the need to see her. The urgency pierced him, the pain unbearable. He circled the hedge with his long strides, making certain he didn't come from the side that would reveal her. When she was ready, he'd vowed.

It was the sound of her sweet birdsong that slowed his approach. Whatever she'd chosen, it was poignant, and as he neared her, the words punched him in the gut. They were riveting, how she asked her lover to help her soar, how she cherished him when she was sorrowful, how he was all she'd ever need for peace to come.

"That is beautiful." He cleared his throat when awe vibrated in his voice.

She squeaked then laughed. He grinned, basking in the sound of her unrestrained joy.

"I didn't hear you approach."

"I hope not. I would not be an Etterian if I did not silence my footsteps." He lowered his bulk to the stone bench and sighed, as if he'd come home. It was a strange emotion, serenity, when he'd nothing to be content about.

"My guards stomp," she said.

"To let you know they are approaching."

"That's so sweet." Her smile saturated her voice. "Are you okay?" Her lips were close to the vine, her palm brushing across the leaves as if she meant to offer him comfort.

"Yes, I am well." And he was.

The darkness that had tormented him had relinquished its barrage. His focus was no longer to exhaust himself to sleep. Now sleep remained elusive because of her, and no amount of training aided. He found himself wondering, throughout the day and at inopportune moments, what she was doing. He had watched the sec vids again, wishing he could see past the filth, to see the suns' rays play upon her hair, to test the softness of her lips, to stare into her eyes and know their color intimately.

"Any new vegetable peelers this wonderful morning?" She chuckled. "Though, if there were, it wouldn't be a happy day for them."

"No, none have tempted me to punish them. For once, I was looking forward to their irritation." There was truth in his words. He had eyed his councilors with an eagerness he'd, until now, never experienced. "Did you leave any blood-bonds or friends behind?" He wanted to know if she'd someone she valued, someone she might be missing, a male she belonged to. Though he didn't like the thought of it, he also didn't like her in pain.

"No, just a hungry dog that will be missing me. Though he probably wouldn't for long."

"Dog?" He waited for his O.D.I. to update him.

"An animal kept as a pet. It was a stray I had taken to feeding until I couldn't afford to anymore." Her voice faded, drifting off on a breeze.

She was so emotive, his Macera. "And that makes you sad."

"Yes," she whispered.

"Your dog looked like the wild dogs Oriana killed in the Arena," he mused aloud.

"Who is Ori-Oriana?"

He frowned. How best to explain? "She is Enyl's Dar Eth."

"Prince Enyl?"

Xeus stilled. Alodon's balls, how was he to know she'd heard of Enyl? And what could he say? Stating Enyl was his son would reveal who Xeus was. And with her fear of meeting King Xeus... He pinched his brow. "Yes."

"How do you deal with royalty? I assume you're high up there, having to work with ambassadors, advisors, and visiting dignitaries." Her breath rushed out of her, though what that meant, he didn't know.

Was she referring to the Sy-mar incident? Xeus swallowed a chuckle. When Sy-mar had revealed she'd run from him, Xeus had to admit he'd struggled to keep his laughter in check. "A royal is a person, *ensa*. No more, no less."

"Yes, but after what happened, I expected to be dismissed, shipped off to some abandoned planet or a prison colony." She rested her temple on the vine, so close her warmth penetrated the leaves.

Straps cinched around his heart and squeezed. Not once had he considered she might be worried about retribution. "Sy-mar is a close friend. He would not harm a female, *ensa*. Especially you."

"Thank you for the beverage."

"My pleasure," he said.

"Did you find your Dar Eth? Or is that a rude question?" Her words tumbled over each other. "I'm sorry if I've offended you."

He shook his head before remembering she couldn't see him. "No, no Dar Eth for me. Some would think I am too old for one."

"How old are you then?"

"In Earth years, I am forty-two."

"That's not old, not at all. Rior's an older Etterian, and he's still attractive. You both deserve to find your Dar Eths." He appreciated the smoky passion in her voice as she defended him. "On Earth, we call the forties naughty."

"Naughty?" His breath hitched. *Did she mean sexually?*

"I can't remember the fifties. Naughty forties, dirty thirties. I turned thirty-one last week."

"Did you celebrate it?" Silence met his question. "Is that a no?"

"Yes."

"If you could celebrate it, what would you do?"

"I don't know. Birthdays sadden me. Something bad happens when it's my birthday. It's why I don't tell anyone. Strangers wish me happy birthday, but they don't know *me*." Her shoulder ruffled the leaves when she shrugged. "Do you celebrate your birthday? Is that an Etterian thing?"

"I do not have a choice. Everyone attends an event held in my honor. As you stated, they do not know *me*. The celebration is more for them than for me."

"Shit, that sounds worse than mine. I only have a few insincere well wishes. You have an entire room." The goblet clinked against the carafe. "Anyway, happy birthday. Hugs and kisses. Hope you have many more." Her sincerity rang clear.

It was the best felicitation he'd received in a long time, even if it wasn't his birthday. "Happy birthday to you too, Macera."

She gasped. "Well done, even with my proper name. So formal."

He chuckled then frowned when Cales approached him. *Was it time?*

"Did you have the meet-and-greet canceled?"

"Meet-and-greet?" he echoed, while Cales wiggled his eyebrows at him.

"Yes, with the king and his court?"

He nodded, then realized she couldn't see him. "I suggested a private session instead."

She thrust her hand through a gap to clasp his arm. A bolt of white fire traversed from his arm to his chest and stayed there. "Thank you," she said, relief making her voice breathless.

He captured her fingers to brush his lips across them, wishing he could do more. "I have to go."

"Duty calls, I suppose." Her shadow remained seated when she withdrew her hand. "If anyone gives you attitude, toss them on their ass." Her laughter was husky sound that twitched his semi-arousal. "It will make you feel better."

"I may do that. Until tonight, Macera." He'd taken to comming her every night, just to let her know he was thinking of her. And Maker, was he.

"Goodbye, Zoo."

He pressed his palm to the thick vine as a farewell. Inhaling one last time to capture her scent in his lungs, he followed Cales.

"What happened now?" He rested a full scowl on his battle-bond.

"Your next appointment." Cales nudged his head in Macera's direction. "I do question your plan, though. As much as her joy calms you, where do you think this is going?"

"Nowhere," he said. Where could it go? "I like her company, and the anonymity eases her fears."

"Did she tell you to toss one of the ambassadors on their asses?" Cales laughed. "I would help."

"And to be firmer with the idiots, as well."

"I have said as much over the years." Cales scowled.

"Yes, but she is an outsider. You hate all the ambassadors, so any violence you recommend, I must temper."

"True." Cales smirked.

Chapter Thirty

Planet Etteria
Issneen, the Royal City
The following morning before the crack of dawn.

"WHAT ARE YOU WEARING?" The horror in Nuos's voice spread to his face, twisting it.

Feeling self-conscious, his stunned question made Macy more so. She wore a white semi-transparent sarong over a vintage-style swimsuit. The one-piece was a navy-blue halter top with low-cut legs. She looked good in it, and it was comfortable. On her feet were dark blue sandals, and she held a wide-brimmed straw hat in her left hand.

"I'm dressed for the beach," she said, aware both males stared at her bare legs where the sarong ended mid-thigh.

"You cannot swim," Azan said, his gaze on her toes. She fought the urge to wiggle them or tuck a foot behind the other. "There are omeika in the waters."

Her disappointment slumped her shoulders, and she thumped her hat on her thigh. "What's omeika?"

"They're carnivorous fish. They leak a red ink which stains the waters."

Like a piranha meets squid? She scowled. Shit, so no swimming at all? "Is that why the oceans are crimson?" At Azan's nod, she messaged Zoo. *Remember when you said you'd take me to a beach? Are there carnivorous fish?*

The omeika? No, ensa, the Galaza beaches are free of them.

She bounced on her toes. So going to the beach wasn't a complete hell-no. *Oh? What color are the waves then?*

Still red.

Nuos leaned closer to sniff her, ending her chat with Zoo.

He stumbled back, his nose wrinkling, as if she'd slapped him. "What is that stench?"

"Stench?" She frowned, anger stiffening her shoulders. Lifting her arm to her nose, she smelled nothing but coconut lotion. "It's sunblock so I don't burn."

With a harumph, she slammed her hat on and grabbed the new beach bag, ignoring them as she hurried to the royal gardens. There had to be a path that led down to the beach. And if this was the way her guards reacted to her outfit, she shuddered to think how the males walking by might act.

At the audacity of it all, she slowed her pace and strolled in the direction of the beach. She greeted every male she passed, ignoring their gawking at her state of 'undress.' Like it damn well mattered? A plain girl with fat legs was an anomaly? The velvet texture of a hahyt petal tempted her to stroke it, causing Azan and Nuos to bump into her. She snorted, wondering why they thought hovering close to her could diminish the effect of a human woman in a swimsuit.

"Do you never go to the beach?" She lowered the bag to the ground to undo the sarong and rewrap it under their watchful gazes.

"No," Azan said, anger hardening his features before he surveyed their surroundings.

"Etteria has reserved the eastern beaches for visitors. Those waters are too warm. The Omeika do not gather there, so it is safe to venture in," Nuos said, his gaze meeting hers and not dipping lower.

He was super pissed with her if she judged the ticking at the base of his jaw. She grinned at him without a smidge of remorse. *What does he have to be furious about? He's acting as if I'm walking around naked. Dammit, you'd swear I'm irresistible.*

"Your loss." She shrugged, scooped up the bag, and strolled in the general direction of the beach. "Please direct me, or else I will remain in the gardens as is. Hell, I might even eat dinner in the hall."

Nuos grumbled but did as she asked.

The ocean breeze greeted her as she took the stone steps to the gray sand. She removed her sandals, left them on the steps, and stepped onto the soft heated sand, moaning as her toes sank. She drew in a deep breath, savoring the almost-familiar fragrances of the sea before she trudged to the middle of the beach. She dug into the bag and whipped out a beach blanket, spreading it on the sand. She then pulled out a small bucket and spade. With those items in hand, excitement coursed through her, tightening her grip. For once, she looked forward to something, even an afternoon spent on the beach.

"Can I dip my toes in?" She shielded her eyes as she peered up the wall where both males had chosen to stand guard.

"Up to your ankles and no more, Macy. I am serious," Nuos said.

She hid a giggle. *He is serious? I couldn't tell.*

Unwrapping her sarong, she tossed it onto the blanket. She grabbed the bucket and spade and raced to the waves crashing on the beach, her braided hair swinging out behind her. The water was cool and refreshing on her bare feet. With a squeal of delight, she scooped up water and threw it a meter or two away from where the waves ended. Once she'd a sizeable section of damp sand, she dropped into the middle of it and began to compact it into the little bucket. This was turning out to be the best damn afternoon she'd had on this silly pink planet.

"WHAT IS THE MEANING of this?" Xeus strode toward Macera's guards. Cales was close on his heels and not looking too pleased either. Every male Macera had encountered had informed Xeus of her attire and her destination. And after her brief comm about Galaza, he believed every report.

Nuos and Azan stood at the stone wall, vigilant yet minus the presence of a tiny human woman.

"We are standing guard, my king." Nuos gestured behind him but didn't turn to indicate her precise location.

Xeus scowled and marched to the wall. He pressed his hands on the top to lean over it, searching the beach. He hadn't expected a semi-naked Macera digging in the sand. Not that he could see her as well as he would've liked. Her back was to him, and her hat shielded her face from him. But her bare skin glowed in the sunlight, upon which her thick braid rested. The vision of her was a thousand times better than the sec vids. And yet, he couldn't see all of her. Just like the vines, he caught glimpses of her.

She filled and emptied a container.

"Alodon's balls, what is she doing?"

She jumped out of the hole she'd dug as a wave ventured closer than anticipated. She squealed with laughter, stamping the water as if admonishing it for its intrusion. Her joy was infectious, delightful to hear, twitching his lips in response. Her profile was exquisite. His breath hitched as white heat flooded his chest and lower, hardening him. He raised his nose to scent her but wrinkled it instead.

"Potion. She has applied it to her skin to protect it from the suns," Nuos said, who must have noticed Xeus's reaction.

He growled when she dipped her feet in the water, just deep enough to fill her tiny container. He zeroed in on her bare legs, all the way up to her backside. Maker. His eyes stuttered shut at the sight of her.

"I have made her aware of the omeika, my king."

At Nuos's statement, Xeus spared him a glance. This he knew already. When she'd asked about the color of the waves, he'd chuckled. "What is she wearing?"

He fixed his gaze on her dark blue-encased backside, unable to resist the urge. His bloodline color on her made his heart leap into his throat with an intensity that snatched his breath.

"She did not say, my king," Azan said, still facing away from her.

Cales drew alongside Xeus, watching as Macy scrambled to her blanket. Xeus wished she'd raise her gaze to him. But she did not.

Instead, she laughed as she kicked at the sand before collapsing onto the blanket. For a few minutes, she lay on her back, staring at the sky. She twisted to grab a beverage out of the bag, took a few sips, then jogged back to the hole.

"She packs the container full of sand then extracts it to build a wall," Nuos said.

"And she finds this enjoyable?" Cales frowned, arching a brow at Nuos.

"Yes, Advisor," Azan said. "She has laughed and talked to herself throughout the afternoon. She speaks to us, knowing we can hear her."

"My king, Advisor Cales, good afternoon."

Xeus faced the female and frowned. She shouldn't have surprised him. Humans didn't move on silent feet.

Lady Cyndi wore a loose flowing dress, her feet sandaled, a hat in one hand, and a bag in the other. "Macy said she'd be here this afternoon, so I thought I'd join her."

"Lady Cyndi, please do not venture into the water—"

She waved her hand at Nuos, smiling as she silenced him. "Stow it, warrior. Iddan has given me the lecture." With a quick curtsey at Xeus, she strode down the path and the stone steps to spread her blanket beside the other. She stripped off her dress revealing a skin-tight outfit similar to Macera's but in pink.

"Cyndi, I need your help. It's the ugliest castle I've ever built." Macera chased the waves to scoop and toss more water.

"Here, give me the bucket, while you rinse off. You have sand all down your back, it's even in your hair."

"I do not." Macera tossed the container and her hat at Cyndi before laying down in the shallow water, across the flow of the waves. She threw her hands back to support her as she arched to dip her long braid in the water. But when a wave hit her, she giggled and collapsed, allowing the water to flow over her. "I'm swapping sand for more sand."

Her wet body caressed by the ocean's waves had Xeus riveted. *Please, look up, my Macera. Let me see all of you.*

Cales cleared his throat. "King Xeus, your next appointment—"

"Is canceled," he growled.

"Warriors, stand guard on the beach," Cales commanded, and the moment they were alone, he gripped Xeus's shoulder. "You cannot go down there. She trusted you not to see her until she was ready to reveal herself."

Xeus frowned at Cales for the reminder. *Yes, I did decide in her time. But the need to see her, for her to see me, is driving me.*

"You are an honorable male," Cales said.

With a scowl at those words, Xeus threw one last glance at Macera and stormed off.

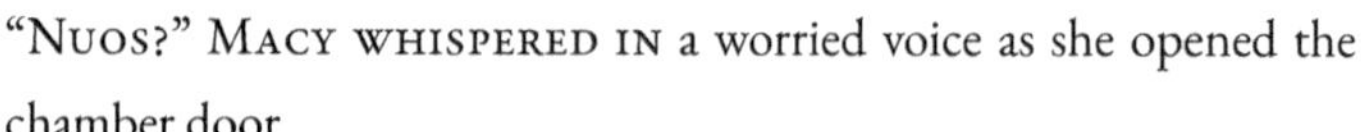

"Nuos?" Macy whispered in a worried voice as she opened the chamber door.

Nuos stiffened but refused to look at her. After the day he'd been through... He wanted to cleanse and climb into bed. The quicker he ended this day, the better. Since she'd yet to attend dinner, they remained on duty.

Sighing, he peeked when she didn't close the door. Her skin glowed red, and even from this distance, heat poured off her.

"Yes?" He faced forward, still furious with her for making him lose his boots and build the sandcastle with her and Lady Cyndi. For the hours after that...torture, she had sprawled on her stomach or back, reading a...book made of paper. Time had dragged on when they'd lunched on the beach before Lady Cyndi had ended the day.

"Do you have a medic I can call?"

At Macy's words, Nuos frowned and studied her.

"I don't think your suns like me." She forced a smile before dropping it.

"Why is your skin red? Is this normal for a human?" Azan's eyes were wide.

"Yes, when exposed to too much sun." She shrugged then whimpered.

Azan typed on his O.D.I. "Medic Aldur, the king's medic, will attend to you," he said.

"You're not burned?" Her gaze traveled over Nuos's face and parts of his upper body. "Dammit." She twisted her lips. "I'll be under a cold shower. You can send him in. I'll be in my swimsuit, so decent." The door closed behind her and in Nuos's scowling face.

"Decent?" he growled. "There was nothing *decent* about her attire."

"At least we now know that she calls it a swimsuit," Azan said.

"Good, knowing its name is so beneficial."

At Nuos's tone, Azan's brow hitched. "You sound like her."

"You did not have to—" He bit his tongue.

Playing in the sand like a *damu* hadn't been terrible. But he was still finding sand in strange places on his body. He commed the king, regarding the name of Lady Macy's garment. He violated protocol, but he suspected that Advisor Cales wouldn't forward this information. It wasn't critical to Etteria, but judging by the king's expression, it had been important to him.

Medic Aldur ran toward them, his eyes narrowed in concern. "What is it?" he asked, drawing to a halt in front of them. He wasn't out of breath, still in excellent shape for a male his age.

"Lady Macy spent the afternoon in the suns, and they have *burned* her," Nuos said.

"*Burned?*" Aldur jerked back.

"Her word, Medic Aldur," Nuos said.

"She awaits you in the cleansing room and wears a revealing garment, so prepare yourself," Azan said. "She considers herself well-covered."

"In the cleansing room?" Aldur frowned.

"Please proceed," Nuos said, opening the door for him.

Aldur entered, striding to the cleansing room.

Nuos trailed him and assumed guard outside that door the moment it closed behind Medic Aldur. He was able to listen in on the conversation despite it violating protocol. He did so for her safety, not that he expected Aldur to harm her, but he did expect to give King Xeus a full report.

"Milady?" Aldur said. "I am Medic Aldur."

"Oh, thank the Lord, you're here," she said with a moan. "Please, help me. I hoped the icy water would stop the burning."

"Burning? Please, step out of the water so that I may scan you, milady."

Her sigh of relief penetrated the walls. "Thank you, Aldur. That feels amazing," she said, her gratitude clear. "Can you recommend a sunblock so this doesn't happen again?"

"Sunblock? We do not have such a potion."

"You don't?" she gasped.

"Are you still in pain, milady?"

"No, thank you so much. In the past, I usually spend a few miserable days in agony while my skin heals. I assume I won't peel?"

"Peel?"

Nuos smothered a chuckle at Aldur's spiked voice.

"Yes, when we burn, some of us peel. I'm one of those lucky few who do."

To Nuos, it didn't sound like a good thing.

"You should not peel. The med-gun has healed you."

"Thank you, Aldur, for hurrying over. I appreciate it."

"I am pleased to aid you, milady," Aldur said, as the cleansing door opened.

Nuos remained where he stood while she escorted the medic to the main door.

"Guys, I'm calling it a night. I'll eat something from the rehydrator if I'm hungry," she said, standing there as if she wore more than a thin...swimsuit.

"Are you well?" Nuos ran his gaze over her normal skin tone. She was wet, with water droplets running down her body. Satisfied that she was no longer suffering, he slid through the door to stand beside Azan.

"Yes, Aldur worked a miracle. Thank you for calling him for me, Azan." She smiled. "Still angry with me, Nuos? Was it *that* bad?"

"No," he said with a frown before grumbling, "...I have sand everywhere."

"Yes, but was it fun?"

"It was...interesting." He couldn't bring himself to remove her smile.

"Next time, Azan can help me." She winked at Nuos.

"Agreed. Goodnight, Macy." After she closed the door, he nodded at Azan. "Never a dull moment."

"The barracks is this way," Azan called.

Nuos ignored him, heading instead to the royal chambers. With the way the king had reacted to Macy, Nuos expected a summons at any moment.

Chapter Thirty-One

THE SMALLEST SUN HAD just risen, and Macy wandered the gardens again. Going to bed so early had her awake sooner. The beach outing hadn't exhausted her as much as she'd hoped. But the sunburn had put paid to her visit with Zoo in the afternoon. With nothing to occupy her days except knitting and ordering furniture, sleeping was becoming elusive. It was still another half an hour until Nuos would torture her again.

The moment she'd opened her door, the two males had come running, grumbling at her about the change in routine. Not that they were disheveled in their military uniform. She wondered if she should mention that, to her, they looked midway between a biker and covert ops. She giggled. *Sure, aliens in black leather, why not?*

She ignored their grumpiness and lifted her face to the sky. The dawn streaked across the dark-pink horizon with several shades of pink and orange. It was so beautiful that she sighed, blissful and content.

She strolled, trying to find the path leading to the white wall parallel to the beach. Nuos had led her to the wall yesterday, but she hadn't paid attention to the route taken.

The path ahead of her grew wider and with less bluish grass. She didn't mind. Her slippers were on the ground a few bushes back, and the soft grass pillowed her bare feet. Maybe the grayish sand marking the pathways would feel as good as the beach had.

Nope, it did not. It was like coarse gravel. Wincing, she glanced over her shoulder to where she'd left her slippers or her guards, but nothing was behind her. *What? Did I take a turn I wasn't aware of?* A *thump* and a grunt coming from ahead, behind yet another blue bush, drove her forward. She picked her foot placement, hissing with each step.

As she rounded a bush, she froze in place.

An Etterian male swung a greatsword. He was bare-chested, and sweat glistened on every mouth-watering muscle. Tight breeches hugged his gorgeous and firm backside, riding low on his taut stomach and revealing an Adonis belt. Clinging to his hips too, low enough to reveal two dimples at the base of his spine. And damn, those large thighs... He had amazing thighs—strong, muscled, sculpted.

His feet were bare. How did he manage that on the rough gravel? *Tough warrior, tough feet?* She smothered a chuckle. He swung his sword with such precision and fluidity that it was like a dance, graceful, perfect. With every swing, his arms and chest rippled. He'd grunt, and his long braid would whip around him, as if it had a mind of its own.

Now, this is a fine specimen. The best Etterian male I've seen to date.

She stood there for who knew how long. Watching him was such a pleasure. And when she said pleasure, she meant *pleasure*. Her nipples were harder than diamonds, and she was damp...down below. She blushed just thinking about...her nether region. For almost a month now, these gorgeous males surrounded her, and only this one had stirred something powerful within her. The Lysarans didn't count. These reactions were all her. Her body hummed, flushing her skin with a tingling heat that prickled her scalp. Just like when she'd gazed upon Zoo for the first time, or when he'd kissed her fingers and knuckles.

Her sexy specimen stilled even though she hadn't made a noise. Maybe she'd gasped? He called for such a response from her. Maybe he could hear her heart beating since it pounded in her ears. He faced her, and her ovaries broke out into full applause. Then to make matters worse, her lady bits clenched with need. *Shit, he's gorgeous.*

Wait. She knew that face. *Zoo?*

His gaze met hers. With a violent groan, he collapsed to one knee. With full force, he plunged his blade into the ground, up to half its length. He clenched his hands around the hilt. He wasn't looking at her now, just kneeling there and trembling as if in agony. Whatever had felled him had to be overwhelming to bring down such a powerful male. She hurried forward, ignoring the rough gravel, and dropped next to him, the loose stones bruising her knees.

"Are you okay?" She raised a hand but hovered inches from his hot skin, uncertain. Without knowing what was causing the pain, she feared touching him in case it was a rash or a sunburn. Although, his skin glowed with health, all bronzed and velvety. He smelled good too, like cut grass.

He groaned again. His knuckles whitened when he tightened his grip.

"Should I get help?"

He shook his head and shuddered.

Helplessness paralyzed her. "Want me to leave you alone?" She chewed on her bottom lip, not knowing what else she could do.

"No," he growled.

She released a drawn-out sigh, sat on her backside, and crossed her legs. As she waited, she drew swirls in the rough stone, content to ogle every inch of him. He was in pain, but he was being stubborn, and short of offering him her back—which was the ultimate in rudeness—she could do nothing else but admire him. This close...was wow. No male should look this good. She sucked in a deep breath and ran her hands over her thighs, itching to touch him.

Down, girl. This is Zoo, remember?

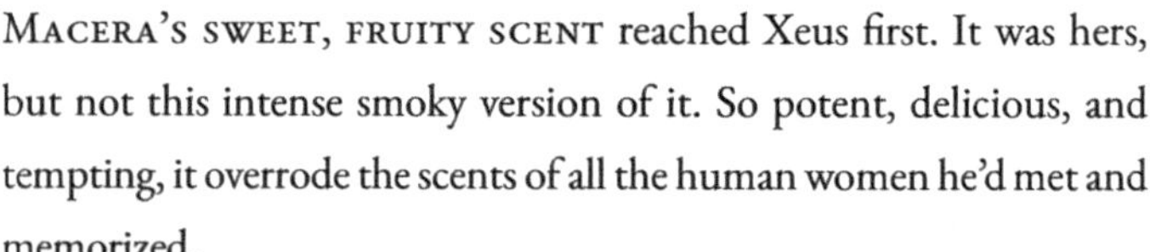

MACERA'S SWEET, FRUITY SCENT reached Xeus first. It was hers, but not this intense smoky version of it. So potent, delicious, and tempting, it overrode the scents of all the human women he'd met and memorized.

Is she aroused?

Fury tore through him, casting his concern aside. He spun to locate her. Why was she aroused? Who would dare to touch her? Her admiring him, her brown eyes wide in her small face, her breasts rising and falling in her tunic, her tiny feet bare, and the richness of her arousal

298

registered one by one. Then the pleasurable torment had lanced his heart and taken him to a knee. The heat curling in his belly was to an unbearable degree. He shivered as a chill ripped along his skin.

A vision of her came next. Her smile, her eyes closed as she feathered kisses across his lips. He could *taste* her soft lips, *feel* her incredible breasts pressed against his chest, the slickness of the heated water, her legs entwined with his. She purred with pleasure. He shuddered, tightening his hold on the hilt, trying to control the urge to touch her, claim her, right there under Etteria's pink sky.

Her scent came with her when she approached him, intensifying with proximity, shaking his control further. She spoke to him with concern, her voice husky and appealing.

His Dar Eth.

Watching her draw shapes in the sand made him release a great, whole-hearted laugh, despite the pleasurable pain burning through him. He was so pleased to have found his salvation and thrilled it was his Macera.

"Feeling better?" she asked after his laughter dwindled, not understanding that he never laughed.

Now he had the urge to. The intense emotions exploding in his chest were liberating yet unexpected and unknown.

"Yes. Thank you for your concern." He frowned as he leaned back on his heels.

"You have mesmerizing eyes." She peered into his eyes; her mouth parted. "What happened to your dark blue irises?"

He groaned, looking anywhere but at her.

"My alcove guardian," she grinned. "Zoo."

His breath hitched, and his gaze flew back to hers. Her smile...so perfect.

"I didn't mean to disturb your training." She shifted to rise, not realizing he was staring at her blue-encased legs.

"You are never a disturbance," he said, frowning at her tiny toes. *I want to suck on each one.* But that wasn't what bothered him. "Where is your footwear?" He gazed upon her upturned face, taking the time to admire her now that he could do so. She was on her knees, half-risen.

It had been a while since they'd vid-commed. But the Ethera made this more potent.

Long brown locks cascaded around her in wild abandonment, falling to her elbows in gentle waves. Her eyes were brown and slanted upward at the corners. She had brown arching eyebrows, and the way they dented was expressive. Her nose was short with a little dimple on the tip, tempting him to press a kiss to it.

Her lips were full, pouting, and pink, the color of his hahyt flowers. They appeared soft...sweet...alluring. They dusting of spots across her cheeks still fascinated him. He must have been silent for too long. She chewed on her bottom lip with her tiny white teeth, shooting a dart of need to his groin. He grumbled, his breathing becoming uneven again.

"I lost them somewhere there." She flicked a hand indicating behind her. "And Nuos and Azan too."

Xeus frowned, trying to recall what they were discussing. "They knew I was here. You are safe with me." He marveled at the many emotions bursting inside him, some he couldn't name.

"I've always thought so."

His chest swelled at her words. He scooped her into his arms, unable to resist holding her, to protect her soft feet from Etteria's harsh stones. She squeaked and latched onto his shoulders. At her touch, he trembled, his nipples pebbling. He ignored his body's reaction and strode to where he could scent her guards waiting.

"Going to tell me your name? Or should I keep calling you Zoo?" She leaned her head against his chest. Her skin was cool, her touch both bliss and torture.

He dipped his head to nuzzle her, rubbing his jaw across her hair. "I like the anonymity. I am invisible but never anonymous. It is a new experience for me."

She cupped his cheek. He marveled at her audacity to do so, to touch him without hesitation. "I see you."

He stopped to gaze at her. "Thank you. It is all I've ever wanted, for you to see *me*." He brushed a kiss across her cheek, enjoying her shiver in reaction before taking that leap of faith he'd advised Xan to do. "My name is Xeus."

"As in King Xeus?"

He nodded, watching her expressions. *I could lose her in this moment, not that I would let her go. I need her more than I can express.*

"Damn," she chuckled, shaking her head in disbelief. "Zoo for Xeus? And I suppose once I reached Etteria, you couldn't tell me because I was nervous about meeting you?"

"I meant to offer comfort, unknowing that I was the cause of your distress."

"I know you meant to help. Thank you for that." She smiled before a thought shadowed dread across her adorable face. "Do I have to get to know the king now?"

"I hope never. I wish for you to know only me, your Zoo."

Her eyes widened with delight as her cheeks pinkened. "Is this serious?" She indicated the two of them with her fingers while she peered into his eyes.

"More than you will ever know." He fought the need to kiss her, even though she was his now.

"Are you sure?" The warmth of hope in her eyes swelled his chest in response.

"You took away my loneliness." His honesty brought such a rush of color to her face, but she leaned up to brush her lips across his jaw.

"You took mine away too," she said, clinging to his shoulder.

"You were sad." He'd known she'd been yet not liking that she'd suffered as he had.

"Not anymore," she said. "Zoo?" Her melodic voice drew his focus. He waited for her to continue. "Is this the same as what Xan and Quin have?"

"The Ethera?" he asked, needing her to know the word.

Her exquisite brown eyes were large in her tiny face. "Yes."

"Would you like it to be?"

"I don't want it to be anything else than what it is, but I also don't want to meet another male, and he turns out to be my Eth." She glanced at his chest before meeting his gaze. Fear and something intense crossed her face. "I don't want to give you up."

His pulse paused at her honesty. "You *are* my Dar Eth, Macera. The mate of my heart," he said, his voice hoarse. "There will be no other male, no other Eth. An Etterian male's eyes change color when they meet their life force, *ensa*."

"Like yours did?" Despite the excitement trembling her body, a frown furrowed her brow. "Does that make me a queen?"

"Automatically." He didn't doubt she'd make a wonderful queen.

"Can't I have you without being a queen?"

Maker. He crushed her against him. *How many females have thrown themselves at me in the hopes of securing that position? And my Dar Eth wants me alone?*

"I do not deserve you, Macera." He gathered her closer, but it wasn't enough.

"Zoo, I—"

"My king, is Lady Macera injured?" Warrior Azan asked.

Both warriors stilled at the sight of his ice blue eyes. They glanced between Xeus and Macera, their jaws slack. Then as one, they bowed.

"My queen," Nuos pledged, with a fist to his chest.

Xeus threw a pointed look at her, to which she rolled her eyes. When she wiggled, he lowered her to the ground, though he kept her back pinned to the front of his body with his arm looped around her waist. The weight of her breasts resting on his forearm made him more aware of her warmth against his harder edges.

"Azan? Nuos?" She folded her arms across her chest. "It's me, remember? The troublesome human female always grumbling at you? Just because Xeus's eyes change color doesn't mean I'll stop irritating you."

"You do not, my queen," Azan said.

"I thought Etterians don't lie," she said.

Azan flushed at her implication.

"I like your singing, my queen," Nuos hurried to add.

She sighed and glanced at Xeus for assistance. He flashed her a lopsided grin—delighted to watch her do anything.

"As your queen, I command you to call me Macy." She turned back to Xeus, "Can I do that?"

He nodded with another grin before tugging her into his arms, succumbing to the urge to hold her. Yet that didn't seem to satisfy the need driving him. He lifted her, wrapping his arms around her back to press her against his chest.

"What are you doing?" She gazed at him from her new position. Where she clasped his biceps, her fingers stroked his skin, her touch arousing.

"Holding you. I am in awe, Macera, and so grateful." He admired her face, attempting to memorize every inch of her. Her scent and her softness surrounded him, at last, making him ache with pleasure.

"You are? It's just me, Zoo," she said.

"Just you is perfect for me." Another smile cracked his cheeks. He marveled that he could, that he wanted to, that the darkness consuming his soul had evaporated. The light within him was almost blinding, and she was at the center of it.

She cupped his face, her fingertips on his temple, her palms at his cheeks. "You are perfect for me too."

He tightened his arms, needing her melded to him. "I would kiss you now, yet I fear I will not stop once I taste you, Macera." His voice plummeted below guttural as he lowered his gaze to her too-tempting lips.

They parted with a gasp under his watchful gaze. "You...find me attractive?"

He frowned at her surprise, at her disbelief. "Attractive? You *are* beautiful, my Macera. Feel how holding you makes me tremble."

"It's my weight straining your muscles." Her teasing crinkled her eyes in the corners.

He chuckled before burying his face in the curve of her neck to inhale her scent. Emotions warmed his chest, overwhelming in their intensity.

"I tremble, I cannot breathe, my heart pounds, and I am harder than our mined rock." He grinned as pink color splashed across her cheeks again. She licked her lips. The dark depths of her mouth called to him. "If you do not want me to claim you here and now, you will behave."

Her mouth snapped shut. "Behave? In what way am I misbehaving? I'm not the one going around picking me up or promising to kiss me yet not delivering."

She returned her hands to his shoulders before wriggling in a silent request for release. He held firm, despite the sensations now flooding his body from her movements. A deep groan shredded his throat.

"You are tempting me beyond my control," he said.

She stared at him. "I am?"

He growled at her astonishment.

"King Xeus, good morning." Cales strode toward them. "I thought to find you here but not so indisposed." He indicated the female in his arms. When Xeus didn't acknowledge him, instead, he nuzzled her hair off her ear, Cales continued, "Your first appointment is—"

"Canceled," Xeus mumbled, expecting Cales to hear him. "Cancel the day, Cales. I wish to spend it with Macera."

"You want to do nothing with me?" She trailed her hands from where they gripped his shoulders to loop around his neck, bringing her softness and scent closer to him. He rumbled his approval.

"I do not care what we do, as long as I am with you." He lifted his head to smile at her. "I could take you to Olivia's."

Macera's eyes twinkled. "Olivia's? Is that like a restaurant? A spa?"

"It is an orphanage we brought from Earth."

"You have human children on Etteria?" The joy on her face was unmistakable.

"Yes, here we cherish them." He lowered her feet to the floor, pausing to ensure she regained her balance. Keeping his hand at the base of her spine, he faced Cales. Touching her didn't appease the Ethera's demands, but it would do for now.

"I assume your training is also canceled, my queen?" Nuos asked.

Xeus chuckled. "As your queen, she controls your future. Keep pushing her, and she might send you to the omeika farms."

"Please forgive Nuos, Macy, he teases as you taught him to," Azan said.

"My queen?" Cales's voice was a whisper. He bolted forward, halting in front of Xeus to stare into his ice blue eyes. "Alodon's balls, Xeus. I hoped. I prayed."

"Thank you, my old bond." Xeus laughed, unable to curtail the joy, the freedom that saturated every dark corner of his being. "This is Macera Mitchell. Macera, this is Cales. He is my oldest battle-bond and most valued advisor."

"A pleasure to meet you, Cales." She held out her hand.

He accepted it with reverence, not shaking it, just holding it. He stared at her upturned face, his dark blue eyes traveling over her features.

"The pleasure, no, the gratitude is mine, my queen."

"Not you too," she groaned.

Cales stiffened. "Have I offended, my queen?"

"She does not want to be queen, Cales. She only wants me." Xeus couldn't stop grinning. When he tried, it split wider, defying his efforts. "Now, if you do not mind releasing my Dar Eth…"

Cales dropped her hand and stepped back, his cheeks darker than a moment ago.

"We will inform the court this evening. For now, I wish to spend the day with my Dar Eth, and Maker willing, without a care in the world."

"Perhaps a tunic?" Cales ripped off his to toss at Xeus, who caught it then pulled it on.

"Nuos, Azan, I shall see you at 0430 tomorrow," she said.

Nuos lowered her shoes, placing them on the ground at her feet. Then with a quick bow, they strode away.

She glanced at Xeus, who watched her slip on her footwear. "I've you to protect me, don't I?" Her eyes sparkled as a small smile curled her lips.

He gripped her tunic's fabric. "You do." But she had no one to protect her from him.

Chapter Thirty-Two

As Xeus led his Macera to the new gardens behind his palace, he snuck glances at her, disbelieving this gift, this blessing. That he held her hand in his helped to assure him that it was the truth. He had been blessed with a Dar Eth, the very same female who had haunted him. Her brown hair flowed behind her when she moved—the freedom of it stirred something unnamed within his chest. He inhaled, hoping to memorize her scent now that she was his, his queen, his salvation.

"You keep glancing at me, Zoo," she said before flashing him a shy smile.

"I never expected to find my Dar Eth, Macera."

"Because you think you're too old?" She arched an eyebrow.

He traced the shape of it with a fingertip, finding it soft too. "Yes, I believed I was lost."

She clasped his tunic, just above his nipples. "Not lost, too impatient." She smiled at him to soften her words. "Look at me then, Zoo. If I am yours, as you say, then you are free to look and touch."

His heartbeat tripped as his gaze traveled over her features.

"As am I," she said, fluttering her fingers up and over his collar-bones to his shoulders.

His eyelids stuttered at her gentle touch. "To look is to touch is to taste, *ensa*. I am not strong enough to resist you."

Tiny bumps feathered over her skin as she shivered. He liked how she reacted to his words.

"If you were Etterian, I would claim you now," he added in a gruff whisper.

"But I'm not." She glanced away but not before he caught the shimmer in her eyes.

"No, you are precious as you are, so soft and sweet-scented." He smiled. "So passionate." He captured her hand in his, eager to move while resisting the temptation to toss her over his shoulder. And when he had her there, he'd take her to Crustiiu—the heated pools hidden in the rocky cliffs behind the palace. "Which is why the children will make excellent guards."

She frowned. "Why are you not claiming me now?"

He groaned as images flooded his mind as per his vision. "I have little control. I will not risk losing it and harming you, my Dar Eth."

Her eyes grew huge.

She is so expressive, my human.

"I'm here when you need me, Xeus." She squeezed his hand.

He was unable to speak. She was there for him when he was ready, and he valued her courage in telling him this. By the pink on her cheeks, discussing such a subject wasn't normal for her. He opened the gate and ushered her through, closing it behind him before urging her down the path to where the children played.

"Uncle Xeus." Lily ran up to him to throw herself into his arms.

He kneeled to catch her but didn't release Macera's hand, unable to do so. "Hello, Lady Lily, how have you been today?"

"Did you hear I have a new daddy?" She gave Xeus many hugs and little kisses.

"Yes, I have. Nerx is a good male."

"He's my daddy," Lily said before glancing at Macera.

"Hello, Lily," Macera said. "Do you like living here?"

"Pink's my favorite color." Lily giggled and gestured to the pink sky, her tiny pink leggings, and matching baggy shirt. "Daddy let me choose this morning."

"Don't tell Uncle Xeus, but my favorite color is the blue of his eyes," Macera whispered into Lily's ear.

He stiffened then slid his hand along Macera's back to squeeze a hip. Her softness filled his palm but also allowed him to draw her closer.

The little girl winked at Macera, gave Xeus another hug, and skipped away. He rose to his feet, and as he did so, he looped an arm around Macera's waist, pulling her into his arms.

"I want to kiss you so much," he mumbled, as he buried his nose in the curve of her neck.

"Juice time." Olivia's voice traveled across the playground. Macera's head shot up. She slipped out of Xeus's embrace, unaware she did so with his permission. "Hello, Xeus," Olivia said and gave Macera a welcoming smile.

"Hello, Olivia." He strode over, grabbing Macera's hand as he swept past her, tugging her with him. "This is my queen, Macera." His gaze remained on Macera's upturned face. Not once did he glance at Olivia, not even to lose himself in her junix-colored eyes like he used to.

"Your queen? I didn't know you had a wife?" Olivia smiled even as her eyebrows dipped in confusion.

"It just happened, within the last hour." Macera chuckled. "The Ethera makes it immediate."

"That...is amazing." Olivia clasped her hands together while beaming.

"I know, right?" Macera laughed, squeezing Xeus's hand. "Found a male yet?" she asked Olivia.

"She will soon. They will come to gaze upon her *junix* eyes." He smiled at Olivia, pleased to be able to do so.

"They are beautiful, Olivia." Macera faced him. "Did you receive a request from Oyaz about communicating my image to all your males?"

"Yes, and permission was given," he said, though the decision had cost him a sleepless night. "I didn't receive the comm. Had I seen your full image, you would have been my Dar Eth sooner." He leaned in to whisper, "I wanted you to be mine for so long."

She gazed into his eyes, then rested her hand palm-down on his chest. Contentment flooded him with sweet warmth. He covered her hand with his, trapping her there.

"Couldn't we do the same for Olivia?" Macera asked before glancing at Olivia to see if she'd agree to such a process.

"Would you be comfortable with such an imposition?" Xeus caught Olivia's hopeful gaze. "I will have Cales attend to it before his departure." He activated his O.D.I. to send the instruction, releasing Macera's hand to do so.

"I'm so pleased to meet you. I've been bored since I got here," Macera said. "Quin is somewhere with Xan, and I haven't seen her since we landed. Cyndi is with Iddan and too busy to spend much time with me. Is there anything I can do to help?"

Olivia patted Macera's forearm. "Come on by whenever you're free, and we'll find something for you to do. Just playing with the children helps."

Macera squealed and hugged Olivia. Her energy vibrated off her and triggered an answering response in Xeus. "If I had only known," she said. "There are many things about life on Etteria I wish someone had told me."

"Come on in. The children are having their juice and cookies if you'd like to join them." Olivia entered the modified barracks.

Macera spun instead and threw herself into his arms. Her unexpected affection had him crushing her against him, grateful for any contact.

"What is this for?" He rubbed his chin back and forth across her temple.

"I hate being bored. Doing nothing drives me crazy," she said into his neck, inhaling his scent as he did hers. "You smell like sunlight and cut grass."

He shivered as she released him, forcing him to lower her down his body. Her expressive mouth parted on a breathless moan before she bounced away from him only to turn back to grab his hand and pull him behind her.

Cales arrived to comm Olivia's image to all his males. In the meantime, Macera played with the children and told them the incredible story of her kidnapping and escape. She often slid onto Xeus's lap as he'd seen Lady Ava do to Kanzo. Protectiveness swirled within Xeus among other emotions he still couldn't identify nor control. Xan's words replayed in his mind, making him realize his control was under attack. Where it had bothered Xan, it delighted Xeus.

Macera sang to the children, the words charming, the rhythm hypnotic. The pace increased, and the children joined in, laughing and bouncing around the room as much as Macera did.

Alodon's balls. She has passion and fire, my queen.

"I've been matched?" Olivia cried out. Her voice silenced the birdsong.

Macera clapped her hands to draw the children's attention to her, then moved over to the display vid to choose an entertainment vid for them.

"Who?" She clasped Olivia's hands.

"He's seven-feet tall?" Olivia gaped at Cales as she stared at the pixelated image on his O.D.I.

Xeus shifted closer, drawn to Macera. He slipped his arms around her for a hug. Her breasts rested on his forearm, pleasing yet tormenting him.

"Supreme Commander Syna," Cales, understanding Xeus so well, said to him when he'd arched a brow in query.

"He is a good male, strong enough to protect all your children," Xeus said to Olivia while he rubbed his chin across the crown of Macera's head, unable to stop himself.

"He *is* handsome." Olivia's smile was slow to form.

Macera snorted. "All Etterian males are handsome. It's to find the one that makes your insides melt." She glanced at Xeus, her lips curling into a smirk. "And before you call a medic, it's just a saying."

"What does it mean, my queen?" Cales frowned.

Thankfully Olivia answered since Xeus drowned in the swirling brown of Macera's eyes. "Your heart beats without a rhythm. You can't breathe when in his presence. You'd pin him to a wall and have your way with him if he let you."

"Yes to the latter," Lady Ava said, entering the barracks. Some of the children cried out in excitement and rushed to hug her.

"Hello, Ava. Where's Kanzo today?" Olivia asked.

"Cales has him running around. If he's too exhausted to tend to more important matters in the evenings, meaning me, I *will* comm you, Cales," she said. "So what's this about melting your insides?"

"Olivia has an Eth," Cales said, unfazed by Lady Ava's threat. He tilted his arm to show Syna's holographic image.

"Let me see?" She tugged Cales's wrist toward her. "Wow, he's amazing. Seven feet? *Damn.*"

"Don't let Kanzo hear you." Olivia laughed. "Come meet Macera, she's King Xeus's Dar Eth."

Ava's head shot up. Her pale-green eyes widened in delight. "If anyone deserves a Dar Eth, it's Xeus. Welcome, Queen Macera." Ava hugged Macera as best she could with Xeus's arms still around her.

Cales glanced up from his O.D.I. "Syna will arrive in three days. He is on the battleship *Usaha* en route to Issneen, having abandoned the battleship *Chikara* to Sub-Commander Cylo." He lowered his arm and nodded at Xeus. "I've commed him and requested he recommends his replacement."

With a whispered thank you, Xeus gathered Macera close.

They had lunch on blankets spread out on the blue grass. He hid a smile. She was aroused. Her intoxicating scent tantalized him, smoky and intense. She squirmed, unable to find comfort. Her pebbled nipples were visible through her tunic, and she blushed every time she glanced at him. Her hooded gaze told him what she wanted to do with him. If it wasn't for the children, she'd be beneath him now.

"Are you not hungry, my Macera?" he asked.

She took a quick bite of her untouched sandwich. If he didn't leave her this afternoon, he'd claim her. He shuddered at the thought. One or two things needed his attention. Informing Enyl of this was the first item on his list. Citus, as well. With that in mind, he leaned across to drag her onto his lap, wrapping his arms around her as he inhaled her scent deep into his lungs.

"Will I see you at our alcove, the usual time?"

Her gaze swung to meet his, alarmed. She studied his face then nodded, letting a small smile tease her lips. "Yes, Zoo," she said. "I look forward to it."

"So do I." He pressed a kiss to her temple and shifted her off his lap, his fingers curling into her hips with a reluctance to release her. Bounding up, he forced himself to leave, his hands clenched at his sides.

MACERA WAS WAITING FOR him when he approached their alcove, this time from the side where she could see him. There was no need to hide anymore. She'd plucked a hahyt blossom and brushed it back and forth across her cheek, humming to herself as she stared dreamily at the clouds.

Maker, she takes my breath away.

She must have sensed his presence since her gaze focused, and she turned to meet his gaze. She gave him such a sweet smile, spasming his balls.

"You came." She bounced on the bench then patted it beside her. "Did you do what you needed to?"

He had commed his status change, he'd cleansed and dressed in appropriate garments, including boots, and he had no other appointments other than to present her to the court this evening.

"Yes, I informed my son and brother," he said, lowering his bulk onto the bench next to her.

Unable to resist, he laced his fingers through hers and drew the blossom out of her other hand, only to run the petals along her forearm. Raising her arm to his nose, he inhaled her and the hahyt's scents combined. He rumbled his approval.

"I met Kanzo," she said. "He adores Ava. It was beautiful and embarrassing to witness. He gazed at her with such an intimate expression of love that I felt like I was intruding." Macera blushed when she glanced at Xeus.

"Love?" He knew what it meant before his O.D.I. informed him.

Strong affection for another arising out of kinship or romantic interest.

As far as I'm aware, Etterians do not feel love. They experience the Ethera, perhaps that is love? This volatile, uncontrollable addiction to another being?

"The Ethera?" he asked.

"Is that your word for love?" Her temple furrowed.

He ran a fingertip over it and marveled as the ripples in her skin faded.

"We train out our emotions and, therefore, cannot recognize complex emotions. What does love mean to you?"

"There are many types of love. The love of a parent, of a friend, a brother. But the love Kanzo has for Ava is none of those. It's an all-consuming emotion... I don't know how to explain it, Zoo."

"Have you experienced this love?" he asked even though the thought of her loving another male gritted his teeth. He blinked away the red haze from his vision and forced his shoulders to relax. She was his now.

"No, but I know it exists." Her belief in this *love* was evident. "To be someone's universe, to sleep, dream, breathe just one person as if your existence rested on their wellbeing? A love like that would be wonderful."

"And you saw this in Kanzo?" Xeus would make sure to study his new advisor and Lady Ava together.

Macera snuggled into his side. He raised his arm to draw her closer, wrapping his arm around her shoulders. Because he couldn't help himself, he pressed his lips to the top of her head.

"About tonight, is there something specific I need to wear? How formal is it?"

"You would allow me to...dress you?" A sharp pain crushed his chest, and he tightened his arm around her, disbelief blurring his thoughts.

"Why wouldn't I? They are your people and customs. I need your guidance, Zoo. I don't want to disappoint you."

He dropped her hand and pulled her onto his lap, wrapping his arms around her to nuzzle her neck. "You could never disappoint me, *ensa*. To allow a male to choose your garments is to announce you are pleased and are willing to mate with him."

"It is?"

"Your garment will be in dark blue. You will look magnificent in my color, my Dar Eth," he said.

Fresh pink stained her cheeks and she lowered her gaze, hiding her expression from him.

"So any garment in dark blue?" she asked, a tempting curl to her lips but not a full-fledged smile. "I can wear my swimsuit then?"

Before realizing she teased him, he drew in a sharp breath. He released it with a sigh of relief. "I will ensure you have the appropriate garment, my Dar Eth. It is my duty, my honor to see to your needs. And as to your swimsuit, it is only for me to see. You are mine, Macera. I do not like to share what is mine," he ground out with utter conviction.

She shivered but the expression she bestowed on him wasn't one of fear but of awe.

"How long do you have this afternoon?" She ran her fingers along his forearm, the softness of her touch settling peace deep within him. "To spend with me before duty calls?"

"I've no appointments, no urgent missives."

"You're mine for the day?" She jumped up and grabbed his hands, as if she could lift him off the bench.

He rose with a chuckle and followed her, seeing that she led him to the beach. At the last few stone steps, she paused to toe off her footwear and rolled up the bottom of her blue breeches. Then, as she sank her toes into the sand, a bliss crossed her features, making him Fuyra hard. He grumbled but removed his boots, rolling his pants up as far as he could, which wasn't far since they hadn't been designed to do so.

And yet the moment he sank his feet into the soft and heated sand, he gaped at the exquisite sensation. *I've never known.* He wiggled his toes, unable to still them in the shifting sands.

"Feels good, right?" She dipped to peer into his eyes.

"Maker, Macera, this is remarkable."

She laughed and laced her fingers through his hand again, then urged him to follow. He did so with more eagerness this time. He marveled at the cool waves then at the heated sand and in repeat, at last understanding her appreciation of this part of his world. His gaze rested on her upturned face she held to the suns' rays, her eyes closed, and with such a peaceful expression. He felt shame then. Etteria was his to protect, yet he hadn't appreciated the true gift that it was.

"Do you think the children would love to come here?" he asked, though he'd need to task more males to protect them. Omeika *did* infest his oceans.

"That's a brilliant idea, Zoo," she said. "I think you should suggest it to Olivia."

"*You* should suggest it." He looped his arms around her waist to hold her against him. A breeze lifted her hair off her shoulders and covered his arm and shoulder with her suns-baked locks. *I'm in heaven.*

"No, you're the sweet and considerate male to think of it. I want all of Etteria to know how wonderful you are."

His chest swelled at the intense emotion in her eyes. "Sweet and considerate does not sound intimidating," he teased.

"True." She chuckled. "All right, I'll suggest it. We can't have our enemies believing you've gone soft in your old age."

"Soft? Old?"

She slipped from his arms to scurry away, her laughter tinkling in the air.

He realized as he chased after her that he was…joyful.

And at peace.

Planet Etteria
Issneen, the Royal City
The Royal Court
That evening.

XEUS STILLED WHEN KANZO and Lady Ava stepped through the doors leading into the court. His avid gaze sought out his Macera, eager to scent and hold her. It had been less than an hour since he'd escorted her to her waiting guards. He'd activated her replicator from his O.D.I. and ordered the ceremonial wrap according to her stored measurements. Even footwear for her tiny feet.

He struggled to calm his erratic heartbeat. Energy coursed through him which made standing still impossible. Not that he cared whether the court accepted her or not. They didn't have a choice. The Ethera had chosen. Not even he, the Great King Xeus, could reject the Ethera. He was simply anxious to be in her presence.

Her brown hair swirled around her as she laughed at Nuos trailing her. Judging by his darkened cheeks, he was blushing. Then she stepped into the court... The dark blue and gold of her ceremonial wrap didn't go unnoticed.

Xeus stared, mesmerized as she strolled toward him. The wrap accentuated every curve, the blue as stunning on her as the swimsuit had been. Pink glowed on her cheeks from their afternoon on the beach, and her eyes sparkled. She bounced as she moved, her vibrant life force so potent he could almost scent her emotions. As she headed for him, a bright smile spread across her cheeks. At that moment, he was the most blessed male on Etteria.

This marvelous creature was his Dar Eth. He held out his hand to her, and she accepted it, content to allow him to draw her into his arms.

"As my final announcement this evening before I embark on a mission for Etteria, please welcome Queen Macera, King Xeus's Dar Eth." Cales gave them a welcoming smile.

Court members pressed in to 'congratulate' them, but their true intentions were to stare into Xeus's eyes, confirming the validity of her claim. His chest swelled as he watched her. But when Ambassador Tamra approached, he stiffened. He twitched to stand by Macera's side. Yet to do so would undermine her authority.

"Breathe, my king. I advised her to be firm but welcoming," Kanzo said from beside Xeus before abandoning him to join Ava.

Xeus wiped away a scowl. Welcoming? His Macera was every-thing he was not—kind, sweet, joyful, and spontaneous. What was he thinking, leaving her to face his stern people alone. But it was too late. Tamra had reached Macera.

Tamra peered down her nose at Macera, who beamed at her, un-aware of the hatred swirling in Tamra's dark eyes. Alongside his queen in his bloodline color, Tamra in pale yellow formed a striking im-age—tall, statuesque, her thick braid falling to her heels. Macera, with her wild hair, lush lips, and stubborn little chin was infinitely more beautiful to him.

"And you are?" Macera asked, clasping her hands in front of her.

"Ambassador Tamra," she hissed.

Duly unimpressed, Macera's eyes twinkled with unsuppressed hu-mor. "Do you like poazo, ambassador?"

Tamra jerked back, a frown furrowing her brow. "I do not under-stand the question."

That she didn't grant *Queen* Macera respect had Xeus wishing he could have a foot of honor taken from the female. *How dare she speak to his Macera that way?*

"Well, *Tamra*," Macera dropped the ambassador title while leaning in as if to whisper, "I once advised my *Eth* that a stint at peeling poazo in the palace's kitchens would do his ambassadors a world of good." She patted Tamra's forearm. "I assume you're not a difficult ambassador to deal with."

Tamra gasped, her eyes wide. "King Xeus would never allow you—"

"Allow? My Eth is most generous." Macera glanced at him and smiled. "Such an honorable male, is he not?"

"Well, he can be stubb—"

"Is he not, Tamra?" Macera scowled and raised her fingers to tap each one. "You haven't addressed me as befitting my title. Strike one. You show dishonor toward your king. Strike two. And just because I'm not Etterian, you think to intimidate me? Strike three." When Tamra gaped at her, Macera gestured Nuos over. "It seems the ambassador has yet to see the palace kitchens. Do give her a tour. Perhaps have her peel a poazo or two."

"As you command, my queen." Nuos thumped his chest before escorting a muttering Tamra from court.

"You may have made an enemy, Macy," Azan whispered.

Macera flicked a dismissive hand. "Humans fight for what is ours. Xeus is mine, as determined by the Ethera. To not accept that is to laugh in the face of your tradition. I won't tolerate either." She grinned at Azan. "But it might be wise to add combat training to my morning sessions."

He chuckled. "Indeed."

Word traveled through the court for what awaited those dis-respectful. Xeus groaned when Ambassador Brenin cut a swath through the gathered crowd. The male took a moment to stare into Xeus eyes before gripping his forearm and flattening his palm on his chest. Such an unexpected gesture from his most argumentative ambassador snatched Xeus's breath.

"This...gives me such hope. My congratulations, my king." Brenin fell into position beside Xeus to survey the court. "A human as queen is not what I expected for Etteria, but...the Ethera has chosen. And she dismissed Tamra well." He didn't glance at Xeus when he said, "A trying female."

"Thankfully, not all our females are so ill-mannered." Xeus grinned when Macera laughed at something Lady Keryr said, their temples almost touching as if they were *damu* planning mischief.

With Keryr on her left and Azan to the right, Macera swept through the crowd. None spoke a harsh word about her or him, fearing a session of poazo peeling.

"Ingenious," Brenin whispered when Nuos returned with an almost docile Tamra. "I shall threaten the same in my house." He thumped his chest and abandoned Xeus.

"When Brenin approves, I cannot but be concerned." Kanzo sidled closer, bringing Lady Ava with him.

"Indeed. Let us adjourn," Xeus said when he realized Macera's vibrancy was fading. He gathered her near and escorted her into his office where they waited for Cales, Kanzo, and Lady Ava to join them.

"You did so well," Lady Ava said, squeezing and releasing Macera's hands. "You were regal and diplomatic."

"I tried." Macera shrugged before stifling a yawn. "I'm so sorry. It's been an exciting but long day." She snuggled against Xeus's chest.

He wrapped a protective arm around her, rubbing circles on her back to ease the tension in her muscles.

"It did go well," Cales said, but his excitement was more for his impending journey.

Xeus scooped Macera up, holding her in his arms as he lowered himself into a comfy. It adjusted to accommodate them.

"Did I...do well, my Eth?" Her wide eyes revealed her uncertainty.

"You are beautiful in every way, Macera. And how you handled Ambassador Tamra was admired by all." He gave her a pleased smile.

She responded with a sweet one, her fingers embedding in his tunic. "Do you depart tomorrow?" he asked, raising his gaze to rest on Cales.

"Yes, the battleship *Usaha* has been burning at full pulse to reach Issneen."

"Isn't Supreme Commander Syna on that ship?" Lady Ava asked.

Cales tapped his O.D.I., no doubt checking on the battleship's location. "Yes, it wouldn't surprise me if Syna arrives sooner than that, using a scimitar to hasten the journey. It is right that an Eth is eager to claim his Dar Eth."

"Regardless of your departure time, Cales, all of Etteria is with you," Kanzo said, gathering Lady Ava within his embrace. She gazed at him for a long unguarded while.

It was then that Xeus saw this *love* Macera had mentioned. A timeless warmth passed from Kanzo to Ava and back, something he was uncomfortable witnessing while being mesmerized by the intense bond between them.

He wanted that connection with Macera, understanding now why she revered it. Wondering why she was quiet, he glanced down. She'd fallen asleep with her face pressed against his chest, her soft mouth parted, her delicate fingers resting over his heart. Warmth flooded him, and he tightened his arms, keeping her near.

"Safe journey, my battle-bond." Xeus bid Cales farewell as he rose from his comfy, giving him a nod before slipping through a side door and out onto the stone passage.

Azan and Nuos ran to assist.

Xeus shook his head and whispered to remain silent.

Azan hurried ahead to hold her door open so that Xeus could stride through to her room unhindered. He lowered her onto her bed and pulled a blanket over her. He sat on the edge of the bed, brushing the curls off her temple to tuck behind her ear.

My Macera.

My Dar Eth.

My queen.

My...love? Dare I hope?

Chapter Thirty-Three

XEUS WAS ON HIS way to meet Macera as per their old ritual. He hadn't seen her, not since he'd laid her down to sleep the evening before. She'd attended her morning training with Nuos, had breakfast in the dining hall, and spent the morning with Lady Olivia. Xeus was too eager to see her at their alcove. He'd just reached the outside walkway when the skies opened, and the rain poured down. He sighed. *Now what?* He hurried toward the other entrance with long strides. Perhaps they could meet in the archives?

It was the sight of Azan and Nuos standing on the covered walkway that halted him. They had their backs to the rain. *She is not out in this downpour? Is she?*

He bolted, bursting into the rain without stopping to look first, the deluge drenching him in seconds. She stood there, soaked through, spinning, and laughing with her arms outstretched. Her white shirt

327

was saturated and clung to her body. He groaned at the sight of her breasts and pebbled nipples. His mouth watered.

"Macera?" he growled as he approached her, not willing to hide his longing a moment longer.

She stopped spinning, lowered her arms, and smiled at him. Water glistened off her eyelashes and plastered her hair to her head, but it was her glorious joy that broke his control. He yanked her against his chest and crushed her to him. One hand clasped her cheek as he slashed his mouth over hers, kissing her as he'd yearned to do.

He rumbled his approval, at her sweetness, the heated silkiness of her mouth, at her soft lips under his. She clung to his chest, and with a roar that tore out of him, he lifted her off the ground, crushing her breasts against him. Now at his eye level, he proceeded to conquer her mouth, accepting and defending when she brought her tongue to meet his.

"Maker," he rasped as he abandoned her mouth to brush kisses along her jaw, to latch onto her earlobe to suck.

She whimpered, fisting his wet tunic.

He traveled back along her jaw to claim her lips again, nipping at them, swirling his tongue in the recesses of her mouth. He was Fuyra hard, but it didn't matter. Nothing mattered but the taste of her, the feel of her against him. He had craved this, as revealed by his morning chore. He hadn't realized just how much.

"I need to kiss you more often," he said into her mouth before plunging in again.

She moaned, wrapping her legs around his hips to cling to him. He wanted her legs spread, just not in the rain and not clothed. Tugging on her braid to arch her back, exposing her throat to him, he pressed open-mouthed kisses along the length of her neck, across her jaw to claim her mouth again, marveling at the sheer joy and heated pleasure coursing through him.

"Your taste is incredible," he said, allowing his breath to mingle with hers, wishing he could meld his soul to hers for an eternity.

"Your taste is addictive," she said, running her tongue along his bottom lip, making him shiver in reaction. She raised her arms to wrap around his neck, then kissed him, claiming him as he'd done her. He crushed her to him, tight enough that a Maloidian dagger couldn't pass between them. He ached for her heat and softness more than he needed to breathe.

When she shivered, he realized she was cold, not that she gave any indication it bothered her. But he minded that she was cold, his Dar Eth. Cupping her backside, he marched, not releasing her lips once until he reached her chambers. He broke off the kiss, trembling for another reason unrelated to the rain.

"Cleanse, dress, and I shall meet you in the archives, *ensa*." He lowered her feet to the floor.

She gasped when she encountered his interest in her, and the heated glance she gave him snatched his breath. He opened the door and urged her inside, fighting his body's demand he follow her. After the door closed, he stared at it, despite knowing Nuos and Azan hovered nearby.

"When she is ready, escort her to the archives," he said before heading to his chambers to cleanse.

He commed Kanzo on the way, informing him to reschedule his next meeting, that there'd been a delay. *Not that I consider kissing*

Macera a delay. Alodon's balls, anything to do with Macera is never an intrusion.

He rushed through his cleanse, and with a fresh tunic, military pants, and dry boots, he was waiting in the archives for her. She arrived after him, wearing blue breeches and a pale pink tunic. She smiled in such a way, it made his heart staccato again.

"Do you know I saw you once," he said to her as she sank into a comfy next to him. He laced his fingers through hers, needing the contact. "You were on the beach in an incredible outfit, a swimsuit. We do not have those on Etteria." He pressed a kiss across her knuckles. "It was dark blue, the color of my bloodline, as you now know," he said, stroking her silky skin. He couldn't refrain from touching her and was incapable of commanding his hands to obey him. "To wear a male's color is to state to all Etterians to whom you belong."

"Oh?" she gasped before shaking her head. "I thought it was your favorite color."

"It means much more to me seeing you in blue. I wanted to meet you face-to-face that day, but I had vowed that you could reveal your identity to me when you were ready to do so."

"I was hiding from you?" She twisted in the comfy to face him.

"Yes, when we met in my gardens, you asked me not to look upon you."

"Oh, no, I didn't mean forever. I'd been crying, which makes my nose red and my eyes puffy. I wouldn't want anyone to see me like that."

"I want to see you no matter what color your nose is." He brushed her cheek.

"Next time I cry, I'll let you see me." Her brown eyes crinkled at the corners as her pink lips parted to smile.

"If my Dar Eth cries then I would be a bad Eth," he said, not wanting her to have any reason to be sorrowful.

"Then you'll be a bad Eth at least once a month," she said, and this time her cheeks splashed with color.

Sharp anger cinched his lungs. "How could you say such a thing?" How had he disappointed her that she would believe him unworthy?

She jerked back, but instead of ducking her head, she tightened her fingers over his. "Because one week a month, I bleed, and my hormones go all over the place. Sometimes I cry for no reason."

"You bleed? Why would you bleed?" he asked. The tests done on Oriana hadn't revealed a fundamental death-defying weakness in humans. He brought Macera's hand to his lips, pressing a kiss to her knuckles. She wouldn't suffer, not when he had excellent medics.

"Because my eggs weren't fertilized, so my body sheds my womb's lining to prepare for the next month."

He blinked at her for a long moment attempting to understand what she was saying and what an impact this would have on Etteria if what he suspected she meant was true.

"Are you telling me you are fertile once a month?" He held his breath as he waited for her response.

"Yes, women are fertile one week out of every month, and we carry the baby for nine months before giving birth," she said. "You need to compile a pamphlet on humans. I can't keep repeating this."

He grinned, too happy to respond to her suggestion. "A child every nine months? Alodon's balls, this is wonderful." He fought the urge to holler a battle cry.

"For Etteria, yes. Now to come back to my point, I don't want you to believe you've been a bad Eth if I cry for no reason. Just hold me, and let me cry on your shoulder," she said.

He dragged her onto his lap. "You ask too little of me." His voice roughened. "Maker, Macera, I would hold you all day if you allowed me to."

"You would?" she squeaked, twisting to meet his gaze. "Who's stopping you?"

"Not who, what...duty, honor." He rubbed his chin over the crown of her head. "And having you in my arms makes me think of other things. This is not conducive to running a nation."

"Mm, other things?" she said as her eyes drooped. She snuggled into his embrace and sighed. "Would it be too bold of me to ask if you could hold me tonight until I fall asleep?" she mumbled into his chest. "I just can't sleep, but I slept well when Illan was in the bed with me." Her eyelashes fluttered open when Xeus growled. "Not like that, my Eth." She caressed his cheek. "Picture two brothers sharing a bed. Regardless, his presence soothed me."

"You wish to fall asleep in my arms as you did last night?" He frowned at how she had his emotions fluctuating.

"If you don't mind. Just being in your arms makes me feel safe, not alone."

He glanced at her pressed against his chest. Her eyes were huge, but the shadows beneath them indicated her exhaustion.

"I do not mind, Macera. Whatever you need, you have only to ask." He wished he could give her more. *Holding her until she sleeps pales against the salvation she is to me.*

"That applies to you too, Xeus." She smiled before shifting to sit up. "I assume you have appointments for the remainder of the day?"

He frowned, not wanting his duty to intrude on his time with her. Allowing her to climb off him, he didn't expect her to place a kiss on his mouth.

"Shall we meet for dinner in the hall? Perhaps then you can explain what my duties will be as your queen." She kissed him again, this time lingering until her breath merged with his. With a deep sigh, she left him.

He wanted to stop her, to call her back to him, to cancel his meetings for the remainder of the week, and to show her how much she'd come to mean to him in such a short time. But she stumbled, with Nuos steadying her. His Dar Eth came first, and she needed to rest, not deal with his amorous advances. At least, this evening, he could hold her for hours. For now, that would have to suffice.

Chapter Thirty-Four

Planet Etteria
Issneen, the Royal City
The palace dining hall.
Later that day.

Xeus strode toward the table where his Dar Eth waited. She wore a dark blue tunic with her blue breeches, and she'd kicked off one blue footwear as she swung her foot back and forth. He knew she'd dressed so for him. This pleased him.

Her hair cascaded over one shoulder, beautiful against his bloodline color. With her fingers, she twirled a strangely shaped glass goblet filled with a deep red liquid. She raised it to her lips. The gentleness and grace with which she held the goblet were magnificent to behold. He watched as she swirled the sip in her mouth before swallowing. It had to be the beverage that tainted her lips a tempting red color even as it flushed her cheeks.

Her thoughts were far away on something that made sadness shimmer in the depths of her brown eyes. He didn't like to see her so.

"*Thamani*," he said, sliding onto the bench opposite her. He needed to touch her, but he also needed to see her face, to read her thoughts, her emotions, to discover the reason behind her sorrow.

"Zoo," she said with a bright smile. He studied her sincerity. She *was* pleased to see him.

"What is that?" he asked, gesturing to her beverage.

"It's red wine. It makes me sleepy..." She pushed the goblet across to him. "Taste, see if you like it."

He picked up the fragile goblet, as she had done. Taking a deep inhale, he noted the alcohol and strange scents he couldn't name. He took a sip, swirled it in his mouth, and froze. The flavors exploding across his tongue were sharp, fruity, spicy, and bitter. He swallowed while gazing at the liquid. The alcohol tingled in his mouth then moved swiftly through his body, his metabolism eradicating its effects before it could take hold. The *wine* was delicious.

"I like it," he said, pushing the goblet to her. "This will make you sleepy?"

"Wine has that effect on me." Her shrug disturbed the waterfall of her hair.

"Are you not sleeping in my arms this evening?" He arched an eyebrow even as he prayed she hadn't changed her mind.

"Yes, I just don't want to disrupt your sleep. You need it more than I do."

"I am your Eth, Macera. It pleases me to hold you, to tend to your needs, whatever they may be."

She blinked, her mouth parted, then her blush deepened. The scent of her arousal hit him. He flashed her a mischievous smile, joyful that she thought of other needs than sleep.

"So, what will my tasks be as your queen?" Her eyes lowered with a lust that made him Fuyra-hard again.

Maker. He squirmed in his seat like a youngin under Remi's stern gaze.

"There has not been a queen for many years. You will need to determine what tasks you deem necessary for Etteria."

"No guidebook? No historical records of the previous queens?"

"Perhaps there are in the archives."

She tapped her chin. "There is one thing. A welcoming committee for the new humans. A support group where they can learn about Etteria, your culture, and not be so nervous about meeting the all-powerful King Xeus. Why I was so nervous, I don't know." She raised the goblet to her lips, though it didn't hide her pink cheeks.

"I agree, to assist in the transition, but it is *our* culture now, my Dar Eth."

She beamed. "Are your marriages like Earth's?"

Xeus waited for the O.D.I. to inform him of her word choice. He scowled at the information that flashed into his mind. "No, when we...*marry* for politics or anything else other than the Ethera, we live apart. You would call it separated?" At her nod, he continued. "When it is a pairing, as we are, then we become inseparable. If you die, Macera, I die. I would choose to follow you rather than live a life without your radiance."

Her eyes shimmered with unshed tears. "That was beautiful. No one has ever spoken to me like that. Thank you, my Eth." She clasped his hand, giving him a watery smile. "But I don't want you to die..." She leaned back and swiped her cheeks. "I'm sorry, I don't know why I'm so emotional."

"The wine perhaps?" he teased her.

"I'm just going to have a good cry," she said, rising to her feet, "especially since you interrupted the last one."

He stared at her. His concern warred with his need to hit something. He didn't like seeing her sorrowful.

"I'll see you tomorrow, my Eth." And she limped away, sans one slipper. Nuos and Azan dropped their eating utensils mid-meal and hurried after her. *What did I say to cause such a reaction?* Stunned, he watched her disappear through the door.

Just hold me, and let me cry on your shoulder.

He burst into a run before he thought to. Not caring that a sprinting king might alarm his people, he ignored anyone he raced past. His Dar Eth needed him. Now. As he neared her from behind, Nuos and Azan jumped out of his way, allowing him to scoop her into his arms. She squealed, her arms flying wild before she latched onto him.

"What the hell?" She glared at him.

But at the sight of her tear-stained cheeks, his heart lurched as pain lanced through him. He didn't speak, simply carried her to her chambers.

Azan opened her door and closed it behind them.

Xeus kissed her temple. "You told me to hold you when you cry, *thamani.*"

MACY BLINKED AT THIS great hulking brute, who cradled her as if she was precious to him. His warmth and tender care opened the floodgates. She clung to his tunic, drenching it with tears. That she didn't know why she was crying made her sob even more.

Maybe she hadn't mourned her gran properly?

Maybe she hadn't dealt with the kidnapping, being stunned, injured, and was now a refugee on another planet?

Maybe being Zoo's anything scared her? To have the Etterian empire turn to her for guidance—her, ex-shop-assistant and underground lounge singer?

Maybe it was the intense emotions in his eyes whenever he looked at her?

Maybe what he invoked within her frightened her? Feelings she'd never felt for anyone?

Maybe all of this was too good to be true? Who could love an unattractive fat woman?

And through her sobbing and wailing, he rubbed her back, whispered soothing words in a language so lyrical, and pressed kisses to her temple.

As her tears dwindled into hiccups and sniffles, embarrassment descended, flooding her with heat from her ears to her chin. Mortified by her red cheeks, swollen nose, and puffy eyes, she hid her face in his damp shirt.

"Feeling better?" he asked.

"No, now I'm hideous," she mumbled past her raw throat.

"Never," he said. "If I had a scar down to my jaw, would I be repulsive?"

"You'd still be handsome." She smothered her face against his chest, inhaling the addictive cut grass scent of him that made her heart staccato.

"Then why would you believe crying would detract from your beauty?"

She sighed. The poor male didn't understand. How could she explain to him that she wasn't as pretty as Ava, Cyndi, or Quin? Even Olivia was stunning.

But she was just Macera Mitchell, with her dull coloring and generous curves. Zoo got the shit end of the stick if she was his Dar Eth. His enemies would pity him. A sob escaped her. She'd embarrass him, or worse, shame him.

Yet he said he'd die without me.

"I'm so sorry, Zoo." She cupped his cheek. "That you are stuck with me." She dipped her chin and tried to pull away. *Dull, unattractive?* She hadn't spoken those words, but they sat on the tip of her tongue. She cursed herself for mentioning her insecurities, forcing him to spout platitudes. But he wouldn't release her.

"I disagree."

"What...?" She shifted to meet his gaze.

Tears pricked behind her eyes again. *Here comes the fake compliments.* She hadn't expected them from him. It would hurt a shit load more coming from him. Since Lysara, she'd hoped to be his. And she'd wanted to find her Eth? A husband? Days ago, she was plain old Macy Mitchell. Now she was Queen Macera. It had happened as fast as she'd wanted it to. Still, her mind reeled while her heart forged a new path.

The responsibility of a planet fell on her shoulders. *How insane is that to put that much pressure on a single person?* Her eyes widened when she realized Zoo must be so overwhelmed. Her gaze shot up to admire his features, strength, and authority.

"You are the most exquisite creature in all the known galaxies, Macera Mitchell. I will not have you think less of yourself. It ends now." He commanded her as only a king could, expecting full obedience. "You are my sunlight, my air. I need you, your softness. Can you not see what you bring with you when you enter a room? When you speak to my males?"

She gaped at him, her skin tingling, her heartbeat thundering in her ears. Never had someone spoken with such conviction that she believed him in an instant.

"The red oceans are magnificent, but so are the gray beaches. Neither is more wonderful than the other." He stroked her cheek, captured her chin, then held her still for a lingering kiss. "Etterians do not lie, *ensa*."

"Zoo," she whispered, dazed. Oyaz and Illan had believed males would want to mate with her. Rior and Xeus said she was beautiful. "All this time, I thought you had sweet males." She moaned, now seeing all their words as compliments. "Oh, no." Shame, hot and accusatory, burst across her cheeks. "And I mentioned my nipples to Oyaz…"

Zoo growled, "Why would you—?"

"He was concerned my clothing would be too revealing. So, I threatened to wear a see-through shirt to show my nipples." She gasped. "That was mean of me. He was trying to protect me."

"Yes, as expected of a male." Zoo's gaze traveled over her face and down to her blue shirt. "I would like to see you in such a garment."

The intensity in his eyes widened hers. A flutter consumed her stomach. He meant it. He found her attractive.

This is real? I have an alien male, an Etterian.

Dumbass, her conscience said using her gran's voice.

"You'd like to see me naked, as well," she teased, regardless of her reeling thoughts and emotions. It was difficult when it was real, to flirt, especially with a male who meant more to her than she'd realized.

He rubbed his chin across her temple. "Yes." His embrace was gentle despite the hard evidence of his arousal pressing against her ass. Physical proof he liked the look of her.

"You can see me naked tomorrow after a good night's rest." She looped her arms around his neck and placed her head on his shoulder.

"AND IF I WANTED to see you naked now?" Xeus slid his hand under her shirt and over her stomach.

He shuddered at her warm, silky skin beneath his fingers. He hadn't considered she'd be even softer than when he hugged her. Under his vigilant gaze, her nipples pebbled, her reaction to his touch instant. She dug her fingers through his tunic into his chest muscles. He glanced down to meet her gaze, her eyes hooded and darker. He watched, mesmerized as she sat up to brush her sweet lips across his.

With a guttural grunt, more animalistic than Etterian, he claimed her mouth, plunging his tongue in, unrepentant with his demand, in his need. He stamped her as his territory even as he marveled at her taste, the addictive depths of her mouth, the heat pulsing off her.

His eyes stuttered closed when she slipped her tongue into stroke his, dueled him for supremacy, challenged him for control. He wrapped his arms around her back, crushing her to him as he tilted his head to the side, gaining better access to her. She tightened her arms around his neck, bringing her closer. This allowed him to feel her trembling body, pounding heart, and moans, which vibrated down his throat. He welcomed the sensation, as if they were merging into one being.

He inhaled deeply, attempting to trap her essence inside his lungs and failing miserably. She nibbled on his bottom lip, and all was lost. The groan that tore from him made her whimper. When she swiped her tongue across her lips, he ravaged her then, not giving her any mercy, unable to do so.

Her shiver penetrated the lust haze in his mind. Only then did he register the dark circles under her eyes. He broke the kiss and rested his temple on hers as he fought for calm. His ragged breaths didn't help, bringing her aroused scent into him.

"Maker, Macera, you shatter my control." Gathering her close, he rose to his feet to carry her to bed, his gaze not leaving her face. After he'd settled her in the middle of the bed, he slid on beside her. He pulled her into his arms, tucking her against him. "The quicker you rest, the quicker I will claim you," he said, even as his malehood throbbed and pulsed with need. "Sleep, *ensa*."

"I don't have a say?" she teased but ruined it with a yawn. She sighed and snuggled into his arms, resting her face in the curve of his neck. Her breath tickled.

"I want to kiss you all over."

He shuddered at her whisper. He ached for her to do so as well, and Maker willing, it would happen tomorrow. As an Etterian male, he must find the strength to last a few more hours. He focused on his breathing, on clearing his thoughts, on anything other than the warm, soft, and sweet-scented female who lay trustingly in his arms.

He wouldn't fail his Dar Eth.

Chapter Thirty-Five

*** Planet Etteria***
Issneen, the Royal City
The palace dining hall.
The following day at breakfast.

MACY STARED AT THE bottom of her cup of giyua juice. She'd just finished her breakfast and was waiting for Azan and Nuos, who were still eating their rather generous portions. As she swirled her alien lemon juice hypnotically, her mind rested on her Eth. Of course it did, with the way her body hummed with need. He had stayed the night, held her close, and left her just before her O.D.I. woke her for training. The indent in the pillow where his head had lain had been warm. Her arms remembered where the ghost of his presence lingered. She'd have liked to have awoken in his arms, to press a morning kiss to his stubbled chin. *Stubble?* She hadn't seen a single hairy Etterian male.

"Nuos? Do you shave?"

He froze just as he shoved kreso into his mouth.

"Shave?" Azan arched an eyebrow.

"As in manually remove the hair from your chin, jaw, and cheeks?"

344

"Etterian males do not grow hair on their faces."

So not on their faces. She swallowed past a giggle. "Where *do* you grow hair?"

Azan's cheeks darkened. Instead of answering her, he took another bite of kreso.

"Okay, how about I list places and you agree or disagree." She didn't wait for their reply. "Chest?"

Nuos frowned but shook his head.

"Underarms?" *No.* "Back?" *No.* "Backside?" *A frantic no.* "Arms or legs?" *No.* "Anywhere else?" *Yes, with another blush.* "Okay, so down there but smooth everywhere else. I wish I was."

"Any medic can remove unwanted follicles," Nuos said.

She gasped. "To never shave again?"

"Greetings, my queen." A deep voice intruded on their discussion.

She glanced at the speaker, then waved Azan and Nuos back into their seats.

The male bowed. "I am Warrior Altu and served on the *Phoenix*. I enjoyed the club event and wished to enquire whether another such evening is scheduled?"

She blinked. A club night hadn't been a consideration, and without Oyaz, she was lost as to how to organize it.

"I've been practicing the dancing." Altu broke into some impressive moves and with a flare she hadn't expected from a warrior. He thrust his hips at her in a stripper move, but she didn't have the heart to tell him so.

Nuos's growl had her glancing at him then the hall to check if anyone had noticed. Azan gaped in morbid fascination. She half expected his eye to twitch.

"I haven't thought to host anything." She shrugged. "I'll ask Advisor Kanzo. Please, give me your contact information. I'll notify you of the outcome." She thrust out her arm, and he diligently scanned in his details.

"Thank you, my queen."

She stared at his disappearing back, ice slithering down her back. Something felt wrong about this. The club night had been a success. The males had loved the heavy beat and bass of the electronic music. But in the broad light of the two suns of Etteria, she wasn't sure introducing Earth's music was such a clever idea. She didn't want to ruin a culture she was growing to love.

"What was that?" Azan asked.

"It's called dancing and is usually done to music. I showed the males on the *Phoenix* what humans do for fun."

"Music?" Azan's eyelids fluttered.

She sighed, navigated to the last song she'd played on her O.D.I. and pressed 'continue.' Humming along her bones, an old pop song played.

"I know this." Azan grinned. "You sing it."

"If you want to learn more, you'll find them under Alien Cultures, Earthians, Entertainment. We have music and story vids too." A twinge of guilt struck, like she was abandoning an addict to their vice. "There's a lot, so choose something and set it to random. Eventually, you'll find something you like. And if you have any questions, just ask."

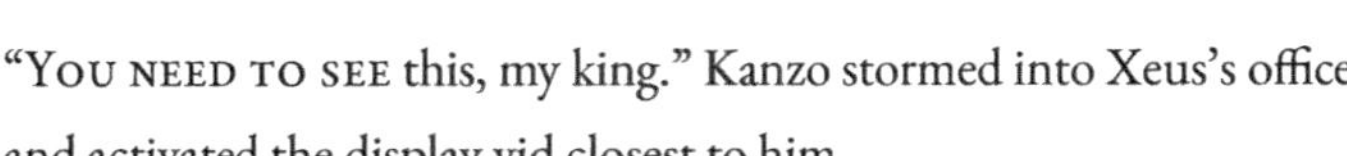

"You need to see this, my king." Kanzo stormed into Xeus's office and activated the display vid closest to him.

Xeus stood alongside Kanzo and waited for him to start the vid. An image of a contented Macera flickered on. He greedily studied her features. Her easy smile and the lack of shadows under her eyes pleased him. But at the sight of a male thrusting his hips at his Dar, a red haze consumed Xeus's vision.

"Get me all the vids from the *Phoenix*," he demanded in a voice just above guttural.

Kanzo typed on his O.D.I., and a few minutes later, the vids queued on the display vid.

They showed Macera wandering the battleship in misery—the sight splintered his heart. And because a disturbance was logged for her quarters, he was able to experience the *music* that had enthralled Oyaz. Every one she'd played was indeed riveting. Her *dancing* to the *music* was also enjoyable to watch, her movements erratic or graceful.

"Honor Oyaz for his contribution to my Dar Eth's joy," he said to Kanzo as Oyaz tasked her to introduce his males to human foods and trained her to improve her fitness.

Xeus laughed at her conversations with Illan. That was his female. But when she did the *sexy dance*, his body burst into flame. He was, in an instant, hard. Breathing became impossible. Seeing her so...sensual was more than he could bare. It had taken a mountain of tasks and hours of sparring on the proving grounds to gain control, to resist returning to her to claim her as she'd promised.

"Alodon's balls," Kanzo said beside him and jolted a mesmerized Xeus.

He stiffened, furious need making him roar, "Send it to my O.D.I."

He stormed out of his office to locate his female. *How dare she do that? Purposely incite another male?* He wasn't thinking rationally and understandably so. His thoughts circled; his emotions catapulted. He wanted...he couldn't say what exactly. He just wanted ...needed... Macera. His long strides made quick work of reaching her chambers. He burst in without requesting entrance and startled a squeak from her. She had just stepped through her bedroom door in a long flowing dress, similar to what she'd worn in the vid.

She splayed her hand on her chest. "Zoo?"

He raced across, lifted her by the waist, and pinned her against the panel.

"What's wrong?"

When he pressed his body to hers, he shuddered at the wave of heat assaulting his overwhelmed senses. "This." He activated his O.D.I. and found the vid Kanzo had sent him. His breath came in gasps as he watched it with her.

Her eyes widened. "It's a sexy dance," she said, glancing from the vid to him.

"You did *this* in front of my males," he snapped, too furious to soften his tone.

"I didn't." She tapped 'continue,' but a minute later, Oyaz and Illan halted her. "So why are you so angry?" She cupped Xeus's face, keeping his gaze on her. "I said I'd never dance like that again."

He inhaled, flaring his nostrils and drawing her exotic scent deep into his lungs. With a growl, he released his anger and buried his face in the curve of her neck. He nuzzled her earlobe and brushed kisses along her jaw to slant demandingly across her mouth. He held her to the wall to slip a knee between her legs, spreading her thighs and her aroused scent.

"I need you, Macera, dangerously so," he said into her parted mouth.

Her breath hitched. "You have me, Zoo. You always have."

At the truth in her brown eyes, he scooped her into his arms and strode into her room. He lay her on the bed, stepping back to gaze upon her. His body trembled. The vision before him, what he was about to do, how much he ached to *know* her... He frowned. "If you want to keep this garment..."

"Rip it off," she said, her breasts rising and falling erratically as she drew in ragged breaths.

He smiled, grabbed the collar of the garment and tugged. It split down the middle, unable to resist the strength of his hands. The fabric parted to reveal a nude human woman before him. He groaned and clenched his fists, taking a moment to memorize every inch of her body, each curve and valley.

"You are perfect," he said, placing one knee on the bed to lean over her. He slanted his mouth across hers again, demanding, needing, and taking while he stroked his fingers from her neck to her collarbone to brush over a pebbled nipple. Her moan encouraged him further. He cupped the breast and plucked at the nipple.

He continued his onslaught, ravaging her mouth, consuming her soul as he brushed his knuckles over the curls of her femininity. Even there, she was so silky. His moan deepened into a growl when he discovered how aroused she was. As per the instructional vids, when a woman's folds glistened, she was ready for her male. Macera's scent surrounded him, making his malehood dribble in anticipation. As he brushed her nub, she cried out and arched off the bed, thrusting her folds into his wide palm.

"Do you like that?" His lips twisted into a smile, his focus unwavering.

"Yes...please, don't stop."

He flicked his fingers. She whimpered. He gently pinched her nub between two fingers. Her eyes stuttered shut, and her mouth fell open with her hands lashing out to fist the bedding. He captured a nipple and sucked on it, the taste of her skin consuming his tongue. When he flicked her nipple, she whimpered. He released her nub and trailed a finger lower. She shivered, with tiny bumps forming on her smooth skin. He sank a finger into her tight sheath and rested his thumb on her nub. She arched off the bed, keening at the triple onslaught.

And her heated channel clinging to his finger drew a grunt from him. "You are so..." Precious? Exquisite? Breathtaking? His? His tongue tied, and the words wouldn't form.

She gripped his upper arms, then brushed her fingers along his sensitive skin, skittered over his shoulders, then down, scraping her nails over his tunic and nipples.

"Please, Zoo... Please." She grasped at his garments, begging him to remove them.

He stepped back to strip off his armor, tearing the fabric in his rush. He paused to allow her to look since he'd taken the same liberty. And she did, her gaze hooded with desire at the sight of his body. When she lingered on his erect malehood, her eyes widened, but no fear darkened her awed features. She parted her mouth to lick her bottom lip as if she tasted him.

"*Thamani*," he whispered before sliding between her legs. He rested his elbows beside her shoulders, pressing the full length of him over her, careful not to crush her. With her trapped beneath him, he placed kisses on her forehead and cheeks while embedding his fingers into her hair in an attempt to gain some control.

She wiggled her hips until the head of his malehood was positioned just right. A throaty moan escaped her, and what control he'd recovered, slipped from him. She wrapped her legs around his hips and dug her heels into his backside, encouraging him to move. Her fingernails scraped his back, sending shivers up and down his body.

"Macera..." he mumbled then pushed his malehood into her sheath and froze. She was so tight, he didn't want to hurt her, but the urge to thrust in, to bury himself deeply was almost unbearable. "*Thamani*, please, do not move."

"Go slow." Her smile was filled with trust.

Maker, he didn't want to harm her. He withdrew all the way and dipped back in a little deeper. And shuddered. Perspiration broke out across his body as he fought for control. Fought for it and won.

"So hot and soft," he mumbled. He opened his eyes to kiss her again.

She gasped and kissed him back. When she tightened her legs around him, he slipped in a bit more. He growled, the pleasure too much. White heat rippled along the length of his malehood. Her touch fluttered over his back, into his hair, and down his chest to toy with his nipples. He moaned into her mouth, as he ventured in a little deeper.

"Just one more," she said.

One...last...time. He pulled out to thrust into her, embedding himself to the hilt.

She cried out and arched into him.

His eyes stuttered closed as sweet bliss consumed him. "You are magnificent," he rasped.

He crushed her mouth with his, drowning in the taste of her, her scent. While kissing her, he withdrew to plunge into her. She mewled into his mouth, her heels urging him on. He didn't need the encouragement. *She is everything and more than I imagined. Perfect for me.*

"I think I'm dying," she whimpered. "So good." She tilted her hips. As he thrust deeper into her, she trembled, panted, and purred. Her nails bit into his flesh. Shivers rippled from there outward to pool in his balls before firing heat along his hard arousal to the head.

"Macera," he groaned as his hips thrust harder, faster.

She clung to him, pressing her hard nipples and soft breasts to his chest. Then she froze before screaming. Incredible wet heat engulfed the length of him as her channel contracted and released around him, calling forth and demanding his fulfillment. She chanted his name, the throaty sound of it smothered by his roar. The pleasure was so intense, so incredible, his vision blurred then re-focused with accuracy on her flushed face, on the center of his universe, and rightly so.

Chapter Thirty-Six

Planet Etteria
Issneen, the Royal City
Macera's chambers.

XEUS AWOKE WITH A start. He lay in bed, staring at the ceiling. A huge involuntary smile formed when every inhale stuttered his heartbeat. The scent of their union still drenched the room.

The swirling sensations barraging his chest were overwhelming and unrecognizable. Just thinking of Macera warmed him with the realization that he had no control over his emotions when it came to his Dar Eth. Not that he cared. She was his, and she was all he needed and wanted.

A strange noise emanated from the seating area. Perhaps that had disturbed his sleep? It sounded like her music. He jumped out of bed and peered through the bedroom door to find her swinging her gorgeous backside and swirling her chest while she set the counter for breakfast.

He grinned at the sight of her wearing his tunic and nothing else. Her hair, in wild disarray, cascaded around her, calling to him to lose his fingers in that mass again.

She was a breathtaking sight.

He leaned against the doorframe to watch her, not caring that he was naked.

Her head snapped to the side when she noticed him. She flashed a sensual smile, promising heaven before dancing over to him for a kiss. Swaying her hips as she stepped back, she popped something salty into his mouth. He chewed the tasty morsel while clasping her by the hips to keep her near.

"What is this?" he asked.

"Bacon," she said.

"Leave the meal." He placed a kiss on her exposed shoulder and roamed his hands down her back to grab her backside, lifting her to press his rock-hard malehood at her feminine folds.

Her eyelashes fluttered over her heated gaze. "Again?" she rasped, stroking his chest and nipples with an eagerness that mirrored his.

"Come to bed," he growled.

"Take me here, now," she challenged while brushing back and forth over his taut nipples.

"Here?" His eyebrow shot up.

She chuckled and tapped the bulkhead to the left of her. "Yes, unless Mighty King Xeus can't pick up little me?" she teased. "Or should I ask my alcove guardian?"

His reaction was immediate. He raised her off the floor and pinned her back to the bulkhead, with enough force to vibrate it. Her entrance drenched the head of his malehood.

Her mouth parted on a moan.

"You are wet," he said hoarsely.

"Only for you, Zoo."

At her response, he thrust into her in one swift movement, embedding his malehood to the hilt, slapping his balls against her inner thighs. She arched her back with a cry of pleasure. Her fingernails scraped along his shoulders and embedded in his hair, which had come loose to swirl around them.

"Take off my tunic. I wish to feel your softness, *thamani*," he said.

She yanked off the garment within the space he allowed her. Once her breasts bounced free, he crushed her to the bulkhead again, grunting at the warmth of her against him. He plunged into her, in, out, with smooth, forceful thrusts, the exquisite silkiness of her stealing his breath, thoughts, and will.

She hooked her legs around him, digging her feet into his backside as she screamed her fulfillment. Pulsating heat gushed along the length of him. As she'd found hers, his ripped through him, splintering his world into miniature worlds, each containing infinite stars and an eternity of pleasure.

"Alodon's balls." He feathered kisses across her flushed cheek. "You take my breath away."

Her shyness under his admiring gaze drew a chuckle from him.

"May we eat now?" she asked, wrapping her arms around his neck. "Or do you want to go again?" She teased him with a swirl of her hips since he was still inside her and aroused.

Again? He stilled. "You wouldn't mind?"

"Let me down..." Her voice was seductive.

Intrigued, he pulled out, instantly missing the heat and tightness of her. She danced away from him to shift the meal to the other counter before throwing the top half of her body over the surface.

"Come, stand behind me."

He did so, eager for the view.

She gestured to him to step closer until his arousal brushed her backside.

His breath caught as she parted her thighs and arched her back, exposing her glistening feminine folds to his hungry gaze, to his eager malehood. Like a blossoming hahyt, her folds had flushed and become swollen. He ran his thumb over her nub, dipped into her channel, then out. She cried out, shoving her backside out when she pressed her temple to the surface. He'd never seen anything more mesmerizing.

"Zoo, please." She wiggled her backside.

He brushed the head of his malehood along her folds, loving how ready she was for him. Then in one smooth motion, he buried himself again. He bent backward at her tight, wet, and heated channel surrounding him.

She keened her pleasure, her thighs trembling as he removed his malehood before plunging into her. Her arms flew out as she latched onto the counter's surface, her fingers splayed out wide. She moaned, panted, begged as he mercilessly took her over and over until, with a scream, she clenched around him again. Her pleasure called forth his, and he roared her name, the sensations too intense as she continued to milk his seed with each ripple of pleasure consuming her.

He collapsed over her, catching his weight with a thrown-out hand while he feathered grateful and affectionate kisses to her trembling shoulder. "I like this one," he whispered, relishing the saltiness of her perspiration and the flavor of her skin that was indefinably her.

"I *love* this one," she said into the counter.

He looped an arm around her waist and lifted her against his chest, keeping himself impaled. When he stepped back, she used her feet to grip the edge of the counter. With one arm, he held her up. With the other hand, he dipped his fingers between her folds to thumb her nub. She whimpered, twisted, and kissed him. He thrust his hips down and up while he kept her in position, losing himself in the taste of her, in the feel of her tight sheath, in the slickness of her folds.

Within minutes, she was screaming his name as she gushed her pleasure. The sudden heat engulfed his arousal and launched him over the edge into a violent ocean of joy. As her shudders faded into tremors, he unimpaled himself and spun her in his arms to crush her against his chest for another thorough kiss. He carried her back to the bed. She writhed, her movements sensual. When she ran a finger along his balls, he sprawled across her and thrust into her again, liking her body under his, her softness sublime.

"You are heaven incarnate," he said into her mouth as he increased the speed and intensity until she arched off the bed with a throaty moan. She splintered around him, her channel spasming so tightly he roared his pleasure. He planted kisses on her damp shoulder, pressed a kiss to her puckered nipple before looping an arm around to keep her near.

"Best lover ever," she mumbled as she rested her forehead on his shoulder.

"You please me, *thamani.*"

"You please me, too...many times," she teased, leaning back to meet his gaze. She brushed a kiss across his shoulder, chin, and nose. "I'm addicted to you." A slow beautiful smile spread across her lips, making his heart skip a beat.

"This pleases me too," he said. "Do you want to eat now?"

"Yes. I suspect I'll need to keep my strength up."

"I agree. I like claiming you, my Dar Eth," he said, withdrawing from her channel. She shivered, her nipples puckering again. *So responsive, his human.*

"I like you claiming me, my Eth." She accepted his offered hand. He lifted her to stand on the bed and at eye level with him. She leaned forward to press a quick kiss to his lips. He rumbled his approval, even as he gripped her hips.

"I thought you were hungry," he chuckled, tugging her against him.

"I am, just giving you a little sample of what's after breakfast." And she brushed her nipples across his chest.

His breath hitched, and his fingers spasmed.

"Breakfast first, *ensa*, but let me give *you* a sample..." And he leaned down to lock his mouth over her nipple, sucking it in so deep.

She moaned her enjoyment, her fingers grappling his shoulders for support.

He released her nipple with a swipe of his tongue, finding her trembling in his arms. He gazed at her face, admiring and memorizing every feature. An intense emotion claimed his chest, overwhelming him with an ache he didn't understand. It surpassed the physical ache to be buried within her and the craving to scent and taste her. He grabbed her by the waist and lifted her off the bed, pausing as she gained her balance.

She raised her gaze to his and smiled—the purity of it speared him.

What is she doing to me, my human?

"Are you hungry?" She strolled out of her room, unaware that he hadn't moved.

He was riveted by this emotion burning in his chest, wishing he could name it.

"Zoo?" she called.

With a sigh, he followed.

Chapter Thirty-Seven

Planet Etteria

Issneen, the Royal City

Xeus's office

XEUS REVIEWED THE MUSIC vids for the fourth time. Every time he watched them, he became too aroused to continue. The music was incredible, and he'd quickly formed an attachment to a few birdsongs. But it was her dancing that stirred something deep within him. This time, he managed to reach the club evening she'd planned with his males finding enjoyment in the act of dancing.

It seemed like such a harmless amusement until he focused on the human women gyrating their curves. Then it became incendiary, and judging his unpaired males's expressions, too volatile to allow.

The Eths wouldn't dance without their Dar Eths, which meant battles would ensue. The only solution was to abolish music and dancing among unpaired males and females. His heart ached for his Macera who loved to sing and dance, so obliterating it from their archives would do more harm than good. Besides, every scan of Earth would update the archives. Preventing music from reaching Etteria would be a constant battle.

He navigated to his favorite scene where she demonstrated a *sexy* dance. His arousal was instant.

She swayed her hips while stroking her body as he would. Her fingers brushing over her breasts caught his breath. She thrust out her backside, as she'd done on the counter that morning. Then she flipped her hair out, cascading it around her as she undulated to finally end with her back arching as her mouth parted in silent demand.

He sighed at her interaction with Oyaz and Illan, and when she threatened to reveal her nipples, Xeus had growled even though she'd warned him. He punched into his O.D.I., requesting she visit.

When the music on the display vid continued, it snatched his focus. He had never seen this part before, had always switched off the vid before this. His Macera danced for herself, and this time, she was uninhibited, with no males in her presence to hinder her.

His mouth went dry as she swung her hips, dipping low to thrust out her backside while trailing her hands over her breasts and down her stomach and hips to tug the dress up. His breath hitched as a naked Macera twirled seductively for him alone. Alodon's balls. His malehood swelled to its full length. He shifted in the comfy. This didn't ease the tight sensation, so he undid his pants to allow a little relief. Through this, he didn't remove his gaze from the vid. He didn't blink, lest he missed a moment.

She skipped into his office. "What is it, Zoo?"

He tapped the vid to pause it. She wore a dress similar to the one she'd just discarded in the vid. He bounded around his desk to pull her into his arms, burying his face in the curve of her neck and unbound curls.

"I need your touch," he muttered hoarsely, drawing in her scent. No matter how many times he breathed her in, it was never enough.

"To ease the Ethera?"

He grumbled as he tightened his arms around her and pressed a kiss to her temple, her nose, and across her mouth.

"Mm," she rasped. "You taste good. I could drink from you for an eternity."

"Your taste is as incredible," he growled, his voice almost animalistic. He caught her hand, spun, and kissed her, his heart leaping when she brought her tongue into play.

"Do you have time to take me on your desk?" She met his gaze, her eyes twinkling.

"I've time," he answered 'casually,' which he in no way felt. "But...not when my males will scent you." He tugged her behind him, hurrying her to the Crustiiu pools hidden in the rocky outcrop behind his palace. At this time of day, the circular indents in the stone floor with heated water bubbling from underground would be, for the most part, abandoned.

She gasped when he ushered her past pools to the more secluded one to the rear of the cavern. The air was damp, dewing his skin.

"You've known about this and didn't tell me?" Despite her admonishment, she yanked up her dress to reveal a bare backside.

"Macera," he groaned, running a trembling hand over a soft cheek.

She ripped the dress off, tossing it on the floor before facing him. Dipping a toe first, she sat on the rim, and spread her thighs, displaying her glistening folds to his hungry gaze. He tore off his armor, uncaring where it fell. Once naked, he waded into the crystal clear water to feather kisses along her inner thigh. Her scent taunted him, thickening the damp air. Succumbing, he latched onto her nub, moaning at her taste. He flicked his tongue over her before leaning back to run it upward.

"Zoo," she begged as she embedded her fingers in his hair, her nails scraping his scalp.

"What do you want, my *ensa*?" he asked as if he couldn't read her reactions.

"You, in me, now," she said, to which he chuckled into her folds.

"Only you dare to command me, Macera." He cupped her backside and swung her around. She squealed but calmed, floating on the surface. He positioned his malehood at her entrance, and stilled, allowing her need to drench him.

Her writhing, arching, and mewling dazzled him, agitating the water so slapped against his thighs. He'd never seen anyone so incredibly erotic, so responsive. He splayed his fingers on her chest, then trailed a fingertip down between her breasts, over her stomach to disappear into her curls and folds. As soon as he touched her nub with his thumb, he plunged his malehood into her, burying himself deeply. She cried out and trembled.

He held still again, malehood and thumb, relishing her channel contracting around him. His balls clenched in reaction, the sensation exquisite.

"What do you want, my *thamani*?" he teased her. Tiny bumps rippled across her skin, puckering her nipples. "My *ensa ra ensa*," he whispered hoarsely, trembling with the effort to remain motionless.

"You, only you, Zoo." She opened her eyes to meet his gaze, "Give me all of you."

Shivering at her words, he growled. He pulled out to thrust into her, his hips colliding with her thighs. The contact fueled him, demanding more, harder. Her channel stroked his length, with softness and heat. Her need drenched his pelvis, and he reveled in his ability to create such a yearning in her.

It took all of his battle-honed control not to find his fulfillment. He'd never thought to extend her pleasure—doing so brought astonishing rewards. His Dar Eth trembled as her body waited for his touch, his malehood. She was taut with need, her heartbeat erratic, her breaths gasping.

Without warning, her channel clamped around him as she imploded, encouraging him to join her. He was forced to follow. White heat burst sweet joy through his body. He roared his release, unable to hold back any longer, the sensations too exquisite. His vision blurred, his heart and breathing ceased for what was an endless moment. But his focus remained on her, on her essence surrounding him, her wet skin touching his. He shuddered at her every move, the breaths she took, her erratic heartbeat pounding in his ears.

He collapsed around her, gathering her close to submerge them into the water. His fingers trembled as he brushed over her eyelids, down her nose, and across her parted lips.

"Do you have appointments this afternoon?" she asked.

Her desire to spend time with him glowed in the warm brown of her eyes. He slumped, displeased that he couldn't give her everything she needed.

"Shall I teach you the game of chess this evening?" She pressed her chest to his and cupped his cheek.

"Yes, you may," he said, brushing a kiss across her lips.

"You could have your appointments around me, as long as you stay as you are," she said teasingly.

He chuckled at her suggestion. He was still buried within her, still hard, as always.

"I could, but then I would have to kill any male who sees you so uncovered."

"Quite a decision you have to make, my king. I don't envy you this," she chuckled, swirling her hips.

A tendril of joy unfurled along his arousal.

"Temptress." He laughed and pulled out of her. Her muted moan almost had him thrusting into her again.

At the sight of his well-pleasured queen, he took the time to memorize her beloved face from her fulfillment. He climbed out of the pool but waved her to stay. Under her vigilance, he gathered her dress, bringing it to his nose to inhale.

"I'll need that." She clasped the rim of the pool and folded her arms along it.

He grumbled but folded her garment, placing it on a hewn-out shelf. "Stay, enjoy the pools." Yanking on his pants, he set to donning his discarded armor.

She ventured to the center of the pool before flipping onto her back to float, the peaks of her breasts rising above the surface. "This pool is amazing. It washed away where I came all over you."

"Came?" His eyes twitched as he waited for his O.D.I. to update him. The images were...revealing. His grin was wide, pleased. He was already dreaming of many such sessions with his Macera. "I adore it when you do."

Kneeling beside the pool, he tapped the rim and waited until she waded over. He caught her chin to feather his thumb across her swollen bottom lip, then bent to kiss her one last time.

"This evening," he vowed, rising to lean against the rock wall to watch her.

This was the vision he'd experienced when the Ethera had brought him to his knee. What snagged him was the emotions she summoned within him. With a sigh, he left her, returning to his office and the endless tasks made mundane with her in his life.

When he sat at his desk, his gaze fell on the halted vid, so he instructed it to continue. He didn't blink as addicted and infatuated with his Dar Eth as he was. Before deleting them from the annals permanently as only a king could do, he forwarded the vids to his O.D.I.

He fixed his gaze through the window to the path leading to the Crustiiu pools. What dominated his mind wasn't her writhing beneath him. No, it was the way her lips curled when she smiled, the twinkle in her eyes when she teased him, and that she had yet to call him Xeus when they were alone.

She'd said she wanted Zoo, not Xeus, and he believed it.

I will see her tonight.

Chapter Thirty-Eight

Planet Etteria
Issneen, the Royal City
Macy's chambers

MACY FOLDED XEUS'S SCARF she'd just finished. Keryr and Ava sat opposite her, discussing how best to form a welcoming committee for human Dar Eths. So much had been left up to chance, and since Macy was now queen, she was determined to have someone mentor each woman landing on Etterian soil.

Hell, she might even compile pamphlets or a checklist.

- Get an O.D.I. implanted. It's painless and free.

- A full-length image triggers the Ethera, so flashing boobs won't work. *Well, I did consider it.*

- Etteria hosts an orphanage if you need to keep busy. Or start a hobby.

- Don't swim in the sea. It *will* kill you.

She harumphed at the short list. *It's a work in progress.* She wanted to touch on Etterian hair and how it was tied to their honor. Ava had just today explained it. There was also what the Ethera meant in terms of marriage. Macy tapped her chin. Maybe they needed to compile a pamphlet for the Etterians too. "What to expect when gaining a human ~~spouse wife~~ mate."

"The twins were adopted today," Ava was saying, snagging Macy's attention.

"For realsies?" she gasped.

"Yup, a brother and sister owning a kreso farm two days ride from here." Ava smiled. "Olivia vetted them first, watched their interaction with the boys, and when Dagon hugged them, that was it. Sealed."

Keryr nodded. "Olivia cried."

"And you, Keryr?" Macy clasped the female's hand for a quick squeeze.

"I help where I can." She laughed. "Kanzo took my image this day. Perhaps I will find an Eth."

"What? No pairing ceremony?" Macy frowned. That too had been a recent discovery. Women paraded like cattle. *Here, folks, step right up and get a wife.* Taking images made more sense. What if the male couldn't make it to the annual ceremony? What if Keryr's mate was stuck on a battleship circling some planet?

Keryr's O.D.I. buzzed, and she jumped, her cheeks darkening. While she read the message, Ava and Macy held a collective breath. When Keryr slumped, so did they. "My father."

"This is nerve-racking." Ava huffed. "I get that your image has to bounce from comm tower to battleship across galaxies, but could it please happen faster."

Keryr laughed as she stood. "I have been summoned." She waved Macy and Ava to remain in their chairs. "I shall let you know the moment I receive the news."

After Keryr left, Ava circled the living room, pausing to finger silk roses Macy had shoved into a pewter vase. "Have I told you how I love what you've done with this space, Macy?"

"Yup, every time you visit." She scanned the room now with a 'Persian' rug, woven cushions on the comfys, a wingback chair, and an ottoman by the tall windows. Despite them not being needed, curtains softened the room. Nuos and Azan had grumbled when they'd helped her install the railings. It had taken long to convince them *and* find a tool to drill. Except for the tapestry on one wall, the others remained bare. She planned to try creating artwork of some sort.

She'd even managed to have the replicator create a coffee machine. The aroma of roasted beans percolating first thing in the morning was worth it. All she needed now was a sink in the 'kitchen.' Washing the coffee pot in the bathroom was all levels of *ew*.

"Would you be interested in helping me decorate my home?" Ava pressed her palms together, added a pout, and widened her eyes. "Pretty please."

Macy laughed. "Sure, but you get to choose the finishes. No point in replicating this space. It has to be all you."

"Deal," Ava squealed before slumping into a nearby chair. "I'll find out from Kanzo if there are any incoming women we need to worry about. Might be a good idea to record a video to send to them as soon as they step foot on a battleship."

"And here I was thinking a checklist," Macy smirked.

"Well, we do need a list of topics to discuss."

"I'd also like to find out how many Etterian females would be interested in mentoring."

"Yes, I love that." Ava leaped to her feet to hug Macy. "I have the children coming over for haircuts this afternoon. I wanted to turn the salon into a wonderland."

"Oh." Macy bounced on her ass. "I have my usual appointment with Xeus. After that, I'll come right over."

"Great." Ava pursed her lips before forming a wry smile. "I might need all the help I can get." She skipped to the door. "And thanks for mentioning the Crustiiu pools." With a wink, she waltzed through the door and passed Nuos and Azan.

Stroking the scarf, Macy prayed Zoo would react as Oyaz had. Clutching it to her chest, she rose and placed it on the kitchen counter. It was nearing time for their usual alcove-meeting, but she wasn't sure if it was still happening after this morning's...sexcapades. She squeezed her thighs together, trying to calm the constant ache. One would think more sex meant fewer urges. Nope, she craved him, his touch, his mouth, that glorious tongue.

She grinned. Maybe it was time to show him what her tongue could do.

She swiveled and punched in her requirements—a sleeveless floral dress, a fresh set of armor for Zoo, and two sets of wireless earphones. After a quick shower, she dressed, donned slippers, fluffed her hair, and strode out of her home to face the biggest challenge—convincing Nuos and Azan to listen to music while she introduced Zoo to her mouth.

"THE ALCOVE," WAS ALL Macera's comm said.

Xeus reread it, wondering what she meant. What about the alcove? He glanced at the ambassadors waiting on him. They were discussing the increasing demand for kreso, not only for Etteria but for export. The great hairy beasts had formed the staple of their meals since the first annals were written.

Ambassador Nasu's bloodline had been farming kreso for generations. He was as revered as Cales. Since Nasu had never allowed his training to lapse, Xeus respected his advice and opinion. Nasu was an honorable and true Etterian male.

"I assume it is a comm from your Dar Eth?" He offered a small smile.

Xeus frowned. "One that does not make sense."

"Does it have to, my king?" Kanzo grinned. "I do not know if females have ever had to make sense, especially human women."

"Truth." Xeus chuckled.

At a timid knock, Kanzo rose to open the door.

Xeus leaped to his feet when a redhead peeked in. "What is it, Lady Ruby?" he asked.

She stepped into the room and smiled sweetly at Kanzo and Xeus then nodded respectfully at Nasu, her green gaze lingering on the ambassador before focusing on Xeus again.

"I'm sorry, Uncle Xeus, but Syna has arrived, and the children are scared. I was hoping you could spare Uncle Kanzo?"

"I will be there shortly, Ruby. Have you fetched Ava?"

"She sent me, Uncle Kanzo," and with a glance at all, she left, closing the door behind her.

"Maker, she is breathtaking," Nasu groaned.

Xeus shot a glance at the ambassador. It was Kanzo who scowled when Nasu's eyes swirled between dark blue and ice. They knew so little about the Ethera, so why didn't Nasu fall to a knee? Xeus stared at the door. Nasu had reacted, of that, there was no doubt. And Lady Ruby was far too young— Xeus stilled. She was too young. The Ethera acted the same with Etterian females.

"She is Lady Ruby, a human woman. Perhaps you could assist Kanzo in dealing with this matter? I will attend to my queen's strange comm. We will conclude this discussion before dinner." Xeus raced out of his office, heading for their alcove.

Macera sat on the bench, patiently waiting for his arrival. As he approached her, he admired the dark blue dress she wore, adorned with white flowers not of his world. No straps held up the top of the dress with her bare shoulders catching the afternoon suns light.

"What is it, my queen?" he asked as he strode toward her.

She smiled at him, the sight of which warmed his chest.

"How long do you have?" she asked when he sat on the bench beside her.

"What do you need?" He gathered her hands into his.

"You," she said, slipping onto the blue grass before him. She grabbed his knees to spread them wider, settling between his thighs.

"To your bed then," he whispered hoarsely, yet as he made to rise, she squeezed his knees.

"Stay," she said.

Frowning, he lowered his backside to the bench.

She stroked his inner thighs through his military pants. He trembled from her touch, as if he was bare. "What—?"

She shook her head and placed a finger on his lips, before trailing that same finger down his chest to the mechanism at his waistband. She pressed it, and his pants parted.

"We need to be quiet," she whispered while caressing the skin his gaping pants had revealed. She slid her hand in and wrapped her fingers around his solid girth, tugging his arousal free.

"Macera," he groaned, wondering what she was doing but willing to be patient. She stroked him with her soft fingers. *Maker, that feels so good.*

"What is this?" She rubbed him but lingered on a hard ridge the width of her thumb that ran the length of him, from tip to his balls. As she brushed over it, he shuddered, with a pearl of need forming on the head of his arousal.

"My denit. The size and texture varies per male. It is...sensitive," he gasped as she rubbed it.

She rose on her knees and pressed her lips along the length of his arousal. Ice and fire lambasted his senses, white need overwhelming his control. He'd claimed her that morning, then in the pools.

"What are you doing?" he growled.

"Tasting you." Then she did, sliding her tongue over the tip before sucking him into her hungry mouth. Hot, silky heat engulfed him. The exquisite sensation squeezed his eyes shut, then he flicked them open, not wanting to miss a moment.

He was so big she'd struggle to take all of him into her mouth, regardless, she seemed determined to try. When she twirled her tongue, he rumbled and groaned. Then she caressed his balls with one hand while the other stroked his denit. He grunted and embedded his fingers in her hair. When his hips thrust upward in tiny movements, he prayed he didn't choke her. She pulled him out of her mouth to run her tongue from balls to tip, all along his denit. Her gaze remained on him, watching him react to her ministrations. He clamped his teeth down on his bottom lip in an attempt to be silent.

Climbing to her feet, she raised the hem of the dress to slide onto his lap, resting her knees on his thighs. She tilted her hips until she had his head at her entrance. Excruciatingly slowly, she impaled herself on his length.

He gripped her hips, now aware of what she was doing. And when she'd taken all of him, she rolled forward and back, running the length of her channel along his malehood. He focused on her face, mesmerized by the blush that stained her cheeks, by the heat in her eyes, by the tip of her tongue dimpling her top lip. He was enchanted by her undulating hips and the exquisite softness, so tight around him. She made no noise, just rode him, the speed increasing too slowly for his liking.

He reached beneath her dress to stroke her nub.

She whimpered then yanked the dress down exposing one perfect breast. He latched onto the nipple to suck into his mouth. The pace increased. She came apart, quietly, her body twitching under his teasing fingers. He grabbed her, twisting to balance her backside on the edge of the bench to kneel between her legs, thrusting into her with such yearning and desperation. Within minutes, her channel tightened around him and tossed him over the edge. He rumbled instead of roared his release, his body shivering, tingling as waves of heat rippled over him.

"Macera," he gasped, crushing her against his body, burying his face in the curve of her neck to place an open-mouthed kiss to her erratic pulse.

"Zoo," she managed, still a little breathless.

"Could you not wait until this evening?" he teased, despite being delighted she'd messaged him.

"Never, my Eth." She leaned back to kiss him.

He moaned and claimed her mouth for a thorough plunder.

"Did I disturb an important meeting with this quickie?" she asked when he let her breathe.

"Quickie? That is what you call this?"

"Yes, it's short and sweet." Her eyes sparkled.

His chest swelled with warm cresting waves of emotion. *She is so beautiful, my queen.*

"No, you did not disturb me. Syna has arrived, and the children are frightened of him."

"Probably his height," she said, stroking his forearms. "You can return to your office now. I think I can survive until tonight."

He was still inside her and Fuyra hard. "I cannot return to the office. I scent of you again." He cupped her adorable face. "And I do not think I can wait until tonight." He withdrew his arousal only to thrust into her. She arched her response, her expressive mouth parting with a gasp. "But I also want you to scream my name." He pulled out completely.

"You promise?" she pouted, her voice husky with need.

"My vow." He grinned at her.

"Rinse yourself in the fountain and change into the spare uniform I brought for you."

He chuckled at her imperious tone. "As my queen commands." He laughed, the sound loud in the aftermath of their union.

She pulled the dress up to cover her breast and let the hem fall to her slippered feet. With a sigh, he whipped off his tunic and dropped it into her waiting hands. He removed his boots, followed by his pants. When her gaze traveled his form, he smirked.

"Keep looking at me like that, *thamani*, and I will take you again. This time I will not care who hears your screams." While he rinsed off her fulfillment, he imagined a blush on her cheeks.

He faced her, donning each garment under her heated gaze. Her unflinching admiration made his chest ache. As soon as he was fully clothed, she sighed and folded his garments. Her doing so pleased him, but he couldn't say why. He dropped a kiss on her lips before hastily stepping back.

"Wait." She hesitated and pulled a blue bundle from under his armor. "I...made this for you, Zoo."

He accepted the blue thing, not sure what to say. No one had made him something before. "What is it, *thamani*?" He dug his fingers into the gift and groaned at its softness. Rubbing it along his cheek, he breathed in her scent only.

"A scarf."

His eyelids fluttered with images of women and men wearing this thing around their necks. He tried to mimic the wrapping and succeeded. "It is...amazing. Thank you." He captured her chin between finger and thumb and kissed her, plucking at her bottom lip before delving into her mouth.

"You like it?" Her wide eyes revealed her anxiousness.

"I cannot believe you made this. Such an art form is lost to us." He stroked its softness. "Yes, I *like* it." He adored it, that she had thought of him, had spent the time crafting it, and in his bloodline color... He opened his mouth to reveal, as best he could, what these growing emotions meant. But no words formed.

"Tonight, *ensa*," he vowed for the second time that day.

"Tonight." She offered a sweet smile.

He forced his legs to carry him away, repeating to himself, *tonight, I will see her tonight,* even as he went in search of her guards. He found them less than ten meters away, within easy listening distance. But they didn't turn when he approached. He had to tap Azan on the shoulder. Only then did the male tug white things out of his ears. The music Xeus had just deleted blared off the tiny devices. They must have had the birdsongs on their O.D.I.s before today. Azan nudged Nuos's shoulder. At last, Xeus had their attention.

He grinned at his queen's ingenuity.

"Guard her with your lives," he said then returned to his office.

Sinking into his comfy, he raised the scarf to cover the lower half of his face, her scent clinging to it. With a deep inhale, he tried not to feel as if tonight would never come.

Chapter Thirty-Nine

Planet Etteria
Issneen, the Royal City
Xeus's Royal Chambers
That evening.

XEUS STARED AT THE chess board, not seeing the pieces. His attention was riveted on his emotional turmoil. He understood the game was one of war and strategy, sacrifice and victory. The king was to be protected, even though she'd said it was the queen. Her hesitation had meant a lie, that she'd changed the rules to suit his culture. In her world, the king was to be protected, yet in his, the queen.

Her consideration made his chest ache. He glanced at her as she fervently studied the board as if the game mattered. It did not. She mattered.

She consumed his every thought. He spent his time wondering when next he'd see her, hold her, hear her lyrical voice, and the sound of her laughter.

He couldn't understand this need and obsession.

His gaze traveled over her features adoringly. She showed no internal struggle, no *need* to be with him. Yet she hid nothing from him, held nothing back. He had to take a leap of faith as he'd advised Xan to do. Xeus ached to tell her how he felt, what she meant to him.

But the emotions crushing his chest were unrecognizable, unknown.

"What's wrong?"

He blinked at her and realized he'd stared at her for some time. "I saw this *love* on Kanzo's face. You were correct. That is not the Ethera." Not that he could say how he knew this. He just did. The annals spoke of the pain and temptation the Ethera invoked. Not once had he seen an Etterian Eth gaze upon his Etterian Dar Eth with the same intensity that Kanzo adored Lady Ava. It had to be a human influence, one Xeus hadn't anticipated.

"Are you tired? I can go." Her offer struck a painful dart through his heart.

Even with her as his Dar Eth, he *felt* more for her, more than the Ethera inspired. He never wanted to be parted from her, not for a moment more.

"I want you to never go. I want you to be with me here, to stay with me." His gaze met hers.

"I can do that. It wouldn't be a hardship for me." She grasped his hand. "Whatever you need, Zoo."

He released a sigh, before flipping her hand, palm upward, to press a kiss there. "I believe I feel this *love* for you, Macera."

Her breath hitched as her eyes grew large. "You do?" she squeaked. Tears formed on her eyelashes. "I...I thought I'd be the only one to love. I planned on loving you even if you never returned it." She sniffed and dashed aside an escaped tear. "I love you too, Zoo."

Her confession exploded a fountain of pure joy and light inside him, obliterating any chance of the void returning. Dropping her hand, he reached across the table and dragged her to him, scattering chess pieces everywhere. He positioned her onto his lap just as he crushed her lips with his.

"I prefer quick victories," he growled a few minutes later while feathering wet kisses along the arch of her throat. "And I *feel* victorious."

"You think you've conquered me?" she teased.

"As you conquered my heart," he whispered into her mouth before he gathered her closer.

Planet Etteria
Issneen, the Royal City
Their Royal Chambers
A month later.

"Zoo..." Macera's moan woke him.

The minus sun had yet to rise.

"What is it, *thamani*?" he asked, pulling her closer to him. He stroked her spine with reverence.

"I...I don't feel well." With a cry, she ripped out of his arms and darted to the cleansing room.

He was close on her heels, in time to hold back her hair as she purged her stomach into the waste receptacle.

"Sorry...," she mumbled, wiping her mouth with the back of her hand. "Wait..." And she gagged.

Xeus frowned. Sickness wasn't unheard of on Etteria, just rare. He punched commands into his O.D.I., still holding her hair away from her face. "Aldur is on his way."

"Thank you," she said, allowing herself to slump to the floor.

As she attempted to rise off the floor to cleanse her mouth, he lifted her. He held her upright, his hand on her waist in case she collapsed again. She gripped the counter with white knuckles as if her knees were weak. When she was done brushing her teeth, he scooped her into his arms and carried her back to bed.

"Why is the cleansing room so far away? Who designed that?" she muttered while he settled the blanket around her naked form.

The door chimed, and from the bedroom, he commanded it to open. Within moments, Aldur stood in the doorway.

He entered the bedroom to scan her. His eyebrows shot up, which meant it had to be alarming. Xeus tightened his hand around hers. He couldn't lose her. No matter what she needed to be healthy, he would get it for her.

Aldur slapped his scanner and tried it again. "My king..." He glanced between Macera and him, his eyes wide.

"How bad is it?" Xeus asked, his voice hoarse.

"Bad?" Aldur chuckled, "Not bad, my king. Wonderful. Queen Macera is with *damu*."

"What?" she yelped.

"Yes, and judging by the heartbeats...two."

"Twins?" She gaped.

It took Xeus a moment to understand. Aldur had said two, but it hadn't registered.

"Two?" Xeus gaped. "How are two possible?"

"The same way one is, I suppose," she teased, rubbing his arm. "My mother was a twin."

"I meant for an Etterian, *thamani*. We do not have twins."

"I have not told you the best news...," Aldur said.

Xeus ignored him and roared as he scooped his Dar Eth into his arms, hugging and kissing her regardless of her nudity. Cales had asked him if he wanted more *damu*. Yes, one thousand times yes.

"Xeus, please, Aldur said he has better news..." She laughed, hugging him back.

He stilled. Not at her calling him Xeus, which she did in the presence of others, but at Aldur possibly having something better than this. "What could best this?"

"One is female."

Xeus froze. Something roared and thundered in his ears. Was that his heartbeat? He tightened his arms and trapped Macera against him. With his mouth hanging open, a tear escaped, blazing a trail down his cheek. He dipped his gaze to hers. "I love you, Macera. You have blessed me as no other."

"No, my God and your Maker have." Her eyes shimmered with unshed tears. "And never to a more deserving male."

He planted a kiss on her that was the beginning of something Aldur shouldn't see. He pulled away to command the medic to leave.

"Kiss me later…" She drew Xeus's attention back to her. "Aldur, I need you to go to Earth and find an OB-GYN."

The male who'd offered his back out of respect now faced them. "A what, my queen?"

"A doctor who specializes in womanhood and birthing babies," she said bluntly. "And with a history in pediatrics."

"Pediatrics?" Aldur mimicked. His eyelids fluttered as did Xeus's.

His Macera was too impatient to wait. "The health of children."

Xeus frowned. "I was not aware you were dissatisfied with Aldur."

She blinked at them then sighed, her frustration clear. "I've never and will never be unhappy with Aldur. I want an OB-GYN here because this is the first Etterian-human pregnancy. A normal pregnancy can be difficult, and twins make it doubly so. Let's rather be safe than sorry."

"This is wise, my queen," Aldur said.

"Make it a female, Aldur. I do not want any male to see my Dar Eth's feminine folds." Xeus loved her pink cheeks and relished placing the color there. "And take Nerx with you. Maybe he will find his Dar Eth and provide a mother for Lily."

Aldur beamed. "We will leave at once, my king."

"Thank you, Aldur." Macera smothered a yawn. "You are a wonderful and valued male."

The medic darkened at her compliment before rushing out.

"You are a wonderful and valued female," Xeus rasped, pulling her against him to feather kisses across her temple.

"Zoo." She snorted. "You're just aroused."

"With you, *ensa ra ensa*, I am always aroused."

Glossary

Etterians worship one God, one Maker, since the universes have only His fingerprint on all of it, a single golden thread through all of creation.

Tokens: intergalactic form of currency

Kliks: predetermined length of distance.

Hatimaye – To bring an end (Hutt-ee-my-ee)

Etterian

Alodon (A-low-donn): who accidentally shot his balls off with his own blaster.

Teacher: lima (lee-ma)

Great teacher: lima kuu: (lee-ma koo)

Directions: semit (semm-it)

Lemon: giyua (gee-you-a)

Young one: damu (daa-moo)

Heart: ensa (enn-sa)

Heart of my heart: ensa ra ensa (enn-sa raa enn-sa)

Beloved: thamani (ta-mar-nee)

Little joy: minus susa (mee-nas soo-sa)

Little cat: minus cesu (mee-nas sess-oo)

Large: magnus (mag-nis)

Orgasm: fulfillment/deite asteri (see stars) / released (day-ta ass-tare-ree)

Starfighter: asteri peju (ass-tare-ree pear-joo)

Collection of glass vials: virak (vee-ruck)

Scum of the galaxies: xemi (ze-mee)

Hair up: malia pa (Mar-lee-a par)

Hair down: malia pado (Mar-lee-a par-dow)

Lysaran

Visitor: kashi (Kaa-shee)

God: Kaiha (Kigh-haa)

King: Kuna (Koo-na)

Orange fleshy fruit: Lemte (Lem-ta)

White flowers: Myameru (My-a-me-roo)

Precious: Delica (Dell-ee-ka)

Sweetheart: Sali (Saa-lee)

Arum Lily-type flower: D'nastu (D-nass-too)

Love Blossom: aroa loulu (A-row-a low-loo)

Maloidian

Title of respect: lommia (Lomm-ee-a)

Stubborn, lethal tree: tewaa (Tee-wah)

Tokauri/Kulai

Blade – Sulac (soo-lack)

Bone – Ukog (you-cog) - bone from some dumb animal, probably an ukog.

Braided – Gisul (gee-sool)

Father – Danno (dan-no)

Heart – Kassu (cass-soo)

Maker – Mugbu (Mug-boo)

Mother – Manno (man-no)

Sapphires – Buha (boo-ha)

Shit – Saho (sa-ho)

Star - stuon (stoo-on)

Stupid – Ungog (oon-gog)

Vessel/ship - sakay (sa-kay)

Pronunciations

Names

Aaro - Ah-row

Adda – Ay-dah

Aldur - Al-durr

Alllero - A-le-row

Balllio – Bah-leee-oh

Bos - Boss

Bry-dar - Brigh-darr

Brynr - Brin-ner

Cales - Cale-es

Cento - Sen-tow

Citus - Sigh-tuss

Coldar - Coal-daar

Cria - Kree-ah

Eriz - Sigh-low

Danic - Dan-eek

Deeezo – Dee-zoh

Der - Durr

Diso - Dee-sow

Diyo - Die-oh

Eira - Eye-raa

Enyl - E-neel

Eriz - E-rizz

Garix - Ga-ricks

Gayn - Gain

Iddan - Ee-dann

Idon - Eye-donn

Illan - Ee-lann

Jarg – Jar-g

Jokta - Jock-tar

Kanzo - Can-zow

Keelu – Key-loo

Keryr – Kerr-eer

Ksal - Ka-sell

Lazu – Lah-zoo

Lurz - Lurr-z

Malo - Mail-oh

Matir - Mat-teer

Myan - My-ann

Myn-ras - Min-russ

Naio – Nay-oh

Nerx - Nurcks

Nuos - New-oss

Oyaz - Oh-yaz

Prex - Precks

Ronin - Row-nin

Saan - Sarn

Sena - See-na

Sy'mar - Sigh-marr

Syna - Sigh-na

Tamra – Tum-rah

Taro - Tah-row

Tenu - Ten-oo

Trav - Trahv

Tinh - Tin

Vytus - Vie-tuss

Vodin - Vo-din

Ulriq - Yule-rick

Vorn - Vawn

Vyar - Vie-arr

Xan - Zan

Xeus – Zeus

Zaro - Zah-row

Ziot - Zye-ott

Places

Argaxx – Are-jax

    Crustiiu – Criss-tee-oo

    Dyuqa - Dee-you-ka

    Etteria – E-tare-rea

    Galaza – Gah-Lar-Zah

    Gikaet – Gee-ka-ett

    Iphara = Ee-far-ra

    Kulai – koo-ligh

    Lysara – Liss-saa-ra

    Mascroba – Mus-crow-ba

    Resia Cay – Ress-Ee-ahh Kay

    Sarvis – Sarr-viss

    Sosu – Sow-soo

    Tokauri – Too-cow-ree

    Yithia – Yith-ee-a

Battleships

Chikara – Chee-kar-a - Force

    Gladio – Glad-ee-oh - Sword

    Kushin – Cush-shin - To Pierce

    Surata – Soo-ra-tah – Beginning

    Usaha – Oo-saa-hah - Endeavor

Shuttles

Celeeri – See-lee-ree - swift

    Denessi – Denn-ess-ee - sodge

    Eshima – Ee-shee-ma - respect

    Kevol – Kev-oll - agony

    Kuta – Koo-tah - modular shuttle.

    Liri-ny – Lee-ree-nye – freedom

    Misaia – Miss-aye-a - memory

    Sasay – Sass-ay - whispers

    Yakin – Yuck-kin - belief

Creatures

Asnu – Ass-Noo – buffalo/donkey

    Eiltur – Ale-turr

    Gracc – Grrr-ack

    Ilag – Ee-Lug– leggy slugs that feast on sol.

    Kreso – Kreh-soo

    Omeika – Oh-may-ka

    Pagsu – Pug-Soo - cocksuckers

    Reshy – Resh-Ee - huge, like the size of a kuta shuttle, with massive jaws and rows of sharp teeth.

    Sogair – Sow-gare

    Wilanegy – Will-anna-jee

About the Author

Sevannah Storm is a fiction writer who immerses herself in fantastical worlds both magical and science fiction. She has a flair for the creative having studied art and interior architecture and spends her time drawing, oil painting, and writing. An avid reader from an early age, Sevannah finds her inspiration from various sources: games, novels, music, and the land of make-believe. The unique versus the practical has brought on numerous debates.

In her spare time, she does Krav Maga, CrossFit, and rereads novels that snatch her breath away. Having embraced the social media world, you can find her on most platforms.

Her home is a land south of Wakanda, where animals roam free. Born in Zimbabwe, she grew up in South Africa. The crisp blue skies with cotton-candy sunsets expand her heart and soul, encapsulating a sense of freedom.

Words she lives by: "Know your pothole and dodge it. Don't work in a pencil factory if you're a vampire."

Sevannah loves to hear from her readers. You can find and connect with her at the links below.

Website/Newsletter:

https://www.sevannahstorm.com/

Facebook:

https://www.facebook.com/sevannah.storm

Instagram:

https://www.instagram.com/sevannah.storm/

Twitter:

https://twitter.com/sevannah_storm

Thank you for taking the time to read Star Forged. If you enjoyed the story, please tell your friends and leave a review. Reviews support authors and ensure they continue to bring readers books to love and enjoy.

https://sevannahstorm.com

SOUL FORGED

THE GIFTING SERIES #1

Know-it-all Oriana agreed to travel with aliens who need women. But she didn't agree to abduction, life/death battles, and escaping with a bossy, arrogant man. She was sabotaged, attacked, and kidnapped, but she is far from beaten. Forced to participate in an alien battle arena with no promise of freedom, she has to forget the loss of her family and focus on surviving.

Enyl has given up hope. His people are dying due to a genetic modification gone awry. Darkness is consuming his warriors, and his world, as he knows it, will end. His father, the king, has rolled out a plan to save them all. But Enyl doubts a solution will be found in time.

And when a compatible female is found...and lost, he must rescue her, a human female capable of surviving despite all odds. However, freeing Oriana serves to anger the aliens holding her captive. Ensuring she is cared for—as per Etterian protocol—he is stunned by the strong connection between the two of them. Such a bond was only experienced between Etterian mates.

Is she his salvation or is that wishful thinking on his part?

Read it here:

https://books2read.com/u/mlAWr9

FATE FORGED

THE GIFTING SERIES #2

Jacqueline (Jack) Dunois struggles to find a man not intimidated by her career as a law enforcement instructor, especially in the small town she calls home. She would sacrifice a kidney to find someone who would make her ovaries clap and didn't live with his mother. Then she meets a supreme commander from another world who thinks the stars in the galaxies shine in her eyes... What's not to love about that?

Supreme Commander Ulriq doesn't believe in love, an archaic term for a volatile and untrustworthy emotion Etterians were no longer subjected to. Until he meets Jack who triggers the Ethera, the soulmate force that irrevocably changes a male when he finds his ideal female. At that moment, his world, his focus, his very loyalty shifts. But when she is taken from him, it is too much to bear. Under the influence of the Ethera, he launches a rescue. He'll start a war and kill anyone who dares stop him, just to have her back in his arms.

Read it here:

https://books2read.com/u/bMY09v

SUN FORGED

The Gifting Series #3

Meeting a drop-dead gorgeous man, who falls onto a knee the first time they meet, sounded too good to be true for Ava. Of course, with her luck, he had to be an alien. Thrust into an unknown alien world, meeting weird and scary creatures, and fearing for her life, Ava tries to survive as best as a hairstylist can.

Kanzo never expected to find a life mate, a Dar Eth. Since he was young, he was taught that pairings were rare with fewer females born. The statistics on finding his Dar Eth would be slim to none. Instead of dreaming and longing for companionship, he focused on being the best male possible, to end his life on a battlefield with honor. But when he experiences the Ethera—the life mate force, and is blessed with his female, he isn't prepared for the level of pain, pleasure, and need she invokes within him.

Unable to save her as she's teleported from him, the dark consuming pain in his chest drives him into a blinding rage. With no idea who stole her or where to begin the search, he will scour the known universe to find her, to hold the female he never wanted.

Read it here:

https://books2read.com/u/3n5vaB

WAR FORGED

Being kidnapped by aliens does not sit well with Quinlan. Not only would her seven guardians give her hell if she doesn't attempt some sort of escape, but she refuses to be at anybody's mercy. With her practiced military skills, the help of an underground lounge singer and a personal assistant, she takes over the alien slave ship. Not knowing how to fly the damn thing, she sends a distress signal. ...The rescue comes swiftly in the form of a bronzed man with exquisite ice-blue eyes. Leaving her to ask the true question: has she just given up her newfound freedom for a gorgeous man who seems determined to have her for eternity?

As Elite Supreme Commander of the Etterian Forces, Xan answers a distress call in Earth English. That is all he did. The female who captured the slave ship shows remarkable skill, making her a warrior in her own right. Said skills should be respected and honored. Except she is his Dar Eth, calling forth the Ethera—the soulmate bond. How can he protect his female when she can do so herself? What can she possibly need from him? What can he offer a female, not Etterian but human? Not that he can think clearly in her presence when she scents so good and makes him want to kiss all of her.

Maker help him.

Read it here:

https://books2read.com/u/bz1QGD

SHADOW FORGED

The Gifting Series #6

Forty-year-old Caroline is too old to start dating and too bored with her vibrator, but what other choices does she have. On the day she burns her shirt and breaks a fingernail, she meets Etterian warriors. As part of her job at E.S.A. (Earth Space Association,) she must 'entertain' the hot-as-apple-pie Chief Engineer she suspects isn't who he claims to be.

Operations Commander Malo, Head of Espionage, must act as an engineer and ambassador, hoping to invite human females to visit Etteria and save his dying race. From Princess Oriana, he has strict instructions to distrust humans. What he finds he cannot trust are his emotions and his body whenever in the presence of the human ambassador, Caroline. She does not believe in soulmates or in a forever with him. Convincing her to choose him is the greatest task ever set before him, one he cannot afford to fail.

Until she is stolen from him. He calls in favors, utilizes all his resources to find her. And *when* he does, he is never letting her off his battleship...or his bed.

Read it here:

https://books2read.com/u/bPNd8j

EARTH FORGED

The Gifting Series #7

Guilt hounds Izzy, who caused her sister's injury and subsequent blindness. But no matter how she cares for Simone or what she sacrifices, it doesn't ease the ache in her chest. With Simone and naive Caro, her best friend, Izzy's role as protector is fully realized. The cost? Hiding behind quirkiness, pseudo-joy, and giving up her hopes and dreams. What she needs is a knight in any armor. After all, beggars can't be fussy. She has no idea that armor, in her case, means black military and that a knight could come in any color, specifically bronze.

Oyaz wants to find his life force, his soulmate, and he'd like her to be human. Earth's females are soft, amusing, passionate, and their scents rival a garden of hahyt blossoms. His task is to guard their planet that promises so many salvations for his males. It's a duty he's pleased to perform, one he would die for. When Operations Commander Malo orders Oyaz to retrieve a human female, he's eager to oblige. That it would lead to his salvation is something he couldn't anticipate. What he hadn't planned for is an ambush that costs him more than his memory, the loss of his soulmate.

Now what? Nothing in their training prepared him for this.

And yet, despite not remembering kneeling for Izzy, he longs to claim her with every inch of his soul.

Read it here:

https://books2read.com/u/31V82D

LUST FORGED

The Gifting Series #8

Ex-socialite Leona wants nothing more than to enhance the mechanics within sex-cybs, not to mention improve their performances with their 'lovers.' It's a job where she's safe in an all-woman factory on Callisto, and far from her matchmaking mama. When the chief engineer is incapacitated, Leona's required to gift—her term would be pimp—sex-cyborgs to prospective clients. On an Etterian battleship, surrounded by gorgeous males, she tries not to think of sex when it's her work, especially with the Sub-Commander Aaro whose neon-blue eyes are the stuff of her erotic dreams.

As a diplomatic favor, Aaro must abandon his task to guard Earth, and perhaps find his Dar Eth or soulmate, all to protect cargo en route to many worlds, including the dangerous and unpredictable Yithia. Princess Oriana is most concerned for the two human female engineers determined to ensure the deliveries are successful. A simple enough mission until one human enters Aaro's cargo bay, dropping him to his knees.

But revealing to independent Leona that she's now trapped in a marriage isn't something Aaro can bring himself to do. He violates all he stands for, every ounce of honor by not telling her the truth. All in the hopes that she will choose to love him.

Read it here:

https://books2read.com/u/3LdA1w

www.ingramcontent.com/pod-product-compliance
Lightning Source LLC
Chambersburg PA
CBHW072004110726
47910CB00005B/1657